Through the Lychgate
A Speculation

BY THE SAME AUTHOR

To the Great Sea: A Story for Christmas (Troubador, 2011)
Checkmate: Three Portraits of Power (Troubador, 2013)
A Time for Role Call (Troubador, 2017)
The Approaching Tide (Troubador, 2021)

Through the Lychgate

A Speculation

Doug Thompson

Copyright © 2024 Doug Thompson

The moral right of the author has been asserted.

Apart from any fair dealing for the purposes of research or private study, or criticism or review, as permitted under the Copyright, Designs and Patents Act 1988, this publication may only be reproduced, stored or transmitted, in any form or by any means, with the prior permission in writing of the publishers, or in the case of reprographic reproduction in accordance with the terms of licences issued by the Copyright Licensing Agency. Enquiries concerning reproduction outside those terms should be sent to the publishers.

This is a work of fiction. Names, characters, businesses, places, events and incidents are either the products of the author's imagination or used in a fictitious manner. Any resemblance to actual persons, living or dead, or actual events is purely coincidental.

Troubador Publishing Ltd
Unit E2 Airfield Business Park,
Harrison Road, Market Harborough,
Leicestershire LE16 7UL
Tel: 0116 279 2299
Email: books@troubador.co.uk
Web: www.troubador.co.uk

ISBN 978-1-80514-478-6

British Library Cataloguing in Publication Data.
A catalogue record for this book is available from the British Library.

Printed and bound in Great Britain by 4edge Limited
Typeset in 11pt Minion Pro by Troubador Publishing Ltd, Leicester, UK

For

In the particular,
GFA
who always believed,
and
JAS
who couldn't

and
in the general,
for all those I have loved,
and those who have loved me at different moments
during
my rich and privileged life.

In gratitude.

Preface

Through the Lychgate has been far longer in its gestation than any of my other books, and as a result has gone through many transformations, both stylistic and in its story line. My hope is that it has gained much too, in the interim, from my writing of *A Time for Role Call* and *The Approaching Tide*, while being a very different novel from either of these – a "speculation", after all, however you choose to interpret that multi-faceted word.

My thanks, as ever, to those who have in their different ways had some input into the novel, but particularly to my partner, Gillian, with her inventiveness and her diligent editing skills.

I can only hope that those who choose to pass through the lychgate will find it to be an intriguing world, unlike any other they have experienced through the written word.

ADT
April 2024

1

Rosalind will be late, of course. Always is these days.
Rosemary sighs. But she's gone there early just the same. She likes the park, so big and open, especially at this time of day with no one about, so she doesn't mind the waiting, wandering along the asphalt paths, past the greenhouses, down through the rockeries, towards the boating-lake.

Passing the Victorian drinking-fountain she stops and runs her hand up its iron-cold smoothness, distractedly caressing its rounded top, liking the feel of it. Impulsively, she jabs at the plunger, but no water comes. She turns up the iron cup, swinging gently on its chain, and looks inside. 'Let this cup pass from me' comes into her mind. She says it out loud, and smiling, she drops it, to clang against the pedestal, clanging, a bell clanging, as she turns away.

A light mist lingers over the water, drifting languorously among the trees over the other side, where all is still indistinct. Although the sun is already well up, above the trees even, the chill of the mist and the dew hang in the air by the lakeside, and she buttons up her coat before sitting on her favourite bench, near the boat house.

Tuesday, it's back to school. She closes her eyes, wishing these next few days could go on forever. If she could only see Val again, just round the close. Not any of the others, though, not any more. Bad enough with 'O' levels, but if the rumours were true, it'd be horrible, just horrible.

A bird calls, and she looks up, vaguely searching for it among the boughs. Apart from old Charlie, the boat-keeper, bobbing back and forth, there isn't a soul about.

But it was going to be hot. And being a Saturday there'd be loads of people this afternoon scrabbling for boats, shoving and yelling and jumping the queue – once, she'd seen a man and a woman who'd even started fighting, their children crying, scared at the sudden outbreak of violence.

'Number two for you,' Charlie would call out in his singsong voice, before starting his muttering and cursing over again as he tried to keep them in order. 'Number three, number four…' And they'd crowd into their little boats and row as hard as they could, trying to get somewhere as far from the crackling tannoy as they could, knowing that soon it would be calling them back, always too soon, over the water.

Rosemary shivers and stands up. Funny how the park always seems to be where her own little dramas take place.

And here comes Rosalind now, hurrying along the path towards her. And Rosemary can see, even at a distance, that something is wrong.

'It's true,' Rosalind shouts, coming up. 'He's back. Saunders has actually *seen* the bastard. That's what Willetts says, anyhow.'

Rosemary's mind empties and for a moment she has no idea what Rosalind can mean. Then, just as suddenly, it's as clear as day, and her stomach lurches.

'He's having you on,' she says. 'Come on, Ros, who can believe a word Willetts says?'

'It was him I tell you, coming out of the public library!' Rosalind snarls, malevolence burning in her eyes, her cheeks flushed; and Rosemary turns away, not knowing what to say.

'He'll be sorry! I'll make the bastard sorry, you wait and see!' Rosalind hisses.

Rosemary glances at her, at her eyes narrowing, narrowing like a cat's as it tenses to spring.

'Why do you hate him so much, Ros?' she asks, her eyes still averted. 'He was a good teacher. Kind, always listened to us, encouraged us.'

'What! Are you stupid or something? It's obvious why. It's what he *did*… as well as everything else. All that stuff he told us… just rubbish. Lies. All of it. Ask anyone! Everybody feels the same. He was a liar and a fake from start to finish! He left, and good riddance! And he should have stayed away.'

Rosemary nods slowly though no longer sure *what* she feels, now that rumour seemingly teeters on the edge of probability.

Rosalind looks up at her in alarm. 'Oh, Rosie, tell me you're not glad he's come back. Promise me you're not glad.'

Rosemary can feel her eyes pricking, and she shakes her head violently from side to side, her hair flashing golden in the sunlight.

'I'm *not* glad he's come back – if he has,' she murmurs. 'Really, I'm not. Things are complicated enough as it is.'

Rosalind smiles her relief, steps forward, and takes Rosemary's face in her cupped hands, then, on tiptoes, she kisses her. For a moment, the two girls stand with their foreheads pressed together.

'You're just like Twiggy,' Rosalind whispers, 'sexy, like Twiggy.' And she giggles as she says it.

'Twiggy? Who's Twiggy? Never heard of her.'

'Oh, come on, Rosie! *Everybody* knows who Twiggy is.'

'Why don't I then? Maybe *I'm* nobody!' And Rosemary blushes.

Rosalind smiles again. 'Bet you don't know who the Fab Four are, either.' But then she becomes serious again. 'You're not *secretly* glad, though… that he's back?'

Rosemary, glancing cautiously this way, then that, gently frees herself from Rosalind's grasp. She backs away a few steps, staring out at the lake, then, half-turning, whispering almost, says, 'No. I'm not secretly glad, Ros. Honestly, I'm not.'

A scene played out long ago but chalked up on Time's slate.

The park is still there.

***

'Please, Mary, could you… would you just be… quiet. *Please!*'

'Oh, Milly, dear, I was only saying… Here – take this.' And she hands her a tiny lace handkerchief.

But Milly Tomelty is far too distraught to listen to *anything*, as she kneels, quietly sobbing, gently patting the small mound of newly turned earth covering her dead canary.

Mary Talbot falls silent then, though only for a moment or two before exclaiming, 'Oh, wasn't that old Professor what's-his-name?' And she strides gawkily down to the gateway to squint from behind the privet, her left eye twitching nineteen to the dozen.

But the lane appears to be empty.

'How very odd! I could have sworn…'

Mrs Talbot walks slowly back up the path, shaking her head, never suspecting for one moment (and why should she?) that this fleeting glimpse of hers would be the very last sighting of Dan Teal, by anyone, ever.

Just now, though, he has merely vanished under the low, interlacing branches where the lane funnels sharply, then darkens and narrows into a long, winding track that takes you, if you bear right, out of a sort of clearing near its end, to an old house.

If you turn left out of it, you come instead to the dense undergrowth of Hall Wood, where…

But that is for later.

As he glances at the wrought-iron gate over to his right – the "postern", they'd always called it – Dan's mind is in a whirl of anticipation and apprehension, and his step quickens, as does his heartbeat.

A moment later, a sudden clapping of wings from above and behind brings him up short, and as he turns, in panic almost, a pair of doves flashes past to alight on the grass beside the lychgate, which you don't really see until you are almost upon it because of the thick hedging. As he nears it, however, they fly off again, over the hedge into the rose garden.

Rifling his pockets for keys, he stops, then calls the code to mind, and begins to negotiate the elaborate locking system. But why so complex? All he'd wanted was for the thing to lock, and surely, you didn't need a bloody mainframe for that!

Jerking his head back in frustration, he notices that part of the hedge appears to be growing coppery, just a few fronds where it abuts the lychgate's superstructure. But yes, last night's storm. Of course. Evidence of it everywhere. Just a bit of the old copper beech broken off and fallen. And he glances upwards, as if to make sure the huge tree itself is still where it should be, towering over the gateway.

Stepping forward he takes hold of the bough to remove it. 'Come on, come on! Don't be difficult!' But only a small part of it gives way, much more of it remaining in the hedge. So nothing to do with the storm at all. Just an outgrowth from the lower trunk thrusting into the hedge.

And breaking through the silence, the leaves of the burnished giant rustle at the sudden gusting of a breeze.

Dan returns to his task, and with the gate finally open, retrieves his briefcase and the carrier with the clock in it from where he'd set them down in the lane, and with the bough fragment still in his other hand, he stands for a moment or two, looking back towards the dark wood before stepping into the rose garden and locking the gate behind him.

This is it, then. The last moment. And the first.

He shakes his head, wistfully. The house. The empty, sloping field – his future vocation – now starkly before him.

Halfway back down the long open field above the house he stops, as the sun, which had delayed all day behind sullen clouds, breaks loose. And he marvels at the miracle of transfiguration it works on grey stone and lacklustre green.

He has not yet ventured inside the house.

At the door he'd paused only to switch off the alarm and discard his briefcase and the clock, before making for the sandstone outcrop cresting the field. And there, sitting on one of the lower rocks to catch his breath, he had laid the coppery bough on the little mound inside a ring of stones set in the lee of the rocks, then knelt beside it, stroking his hand slowly across its shiny, close-knit, sedum cover. '*Hic incipit vita nova*,' he had murmured.

Premature, as it happened, for the very next moment ushered in, seemingly from nowhere, the vision of a girl in a gymnasium, a scene from that long-ago enchantment which had ambushed him, enraptured him, transformed his life. And then it was over. And he was left…

But why now, suddenly, here?

After retrieving his things from the step, Dan enters the house, leaving the back door wide open. Sunlight floods through the kitchen to the hallway beyond, illuminating the face of the quite majestic grandfather clock, and he stands there for a moment or two, contemplating its motionless hands.

Clocks. Time. Our prison, no less.

The grandfather had been in a piteous state when they'd stumbled across it at a car-boot sale, but an old friend had patiently restored it to the elegance its maker had intended a century earlier, and it had kept tolerably good time. Or it would have, had he been there more often to wind it.

He shakes his head and thrusts his hands into his trouser pockets. Well, he will need a similar unwinding, won't he, in this new beginning? From now on, time will be within *him*, regulated by his own physical strength, by his will or caprice. No more chasing after it, after the train just leaving the platform or the meeting already begun – those daily irritants that can gnaw away at any creative endeavour.

Reaching out his right hand, he traces a finger, affectionately, along the fine grain beneath the clock's face. 'No more time for you, old friend,' he whispers. 'As of today, you're retired too. *You* are something else, too… from today.'

Then he turns and runs up the stairs. Breezing into the front room, his study, Dan puts his things down on the end of the mahogany desk, which is framed by the huge window, and looks down at the gravel path leading through the graveyard back towards the lychgate. Then he slips off his wristwatch and pushes it to the back of a drawer.

Turning away from the desk, he crosses the wide corridor and enters the large back bedroom, removing his jacket and tie as he goes. Opening the built-in wardrobe that fills the wall at one end, and taking hold of a coat-hanger, he places his jacket on the rail, and rolling up his tie lays it neatly with others in a drawer, before reaching for a beige sweater on a high shelf and pulling it over his head.

Off with the old and on with the new, is it?

Then he goes back to the study for the mantel clock. 'Sorry, mate, but you've turned up too late to be of any use, just another dust-gatherer, so regretfully...' and he thrusts it, still in its carrier, into a corner at the bottom of the wardrobe.

***

Emerging from the park, Rosemary hurries across the Market Square, enters the bus shelter, and anxiously scans the scuffed, almost illegible timetable.

It jolly well better come soon, she thinks. Or mam and dad'll back home with the shopping, and if she's not tidied away the breakfast things, laid the table, and been for the fish and chips, she'll not hear the last of it the whole weekend.

Why did Rosalind always have to make things so awkward?

So moody and selfish, and so... extreme in everything, even if she brought *some* smiles, every now and then. But all this fuss about Mr Teal... She sniffs. *Bound* to be unpleasantness if he *was* back, back from wherever he'd been. Always trouble when Ros got a bee in her bonnet.

She looks down the hill, willing the bus to appear, then scowls at her watch. Stupid things, always late... So is it good if he *is* back? She isn't sure if it is. Scary though, scary to see him again, when she'd thought she never would, not ever.

And she sighs, long and hard. All ups or downs, pains or pleasures, that was what being around Rosalind meant. Her friend's life a million miles from her own – chapel and Sunday school and all the prayers and Bible-readings and long, dreary hymns – well, not all of them, but most. All that straight-laced stuff her mam and dad go in for… Better Ros's Fab Four any day! And her lip curls and she groans then, remembering the stupid whist-drive after tea, and spending long boring hours with kids half her age. Unpaid childminder, that's what she is, and so unfair! Taken for granted she is, that's what!

Oh where has the stupid bus got to?

Rosemary sighs and almost stamps her foot. But then she sees it, out of the corner of her eye, trundling towards the stop as though next week would do!

As it grinds to a halt, she steps up smartly onto the platform, rummaging for her purse. She makes towards the stairs, but then changes her mind. Only three stops, after all.

But Ros and… Mr Teal. Had it really been like she'd said? Had they really done… those things, together?

She shakes her head, not really wanting to think about it, but not able *not* to think about it. Ros, though, she'd never talk about it. Just went all red and blotchy if it was even mentioned.

Oh why, why in God's name does she have to go back to school on Tuesday?

Yes, she was full of foreboding, but a tiny bit smug too at her daring – saying 'God' in her mind like that; she'd have got a slap from mam, as well as a sermon full of 'thou shalt nots' from dad, if they'd heard.

Rosemary stands up and signals smartly to the conductor, who rings the bell.

II

It is a grandiose scheme, right enough. And one morning, deeming the time right, Dan goes round to the long shed by the "postern", and takes down the new spade. He slits the oil paper at the handle, then all the way down the haft, and holds it, contemplatively. Then he walks back purposefully past the front of the house, and up the steps into the empty field.

Several weeks have passed since his arrival at the house, and one problem he has been wrestling with is what to do with all the turf. Initially, he can just tuck it under the curtain hedges, those nearest the point where he's working, but later, he will need to think again. Anyway, his first task, now, is to cut the steps up through the bluff, above the high containing wall between the field and the north side of the house. Then he'll work his way back down again, gradually uncovering the central pathway marked out in his mind, right back to where he stands now, at the first step.

Titania, the first step.
Deeming the time right.
A whirl of anticipation.

The spade jolts and clatters in the wheelbarrow as he pushes it round the side of the house, over the uneven ground. It is a beautiful, azure morning.

Outside the back door he sets the barrow down and goes inside for a moment. He is looking for his old Aussie bush-hat, but in the search becomes distracted, turning up anything but the hat. And somehow, his resolve weakens. There may not be very many days left this year as splendid as this one, he muses, and hasn't he worked every single day since getting here, unpacking and preparing? And besides and besides…

Some little time later, Dan re-emerges with the shapeless old hat he'd gone in to find, but also with a book, a cassette recorder, a box of cassettes… and a deckchair, tucked awkwardly under his arm. Smiling contentedly, while shaking his head, bemused, he has decreed that today will be a holiday.

Looking for a place where he will not be disturbed too soon by encroaching shadows, he glances, towards the trough, then left, in the direction of the graveyard, and finally settles down nearer the latter, just beyond the corner of the house. Ages since he has listened to music – hadn't given it a thought when reorganising the study and his books; a pity, for it might then have helped take the edge off his many frustrations.

Reaching for an unlabelled cassette, he inserts it, just to test the batteries. But no, there it is in an instant. And he freezes, as if in shock.

> *Words are all we have to use,*
> *our lives change with their tone.*
> *They decide, we win we lose,*
> *Yeah, sometimes – I hate bein' alone…*

That voice. Deep and resonant. Casella's voice.

Abruptly, he switches off, unable to bear the wistfulness of the words that would follow. At the Cajun Festival, wasn't it, in Lafayette? And what a day that had been! So many years back. He smiles to himself, at himself, still grappling with ghosts.

To lay… or to hold on to?

Giving the spade an apologetic look, Dan settles back deep into the deckchair, and closes his eyes, savouring the memory. And in no time at all he is asleep.

***

In an infinitely more distant dimension, a young woman (let *us too* call her Titania, for that is who she always was for Dan) lays aside her book and with it the cares of Perdita, the tricks of Autolycus.

She sinks deep down into the deckchair, at the same time tilting her head backwards to look up into the apple tree, at the wisps of cloud slowly teasing out across its blue-backed tracery. She scrutinises them intently, looking for any change in their pattern, but they remain well-nigh motionless. And still watching, she becomes gradually aware of the coolness of the grass under her bare feet, which she presses hard down on the earth in a surge of exhilaration, stretching back, pushing her shoulders against the chair back, knowing the strength of her body.

A bee comes near, hovers an instant, then darts away again. A moment in which everything is still and silent in the gathering heat of the morning.

She closes her eyes, smiling contentedly, and her mind empties. But then Perdita comes creeping back, and Autolycus. There was another Autolycus though, wasn't there? But she can't remember anything more; just another one, read about, somewhere…

And suddenly she is falling, hurtling earthwards from the wisps of cloud that can hold her no longer, and she wakes with a start. Prince jerks up, fixing her quizzically before gradually settling back once more, stretching out flat and low, to hug the cool earth under the apple tree.

The sound of a distant mower coughing, spluttering, starting up. Was that what had startled her out of her momentary drift?

Or her mother, smiling down at her, now, proffering a glass of cordial?

'It will be nice at the sea. They're saying the weather is going to hold all this month.'

Titania smiles her pleasure, struck by her mother's fine features as she stands just beyond the tree's shadow, glowing in sunlight.

'I bumped into Mrs Kelday, in town. She says they've appointed someone for History for next term. Somebody who taught general arts at the school a couple of years back, she said. I can't quite remember... it was an unusual name – Tillotson, was it? Tyldesley? But no, it was shorter than that. Anyway, I hope...'

Still intent upon her mother's features, Titania barely heeds her words.

'...and I hope you have Mr Kelday again for your English, this next year. It's so important, your "A" levels...'

'Don't worry, mummy, that's all settled.' Titania sits up. 'Mr Kelday told us so himself, at the end of last term... Let me come and help you get things ready.'

'No, you stay here. I'll call you if I think of anything. I'm almost done now, anyway.'

So Titania, eyes closed, drifts away again, to the sea. And there is the sandy beach; and behind it, the wind-blown dunes she has been scrambling over ever since her memories began, the scene of so much happiness in her younger life, the quiet setting for more recent reveries.

Will I ever stop going there? she wonders. 'Will I, Prince?' she says out loud, and the dog leaps up to nuzzle his way under her outstretched hand.

***

Dan's head jerks forward, and he wakes with a start, lost, verging on panic. After a moment or two, he picks up the unopened book, which had slipped from his lap, flicks quickly past the Introduction, and begins to read at the first line of Act One, Scene One:

'If you shall chance, Camillo, to visit Bohemia...' But now, inexplicably, he has lost all appetite for it.

'Perhaps today is not a holiday, after all,' he mutters, snapping the book shut.

And this sudden disturbance startles a flock of woodpigeons pecking at the grass, scattering them away in all directions up the field.

It is no easy matter getting the wheelbarrow up the steps into the field, even when empty. The steps are narrow, as well as steep, so that it is some little time before he stands, panting hard, at the top of the containing wall, uncertain whether to go on up to the bluff with the heavy barrow or back for the spade, the turfer, and the fork, which are still leaning against the house wall. Catching his breath, he continues diagonally up over the rough grass, soon finding it easier to pull the wheelbarrow behind him, rather than push it. Reaching the rocks, he slumps down beneath them, again breathing hard, clasping his knees, which he has drawn right up under his chin.

Bound to be hard at first, so out of condition is he. But the higher he works his way up the open field the easier it will become, surely?

For the moment, though, Dan is disinclined to move, distracted by other memories bubbling up, unbidden, out of nowhere.

Poor Rosemary. Rosemary who had ended so badly.

After she had left school in mid-term, to take a job in the nearby city – at the town hall, if he remembers correctly – the girl had taken to writing him long, convoluted letters in which she'd confided many things, personal things, and about her erstwhile classmates, too. But in the end, it had dawned on him, and he had asked her to stop. Whatever the letters' apparent subjects their real message was her schoolgirl crush on him, her struggling, adolescent emotions. And he sighs, sadly. But why should he be thinking of her now? Or the girl she'd gone around with, or other things, all from a period of his life that had, after all, been quickly over?

But poor girl, poor troubled girl. If only he had been aware of it – of her – at the time.

If only he'd been aware of a lot of things.

He frowns then, remembering something else, something she'd said in one of her rambling letters from that long-distant autumn, about an evening that had started in a sort of gazebo in the park.

***

Rosalind turns up her card – the joker.

Rosemary gasps.

Willetts almost chokes.

For an eternity Rosalind's eyes fix on the card, lying there gay, innocent, cradled in the soft pink phosphorescence that barely penetrates these shadows from the streetlamps beyond the park railings. Then she looks up and is met at once by Saunders' eyes, and he holds her there, a smile twitching at the corners of his mouth. But she returns his gaze steadily, unyielding.

'Come, come, Rosalind. Do we get to or don't we? If it were… well, let's say, our good friend, old Ulysses, who was viewing, would there be all this prevarication?'

'Saunders! That isn't fair, that's a rotten thing to say!' cries Rosemary in dismay. But Saunders, with a slight movement of his hand, wafts away her protest.

'Well, Rosalind?' he taunts. 'Do we… or don't we?'

'You're a pig, Saunders, you really are,' Rosalind hisses. Then, she stands up, and is instantly outside the gazebo. One or two steps along the path to the right, then again to the left, sufficient to reassure herself there is no one about.

She comes back inside.

No one has moved or broken the tense silence.

'All right,' Rosalind says calmly, firmly.

'Oh no! Don't do it, Rosalind! Don't, please don't!' Rosemary groans.

'Just you shut up!' Rosalind snaps at her, sitting down again. Her narrowing eyes never leaving Saunders' impassive face for one moment, she begins to unbutton her blouse, and when that is done, she slips it off and lays it beside her, on the concrete bench. Stretching back, she unclasps her bra and slips that off too, all in one deft movement. Then slowly, she settles into an upright position, with the wan light flickering on her naked breasts and shoulders, her eyes not leaving Saunders' face for an instant.

A suppressed choking, becoming a curious gurgling sound, out of the shadows where Willetts is sitting.

'Yes, quite; quite so, David,' Saunders mocks. Then he leans forward into the pink light. 'Not bad, Rosalind! Not bad at all!' Still mock-serious, his head nodding sagely, he continues his scrutiny. 'Maybe just a teensy-weensy bit on the scrawny side, but certainly more there, yes, than ordinarily meets the eye. Hm, not bad at all. Seven out of ten, would you say, David… or eight maybe?'

Rosemary cannot bear to look, perspiration prickling, and she is shivering too. She is sure she is going to be sick.

Willetts leans forward and stretches out his hand to touch Rosalind. But she is too quick for him and bats the hand away.

'You look with your eyes, Willetts, not with your hands, and don't you forget it!'

Saunders, released at last by her movement, jerks round.

'What's matter, Rosemary?' he drawls. 'Haven't you ever seen a pair of – he enunciates the word crisply – *tits*, before? Don't suppose you have!' He smirks at Willetts. 'No superabundance of that commodity in our Rosemary's case, is there?' And he looks up and down her thin frame, peering hard, mocking.

Rosalind sniggers.

Rosemary feels confused, ridiculous, humiliated.

'Well, let's see if that's true, then,' says Willetts, excitedly, almost gulping for air.

'Good idea, David!' exclaims Saunders. 'Come on, Rosemary. Off with your jumper, and let's all hunt for the needles in the haystack, shall we?'

All three begin to laugh, as Rosemary shakes her head violently from side to side. She is sweating hard, and tears have welled up, stinging her eyes.

'She couldn't do that for anybody,' Rosalind sneers, turning in Rosemary's direction. 'You couldn't, could you, Rosie? Not even to save your life!'

Stung to the quick by this so-casual cruelty, Rosemary jumps up, banging her knee hard against the concrete table. And as the tears brim over, blinding her, she gropes her way outside, lurching away off the path, shrieks of laughter ringing in her ears. Dizzy and sick, she stumbles along, until finally, slumped against a tree, she slips down its bole, moaning and shaking her head from side to side.

She sits there, among the roots, her cheek pressed against the cool bark, until she feels her senses wheeling.

And the ground seems to heave beneath her as she faints away.

***

Poor, poor Rosemary, so kind and gentle. Always out of her depth; awkward, angular, a misfit anywhere, but especially among those hard, unfeeling fifth-form boys.

It had not ended there, though. There had been a reckoning of sorts, that same evening. The endless retribution. She'd written it down in 'a sort of poem', she'd called it, and he must have it somewhere still, for it had kept turning up among his papers over the years.

Dan rises stiffly to his feet, suddenly, painfully aware he has been crouching in the same position for far too long.

And dismissing these images, he sets off back down the field to fetch his tools, stretching and flexing, and forcing himself to think about the arrangement of paths and beds and the different levels, and not about Rosemary… or anything else. So yes, there will be many paths, some of them leading nowhere at all. Paths and beds. But will the paths determine the shapes of the beds, or be determined by them?

He shrugs. No matter, for the moment. For before then he must lay bare the soil.

III

Dan's first evening at the house had felt both strange and welcome. Finding homes for things, a makeshift supper, and then clearing away, as he'd so often done wherever they'd lived, apart from in the Far East, when they'd had... what was her name? Lim that's right. And he smiles, remembering their amah, her ways, and how good she'd been with the twins.

That time had been strange at first too, and welcome on all sides – as a fresh start after the emotional storm that had ripped through their lives: his life, after his second stint at the school, and then theirs...

Slowly, methodically, savouring the aroma of a freshly opened packet of coffee, Dan prepares the mocha and lights the gas. Exploring Singapore and southern Malaya had certainly been an adventure for them both... even if it couldn't last, or it wasn't long enough, or just not enough. Day had followed day, long empty days with no word, no news, just the girl's unbroken, inexplicable, total silence.

Two years later they were back in England. And he'd had *another* fresh start: a university job this time – with the ache still there, an ache become an empty longing, become grief.

And now, suddenly, in the batting of an eye, seemingly, "university" was behind him too. Thirty-three years of it! All to be shelved in the past, as his life takes yet another uncharted direction.

Is it truly what he wants, or a limp acquiescence, an eternal making the best of a bad job?

The very last act of his university career had been the farewell sherry "do", which might have been a pleasant enough affair if the Vice-Chancellor, damn the man, hadn't shown up, taking over the proceedings from the Dean and seeing off his career in less than four minutes… including the presentation of the mantel clock, thrust into his hands with great solemnity as though it were the Holy Grail.

Dan had skirmished with the VC at Senate meetings often enough, disapproving of his mode of management and its corrosive effect on the University's *modus operandi,* though all to little effect. At least at that last meeting he'd attended, he'd had the satisfaction of seeing the man thoroughly riled. Oh yes.

The VC had been *smugly* lauding the Chemistry Department for its latest triumph – another lucrative Ministry of Defence contract. And Dale-Denton, of said Chemistry Department, had *smugly* responded, oozing self-importance. All very cosy.

But then Dan had stood up.

'Professor Dale-Denton, tell me: Do you or your staff ever ask yourselves to what uses your research is put by the MoD?'

'That really is no concern of ours, Professor Teal.' Dale-Denton snorts, dismissively. 'We take on a contract and we fulfil it. And we bring in considerable sums of money to the University, which, unless I am misinformed, is *not* the case with the History Department.'

Dan inclines his head graciously. 'Indeed, it is not. And thank goodness! For I should hate to risk having hundreds of deaths on my or my colleagues' conscience… a faculty which seems to have been misplaced in your own department's marketplace ethic.'

The colour drains from Dale-Denton's normally florid features. 'Vice-Chancellor, I protest!' he blusters. 'What we do is perfectly legitimate and above-board, in service of our country and our university…'

'But Professor Dale-Denton', Dan interrupts, before the VC has time to frame a response, 'to what precise uses are these "legitimate" and "above-board" *defoliants* actually put, and where? For I cannot think you are entirely unaware…'

'Gentlemen, please!' the VC thunders, making no secret of his displeasure at the tenor of this exchange, and doubtless to save Dale-Denton from further spluttering protest.

Dan looks round the room, seeing the VC's displeasure shared by most of those present – though perhaps not in the spirit he had intended. The two student representatives stand and walk out, as do a dozen or so other members of Senate, while some of those remaining heckle Dale-Denton, who, blushing furiously, resumes his seat.

It had been quite a spectacle. The students had then got to work, organising petitions and demonstrations, which had duly been reported on, with plenty of front-page speculation. But then, as is invariably the case with press-fuelled storms in teacups, it had all fizzled out. Or there'd been a certain amount of governmental pressure – the MoD, after all.

And then a couple of weeks later Dan had been waiting for a colleague in the staff bar, when a stranger had come up to him.

'Stuart Candley, Chemistry,' the man whispers, almost, holding out his hand. 'Sorry to intrude on your time, Professor Teal, but could I have a brief word? Something I think you should be aware of.'

'Yes? Please tell me... Can I get you a drink? A coffee?'

Candley shakes his head as his eyes sweep round the bar. 'Well, a couple of days ago, our professor – your *friend*, Dale-Denton – summoned me to his office. I'd hardly got there before he was called away, so he invited me to be looking through a file that was open on his desk. And this I did, *not* by taking it over to the seat I'd just been assigned, but at the desk, in his posh swivel chair.' He shrugs. 'Stuff relating to departmental meetings, procedural stuff, all pretty humdrum. But he was gone some time. And my eyes... strayed.'

Dan looks up. 'Go on.'

'There was this letter, on Ministry of Defence headed notepaper – that's what drew me to it. And in one paragraph, highlighted in red marker pen, it was suggested that the Vice-Chancellor... that's who the letter was *actually* addressed to by the way... should "find some pretext" for the dismissal of "troublesome staff" to ensure that sensitive MoD matters did not reach the press again!'

'Really!' Dan cannot hide his scorn.

'Yes. It shocked me to the core. And frankly… well, I thought *you* ought to be warned about it.'

And that was it. Troublesome staff retired, peaceably.

In the hours that followed, Dan could cheerfully have committed murder, or at very least confronted the VC with his duplicity. Pointless, though, he finally decided, since this kind of shiftiness was fast becoming the norm, in management. Instead, after a weekend's weighing up of the pros and cons, he'd handed in his letter of resignation.

'This is all rather sudden isn't it, Dan?' the Head of HR observes, affecting great surprise, and making a show of persuading him to take it back again, to reconsider. 'It's a huge step to take, especially in today's financial climate. And I doubt you'd be replaced.' He shrugs. 'At least think about it a bit longer.'

The Vice-Chancellor, doubtless informed that same day, had remained silent, presumably thanking his lucky stars.

And so he'd suffered the sherry party, the well-wishing and goodbyes, after which he'd left for good and all – declining the VC's invitation to lunch, since he 'had to be off early next morning.' A spur-of-the-moment pretext, rather than an untruth, as such.

Dan smiles wryly. For his eventual destination would certainly have bewildered his colleagues, it being so apparently out of character. Not Yale, or Melbourne or the Vales of some other Academe. Just an empty, open field barely ten miles from the campus: that's where he is!

Once here, however, there'd been the problem of regular provisioning, and of his books, before his real "departure" could be said to be imminent. The books, hundreds of them, had been deposited in the long shed inside the postern gate, by the Estates' people. And thus he'd set to work. And he'd sorted and shelved and catalogued, wondering all the while what the point of it was. Sentimentalism? Creating a museum for posterity, where all lost words are?

As for provisions, he'd drawn up lists, written letters and made phone calls, finding latter-day grocers and milkmen somewhat less than amenable to the perfectly reasonable requests he made of them, regarding delivery and payment.

All this, before he could even start on the field.

By the time Dan had reached the third week, the struggle with his will and the unreliable outside world had taken a greater toll on him than all his physical exertions. The very opposite of the freedom he'd imagined would be his once the world was pushed back beyond his gates.

So the ghost of time had lingered, still, about the house, a stubborn syntax steadfastly resisting its own threatened demise.

***

With the first glimmers of light – "before the morning watch", he thinks – Dan dresses quickly, and leaves the house. Climbing the hill, he sits for a while beneath its crown of rocks, out of the dawn wind, looking back down at the house. And he senses that his *vita nova* really is underway, at last: to seek out whatever lies the other side of his elective silence.

And he will begin today.

The moon and the morning star are still visible, even as the early greyness is transforming into sapphire. And as the red rim of the late summer sun rises over the Gog Magog hills, away to his left, it spills its ever-intensifying light out over the whole intervening valley.

The seventies' alterations to the building's west end had quite disguised it, but from this angle one was left in no doubt as to its original form and function: the rounded arches of its doors and windows, the corbels – gargoyles beneath the eaves – and the cross perched at the gable end, ensnared, almost, in the branches of the oaks which had been planted much too close at the eastern end.

And in a flash, he is transported back to the very first moments of that unexpected discovery. Just a month or so after their three-week voyage home, from Malaysia.

'Just look at this! Just look!' Penny had gasped, pushing open the groaning lychgate.

And they had indeed just stood and looked.

Yet amazement had soon given way to anger – at the neglect. The door, when they finally reached it, pushing through the tangled thicket, and nettles shoulder-high, had clearly at some time been forced, and hung, swinging elliptically on twisted hinges. There were even signs of old fires on the medieval tiles in the centre of the empty nave! A circle of stones, some ash, still. The whole place stinking of cats.

And the dust, suspended in the air, was caught in the wan rays of sunlight which barely penetrated the thickly cob-webbed, stained-glass windows.

How many years ago now? Over thirty, at least.

They had known surprisingly little about it at the village store.

'Never been up there myself, so can't tell you nothing much.'

'Bad, is it? My kids used to play up there, years back. They all said it were haunted.'

Haunted? A childish titter had fluttered round the handful of customers.

'Old Mr Johnson could tell you more, likely as not.'

'Weren't he caretaker or something like, at one time?'

'I do believe he were, now you come to mention it.'

And so they'd gone in search of Mr Johnson who had indeed proved "old" – blind, and almost completely deaf.

Who did they say they were? Had they come from the Water? The Gas, was it?

But when his anxieties were allayed and his importance established, he'd told them a great deal, in his ripe, fenland burr.

The land, he said, was owned by an Oxford college.

'Oi've not been up there in years. Don't get about like oi used to. But in the thirties – early on mind, when times was bad, when even them down London was feeling the pinch – some Church big-wig, down there, in London, he decided they couldn't pay the rent no more. It'd have been different, maybe, if the congregations could've been bigger, you see. But they wasn't, on account of all the people leaving the village, looking for work – it's a lot smaller now, but I can remember when… But anyhow, they wrangled on a bit, but it'd had to close down, in the end.'

'When was that?' Penny asks.

'Well, the very last service… it were just after the old king died. They come here from all over to that service – packed out, it were! But it were shut up that same day and not opened again till during the War, when the government had it. Nobody in the village ever knew what for, mind – still don't, to this day! And then, well, after the war, maybe kids broke in to play there. But apart from that…' And he shrugs, maybe at the waste of it.

'And the field?' Dan interrupts, his curiosity insistent.

'Well, that were used for grazing, off and on – hens and geese and what-not. Let out to one or other of the farmers round about. Too steep for much else, mind. Somebody started up a bit of a poultry farm, and that lasted a while, afore it went bust. Trouble was, th'only road in were the lychgate, you see. The poultry people, they'd wanted to get another right of way, but the Council wouldn't have it, and nor would her ladyship neither – she's dead-and-gone now, God rest her soul! She owned most of the woods around. There was just a goat or two, geese sometimes, hens, so… no, the field didn't get used much. I don't suppose you ever tried getting a herd of cows through a lychgate, and then up a ladder?'

And the corners of Mr Johnson's blind eyes had wrinkled into a sudden smile.

'The lychgate,' Dan murmurs, remembering that long-ago conversation: its function, always, and even now perhaps, the narrow way between the here and now, somewhere and... well, who could say what for sure?

And he remembers too, how they'd phoned the college bursar to find out more, dismayed at the neglect, and the man's initial blustering and excuses. But by the end of the call he'd found himself blurting out an offer.

'An offer? You've made them an offer – are you mad?' Penny was shocked. But only a moment later, captivated by the thought.

It would give them a new focus.

The old building had certainly been in need of restoration, initially to secure it against the elements, and then transform it into a house. Long hours of hard, physical labour at the weekends, and especially during vacations, which left them exhausted, yet exhilarated by what their hands were shaping together. And gradually, the house had become more than just a place to be in, at weekends, in the summer months, important though that was. With it, imperceptibly, they had redeemed the dark period their marriage had gone through since that year back teaching at the school and the following two in Malaysia, trying to put it all behind them... when they had believed they could.

Outside – thanks to the imaginative positioning of a pipe, a trench and a cast-iron horse trough they'd come across – a "troublesome spring" was rerouted, the water taken off down into the wood on the eastern side.

And the graveyard on their doorstep? What were they to do about that?

'Our silent neighbours, we can't just ignore them, can we?' Penny had worried, only half-jokingly.

Round and round it they'd gone, until one day...

'How about a rose bush for every grave? Would that do it, do you think?'

And thus the rose garden had come into being.

'The Taylors are covered in greenfly!'
'Miss Earnshaw has a touch of mildew!'

And a curious sense of neighbourliness had grown – feeding their rose families, spraying them, keeping them clear of weeds and tares.

Dan smiles at the foolish memory. Strange though, that he alone, now, will live out the consequences of this and so many other decisions they'd made together, back then.

Did Penny ever remember things like this?

All such a long time ago.

Standing now by the trough, contemplating his reflection in its crystal-clear, gently rippling water, Dan is distracted by something else.

His grasshopper mind up to its tricks, is it, or just a momentary effect of light glancing off a watery mirror?

Resonances, anyway, wrinkling across time.

IV

The sky is full of stars, despite the dull glow from the nearby city, but there is no moon. And here he is going along a dark street with... Johnny Stone, of course... back for the summer from his cushy teaching job in Abadan. And Johnny is swearing he can't go another step. 'God help us, but I'll burst if I don't.' But now, they are at the end of Holly's street and Dan is urging him on. 'Hold out, Johnny, not far now. Grit your teeth, cross your legs. No Aintree Iron, alas! but there *is* Freddy's shiny new motor car, see? Never shut up bragging about it has he, all evening?'

'Well I could never stand him, when I was at the school,' says Johnny. 'So yes, why not!'

Laying their bundles of fish and chips ('nine times love, three patties and two extra portions of chips') on the gleaming bonnet, they take up their positions and in unison unzip.

Delirium of relief. From pent-up, aching rivers. Dan starting from the radiator, Johnny from the boot, in a slow, clockwise gyration. An endless stream of devotion, dripping from the fenders and sills, steaming in the cold starlight.

'Libations,' says Johnny, contemplatively, 'libations, yes – that's what your Ancient Greeks called it, didn't they?' The relief isn't just physical, though. Freddy's shiny new blue motor car; scapegoat for what, exactly?

Turning away from the trough – smiling at the distant memory, and the silliness of what they'd done – Dan walks slowly back inside the house.

Coffee, he thinks, and shakes yesterday's grounds from the mocha into the pedal bin before refilling it and setting it on a low light on the stove. He stands for a moment or two looking through the window, back up the field, at the warm glow of sunlight steadily expanding.

'Today, I'll make a start on cutting out those first steps.' He says the words out loud, as though it were a public announcement, and therefore maybe even binding.

But images of the before and after of that distant evening with Johnny and other erstwhile teaching colleagues still tug at the edges of memory, demanding attention.

'OK, you guys! The big pay out!' yells Johnny, as they burst in on the smoke-filled, speakeasy movie-set of Holly's bed-sit, and drop the bundles of fish and chips on top of the cards littering the centre of the table.

Holly leaps up from his chair. 'For Christ's sake, Johnny! Dan! Mind those glasses! The bottles, for God's sake!'

So what's eating Holly?

But of course, it's Freddy, isn't it? Holly and Freddy: Abbot and Costello. At it, hammer-and-tongs, even before they'd gone off to the chippie. Holly throwing down his cards, eyes burning like red-hot coals, almost starting from their sockets. Just as Dan remembered it from their staffroom bridge sessions, previously.

'Idiot! You blithering idiot, Freddy! You've thrown it away again!'

The same old worn-out farce. Bridge-time blues!

'Good to see nothing's changed, then,' Dan quips.

But Holly rounds on *him* now, in his fury.

'Oh, you'll find a great deal's changed!' he yells. 'You know, *you* had a lot to answer for, especially where young Saunders was concerned. You skipped off to… wherever it was, but you left us with a heap of problems, starting with Saunders.'

'Cocky little bastard!' Freddy chimes, rolling another of his matchstick cigarettes. Seeking unction, maybe?

'Who is, Freddy?' someone chips in, all innocent like.

'Saunders, of course!' Holly spins round, crimson with anger and alcohol, and he pauses only to wipe away the saliva running down his chin. 'Saunders is who we're bloody-well talking about, isn't he? Discipline! That's what he needed, the opinionated little runt!'

'The National-Service, Sergeant-Instructor's brand, you mean, Holly?' Dan jibes back, ruffled by Holly's insinuations.

'That's right!' Holly growls. 'Speak when you're spoken to. On your feet when a teacher comes into the room. And "sir" every time.'

Johnny shakes his head, slowly. 'God help us, Holly! And how did that work out?'

'Saunders – he speaks only when he's spoken to, now. Can't get on his feet fast enough when a teacher comes in. Never, but never, forgets the "sir".' Holly looks round, beaming in triumph. Ever the preening peacock. 'He's seen, but seldom heard.'

'Well, there *are* other ways, Holly,' Dan says, loftily, still bewildered, and irritated, by this response to what had been intended as a joke, after all. 'But then, it depends on what you believe education is all about, doesn't it? Personally, I don't buy into the "spare the rod" creed, producing kids who "speak only when they're spoken to."'

But Holly couldn't let it rest, could he, even after they'd returned with the fish and chips?

'And it wasn't just Saunders when you buggered-off. Half your bloody class seemed to think they were owed special treatment. Well, they got it right enough, those third-formers!'

Irritated, Dan turns away to take one of the newspaper-wrapped packages.

Others follow suit, taking refuge in eating, or adding more salt, vinegar, sauce... And for a short while there's an uneasy silence.

But then Holly starts up again.

'You ask Alvin, here,' he mumbles, stuffing chips into his mouth. '*He* had the messy job of picking up the pieces, after you upped sticks...'

'Don't bring me into it,' says Alvin, with an oleaginous smile. 'This is your show, Holly, old chum. I'm absolutely neutral.'

'Neutered, more like,' Johnny mutters in Dan's ear, none too quietly.

Snap, snap, snap.

Later that evening, Johnny warns him about Alvin.

'Watch out for that greasy git! From what I hear, he really raked the muck about you. Grilled some of the kids, spread rumours.'

'Grilled the kids, you say!' Dan frowns. 'But what on earth about? And what sort of rumours? What are you on about, Johnny?'

And yet, they'd reappointed him, hadn't they, *and* without interview? So, what on earth was going on?

'Alan will fill you in about it. He told me when I was back here last summer. But that guy must be shitting bricks right now, behind that facade of *bonhomie* – I'll bet you're the last person on earth he ever hoped to meet! Anyway, Dan, it takes a courageous man – or a fool – to go back anywhere. So, which are you, then?'

Dan laughs. 'Ah, well. It was just a convenient coincidence or, you're now making me think, maybe not so *convenient* after all. Applying for jobs from abroad isn't easy – as you may well discover yourself if you ever think of coming back permanently. It was the only one that came up trumps.' He frowns again. 'But hold on a mo', what about you? Every time the Persian Oil Pashas send you off on your over-long, over-paid vacations, you make a beeline for this place, don't you?'

'Sure! I do.'

'So?'

'Nostalgia, Dan. Old times. Old mates. But I would never dream of *working* at the place again. Whereas your coming back, well, it looks to me like a clear case of insanity, a leap from the sublime to the... What went wrong with Greece, anyway? The Colonels, was it?'

Dan lifts the hissing mocha off the stove, pours some coffee and sits down at the kitchen table.

Yes, Greece had crumbled around them with the coming of the

Colonels. Greece, their first new start into something more exciting, more in line with his academic aspirations than school-teaching in a northern backwater, rewarding though it had been, in its way.

The sparkling, moon-white sands at Isixia. Midnight water warm on their tanned bodies; the air breathing rosemary and thyme. And then the awful contradictions of those last few weeks. All that beauty cradling such savage cruelty and fear. Colleagues who suddenly weren't there anymore. Friends beaten, some tortured, humiliated. People disappearing, being killed. The age-old cycle of ferocity starting up again. The Horsemen abroad again. As if the country hadn't suffered enough of that already, in the forties and fifties!

Dan finishes off the coffee and sets his cup down in the sink, before jetting it with cold water.

And then, of course, in the wake of that disturbing evening with Johnny Stone and co, the bewitchment that was soon to follow, when, for a time, '*methought I was... And methought I had...*'

But Holly, Johnny and Alan, Alvin too... whatever became of them?

***

Summer slips inconspicuously into autumn. And each shortening day Dan spends between field and shed, shed and greenhouse, greenhouse and field.

It had been easier when he left the turf where it was, or under nearby hedges. But his decision to cart away all the grass sods as he removes them, first from one side of the centre path, then from the other, preliminary to eventual manuring and planting, doesn't last long: the work is too slow and heavy. Each time he plunges the fork into the earth he encounters resistance – compacted turf, the tough clay, endless stones, and rocks. Not to mention the distances he must traverse to dispose of the thick sods, and the stones. It all slows his progress, and leaves him exhausted, disconsolate.

Sometimes, as if to compensate, he works on after darkness

has fallen, the long habit of impatience gripping him, still. But his resolution is then at its weakest, the voices whispering that this is all folly, that no one but he requires it – no one. So why go on? And eventually he collapses into bed, often too tired to get himself some supper even.

And then next morning, as he rises at dawn and looks out of the upstairs windows, scrutinising his gradually changing landscape, his spirits soar. And once more he is eager to be out and doing.

Gradually, his tactics change. Cairns of stones and rock now dot his landscape, as if waymarks to something. And distinct islands appear in the slowly diminishing sea of green on either side of the central path. And as the first leaves begin to fall, gradually piling in golden drifts about the margins of the field, he senses he must soon call a halt, that this frenetic cutting away must stop if he doesn't want to miss the autumn planting, minimal though it must be in this first year.

And here they come again, these entrancing stills from the past, these ghosts, rooting themselves deep in the unfolding garden.

***

He is in the park, heading along the path leading to the boating lake, walking fast. Going home for his lunch.

Several minutes later, as he passes the far end of the lake, there is a sudden commotion, and he looks back. Someone (it sounds like a man's voice) is shouting angrily, but the curving path, the screen of shrubs and the strong September wind lashing the trees make it impossible to find out without going back, which he cannot do because of the time, the time…

'That's the new history teacher, isn't it?' Andrea whispers to Titania, as they watch him pass through the park gates, just ahead of them. 'He doesn't look very old, does he?' Then, with a giggle: 'Do you fancy him? I do!' She sighs, but before her invitation to like confession can be taken up adds: 'But… he'll be married. The best ones always are…'

Once inside the gates, the two girls go their separate ways. And even before Andrea has shouted her goodbye, Titania is thinking back to the morning, about the part Mr Hollywell has asked her to play in this year's school production. She dawdles up the steep slope, excited, anxious, and wholly immersed in her thoughts.

What an odd little bantam-cock of a man Holly – as everyone calls him – is. Does she like him? She's never sure, though today is different, for he has offered her the part: *the* part. Before the summer, when they'd read for parts (and Mr Kelday had encouraged her himself), it was all different, winding down. Now, everything is winding up. Then she sighs, knowing well enough what her parents will say. 'If only it were the *Winter's Tale* or *Lear,* one of your *exam* plays, dear.' Then they might have given her their blessing. As it is, well…

She turns and looks back down the hill towards the water. She can see Andrea hurrying along, and way in front of her, the gap ever-widening between them, the new teacher, already well past the end of the lake.

Mr Teal. Yes, maybe she does fancy him a bit, whatever that means. And she laughs at herself, at her lack of experience of such things. Of most things really, other than school and home and being at the sea.

At morning break-time, going slowly along the corridor in the direction of the staffroom, with Holly's arm around her shoulder, listening carefully to what he was saying about the play, he'd been there, the new teacher, hadn't he? She'd seen him out of the corner of her eye, yes, talking earnestly, familiarly, it seemed, to a girl she didn't know, a fifth-former maybe. Odd – the thought had flitted through her mind – a *new* teacher having that sort of, well, intimate-seeming conversation, on only the second day back at school.

But her thoughts are suddenly scattered. There's some shouting; and… was that a scream?

She stops again, gazing back down towards the boathouse. And there he is, the teacher, also looking back, though only for a moment. A crowd of boys, running, strung out in a line along the edge of the lake, and two of them carrying... carrying what? Oars. They're carrying oars: holding them high above their heads, like banners.

For a split-second she is sure someone must have fallen in the water and her heart skips a beat. Then she sees old Charlie, the boat-keeper, hobbling away after the boys, shaking his fist, and shouting. Every now and again one of the boys stops and turns, shouting back at him, at the same time slapping his haunches, spurring on his imaginary steed, taunting, then off again. And instantly, her fear turns to anger. Their cruel, senseless tormenting of the old man is contemptible.

Titania turns away in disgust.

***

Lingering on in his mind, still there all these years later. A trivial, inconsequential moment. But in what circumstances, and with what separate imaginings had they come to share it, he and Titania?

That now was beyond knowing.

Taking out the last turf from a long, snaking bed, Dan decides to call a halt for the year. Other beds would come later, and road making – when most of the "cairns" of stones would come into their own and eventually disappear – that must be for the winter. There would be yews *above* the steps leading down towards the house, and again in the shallow coomb near the bluff. But hitherto Dan has not thought out in any detail what plants he will place in this bottom-most section, and the rest, too, is unformed, blurred in his inward eye.

A blind renaissance, since there are no blueprints extant, only ancient rumour, ancient yearning. The quantum leap.

And with that beguiling thought, he hurries off indoors and, collecting pencil, paper, and drawing-board, sits at the wide window on the upper floor, looking down on the shaping garden, sketching a plan of the mazy pattern of borders and islands he has thus far created. It isn't to scale of course. But he can see already that despite his industriousness – the huge order of plants from the nearest nursery, his poring over his books about seeds, about cuttings, and the satisfaction of successfully applying this new knowledge – the contents of the greenhouse will still leave a sense of emptiness. Of course, there would be eventual self-seeding, he reminds himself, eventual addition; and besides, the sparseness would give time for reflection about other possibilities in his continuous probing upwards.

Yet, adjusting his mind, his whole temperament, to the long-term, instead of lusting after the immediate, is no easy matter. Remaking self is as hard as refashioning the earth, he well recognises. For now, however, he will imagine borders of rosemary ('that's for remembrance...') leading on from the yews to a single Judas tree, at the very first bifurcation, the opening exchanges of a complex discourse.

But between this and final clarity there lies a still tortuous labyrinth of paths, beds, and undefined ambitions, further back in his mind.

As his fish bakes in the oven, Dan takes the edge off his hunger with a bowl of cornflakes, and unaccountably, Rosemary's poem sidles back into his mind. He'd been too tired to look for it the other day. Does he still have it? Or her letters?

When later he starts to turn out drawers and boxes, stubbornness and impatience drive him, a hysteria almost, gradually mounting as the possibilities diminish.

Oh, come on, Teal, he chides himself, this is ridiculous! What do these elusive bits of paper have to do with anything, anything that matters now?

He sits down, having almost forced himself back into reason, and then the telephone starts to ring, down in the hall. Turmoil boils up inside him. His heart churns, his palms sweat, and, struggling to subdue his curiosity about this incursion, he grips the arms of his chair, then rubs his hands along them to wipe away the tumescence.

Then he leaps up and slams the door, instantly transmuting if not quite banishing the sound to the outer edges of consciousness.

Sitting down once more, he wonders again at his fixation with this poem, and the events which lay behind and beyond it. Is it really just a pointless curiosity?

The distant ringing ceases altogether, and in that instant, it comes to him.

On his feet again, he opens the filing cabinet behind the door and takes out a bulky envelope file bearing the faded legend, *The British Infection: Notes towards a novel*. And here it is. Rosemary's large, rounded, schoolgirl hand, equally faded. And as his eye runs down the page, he realises that only he, now, can have any inkling of its conjunctural significance, then, this desperate, now meaningless message cast up by a tide that had receded long ago. Poor Rosemary! What it must have cost her, that night; that, together with everything else she suffered daily. Too much for anyone to bear, let alone a sixteen-year-old schoolgirl.

And a strange thing it turns out to be, more so than he had remembered it.

> *Swirling blackness whirlpooling blackness timeless void*
> *headlong down*
> *bloodswirling vortex downrushing leat blackwholing I*
> *darkling here*
> *neverendingly turning neverendingly turning turning*
> *centrifugalling I*
> *river of darkness river of light confluencing I*
> *am Rosemary*
> *moonflowering, I marbled hand plucking me out of my*
> *darkness*
> *smooth bark wrinkled hand symbiotic I am the tree am the*
> *light*
> *rooted in darkness*
> *shaken from an empty dream.*

He marvels, wholly perplexed. Could Rosemary *really* have written this, such mature diction, conception? But if not, where had it come from? Had he perhaps written it himself? But no, the handwriting… Frowning he quickly scans the rest before returning with it to his chair to reflect on what else he remembers, if it is memory, about the poem's context.

That terrible Sunday evening.

V

Rosemary's face turns upwards, globules of light trembling on her lashes, her body cold and stiff. She stretches, uncomfortably. Had she fainted? How long has she been here?

Away to her left, suddenly, for a moment, the purr of voices. Then silence. And through this cold, cloying silence it all comes back to her.

She listens though willing them to be gone. But the voices drone on, the laughter rising and falling amid silences.

Cold, alien laughter.

She sits up a bit, and turns her face from this laughter, which is pushing her out into the cold again, outside their precious little circle. But it wasn't "again", was it, for she'd really never been anywhere but outside, not really.

So why had they seemed to admit her?

And what did being "inside" mean, anyway? She snorts. It meant saying 'yes' to what she doesn't want, wearing her silence like a... yes, like a shroud. Oh, to hell with them! Saunders, Willetts. And especially vain, ridiculous Rosalind, flashing her... tits – *she* was the worst. Pretending to be her friend, when all she wanted was someone to listen to her, or to boss about, or adore her!

And *he* hadn't helped either, had he, their Mr Teal? All that trying to inspire them, and get them to think about things, to *really* think, to discuss them like adults – not like 'wooden puppets dancing on examiners' strings...' Making them do what he called his 'analytical thinking' and see connections between things.

It had made sense then, been exciting for the second-year pupils they'd been then, when she'd started to think school was really worth bothering about after all.

And then he'd gone. Abandoned them. Broken the spell.

His wooden puppets, that's all they'd been, in the end.

They'd given him his leaving present and said goodbye and it had felt so strange, so final, like a… funeral. Certainly, *she* had cried.

Rosemary thumps the ground to her right with her closed fist. She'd kept telling herself she didn't miss him for two whole years, that she wouldn't miss him, hated him, even. And she still did hate him. Because the world was *not* what he'd said it was, it just wasn't! Everything that happened, in every moment, proved it. At school, at home…

That summer, after he'd gone, Val, her only real friend, had got ill and died. How did that happen, in just a few weeks?

After that she'd been scared, so scared of going back to school. No more Val. And no nice teacher, just mindless rules without reasons, being herded about, and being no one, again.

Choking back her tears, she stretches out her legs, and thinks she should be getting home. But before clambering to her feet she listens out again.

More laughter. The three of them, laughing. Something witty sardonic Saunders has said, very likely; probably about her.

He'd been different back then, though, clever-clogs Saunders. Two or three of them, him included, had almost been in tears that first break time, when Rosalind had made those incredible insinuations, said things that had made them all gasp.

Rosemary winces, remembering hearing all the insinuations or confessions or whatever they were, and how she'd hardly been able to stop herself crying, trying to hide behind her desk lid, shut it all out.

And then the miracle – or it had felt like one!

Rosemary lifts her chin. *She*, the girl whom nobody gave a thought about, had given *them* just the right words – which they'd battened onto, all of them! A little thing, really, but maybe big in that moment of… of their sort of… collective misery. Her timing had been just perfect. Oh, if only she could live *that* again, that feeling of being… someone who mattered.

How on earth had she managed it?

'A callous manipulator of vulnerable emotions,' she had declared, standing up and stepping in among them, trembling but unafraid. 'That's what he was! A callous manipulator of emotions.'

It was something she'd read in the *Mail*, a few days before, about a man who'd been tricking old people out of all their savings and jewels.

But whether she believed it or not, meant it or not, she'd been "in" after that. In the "in-crowd".

Or that's how it had seemed.

***

It has been one of those still, bright days in autumn when there is so little movement of air that the pockets of mist gathering before dawn never really disperse, suffusing with slowly curling smoke from leaves and twigs smouldering and flaring by turns, in his garden fires.

Coming slowly up to the bluff, heaving at one last barrow-load of wet cement, Dan pauses to rest in the shallow coomb between the two slender, newly planted yews. Setting the barrow down, he scrambles to the upper edge and gently shakes the trellis he had put up a few days earlier for the jasmine he will plant there in the spring. Firm as a rock. And he congratulates himself, while knowing the real test will be the winter with its increasingly frequent gales.

Taking up the barrow, he moves on a few steps, but stops again. The birds in Hall Wood have been twittering incessantly since sun-up, gathering in whirling clouds above the trees, making ready for off; but a sudden, deep hush has fallen. From one moment to the next, this fathomless silence.

'What is it?' he asks out loud, maybe to dispel the ridiculous, fearful half-thought that total deafness has descended upon him. Abandoning his load, he goes on up towards the ridge, to see better. At first, nothing, for the westering sun, lowering in the sky, blood-red, turns his vision black, but then as sight is restored, he spots it, the hovering hawk in the fiery haze above the trees, waiting for the moment to swoop and snatch.

And there is nothing at all to be done about it; the hawk knows, as the espoused victim knows: this life-giving death, the endless gathering up of myriad particles of being into the all-digesting darkness.

Yet, even as these thoughts are forming in his mind, the hawk veers off and glides away out of sight.

And, as though day has failed to follow night, he stands there amazed, eyes pinned on the silent wood over to his left.

A link broken in the chain.

Then incredibly, out of the dying sun they come. Three huge Montgolfier balloons!

For an instant the sun itself seems one with them as they glide behind gauze, *larghetto*, seriatim, like slow thoughts evolving. In the van, silver and green stripes; close behind, a humbug black and white; then trailing just a little further off, a scarlet *doppelganger* to the sun. Gaily coloured, and begetting an instantaneous, miraculous transfiguration on this petrified world.

And Dan gapes and smiles in spellbound fascination, while the birds, spasmodically at first, still cowering among the trees' almost-threadbare branches, take up their chorusing again, as if in praise of these knights-errant that have routed their tormentor. A seeming miracle.

Yet still he stands there, absorbed by them, by their dreamlike drift across the sky, taken up into them and transported to a higher reach of intensity – until they pass over the crest and fade into the dusk; and he slowly descends to awareness of his neglected task, fearing now for the cement already hardening in the barrow.

Inhaling deeply, still wondering, he strides back down the slope and plunges a finger into the khaki-grey mass: stiffening all right, but still workable.

'Must get a move on,' he mutters, seizing the barrow's handles, 'or it'll be too dark to see.'

And with renewed vigour off he goes, almost at a canter, up to the bluff. And by swift, decisive flicking movement of his trowel – a deftness lately acquired – he manages to have two of the three steps nicely in place before judging the day, and the cement, too far gone to progress further.

Then he heads back down the hill, tools clanging and clanking in the wheelbarrow.

Near the house, the smoke-laden mist seems thicker than before, having an almost physical quality about it, in the softness of the advancing evening. Dan rakes up leaves, curled, rusting, rustling, brown-edged memories, and heaps one last load into the incinerator, before replacing his tools on their hooks in the shed, rinsing out the barrow, and turning finally towards the house.

But as he rounds the corner his mind is jerked sharply away and his spirits plummet: the telephone is ringing.

He hesitates, hurries forward, hesitates. And it irks him that the world beyond his gates can throw him into such a dilemma still, that this intrusion – if he makes the wrong decision – might lead to others whose consequences could be even graver. But what irks him most is his sudden upsurge of curiosity, which tells him that despite his best endeavours to the contrary the old ties linger still.

He opens the door. But before he has reached either the door or a clear decision, the ringing has ceased.

Once inside, he goes upstairs to the bathroom, changes into cleaner clothes for the evening, then enters his study, where his eye alights on Rosemary's poem.

Such a terrible pity. Yet he sees the inevitability of it now: his departure for Greece, born of personal ambition, had left his pupils vulnerable, too young still to cope with the heavy burden of authority that had subsequently descended upon them – singled them out – with Holly the Sergeant-Instructor maliciously directing operations.

Dan puts the poem back in the folder, mildly curious, since he has it in his hands, about what sorts of things might then have constituted *The British Infection*. He leafs through the uppermost pages, and there, on one typewritten sheet, numbered 11, he reads:

Rosemary suddenly realised she had been walking for a long time, she did not know how long, nor had she made any conscious decision about direction or destination. With her mind searching the past, she had climbed up out of the town and found herself, now, some way along the moor road. There was a bench a bit further on, set on a hummock, she recalled, from which, on a clear day, you could see for miles around, and she decided she would make for that. It was still raining lightly, but now she was moving she felt better.

Reaching the bank, she scrambled up to the bench. It was very wet, so she couldn't sit on it, but leaning against its back she peered down into the little she could see of the town. The mist was heavy. There was the wood just below, which was stark and black, even before it was lost in the grey pall which hung over the valley. Here and there, though further off, were stabs of light, and for just an instant she thought she could make out the town-hall clock and the curve of the streetlights that swept round one side of the park. But the mist closed round again, and the void reclaimed them. Everything was dark and dank. She thought of Rosalind down there in the blackness, in the park. For an unthinking moment she panicked at the thought of Rosalind, down there. Would she... would she have... covered herself again, or what? But Rosemary could not go back. Not now, not ever. She pulled up her sleeve to look at her watch and was stunned to find it wasn't there!

Dan looks for the page's continuation but there is nothing. And he is perplexed. Clearly, he had written this, but was it the result of things Rosemary herself had told him in one of her letters, or had he imagined this whole episode himself? And how might it have fitted into a novel bearing such a title? There had been so many false starts, and none of them conclusive, he recalls, and as the folder's bulky contents confirm. But what does it matter now?

And yet, a continuation there had certainly been, later still that same night. He distinctly recalls a plangent letter, full of a sense of injustice, spelling out the cruel details.

***

'Where have you been until this time?' Her mother is white with rage.

Her father's eyes open, and he rises from the settee. 'Don't you know your mother and me have been worried sick something awful had happened to you?'

'She doesn't care. The girl's far too selfish to care! And your clothes, just look at your clothes! They're covered in mud. Your best coat, your good skirt, your stockings laddered. Just look at them!'

'What have you been up to, to get in that state?'

'Have you been doing something you shouldn't, young lady? You must have, to look a sight like this!'

'A tramp. That's what you are!'

'Rosalind was home hours ago, so who have you been with since you left her?'

'What have you been up to?'

'If you get yourself pregnant, you're out of this house, you'll get no sympathy from us. The shame of it!'

Rosemary begins to cry silently.

'So that's it, is it? You're no better than a prostitute!'

'Twenty to one you walk in here and think it'll be quite all right. Well, you're wrong, it isn't all right, young lady. It never occurred to you, I suppose, that I have to be up for work in less than six hours' time...'

'... Nor that you have school, tomorrow!'

Rosemary jerks her head up and looks defiantly at her parents.

'I'm not going back to school. Not tomorrow, not ever. I'm going to get a job. I'm going to get as far away from this place as I can, as quickly as I can. I've had enough of your... Owwww!'

With the flat of her hand her mother has fetched Rosemary a stinging blow across her mouth.

VI

The crows and choughs that wing the midway air show scarce so gross as beetles...

Choughs? What on earth are choughs? Some sort of bird, obviously. Never heard of them. And Titania marks the book lightly with her pencil.

Back in August, it had been gannets, terns and razorbills cutting and wheeling in "the midway air" between the beach and the cliff tops.

The serene horizon, its azure band, its pearly radiance – those unforgettable days by the sea.

And yond tall anchoring bark diminished to her cock, her cock a buoy...

Oh dear! Whatever can all that mean? Let's see. She consults the notes at the bottom of the page. *Cock boat: a small ship's boat... almost too small for sight.* Hm, yes, that makes sense: the tall bark too small, almost, to see, but still visible – just – there, on the water. Hm!

The murmuring surge... I'll look no more, lest my brain turn, and the deficient sight topple down headlong...

"The murmuring surge." She likes that. It makes her think of the trembling, silvery sea that glorious day along the cliff tops, by the golf course, the seabirds high, diving and dipping, Prince barking and darting everywhere at once, and mummy saying that David and she were not to go any nearer the edge.

She smiles, closes the book, and lingers in the memory. Mummy does always worry so, even on the brightest days.

And suddenly she remembers this new thing, the thing at school she has not yet had the courage to tell them about. She *so* much wants to be Titania. Mummy always means well, of course, but she doesn't always understand, even if she thinks she does.

And the would-be seventeen-year-old actress frowns and sucks in her cheeks momentarily, startled by this hint of defiance in her thoughts. But she just has to make them understand, somehow. She has to!

Titania takes up the book again but does not open it, for something down by the boating lake has caught her eye, fleetingly. A crow, perhaps, or the old man, pottering about as usual, on his own, his sharp, copper-tanned features seeming to glow as he faces the morning sun. He sees her looking and waves, so she waves back, and she watches for a while as he goes about his work, calmly, unhurriedly. There is something about him that fills her with a sense of… well, it must be respect, she supposes. Then he disappears again, behind the boathouse.

In an instant, she has passed from shadow into sunlight. The darkening thoughts which had threatened a moment or two before flee her mind, and she smiles her contentment as images of that month at the sea come crowding back. There was that long white boat they had watched rounding the headland, so light and swift it hardly seemed to touch the water, and as it steered straight for the shore far below them the singing voices of its occupants had drifted up towards them on the breeze.

Titania stands, then saunters down the hill to the lake's edge. All around its sides there are patches of reeds growing in the soft mud. And then she notices that the mud is all churned up close to a bench, and she thinks of cattle straggling slowly down to the lake to drink, like some painting she vaguely remembers, so quiet and peaceful is it. But, of course, that's silly. There couldn't be cattle in a park! Then she remembers the fracas the other day, when the boys had been chased by the old man. But that had been further round, surely?

The steeply rising sun is already hot on her face, and she feels a sense of relief when the path at last leads her in among the trees, where it is noticeably cooler and where the dew still glistens, shielded as yet from the warming day. She bends down and lightly lays her outspread palms upon the dewy grass, then presses them gently against her burning cheeks.

Yes, that's it! She'll take mummy a cup of coffee, and... 'Mummy, this play, it's something I have to do... No, it's not one we have to study for A-levels... Yes, I know. But the important point is that it will help me understand much better the ones I *am* doing, like *Lear*. Mr Kelday says Shakespeare's like that. He says the more plays you know the deeper your appreciation of any single one of them.'

Well, he did! Titania justifies, to her less truculent self. And she laughs. But yes, it was the way to do it. They'd approve of that. Surely, they would – with that little bit of help from Mr K, they would. They must!

And as she continues her musing along the deserted pathway by the shore, Titania plucks a reed, and absent-mindedly wraps it around her waist, as though it were a belt, a cord.

***

Trees, bereft and tattered in the woods around; gentle mists easing into fog in the late afternoons; hoar frosts carpeting the hillside – these are sure signs that the year is ending, and Dan, a novice gardener still, starts to fear for his tenderer shoots only lately transplanted. And the "special order" forms for Christmas fare slipped in among his groceries and the "Post Early for Christmas!" reminders on every envelope he takes from the box by the postern. These too are signs, small intrusions. But each time he finds one it sparks flashes of anger and resentment in him – the presumptions, the presumptuousness of the commercial world.

Letters, and especially postcards, are the hardest thing – readdressed by his former neighbour in town, no doubt thinking to do him a kindness, still. And only when his mood of rejection is at its fiercest, a mood Dan has quickly learned to value, does he find the courage to outface them.

Anything hand-written he burns without opening, though sometimes, oh sometimes, if it is a hand or a stamp he recognises, the temptation is overpowering. From Calgary. From Melbourne. Even from Ireland – for in spite of Penny's insistence that the break should be final, there have been cards every April, and then at Christmas. Like it or not, by one means or another, he can't help knowing another year has passed.

Commercial junk-mail, on the other hand, he tears instantly to shreds and consigns to the hottest flames of the garden fires. Occasionally, though, he has to open things, particularly envelopes with a fiscal smell about them, before he can dispatch them to bank or accountant, or the flames. Dan shakes his head wryly. He can't afford to make a slip: just one failed payment or an official form overlooked could lead to an invasion.

And when this kind of thing happens, having to open things just in case, he finds himself reasoning that despite all his precautions and denials he is still engaged in a rear-guard action against the despised, modern world, effectively a race against time. And one he may not stand a chance of winning.

Winter arrives, when good sense should dictate that he avoid working long hours out in the cold and rain, and that even on the brightest days he limit himself to the hours of daylight, despite the steadily reducing number of hours this means he is able to work.

He shrugs. It's not that he can't usefully use his days, even the wettest and the coldest, for there is always plenty to be done inside or in the greenhouse and potting shed, preparing for the spring planting. No, it is simply that his main task, completing the layout and first turning of the soil in the lowest section, is taking so much longer than he'd imagined.

He sighs his frustration, and quickly comes to the decision that if he is not to lose a whole year's growth he just has to keep working outside. The ground needs to be broken and manured, to weather away in the extremes of winter and be ready for hoeing into a 'workable tilth' in the early spring – or so the books say! And then again, over on the right side of the hill, the slope is noticeably steeper than elsewhere, so terracing it will be essential.

Day after day, therefore, Dan continues to give every possible moment to these and other tasks. Yet, with the rain, the ground becomes heavier and heavier, and progress, when he can go out, well-nigh impossible.

And soon his body – stretched, contorted, crouching unnaturally, for over-long periods – knows real exhaustion, always pressing against the limits of time in its urgency, eager as he is to ascend, but painfully slow in the climbing. And his body, at least, is thankful for the heavier rain when it comes, truly thankful, for the enforced respite it brings.

Winter was a traditional time of relaxation, wasn't it, a time to take up long-abandoned interests? Retirement was supposed to allow one time for reading and painting, and indulging a fancy or two, such as wood carving.

So far, all he has managed is a small head of Janus, roughly fashioned over the course of a month from a root of yew, then placed at the foot of the Judas tree, where the bottom pathways divide.

One bright morning, early, when a heavy frost has put paid to any levelling on the slope, Dan strides up through the emerging garden, up the three steps now surmounted by his trellised arch, which supports newly planted climbers – red and white the label promised – and up to the still empty area before the rocks.

Any attempt at cultivation on the slope that fell down the other side, a little way beyond the rocks, he had always seen as pointless – enclosed as it was on three sides by dense woodland – and way beyond his physical capabilities. And he avoids it mostly, to look back down the gentler southern slope towards the house.

To his surprise, he sees how the prospect has already changed. It is not so much the effect of the shrubs and other plants, for they are still small and slender, but of the arches and pathways. Though in part tricks of vision, perhaps, they are steadily translating the house below into this new context he is shaping.

And as his gaze wanders over the land he smiles his pleasure. Yes... maybe this garden, if he can complete it, will, in some arcane way, have the effect of connecting his as yet uncertain future with all his pasts.

What would Penny have made of it? Of his decision to quit the University, and end up living here? Fifteen years now... when for months after she had gone, he would find himself wandering about, here or at their town house, still half expecting to find her there. Fifteen years!

Like a death, it had been, made bearable in its familiarity only by time's passing.

He stands for a while still, contemplating that long, agonising time in his past, before walking slowly back down, pausing under the oaks by the apse of the building, then passing through the gravestones to then stand before the lychgate.

And once again in his mind's eye he sees her, in a sudden, distant memory sprung with flowers.

She is standing at a window looking out into the sunlit garden of a prospective house they didn't buy, while upstairs the children's feet thunder across the vast floor, their gleeful screams and whooping coming ever more frequently as they pick up echoes in the empty rooms; back and forth, stamping and shouting, wrapped in their moment of joy.

'Under those trees,' she is saying, 'under those trees, there, I would plant aconites, daffodils and snowdrops for the spring.'

And so she had, one day – not there, but here. Penny and her flowers.

And Ben and he, how many times had they ended their long rambles over Hare Hill or through the woods sitting up here on the rocks, Ben panting at his feet – there where he now sleeps his final, earthly sleep. And Penny, knowing they must soon arrive, would come to the door, and raise her hand when the kettle was singing. So many times, over those few short years.

But from up here by the rocks the door, he suddenly realises to his dismay, has been somehow obscured by the bottom-most arch and its yews. And a stab of remorse brings him yet again to the question that has plagued him since even before the outset of this journey: the inner struggle between the desire to preserve everything as it always has been and the intuition, for it is no more than that, that he must transform it all gradually, purposefully, into something very different.

Nostalgia. Fond memories baulked at the destruction of detail, at lost associations. But then he shakes his head. Objectively destroyed, well yes, but he need only close his eyes and there it all is again, remade, passing through him once again. And it must suffice, for change is the nature of all things.

The open door, Penny waving, Ben panting at his feet... These worlds, willed or willing, co-exist beyond that endless point of intersection between then and tomorrow, for they are what we are. They are us.

***

Somewhere, earlier in the morning of the boatman's midday chase, there had been another, unseen watcher in the park.

Standing among thick bushes, hidden behind the leafy bole of an elm, Rosemary. Tense. Waiting.

But waiting for what?

In spite of the bright sunlight, the morning is dreary and empty. Trembling a little, she approaches the gazebo, afraid, unsure, conscious of seeking something more than just her missing wristwatch. At least her mam hadn't noticed that.

Is it here? It must be!

Slowly, carefully, her eyes move back and forth over the whole, mute scene: from the chair she had sat in, to Rosalind's, the concrete table, and finally, the bench where Saunders and Willetts had sat swathed in shadows. Nothing. And yet, shutting her eyes, even momentarily, there is Rosalind, the flickering, pinkish light playing on her naked shoulders, and Willetts leaning forward into that light, hand outstretched, eyes popping. And once again, Rosemary flees from that awful place.

As the morning wears slowly on towards noon, a new anxiety overtakes her, like that of the fox scenting the hunters, even before it hears the baying of the hounds. She scurries here and there in search of a refuge from which to watch and, if needs be, quickly withdraw, should anyone come too close.

The park is supposedly out of bounds, but there are always a few who come here – the smokers, for sure. And there are others, too, those who pass on their way home for lunch.

And it is *this* thought which has brought Rosemary to these bushes – not without changing her mind over it a hundred times; to this tree some little way beyond the end of the lake, just off the asphalt path.

Will she catch a glimpse of him? Of... Danny, as she can't help but think of him, still?

It *is* possible; it is!

Rosemary closes her eyes, becoming conscious only of the wind as it moves moodily through the upper branches of the trees, moaning continually like the sea in a storm, at Filey, wasn't it? Once, she thinks she hears a cry, then another, but she cannot be sure, for all sounds dissolve in this fretful, sighing wind, which after a time begins to tell on her nerves. She opens her eyes.

And there he is! Momentarily framed against the restless backdrop of leaves and branches. Here!

And then gone in an instant.

Unbelieving, Rosemary rubs her eyes, wondering if she has recognised *him* in that moment or the *image of him* imprinted on her mind's eye... after he had already passed, that is. And so *not* what she had hoped for. A moment later, she is not even sure it was him. Was it Danny?

In panic she dashes forward, but even as she moves, she senses that someone else is coming quickly along the path, and in a moment she sees her, a sixth-form girl she vaguely recognises, and she ducks back behind the elm only just in time, her heart pounding, as the girl goes by.

Convinced she has given herself away, Rosemary holds her

breath, for what seems forever. Then, with her ears ringing, the pulse throbbing away in her temples, she can hold out no longer and begins to gasp noisily for air. She sinks to her knees, leans slowly forward, and smothers her face in the lush, cool grass.

But the terror, the terror inside her, is always there.

'...And we could paint the back bedroom. Yes, it will be half-term soon, we could do it then.' Penny passes him the remains of the semolina pudding. 'Or next weekend – if I can salvage something from the housekeeping. And then you'd have somewhere to work, or set up an easel.'

'Yes,' he says, looking up. 'Maybe I *could* start painting again.' But he is morose, preoccupied.

After they've eaten, Penny goes out to shake the tablecloth and he hurries up to the cold, unwelcoming bedroom. Could he really paint here, after all the light, the colours of Greece?

Tea chests, wooden and cardboard boxes everywhere, magazines and papers dumped on every available surface or on the floor, just as the removal men had left it all, back in August. Still so much to sort through. He picks his way around the boxes with some difficulty, delving first into one then into another, conscious he'll have to be back at school in quarter of an hour.

He takes a sketch book over to the window and starts to flick through it. Pencil drawings of Isixia and the limestone hills around. Outside, the huge sycamore, which rears up at the side of the house, tosses about in the wind and casts its shifting shadows into the room. He looks down onto the little lawn where a flock of starlings sweeps in upon the crusts Penny has just scattered there. Others keep swooping in, hurled by the gusts of wind which, in the silence that surrounds him, seem so incongruous, so remote from the sunlight. The birds peck and squabble then dart away, one by one, like thoughts, so light upon the wind.

When the starlings have departed he looks down and sees the pages he has been turning are all empty.

Simultaneity. Coincidence, even. Dan shrugs. Instinctively, we cleave to these suggestions of a hidden, ordered purpose, the grand symmetry which common experience, the acid bath of reason, is forever dissolving.

Rosalind was like a bird pecking. Yes, at the staffroom door. Her head jerking back and forth at him, stabbing away. 'Why are you here?' she'd pecked, 'Why have you come back here? We don't *want* you here!' Then off, lost, an alien thing, quite unrecognisable as the sweet little second-former he had known, only two years before.

But back at the *very* beginning, it hadn't just been about career, had it? It had been life, being there at the start, with everything before them, that first gathering outleap.

And Penny, of course; building their new life together – even furnishing a little flat had seemed an adventure. Her unplanned pregnancy *certainly* was! And twins, at that! Their future life closed off, in a way, before it had got going, except that they'd soon learned, as you do, how to accommodate the doubling up of their family.

And it had proved no impediment at all by the time they'd got round to thinking seriously about Greece.

That night, something wakes him.

He has been dreaming he is back at the school for his second innings, after Greece. He has a classful. He can make out Saunders and Willets, but hardly any of the girls as there is a fuzziness to their faces. And then a girl comes in, walking backwards, awkwardly. At his desk she turns, and it is Rosemary.

Padding to the bathroom Dan becomes aware of a flash outside, and then another. He goes across to the window and stares out into the darkness. Yes, over in Hall Wood. Little lights. He rubs his eyes then looks again. Yes, to be sure, small, intermittent lights, getting smaller; but what can they be? Fireflies? Already too late in the year for them, but lights, yes, definitely, but lost now in the thick, dense undergrowth. He can think of no rational explanation.

But what is it about Rosemary that she keeps intruding on his thoughts, and now even trespassing in his dreams?

VII

When Rosemary's breathing has calmed to normal, she straightens up, and after a moment's hesitation begins rummaging about in the bottom of her schoolbag, looking for the apple she had filched from the bowl on the sitting-room table, snatched up when her mother wasn't looking.

She brightens a little at the thought of the apple, turning it over and over in her hands, rubbing it on her gymslip until it shines like emerald. Then she can resist it no longer, and taking one last, admiring look at its green wholesomeness, she bites deep into the crisp, firm flesh. As she kneels there with her back to the tree and the path, pecking away at her apple, she peers intently into the gloomy confusion that stretches away in front of her.

Trees and bushes grow thickly hereabouts, left wild, unattended by the Corporation gardeners. It is dark and dense and scratchy. And as her eyes adjust to the half-light, she wonders how far it is possible to go before you reach a boundary, because a park doesn't go on forever, does it?

All too soon, the apple is finished, and Rosemary finds herself wishing now she had known how to resist it. She thinks of the others, pushing and jostling one another in the lunch queue, collecting their trays, their cutlery, and their plates, sitting down together in their usual corner at one of the long, spell-ridden trestle tables in the clatter and clamour of the assembly hall, and with a stiff, clumsy, upward movement of her arm, she flings the core away into the bushes.

Unsteadily, she gets to her feet and clutching her schoolbag to her body begins pushing her way slowly through the undergrowth which, for a time, seems to become thicker the further she goes. The oak and the elm which grow nearest the path gradually give way to willow, and some way in front she recognises the tall heads of a line of poplars – sixty gallons of water a day they drink, her grandfather had once told her. He used to always tell her things, like to really look at a leaf, at the shape, the veins. Looking now, among the leafy branches of the willows straight ahead, she catches sight of the lake and makes her way towards it. Coming to the water's edge at a break in the trees, she realises she has arrived at its furthest, darkest corner.

The undergrowth ends abruptly in a small, semi-circular clearing, where the grass grows sparsely for want of light and moisture, and she can see now that the poplars are lined against a high wall which is capped by sturdy, sharp-pointed iron railings, a hundred yards or so beyond this further end of the lake. It seems pointless going on, so she swings round to look at the water.

With this sudden movement, she is taken completely off her guard. For in the silver sunlight slanting across the water there is a figure emerging from the reeds on the further side, wading slowly outwards, trying to keep balance in the brisk breeze whipping over the water, and all the while flailing at the rippling surface with a long, slender branch. And Rosemary recognises old Charlie, the boatman, swearing loudly enough for her to hear him, even at this distance, and in spite of the wind. But it is not his actions which hold her transfixed in fascinated horror, strange though they are, so much as the realisation that the old man is completely naked.

She stares at that fearful whiteness, at the water's edge: the emaciation of his body, his wilting shoulders sunk beneath a jutting collarbone too large for that puny little body, like the high cheek bones for his face; the fleshless ribs, and the slack, old man's belly; those random little tufts of grey hair, and… and that funny little thing between his legs. And still he thrashes at the water. Suddenly, reaching forward, he almost stumbles, then grasps at something she cannot see, once, twice, at the same time letting go of his flail, which remains all but motionless on the surface. Then, edging slowly round, he begins to pick his way back towards the reeds.

Rosemary cannot help but watch. That dreadful whiteness, she realises, is also the crackling voice across the water and the whispers too, the incomprehensible whispers, nods and knowing looks of the grown-ups whenever Charlie was mentioned, when she was little.

With his back towards her, he straightens up on the grass, dragging what she can now see is an oar from the water. He pauses for a while, standing motionless, as though scenting the air. Then suddenly, in a flash, he has swung round and is facing her, and is pulling the oar slowly from behind him between his legs, slowly, slowly, endlessly. His eyes are on her, smiling; and gripping the clamped oar with both hands he begins to wave it up and down, to rotate it, pointing it in her direction, never taking his eyes away from where she is standing in amazement, and a paralysing fear.

Rosemary cannot believe he can be aware of her, much less see her, not at this distance, not against the thick backdrop of undergrowth, so her curiosity holds her, still. Yet, even as she watches, she begins to doubt and starts to back away into the bushes. She stumbles over a tree root and falls heavily on her satchel. Winded, she scrambles to her knees, peering in panic through the undergrowth, only to find he is no longer where he was a moment or two before. But then she finds him again, closer, coming in her direction, the oar still fixed between his legs, jutting out in front of him, clasped tightly in his huge hands. She gets to her feet as quickly as the pain will allow and rushes headlong back through the bushes.

Almost at once, she finds herself facing the high, curving, perimeter wall. Panic-stricken she dashes along beneath it in the leafy gloom, continually glancing back, expecting at any moment to see that bizarre, shambling figure behind her. Mercifully, the wall begins to slope gradually downwards and soon the bottom of the railings is level with the top of her head, so she can now see, yes, into the silent, suburban gardens which lie in another world beyond. Further along, there is a wide, wrought-iron gate, similar to the one at the market square, she realises, though this one has an inscription on it, its lettering reversed to her, and she guesses it must be in Latin.

The gate, however, is unyielding, fastened with a rusted chain and padlock.

On a bit further, and now Rosemary is looking down onto a patch of green, bounded on the other three sides by a chaotic fence composed of rusting sheets of corrugated metal, mildewed planks of wood, stout tree branches, bits of tattered tarpaulin, all seemingly haphazardly thrown together. In the middle of the green there is a hut in an equally ramshackle condition, while over in the far corner is a solid-looking brickwork construction, waist high, from which a thin wisp of smoke is curling languidly up into the overhanging branches of a huge willow in the garden beyond.

Rosemary stares back once more into the trees, then begins to pull herself up onto the wall top, to see better whether she is still being pursued. She is suddenly aware of a sickeningly sweet stench. And almost simultaneously a pair of enormous, bristling pigs lumber into view past the end of the hut, pursued by a dwarf of a man, not much taller than the animals, limping along behind them, poking at them with a long stick. The dwarf is wearing a khaki greatcoat which almost touches the ground and a long woollen balaclava pulled down over his brow, almost covering his eyes.

Round the other end of the hut a woman appears, and Rosemary stares at her long straggling hair, greasy looking, as if never washed, black with streaks of grey; and she too is waving a stick, though hers is much shorter than the man's. The woman begins scolding in a loud, piping, bird-like voice, which seems not to belong to her, and her words are gibberish. She comes on at the dwarfish man, poking at him with her stick, still shouting, until he stops chasing the pigs and limps off out of sight round the side of the hut. The woman becomes noticeably gentler, barely touching the animals, making soothing noises at them in a strange, clucking voice, as she coaxes them over to the steaming set-pot in the corner of the pen. There, she begins ladling a foul-smelling slop into a long wooden trough, chanting away all the while in a thin, almost tuneless voice.

In a little while, the dwarf returns, carrying a bucket of water in each hand, and lurches towards a shallower trough which stands close by the other. He sets the buckets down, kneels beside them and begins scooping up the water from one of them into his mouth, gurgling and spluttering, until the woman screeches at him again, whereupon, still on his knees, he empties the buckets into the trough, and then, with a shock, Rosemary realises he is staring up at her. But his eyes seem to cloud over as though looking without seeing and he slumps down onto his calves, his body sagging visibly, and his head drops forward till his chin is resting on his chest. And there he stays, quite motionless.

Rosemary glances across at the woman, whose back is still turned towards her, then silently begins to lower herself from the wall, glancing back the way she had come to make sure she is no longer being pursued. She has already let down her satchel and is ready to spring back down herself when she is startled by the woman's monotone.

'You got some trouble, girlie?'

Clearly, the words are meant for her.

Even then, she could have dropped out of sight and run off, back through the trees; she could have been away in a matter of seconds. But she stays crouching near the wall top, watching the woman through the iron railings.

The words come again, but there is no question in them this time.

'I say you got some trouble, girlie.'

Rosemary does not know how to answer. The woman's voice is gentle now, cajoling even, but Rosemary can only shake her head, suddenly aware she is close to tears. The woman carefully replaces the wooden lid on the set-pot and turns to face her.

'What for you want cry, girlie?' she demands.

All of a tremble, Rosemary shakes her head again. And the tears shimmer like distant crystals on her lashes.

'You cry then. Go on, you cry.' Spoken quietly, gently, with no rebuke.

As the tears are released, Rosemary grips the railings tightly, pressing her forehead against her hands.

The woman is now standing behind the man, who has not moved. She touches his shoulder lightly with her hand; he turns his head up and back towards her, then slowly, with obvious difficulty, begins to push himself up from the ground, with the woman steadying his elbow. He stoops then to pick up one of the buckets but in reaching forward is almost bowled over by the larger pig, for having noisily emptied the one trough the two animals rush towards the other, jostling, snuffling, squealing, in greedy haste.

Rosemary smiles involuntarily behind her hands, which are wet with tears. One of the buckets is overturned, rolling away to clatter against the ramshackle fence, and the woman leads the limping dwarf away round the front of the hut, out of sight.

She is back in a trice, though, carrying something, unfolding a greaseproof wrapping as she comes towards the foot of the wall. Bread, yes – the pigs, distracted by the rustling paper, leave their squabbling at the water trough, and bound after her, howling like great, pink, ungainly dogs, nuzzling at her legs. She ignores them, seemingly unperturbed by their peevish impatience, which immediately turns the one on the other, both snapping viciously.

'You like nice sandwich, eh?' she asks, holding it out at arm's length up towards Rosemary.

Rosemary looks at the woman's grimy hand, her black fingernails, remembers the slop from the set-pot, and smiles weakly, greatly embarrassed, and shakes her head.

'Still warm,' the woman cajoles. And as if to demonstrate the truth of it, she tucks the bulky packet under one arm and feels at the proffered sandwich with the hand she has thus freed. 'Yes, still warm. You feel.'

Again, Rosemary declines, smiling nervously. 'You are... so kind,' she manages to say, 'but I'm really not at all hungry just now, thank you. I've... just eaten,' she adds, crouching ridiculously up against the railings, making as if to leave, yet embarrassed still.

The woman nods her understanding, and keeps on nodding, and muttering. Then she tears the sandwich down the middle and tosses the pieces towards the pigs, which devour them in an instant.

'Maybe you not like bacon?' the woman persists, still trying to fathom Rosemary's refusal.

'No, it's not that. Really it isn't,' Rosemary protests. 'I just... I have to be going, that's all,' she lies, not very convincingly.

The woman stands looking up at her, smiling, and nodding her head backwards and forwards, quite mechanically, as though she has no control over its movement.

'You will come back,' she says.

And Rosemary assures her she will.

The woman resumes her high-pitched, whining incantation, concentrating her attention on the packet of sandwiches and the pigs, as though her visitor has suddenly ceased to exist.

And still Rosemary hangs there, looking down, uncertain, until she feels the perspiration prickling in her armpits, and can stand it no longer.

'Well, thank you again,' she mumbles, trailing off into triviality about the weather, yet sensing, guiltily, she has violated something... intimate, private even, in the newly gathering silence.

The woman looks up, seemingly startled, and holds her for a moment with narrowed eyes, then slowly, enunciating carefully, she issues a warning.

'Be careful who you trust, girlie. Be careful...!'

And Rosemary nods vigorously, making a show of taking her advice to heart, while thinking it such a strange thing to say.

'You will come back.' Leaving the park, a few minutes later, it occurs to Rosemary that there had been no question in the woman's voice, nor had she been issuing an invitation. No, there had been only certainty, perhaps even a hint of command in that simple statement. 'You will come back.'

***

When had Holly first invited him to take part in *The Dream*? And why had he so readily agreed?

Holly was always directing something, for the school or locally. A born actor, he seemed to make no clear distinction between life on stage and life off it. And, returning along the lane from the post box, having dispatched papers to the bank, Dan can see him leaning against the staff-room mantelpiece haranguing his colleagues, whose lives were so much duller than his own, with all his tales and jokes, usually from his latest Civic Theatre production. Holly was somewhat eclectic in his tastes, and for the school's annual productions he had veered wildly between Sophocles and Shakespeare on the one hand, and pop musicals and a bedroom farce on the other.

'My farce caused considerable consternation, as you can imagine,' Holly laughs, 'our head being a gentleman of the old order who believes. "The annual school production should reflect all that is best in our national culture, my boy, all that is best."'

With *The Dream*, at least, he wouldn't have been disappointed.

Dan walks up through the rose garden, frowning. He had always been wary of Holly, all too conscious of that knack of his of making you feel important – if he wanted something from you. Yet he'd still allowed himself to be drawn in. And why? An attempt to alleviate his day-to-day routines, he supposes, or even, maybe, out of a need for make-believe. And if that, then he too was not to be disappointed, at least not while *The Dream* was in the making, not until after it was behind him.

The performance had been in late February, but rehearsals had got under way almost at once, in September. They must have, for he clearly recalls light summer evenings as well as cold, frosty nights, after rehearsals.

But there were endless grey days, too, days with their lonely footpaths merging into mist, seeking in vain her sweet face.

All of it now a series of jumbled stills, their fading images projecting onto the flickering, silent screen of memory.

***

'I don't believe a word of it,' Rosalind taunts. 'You're making it up.'

Rosemary stays silent, staring at the ground between her feet, her face contorted, as if she's in pain.

'Anyhow, why haven't you been to school? What were you doing?' Harsh and remorseless, Rosalind scrutinises Rosemary's face in the gathering darkness, gouging out answers.

Her questions, these, and more, echo round in Rosemary's mind. But before she can get anywhere close to an answer, the inquisition intensifies.

'Right then! Show me where it happened. Now!' she commands. She stands up suddenly, and marches off along the lakeside, towards the trees.

Rosemary must stop her. But fear and confusion make her agonised cry stick in her throat, so it comes out all distorted, as if she were choking.

Rosalind turns and takes a step towards her, then stops, surging anger stifling momentary concern.

'What's wrong? Scared are you I'll find out you're lying?' Her voice is loaded with scorn. She spins round again, away again, into the mist which curls and billows out from the surface of the lake.

Rosemary rushes after her. She has to stop her. She has to!

'No, Rosalind. Listen to me. I can't go back there, it's sort of, well, creepy. It's nearly dark, and besides...' And she catches hold of Rosalind's shoulder from behind, trying to pull her back. Begging her. Begging.

Rosalind jerks free, striding away again, sullen, obstinate, unheeding.

Rosemary catches hold of her arm. 'No, Rosalind, no, I...'

Rosalind rounds on her and begins pummelling her shoulders, her arms, her chest.

Suddenly the two girls feel the ground slipping away beneath them, and they realise, simultaneously, that they have slipped off the narrow path into the mud among the reeds.

Rosemary panics and screams.

Rosalind howls in anger.

And as they twist and turn in the deepening ooze, Rosemary clings tightly to Rosalind, who swears and punches wildly in the fast-gathering darkness, blind rage taking her over, spilling over.

'You fucking stupid cow! Let go of me. Let go of me or I'll fucking well kill you.' And Rosemary's head and shoulders and arms feel the force of Rosalind's clenched fists, her blind hatred. 'My shoes, you've ruined my fucking best shoes. You stupid cow!' She begins to sob uncontrollably, and as if drained in an instant of all energy, slumps against Rosemary and clings to her, heavy upon her shoulder.

Rosemary feels the tremors surging through Rosalind's body being absorbed by her own. She folds her arms around her, holds her tightly, feeling the mud seeping, soft and cold, through her stockings.

And they stand there, leaning together, their feet sunk deep in the ooze.

And then, after what seems an endless time, when Rosalind's sobbing has subsided into a spasmodic whimper, Rosemary leads her back gently, silently, to the bench from which they had started, both of them shoeless. Then following their muddy prints she returns to the reeds, and kneeling, plunging her arms into the ooze up to her elbows, she manages to retrieve the precious shoes – as well as her own. She washes her arms, then the shoes, in the surface water, drying them as best she can on her skirt, before placing the shoes, like an offering, on the seat by Rosalind's side. She sits down and slips her arm once more around Rosalind's still trembling shoulders.

Rosalind takes hold of Rosemary's free hand and guides it inside her blouse to cup her breast, gasping in shock at its coldness. She nestles into the warmth of Rosemary's body, sighing her contentment through the silent spasms still shaking her own small frame.

Neither speaks a word. For several minutes neither speaks.

Eventually, Rosemary feels Rosalind begin to shiver with the cold night air.

'Why are we always going deeper and deeper into… pain, Rosalind?' she whispers, at the same time gripping Rosalind's shoulder tightly.

Rosalind shakes her head from side to side, but her face remains buried in Rosemary's shoulder so that her muffled voice seems to come from inside Rosemary herself.

'It's all my fault, Rosie, I know it is. I don't know why I'm like this, but… I just am.' And she sniffs, miserably. 'I think maybe I'll always break everything I touch.'

One day, she would take Rosalind there, to the pig woman's pen, but in circumstances she could never have dreamed of, not then.

VIII

It is one morning after a light covering of snow has overlaid earlier, deeper snow, one of those winter days when the mist never bothers to clear, that Dan first notices the footprints.

Squinting at the white desert, which stretches away above the three steps and its rustic arch, he spots them, passing straight across the field in a westerly direction towards Hall Wood. He follows them down to the thick hedge, where they disappear from view though leaving tell-tale wisps of coarse red hair caught in the sloe thorns at the gap where the fox must have squeezed through.

A fox, yes. Curious, excited even, he continues up along the gully beside the hedge, over the top and down the shorter, steeper, wild side of the hill to the bottom, where he bears right, still following the hedge. He has not gone very far, however, before he comes upon a new set of tracks leading to the far, north-eastern corner of the field – her return journey, then. Occasionally, the tracks are punctuated by spots of blood, and once even a long smear where she had evidently dropped her prey, to change her grip, perhaps, or rest her aching jaws. And he realises it is years since he's seen a fox, here or anywhere, not since Ireland, when even in the middle of the day he'd pass them on his way up to the airport, scavenging on the city refuse dump, emboldened, scornful, and yes, he remembers always thinking, also defiled.

So, they were hereabouts too, then. But of course they were, for those who donned their annual scarlet and blew their silly little horns through the winter fields and woods, were not just a riding or a drinking club, were they, openly despising the law they flouted.

At the hawthorn brake are more blood smears, and Dan stands for a moment, imagining his nocturnal visitor dropping her prey to pull it through, the thorns being fewer, the confusion of twigs and branches being less, nearer the ground. And contemplating her passage, he wonders about this world outside his own, and he feels, yes, privileged, hoping she will come again.

Continuing round the edge of the field, he crosses the start of the fox's tracks not far below the point at which she had subsequently made her exit. But what chance will she and her cubs have – and for how long – in a human world bristling with other, more obscure hazards and snares, in their way every bit as deadly as the hunt?

And what of the nightly screeching owls, the clicking blackbirds, the bluetit tapping at the window? Or the old bullfrog who… and he smiles at this unthinking anthropomorphism… who, is surely, even now, beneath his habitual slab of limestone, in the ooze, immersed in winter's sleep, as long a resident as he is himself, if not longer?

It is not that Dan has been unaware of these other, ordinary things, rather that his awareness seems suddenly to have undergone a change in focus – not just of vague, marginal presences beyond the bounds of the human, but of real coexistences, of lives almost touching, albeit blindly; akin to the occupants of the rose garden.

And having reached the point, the only one, where the hedge is low enough to see into the eastern wood beyond, he comes to a halt. Near the containing wall, with the bull-frog's marshy residence immediately below him, he has caught sight of the swing, hanging motionless from a high, thick branch of one of the oaks, its ropes now visibly fraying.

* * *

'They're asleep at last,' Penny is telling him. 'So I'm sitting down to do nothing – for the first time today!'

She is tired, irritable, frustrated. She wants perfection and she wants it now.

But a small tin of paint to transform a junk room into a studio will hardly bring that about, he thinks.

'It will be better than just staying still,' she says, 'always the same.'

Penny needs things, to give shape to a vision that has little to do with things. And the lack of the financial means is a constant frustration.

Realistically, he can't imagine a tomorrow much different from today, but he knows what she'll say, that dwelling on that thought means spiralling down into depression, with its rainstorms and shadows dulling your mind.

Suddenly, she leaps up, jerks open the French windows and bursts out into the silent garden.

'If only there were a swing under the apple tree,' she is saying. 'If only there were an apple tree…!'

***

Dan shakes his head and smiles. More co-existence, though not here, of course: the absent swing had been long before, at the house they'd lived in after Greece, when he was back teaching at the school. Here, the swing had been for the twins, though in his mind for her too; sentimental reparation for that hurt long past. After Titania, and Malaysia; going away seeming the solution to everything.

He turns away and goes back towards the house, snow crunching underfoot.

Remembering is twice living, he thinks, and yes, twice suffering. And, sitting motionless like this, intent entirely on their prey, he wonders whether the patient fox or owl remember; or the scuttling field mouse, even as the owl swoops.

An owl, yes, he might attempt to carve one, one of these days, when the work-shed door is closed on the bleakness outside.

A few days later, settling down after supper, the lines come to his mind, unbidden.

*Up and down up and down
I will lead them up and down
I am fear'd in field and town
Goblin lead them up and down.*

He picks up the dog-eared copy from the small table beside his armchair, trying to remember names and faces.

Titania, of course. Oberon, yes; Theseus and Hippolyta. But neither Lysander nor Demetrius will come to mind, no Helena, no Hermia, no anyone else; not even recollection of moments in rehearsal or performance when these shadows had flitted across the stage, pursuing, or pursued.

It was a black hole become an obsession. Remember, remember, at all costs.

But why? Wasn't forgetting a part of the cutting loose? Of the slow, slow drift from the shoreline into mist?

But no, not even their many repetitions will suffice to energise them now, those shadows; though without doubt they had been led up and down up and down many times in those now seemingly threadbare weeks when the play was in the making; when he was still trying to make sense of the newly-realised, overt hostility of those fifth-form pupils – Rosalind, Saunders, Rosemary, and others whose names have also long since slipped away beyond the bounds of memory.

And now, Dan's mind hurries headlong down yet another fenny path, trying to penetrate *its* mists.

Titania.

In that concatenation of forgotten events and inner turmoil, there must have been a precise moment in which those arcane pulses and charges which project us had revealed her as the one, had named her to him as what, his ideal fulfilment? His Beatrice? But, when? In what circumstances could they ever have arrived at it?

Was it that day just before Christmas, the last school day before the break? Was that the moment, the start of…?

It is quite late in the afternoon, already dark.

'They've arrived!' Holly shouts, across the staff room. 'The costumes from Stratford – they're up in the gym, in the staff changing rooms!'

Later, Dan mounts the steps to the gymnasium, and Titania is there, in a yellow jumper and a tartan skirt, her back towards him, no longer a schoolgirl.

It is the first time he's seen her in other than her regulation, cream-coloured blouse, navy-blue skirt, and light blue sash, and he is bowled over by the transformation. She is holding a long, pale blue robe against her, reflected in the cloudy, brown-speckled mirror, quietly contemplating its effect. Lowering the robe, suddenly aware of his presence, she wheels round and smiles shyly, lips parted, as if to speak.

Was that it, the moment?

But if it was, if he was overcome in *that* moment by her gentle mien, surely it was because he had already been bewitched. For the urgent impulse he had felt, that inner surge, had been much more than incipient. Surely it had. His arms raised to her then just as quickly checked.

Earlier then, in another room, at a time before the costumes. Dan, as Bottom, folding his arms imperiously, *'yet my chief humour is for a tyrant. I could play Ercles rarely'*, he boasts, or tries to, having the greatest difficulty co-ordinating words and movement, tying his arms in knots and the others in stitches of laughter. Titania's tinkling laughter, the knowing looks darting between her and Hippolyta… Yes, he well remembers the mark they left on him. So not *then*, for those glances were not the first he had noticed.

So, when?

There is a storm getting up, and Dan goes over to close the window. It is already dark outside, so he draws the curtains and switches on a second table lamp, then returns to his chair, and his pondering. There had, of course, been quite a lot of rehearsals between the end of September and that afternoon in the staff changing room, with the costumes. Titania's blue robe.

***

The swing-doors open noisily, and Titania looks up from where she is sitting on a pile of coarse copra mats in the shadows, her knees pulled up beneath her chin, her teeth sliding along the back of her hand. And she watches him as he stands for a moment in the half-open doorway.

Then he enters, easing the door after him with his foot, though not slowly enough to prevent it shutting with a dull thud, and she catches the flash of annoyance in his face. He tiptoes across the gymnasium, and hoists himself onto a windowsill in a distant corner, not seeing her at all.

Holly too frowns at the squeak and thud of the door. And then there is silence. Theseus has forgotten his lines again.

Standing between Egeus and Hippolyta, he falters, starts again, shakes his head, then stops, his concentration all broken. He makes a vague wafting movement with his hand, as if to apologise. But Holly seems in no mood for such niceties. He stands there, as if petrified, his book open, his hand outstretched, waiting for Theseus to speak, to say the words that will not come.

And Titania, swathed in shadow, stares into the wide amphitheatre of light at the far end of the gymnasium, watching the actors, insulated from their remote, alien world, and waits for the storm to break.

She can feel her pulse racing, an uncomfortable tingling, cold up and down her spine, her teeth now closed firmly upon her wrist.

Then from Theseus, instead of words, comes a muffled snort. A moment later, a second one breaks through, which he instantly checks but too late.

'Davidson!' Holly bellows, white with anger. 'You're wasting my time – and everyone else's.'

Titania closes her eyes. She doesn't want to see or hear this other drama that is beating back *The Dream*. But on it goes despite her, crushing her.

'Now listen, will you, and get this into your thick head once and for all,' Holly thunders. 'You turn to your *left*...You do remember which that is, do you, Davidson? Then you say: *"Go one of you, find out the forester."* Then you take three steps to the right *not* the left, ok, towards Egeus. Got that? Then it's: *"For now our observation..."'*

Holly carries on with his instructions, but Titania loses him, anxious now about her own lines. It's not that she doesn't know them, she's been over them too many times for that... in the quiet of her bedroom, in the garden... over and over, up and down, round about and up and down. But in this horrid, tense atmosphere, she feels she may lose them too, like Davidson, when really there is no...

'"*My love shall hear the music of my hounds. Uncouple in the western valley; let them go...*". You say that bit, Davidson', Holly commands. 'Then after two or three seconds, seeing no one has moved, you turn to the *left* – if we can still remember which *is* our left – and *impatiently*, you say: "*Despatch I say and find the forester.*" Now, Davidson, do you understand these few, very simple, very clear, directions?'

There is another, awful silence. Then Theseus clears his throat and Titania exhales the breath she has been holding.

'Yes, I understand them. But, with respect, that's not what you said the last time we rehearsed this scene... sir.'

Titania gasps. And in her shadowland, she nervously wonders at this 'sir', so adrift, so daring, pointedly reminding Holly that Theseus has rather more substance in the real world than he does here, in these fleeting moments of *The Dream*.

Why, oh why, can't they just get on with it?

Holly glares hard at Davidson. Then he turns on his heel and marches over to the window. The muffled voices of the two masters tease the shadows where Titania is crouching, still tense and shivery, and irritated by the winks, the grins, and the grimaces of the others, on the other side. Fifth-form boys just so immature still, and... silly.

Holly laughs, suddenly, and steps away from the window. A few more paces and, shielding his eyes from the glare of the arc lights, he starts peering blindly into her private space, her shadows.

Quietly, therefore, she manoeuvres herself onto her knees, heart pounding, newly expectant.

'Titania', Holly calls. 'Titania, are you hiding away up there, somewhere?'

Her mouth is dry of words.

'Titania', he repeats, now chiding almost.

Making a bit of a commotion, the Queen of the Fairies scrambles to her feet. 'Yes, sorry, yes, I'm here.' And soon she is beside him.

Holly chuckles. 'I thought maybe you'd got tired of waiting and gone off somewhere. I wouldn't have blamed you.' Although he would, she thinks. He turns and looks the other way, back to the action – or lack of it.

'Anyhow, so as not to waste any more of everyone's time…' And he glares at Davidson, now hanging upside down from the wall-bars, chatting with some of the girls, and quite oblivious to the master's sarcasm.

Holly spreads his hands in a gesture of resignation, then turns back to her. Relieved, she smiles weakly. But never could she have anticipated his next words.

'Now then, whilst I – he gives her a wink – whilst I try and knock some shape and sense into this lot, you and Mr Teal can go and practise the Bottom-Titania scenes, next door. Because – he raises his voice – *some* of us are not going home tonight until we get it right. *Are we Davidson?*'

Davidson, vertical once more, turns to face Holly. 'I don't know. Aren't you, sir?' His face is a picture of innocence.

But Davidson's expression and words elicit a sudden eruption of relief-bringing laughter, from Holly too. And Titania lets out her own sigh.

***

Dan takes up his tattered text, barely holding together now, and flicks through its fragile pages, attending to his faded pencilled notes as much as to its words. So, Titania's kiss, where does it come in the scene?

But he can find it nowhere. *O how I love thee! How I dote on thee!* And that is all; the kiss is nowhere!

Dan lays the book aside, perplexed by these long, chequering shadows.

Methought I was... And methought I had...

IX

The telephone.

Dan jerks to his feet, recalled to the present moment of a dark winter's night and a gale still gusting about the house.

Listening to its baleful angelus, he is appalled, though fascinated, by its power and its squat, black stupidity. And when, at last, silence is left like a gaping hole all about him, he is relieved, relieved that the outside world's capricious attempt to snare and harness him has once again come to nothing.

Was it the same phantom calling as that first time? Or some other phantom? And why at this hour?

He replaces the Shakespeare text on the shelf.

After the first week or so here, he has not used the phone, and it has sat there, a redundant household deity, gathering dust. Scribbled lists have sufficed to keep him provisioned, and the post box, at the lane-end, to keep potential intruders at bay. Yet the phone remains. For somewhere along this road he has chosen, there may come a time when a need pulls him back down into *their* time, one that will compel him to pick it up, form a number, and hope that they hadn't all gone away as he has done. A vague, remote fear, but there, none the less.

There is lots of space at the front, so they don't need to push back much of the furniture. The sixth-form room, is it?

Looking at it now in his mind, Dan sees it without any distinctive shape or dimension. The bookcases peter out into mist. The window wall is mist. And in truth this incomplete room, struggling for admittance at the checkpoint of memory, may yet be some other. Or a sort of jigsaw room, compounded from pieces of several others.

For of course there would be many, many others.

Systematically, under his guidance, with attention to every detail and nuance, the two of them have worked through the words of the few scenes in which Titania and Bottom appear together. If not quite word perfect (he, at any rate, for Titania seems never *not* to have known her lines) they are soon satisfied. Yet still they remain there, going through scenes which play their own part in this other, slowly composing drama, expressing it in each dry-mouthed, faltering start, in each combing of memory for words that might help them along, or might not say too much too soon, and collapse into embarrassment.

But if they are here, still, it is surely because neither has any wish not to be – sitting on their separate desktops, facing each other across the aisle, Titania's legs swinging gently.

***

'I remember seeing you in the Sophocles Holly did,' he says.

Titania looks up, puzzled. 'But that was two… over two years ago. So, how could you? I mean…'

He laughs, understanding the cause of her bewilderment.

'I *was* here then, you know, just for a year. Then I left. We went off to Greece, and I only came back a few months ago. My second coming…'

'Oh, I see. And there was me thinking you were new.' She nods and smiles, her brow puckering, as if half-recollecting something that's no longer quite within reach. 'You must like it here, then.'

He pulls a wry face. 'Well, I did. Now, I don't know. But it'll do for a while, a couple of years, maybe.'

'And then what?'

'It all depends on the two years, I guess, what I do with them, how they work out. Not school, so much as other things.'

At this she laughs a little. 'Meaning?' And the look of puzzlement is there again, in her eyes.

'Well, I keep trying to convince myself I'm really a painter, but so far I've not got much to show for it. And teaching doesn't leave me much time to develop a style, or...'

'So why are you doing this?' She frowns, gesturing vaguely around the room, then at their scripts. 'Surely it takes up valuable time, time you could be...?'

'Because Holly asked me, I suppose.'

'That's silly!' she says, then blushes deeply. 'Sorry, I shouldn't have said that.'

'It's fine, honestly.'

'No, I mean...'

'If you believe it, best to say it.'

'Yes, but I shouldn't have.' She shakes her head slowly, looks contrite.

Amused at her forthrightness and confusion, he is also all too aware of being entranced by her grace, by the delicacy of her movements. And he looks away, thinking how lovely she is: her fine features, her long, chestnut, shoulder-length hair, that sparkle in her eyes.

'I didn't explain myself very clearly, anyway. I felt I needed something different, different from work and home, that is. Also, because I rather like him – Holly, I mean – and I suspect he was desperate to fill the part.' He smiles. 'That bit's not silly, is it? In any case, I can't paint at night.'

'No, of course not.' Her eyes look serious. 'But if you really want...'

'To paint?' he says. 'Yes, of course, but friends are important, too.'

She nods, slides down from the desk to straighten her skirt, then hoists herself back again.

'But do you actually like acting? Or...'

'Yes, I do. I've done quite a bit in the past.'

'Shakespeare, or...?'

'Yes – and other things. And as a teacher, well, I'm acting all the time.' He looks at her directly now, watching for her reaction.

And she laughs, clearly recognising the truth of it.

'And I'm *certainly* enjoying this,' he goes on, stealing another glance at her. But she has looked down, and he looks away, not wishing to startle her with this growing intensity of his.

There is a silence. And it occurs to him she may be embarrassed, doesn't really want to be here but dare not say, or make the first move to leave, for fear of offending. He should at least give her the opportunity.

He stands.

'I'd love to see some of your paintings,' she says suddenly.

He starts out of his dilemma, sits back down. 'Would you?'

'Yes.'

'Don't feel you have to say that.'

'Aren't they to look at, then?'

'Yes, they are, of course they are,' he says, not missing her touch of sarcasm. 'Only... don't people always feel obliged to say that, when they find out someone paints... or chips stone, or scribbles?'

'I don't know, do they?'

He shrugs and apologises, wishing he hadn't sounded so patronising.

'Did you paint much in Greece?'

'No, not much.'

'Why not?'

'I didn't go with any intention of painting. I did a lot of pencil sketches, though, eventually. And it's these I'm working from at the moment. Or rather, not working from.'

Titania laughs, then stretches, rolling a stiffness, perhaps, out of her back and shoulders. And in this moment, with her breasts momentarily thrust forward, firm and shapely, he has the overwhelming urge to take hold of her for real, and he knows he won't, can't, mustn't, and yet...

His heart is thumping so hard he fears she must hear it.

'What do you try to say in your paintings?' She leans forward with what appears to be genuine curiosity, then settles into a more relaxed position.

He clears his throat. 'I don't think painting's like that,' he says, slowly. 'At least not for me. It's more a sort of, let's say, finding out what I can do with colour and shape.'

'I see.'

'Sometimes a painting says things,' he goes on, 'but maybe only when it's finished, and it can be as much a discovery for the painter as for anyone else.'

'Can it? Yes, yes I see what you mean,' she says.

They lapse into silence.

'But... what about you?' he asks, suddenly. 'University next year, is it?'

She giggles and shakes her head, though he's not sure if from surprise or embarrassment.

'Heavens, no! Teacher Training College for me,' she says. 'I've always wanted to be a teacher.'

And he can see why, of course, with her gentleness and her patience. 'Fine, but why not university?'

'University?'

'Yes.'

'I don't know.' She pulls a face. 'Maybe because no one ever suggested it.'

'But...'

'Anyway, it would be a waste – it's little ones I want to teach. Three years then out into bedlam. Running noses... and far worse, I've no doubt!'

'Education is never a waste...'

'I don't...'

'You have intelligence, talent, and sensitivity. And anyway,' he continues quickly, 'it's not just about the job you will do, it's about the person you become, the possibilities it opens up. It's not too late,' he insists. 'There's still time to apply.'

'No, there isn't,' she says, turning to him again. And she looks at him directly, so very earnestly.

And he wants to lose himself for ever in that gaze.

'I've already been offered a place,' she says, 'which I've accepted.'

'Oh. Well, I'm not surprised… about the offer! And I hope you'll be happy, and fulfilled. I'm sure you'll make an excellent teacher,' he says, and he means it sincerely, yet regrets for her what he knows from his own experience that she will miss.

***

It had been Albert Kelday's doing. Albert, whose commitment to the school and to his pupils was unquestionable, but whose mind operated like a railway network, with everything moving in predetermined lines towards unvarying, immutable destinations.

'Limited, Dan. Not the right material.'

'Training College,' one of the older colleagues had muttered. And two of his cronies had agreed as mechanically as they crossed and ticked their piles of exercise books.

And, accepting her mentor's presumed wisdom, Titania had followed his advice, having no means of knowing otherwise.

But Albert had put Titania, as doubtless many other talented pupils over the years, on the wrong train. And the tragic irony of it was that his judgement was based on a knowledge of how universities had functioned in pre-War days and was here so woefully inadequate.

And then Titania, suddenly coming across someone who saw the world rather differently, this unconventional teacher, maybe that had played its part in drawing her to him. And for her too, perhaps, the attraction had been just as confused at first as Dan's own.

That evening in the sixth-form room had certainly forged an openness between them – maybe also because there had been something else. Something quite incidental, certainly accidental. Comic too, in a way.

As though Puck, slipping out from *The Dream*, had got up to his infamous, age-old tricks again.

***

'I suppose we ought to be getting back,' he says, glancing at his watch.

'It's gone nine o'clock already. Let's hope Holly and Davidson have sunk their differences, by now.'

And as he is following her out of the room into the dimly lit corridor, approaching the doorway he suddenly thinks to switch off the light.

Titania, already beyond the threshold, has had the same thought, and, ducking backwards into the room, bumps into him in the instant when his eyes are averted, intent on the switch.

'Oh...!'

Their hands reach the switch almost simultaneously, hers closing over his, while he, thrown off balance by the impact of her body, instinctively clutches at her to save himself from falling.

And with his left hand thus momentarily across her breast, though slipping instantly to her waist, he staggers back, pulling her with him, both pivoting on their right arms still outstretched to the wall, until they end up slumping down onto a desk just inside the room, in the sudden darkness.

Or rather, he is half sitting on the desk, she half sprawling upon his lap, laughing nervously.

All in the batting of an eye.

His face buried in her long, sweet-scented hair.

'I'm so sorry,' she says, checking her laughter, 'how silly of me.' She strains round to look at him. 'Are you all right? You're not hurt, are you? I do hope you're not hurt.'

'No. No, I'm all right, I think. Just a bit... shaken.' Shaken and absurdly, joyously tremulous. 'But, what about you?'

'Shaken, that's all, yes... It all happened so... quickly.'

And he can feel her body trembling as he holds her, hoping she cannot sense his sudden erection against her thigh.

Later that night, as on so many occasions, he would go over and over these moments, recalling her every word and look and movement, pondering what might lie behind them.

'Shaken, that's all. It all happened so... quickly.'

Titania had made no move to free herself from his encircling arm. Was this an expression of expectancy or of a desire not to embarrass further through a show of mistrust? Or was it something else?

His hand does not move back up to her breast after that first, fleeting contact. She does not turn and seek his face again, in the dark. For the moment, in an atmosphere become electric, all futures remain suspended, and possible.

Slowly, gently, reluctantly, he removes his arm from about her waist. Slowly, though not immediately, she stands up, then after a moment's hesitation moves towards the door.

'Yes,' he laughs, pushing himself up from the desk, 'as I was saying, we ought to go and see how the others are faring. And…'

But she is already out of the room, moving along the corridor to the gym, with who knows what thoughts passing through her mind, while he can still feel her body trembling as he held her.

***

Dan had often wondered about the moment as "process" – that moment, and many subsequent moments as the play progressed; the significance of an attitude, lingering over time, or created in one instant to be translated into a new, often dramatically different one, in the next.

What was it that had permitted them to remain just as they had fallen, his arm tightly around her waist, his face consciously straying back towards the scent of her hair, in silence, their eyes adjusting to the darkness? And then, with the ticking away of the seconds in this dark into which their joint action had plunged them, what was it that had brought the awareness of the inappropriateness of this chance intimacy?

For without any doubt they had encroached upon the "inappropriate". And by prolonging it, by trespassing further on time, if only for these few seconds, each had received a signal of other possibilities, far in advance of the current state of their formal relationship. For him it had proved a crossroads, a threshold gently crossed. But for her, for *her* then, what had it meant?

And yet neither could be sure that this signal had emanated from the other, and not merely from self… unless she had felt his aroused passion momentarily against her thigh. But a question mark had remained, enough in itself to engender wholly new circumstances in which anything might happen.

But the darkness. In those uncertain moments, thank God for the darkness.

X

Dan wakes suddenly.

There had been others in the room with him. Penny, certainly. And then Titania had arrived, with a man whose features were too blurred to be recognisable, but who seemed friendly, jovial even; and Dan had wondered about him and Titania, and become aware of a growing tension inside him, the more acute because of Penny's presence. And then he'd noticed that Titania was dressed oddly, flamboyantly, rather like a Spanish Flamenco dancer, so maybe she was on her way to a fancy-dress party. But then she smiled her usual, gentle smile at him and came and sat on his knee. And he'd frozen and looked around, tension at breaking point. What was she thinking? But her companion seemed not to be put out, and Penny was smiling too, and a new world had seemed to open up, in his dream.

The glimmer of light suggests it is later than usual. But he lies in the warmth, the dream fading fast, and he takes his time to adjust to the brightness and to the sporadic sounds outside. The panicking blackbirds tell him the owls are still about, quite likely settling down now in one of the yews by the lychgate, or in the holly.

He lets his eyes rove about the room, separating objects one from another in the gloom now fast diminishing. Tallboy, wardrobe, dressing table, taking shape. But then he realises, almost simultaneously, that the penetrating light has lost something of its sharpness and that beneath the chirping of the birds is another, less compelling yet more insistent sound: that of faintly dripping water outside. And not just in one place, judging by its different notes and tempos, but from many, and from different heights.

The thaw. Even before he ventures over to the window to draw back the curtains, he knows it has come in the night.

He pulls on his dressing gown and hurries downstairs, quite forgetting the burglar alarm, which startles him, and he hastens to switch it off, cursing it, and deciding there and then to set it no more, for what is its relevance to him now? Then he pads through the kitchen to the back door, fumbles for a moment with the keys in the locks, and jerks it open.

Everything is awash. The snow in the yard beneath the field's high wall has almost disappeared, while up the hillside it has separated out into islands, which seem to shrink even as he watches. He steps awkwardly into his wellingtons and paddles round to the rear corner of the house, near the marsh, which is now, goodness, a swiftly moving stream, tumbling down the embankment into the wood below! Behind the gable end of the house, an intricately patterned tapestry of aconites and snowdrops has appeared – Penny's aconites – and he gasps in surprise and pleasure, newly amazed that these first little flowers, brightly defiant, have managed to push their way up through the frozen snow, presenting themselves fully formed in their green nests, affirming that everything is about to begin all over again.

Soon, he knows the warmer air will usher in the springtime proper and the gold and white and purples of other flowers will take up the mantle from these. But these are the first, the harbingers, and he is fired by their brightness, and their resilience.

Though outwardly, time has been banished – his clocks have long stood silent and motionless – the internal habit fades more slowly, he recognises: the cyclic appearance of these flowers suggests it may now be about the end of January; and earlier, not too long ago, hadn't he heard the bells ringing on what must surely have been Christmas morning?

And this morning?

Dan hurries inside, eager to start again, impatient at the obstacles of hygiene, food and household tasks that yet stand between him and his new beginning at the second terrace, where everything is already marked out in his mind.

Gulping down the last drop of coffee he abandons his breakfast things on the worktop beside the kitchen window, and scurries round to the tool shed thinking how sequence and consequence are time also, and that every action or inaction perforce registers its frustrating duration within him. So, the longed-for sense of harmony with all about him must wait, to be located still much further up than the terrace where he is about to begin, to begin all over again.

'Shit and derision!'
After slipping and slithering repeatedly, hardly managing to keep his balance on the treacherous surface, Dan throws down his spade. Impossible, like this! Instead, he makes his way up the slope to the still distant rocks, the future goal of his transforming life.

'We'll just have to wait, Ben!' he says, as he comes up to the little grave. 'We'll just have to be patient.'

But patience is a struggle, and any sense of calm lies way beyond.
And yet really, he is in no hurry, for there remains much that he must still plan and accomplish, unravel in his mind, and understand.

The sun is now well up over the house-top and blinding him as he looks back down the slope. Shading his eyes, he can see other drifts of aconites beneath the hedges, Penny's legacy, and phalanxes of shining snowdrop spears in among the gravestones – the latter forcing winter to turn tail, he thinks, and a surge of pleasure grips him yet again. 'Winter's done for,' he murmurs, 'it is finished. This *is* the moment.'

Ironically, it is also the moment in which Dan first becomes aware of the high-pitched whine of a distant power-saw which has started up, in the wood over to his right.

He thinks little of it, there and then, but the next time he comes outside he hears it again. And it is there all the next day too, and on the following one, when it is joined by a second, the two saws seeming markedly nearer than before.

So, obstinate old Higgins had finally got round to thinning out some of the undergrowth in the wood, had he? And about time, too!

He'd mentioned it to the farmer on several occasions, going back years – about how dense it all was. Not that he ever had a proper response, other than the old man's habitual rejoinder to every suggestion, no matter where it came from – 'Aye, well, maybe; then again, maybe not,' implying a deep wisdom, born of generations of experience of country life which, in truth, Higgins could lay no claim to.

But at last, for all his pig-headedness, he had finally got round to it.

'Aye, well, maybe; then again, maybe not.'

And in fact, Dan couldn't be more wrong about the thinning, as old Higgins had himself been pruned by the Great Forester several months before. And his wife, who was a year or two older and more or less housebound, had sold up and gone to live with her widowed daughter, in Kent.

Late one night Dan steps out, waits a moment or two, then heads to the post box at the end of the lane. He posts three letters – to his bank manager, his accountant, and the Inland Revenue, and has just turned away to walk back, when he stops and points his torch at the post box, then the telegraph pole beside it. A notice? Two?

He moves closer, shines the torch on one of the bits of paper and reads it with some difficulty. And as he reads, his shoulders sag, and for a short while he stands there, quite bewildered.

The first, dated "28th November", and faint because of weathering, is a County Council notice detailing a request for planning permission "to build thirty-one superior, executive-style houses on the site known as Manor Hall Wood, and to widen and substantially improve the access road known as Hall Wood Dray." Any objections to the plans, available for public inspection at Shire Hall, to be registered there before the last day of January, which would be....

Helpless, Dan stares up into the dark, starless sky.

The second is a hand-written invitation to a public protest meeting in the Village Hall, on "Thursday, 18th January", signed by "A.J. Wilkinson, Clerk to the Parish Council."

He frowns. So... but if the 18th has been and gone, so perhaps has the meeting.

And the power-saws?

Dan feels sick. Sick and angry and helpless, seeing in a flash all the desecration, and the irruption of machinery that will soon destroy his seclusion – the very premise on which his new life depends.

Is it too late? Can anything be done?

Slowly, as he stands there, as he wills his mind to cease its dark descent, the rhythm of his breathing returns to normal.

One thing is clear: whether the date was past or not, the "developer" had begun cutting down the wood, and in earnest. Very likely to ensure a quick return on his investment through the sale of the timber, confident there would be no substantive obstacle to his design. And if there were to be any objection, still? He sighs, wearily. Well, the investor's "pals" on the County Council, and then their pals at Westminster, would just brush it aside, wouldn't they, as they seemed to do now, and with appalling frequency?

Can *he* do anything? Will others?

Dan trudges home. And even before he gets to the gate he has dismissed the idea of writing to Wilkinson or the Clerk to the County Council. Even a request for information would necessitate involvement with these people... with people. No, he will just have to trust in the strength of the villagers' outcry – for outcry there would surely be, or have been. Hadn't he – and he comforts himself briefly with the thought – once organised a petition against the closure of a public footpath? A mere thirty signatures had sufficed to quash it!

But – and he shakes his head – the political climate had been different then. Philistinism had not yet been institutionalised and reclassified as "enterprise."

Inside the house now, Dan thrusts the matter to the back of his mind. And for the next few days, planning and preparing the ground for the second terrace absorbs him totally.

***

The snow has gone completely, and a succession of dry, sometimes even windy days and nights has made the earth firmer and more manageable. And while the buzz and whine of the power-saws continues intermittently, reminding Dan of the destruction of the wood, he closes his ears to it, and labours to make his own progress.

He cleans and sharpens his tools, stakes out more beds, and thinks how best to dispose of the turf he will remove, so that it will not unduly hinder his progress.

Then, one morning, while he is burning rubbish down by the lychgate, his eyes open wide, in panic. Men's voices… just the other side of his hedge, and he cowers instinctively, even though he can't be seen, sharply reminded that the problem of the wood has not gone away. How could he ever have believed it might? And almost at once the saws start up again, followed, minutes later, by the creak and crash of falling trees or heavy branches.

They have to get the timber out, of course, and there is only one possible place where they can do so. But he can't just let things run their course. That is certain.

And with this recognition a calm comes upon him, and he goes indoors and thinks the whole thing through once again.

Yes. To start with he will write to a former colleague in the Law Faculty.

> *Dear Scott,*
> *I am writing to ask whether you could give me some advice. I'd fondly imagined my retirement home immune from any sort of incursion. However, the wood flanking my property has lately been sold to a "developer" who is intent on destroying it in order to build a housing estate just over my hedge. A bloody housing estate…! And so I was wondering…*

And that night he slips out of the gate again, feeling almost like a fugitive.

The County Council notice is still there on the lamp post, but the one advertising the protest meeting has been ripped down, leaving just two tattered corners held by rusted drawing pins.

Somebody wanted to make sure there *was* no meeting. Or the date had simply passed.

On his way back, instead of turning in at his gate Dan crosses the lane into the wood. No one about at this hour, of course. Flashing his torch here and there, he confirms that they are indeed cutting a broad swathe through, right into the heart of the wood, and he scowls at the giant excavator, brought in, no doubt, to rip out roots and tree stumps and God knows what else.

The felled timber is stacked to one side, pile upon pile of it – the amount they have cut through already. Sickening!

Deforestation. Happening the world over, now: in the Amazon, Indonesia, even in Malaya – in Johor and Pahang, where those tangled, impossible jungles he'd known a quarter of a century ago had seemed to be forever... But here, it wasn't thought of as "deforestation", was it? Just the necessary, preliminary preparation of a building site.

O if we but knew what we do
When we delve or hew –
Hack and rack the growing green!

Gerard Manley Hopkins, he thinks, setting off to follow the course of the new, rudimentary roadway, which, he soon realises, moves diagonally away from the end of the lane abutting his own hedge, at an angle of roughly forty-five degrees, thus leaving an ever-widening triangle of trees between his garden and the road. Hm, well, better than nothing. It would offer *some* protection from the inquisitiveness of any future neighbours.

Always presuming it remained, of course.

Dan turns and walks back towards his hedge and the lychgate, saddened, if hardly surprised, by this manifestation of greed, ignorance, and complete disregard for tomorrow, for its young people and the kind of world *they* would inherit.

Civilisation. It rarely civilised.

Hall Wood had existed and been coppiced since at least the late fourteenth century. There were manorial documents from that period, both at Shire Hall and in the Public Record Office, in Chancery Lane, in which it was named – as his own research had told him, years ago. And now, within a few short weeks its ancient trees were being obliterated. And he exhales, his breath whistling through his teeth. Their loss was irreparable. And there was real tragedy in the knowledge that those responsible had neither the wit nor the sensitivity to know it. These were the new Vandals, the new Tartars whose depredations won them knighthoods and national awards.

Retreating to his lychgate, he stops.

And standing there, he realises how this part of his garden, directly facing the estate's entrance, will be quite exposed, despite the amount of undergrowth already partially masking the gate.

Then suddenly bethinking himself, he begins to laugh. Was what the "developer" doing so very different from his *own* deconstruction of his environment, to transform it into another?

The next day, resting up at the top of the field after a particularly arduous couple of hours, Dan looks down at the terrace he is "developing" out of the empty hillside. He squints and shades his eyes from the sunlight, but the terrace, though incomplete, feels austere, imposing its own silence conjured by the dazzle of slowly accumulating Cornforth white stone, gravel, and sandstone rocks; it suggests the starkness of a desert, or an image of humanity's relentless asset-stripping of the earth.

He wonders at this and then nods in recognition, and with some sense of satisfaction. But there is still a lot of turf to be removed and carted away, and paving slabs, sand, and stones to be barrowed up: all monotonous and immensely tiring occupations. And so he turns his mind to these practicalities, realising that his own dedication to the process, and thus his momentum, may be better maintained through varying his tasks.

So… what if he were to barrow away five or six loads of turf instead of removing all of it from an area. And then allow himself a lighter task for an hour or so: hoeing and manuring a new section for planting, or setting the smaller, riven paving-stones in patterns, or even planting arum lilies, a Corylus, a broom tree? The large, sandstone boulder towards the end begged a broom, as in the painting by… Giotto, is it? Yes, a more sensible, more workable plan.

Sitting on there, still, ruminating on his newly devised scheme of work, Dan's mind drifts and settles, floats and sinks.

Whether the developers can be stopped or not, all he can do is wait, and continue to carve out of the hillside the images figured in his mind's eye.

And suddenly, there is Rosalind walking off at an angle, hard-faced, haughty, full of scorn, and Rosemary tiptoeing away at another, head bowed, mute. And smirking Saunders, lumpish Willetts, and the others, heads together, plotting and scheming their silly, hurtful, adolescent myths, their content unknowable, their effects known all too well.

Terrible, they had been, those fifteen- and sixteen-year-olds, in their cold conspiracy of contempt, their dumb obedience to him in class. What had their Mr Teal said or done or been that in their eyes merited, exacted such an exile?

Oh, he'd tried to get to the bottom of what was behind it that autumn, of course he had – even keeping Saunders back one afternoon after school, on the pretext of his shoddy, inadequate work (and not just a pretext, at the time); Saunders, the undoubted, malevolent architect of all his discomfort. He had imagined they could sit down and talk it out, whatever 'it' was. Calmly, rationally. Of course they could.

***

Saunders enters the classroom, a supercilious grin on his face, and sits down, at the back. Dan – sitting on the master's desk rather than behind it, signalling his approachability, he hopes – motions him to come forward: he is certainly not going to engage in some sort of shouting match.

Saunders, sighing audibly, moves up three rows, all the while gesticulating over at the window, where Willetts is peering in or pressing his face against the glass, then disappearing, only to reappear, grinning idiotically, at the door. Saunders sitting there, keeping the lower part of his face covered, signals to Willetts to go away, while grinning back, raising his eyes to the ceiling, precisely to keep him there.

All of this as though the master were of no account or had ceased to exist.

'Saunders.'

'Sir?'

'I thought it time we had a talk… about your work. Is something… wrong?'

'Wrong, sir?'

'Do you maybe not have a… suitable place in which to work, at home? Or is there something bothering you, perhaps?'

Saunders shakes his head, blankly.

'That last essay you did. You wrote a single page, Saunders, exploring *none* of the issues we'd discussed in class. Quite unlike you. Were you not paying attention? The examiners are going to need a good deal more than that, as I'm sure you know.'

Saunders raises his eyebrows, affecting surprise at this information.

Calmly and patiently, Dan tries another tack, and yet another, rephrasing his questions, trying to draw Saunders out, trying to ease his way in – to the real issue.

But Saunders is stubborn, unbending.

'My work not up to scratch… sir? Not grammar-school standard, you mean?'

Too late, Dan sees that this ill-focused dialogue is simply compounding his humiliation, for undoubtedly it would all be relayed triumphantly to the rest of the conspirators, the following day.

Lamely, therefore, and hypocritically, as he well realises, he retreats behind the mask of "Authority", to salvage some shred of dignity.

'Well, Saunders, I shall be watching you from now on,' he says, sternly, 'make no mistake. And if I get less than 100% effort from you, you'll be in serious trouble – do you understand?'

Saunders, his eyes fixed on some nebulous point on the desk in front of him, screws his face up, twists his mouth this way and that, as if weighing up this threat, yet faintly smirking all the while.

The silence grows and billows about them.

'Saunders,' he thunders, at last, 'do you hear? Do you hear what I am saying?' He stands up and goes towards Saunders' desk, places his hands upon it, then leans forward, to reinforce the point. 'Well, Saunders?'

Half-rising, Saunders stares to his left, timidly, it seems, for a moment. But then he raises his head.

'May I go now, please... sir?' he says, a shade too politely, too meekly.

And his 'sir', ever so slightly detached, jolts Dan back to the confrontation, weeks ago now, between Holly and Davidson, at that other rehearsal.

And a wave of anger surges through him.

'Get out!' he spits. 'Get out, Saunders!' And he grips the desk tightly to restrain his itching hands. He has never struck a boy in anger. But this is personal.

Solicitously replacing his chair under the desk, Saunders strolls haughtily from the room, not bothering to close the door behind him.

And Dan can hear the two boys sniggering in the corridor, then a moment or two later, their raucous guffaws, as they make no secret of their contempt.

The deliberately unyielding Saunders had led him into, and trapped him behind that mask of Authority, the very mask he abhorred, ensuring that an unbridgeable gulf of formality would divide them henceforth, and make any approach to understanding impossible.

He'd gone home, then, not staying behind as he frequently did, to do his marking. And his frustration and sense of humiliation had dissolved into a depression that gripped him for many weeks, forcing his retreat to blackboard, textbook and yes, an unaccustomed formality.

As yet, there had been no Titania to lighten his days. And in class, his habitual perch on the edge of the desk had remained conspicuously vacant.

XI

The mild spell, having lasted a fortnight, has allowed Dan to work tenaciously at the terrace, and its final form – its sparse, austere beds, its carefully placed stones, its seeming aridity – is now confirmed. And so he rests a little, considers his progress, imagines the colours to come.

And there *is* a difference, of course there is, between what he is doing as opposed to the "developers". He is planting, not just uprooting, working in harmony with natural elements: the soil, the seeds, the sun and the rain, even his home-made compost! The results of what he is doing will be nothing taken away from, but something added to earth's store. What he is doing will transform a natural emptiness into a natural presence, into something visually, intrinsically, pleasing, he hopes; something for anyone to stop and wonder at; and might not even the owls and foxes appreciate it in their own way?

This morning, though, a blizzard has greeted him with its fierce, squalling gusts, and snow piling rapidly against every obstacle in its path.

Winter's icy fang bared once again.

And so he has retreated indoors, been tidying things, reading, or just wandering about aimlessly until, after a while, he is drawn out into the whiteness of that other, harsh, perpetuating winter, long ago.

***

Endless hours spent searching for her along the foggy, circular pathways of the park, or in the maze of dark streets and lanes around it, forever disconsolate. Then, more than once, following her at a distance from school to home in the darkness, after rehearsals. And each time, long after the door closes behind her, standing there hopelessly, outside the house, outside her life, still. And when he's in town, at the library, the bread shop, crossing the market square, eyes everywhere, longing always to see her.

Weeks pass. Then, just two or three days before Christmas...

'Look, there are some seats up front.'

'Oh yes, I see them.' And Dan makes his way down the aisle to the front of the bus, struggling with bags and parcels, while Penny guides the twins. They're off early, on their way to his parents' for Christmas.

With the two boys babbling excitedly, he wrenches an arm free to help them up onto the seat beside him. 'There, now, you can see out of the window.' And his gaze wanders over the grey-white streets.

Soon, as the bus approaches the top end of town, his eyes dart in all directions, and when the bus stops, so does his heartbeat. For there she is in the queue, in her blue anorak with its Post Office armband, the bulky post bag, going to her round.

He turns, casually, to watch her get on, and sit near the door, at the back of the bus. She doesn't look up.

And if she does?

His heart is thumping. He turns back, the tension unbearable, the overwhelming desire to turn round again, just to look, be seen. And equally, the fear of hurting, hurting where he has no wish or right to do so.

And he stares out at the snow, filthy with oil and dust, slushed up by passing vehicles, recognising the impossibility of the dream.

***

Dan shakes his head. The same grey desolation can grip him even now. *Où sont les neiges d'antan*, the white snows of yesteryear?

A few mornings after the blizzard, this numbing return to winter, Dan returns from the letter box at his gate, with a slim, hand-written envelope.

Over breakfast, he scans the first densely-written paragraph, relieved to find that his ex-colleague Scott, who is clearly much more aware of the legal ramifications than he could have been, has himself undertaken a preliminary investigation of the plans for the ancient wood, at Shire Hall. So far so good.

But as he reads on, Dan's face darkens. The protest meeting, he learns, had been poorly attended. And only a trickle of objections had come in. Perhaps that pinned-up notification, on the very outskirts of the village, had been the only one.

> ... *All of which, Dan, leads me to suspect that our Mr Wilkinson, so publicly correct in calling that meeting, is privately not as impartial as he should be. Interestingly enough (though it may be of no relevance, of course), he and Peter Marshman, the speculator, are members of the same Masonic lodge.*

Dan closes his eyes, then rams his chair back so hard that it tips over. He strides across to the window and stands there, looking out into the blurred whiteness. What Scott has discovered boded ill, very ill indeed: for the wood, for all living things within it, and for his own tranquillity.

He turns back listlessly to his cold porridge and toast. And after placing his things in the sink and shaking the cloth outside he reads the rest of the letter.

> *Now, the fact that a petition did not emerge from the meeting is pretty odd, for unless one is organised very quickly, planning permission for a development tends to be given, with little reason to delay; and surely, the villagers can't want that! So if you want to organise one, try at the village post office. But what was recommended at the meeting, to those few souls attending, were individual letters to the Clerk to the CC, as a 'surer' form of protest. But Dan, it rarely is, which lends*

> *weight to my suspicions about Wilkinson… Anyway, above all, it's numbers that are needed in such cases. But people, alas, rarely get around to writing individual letters, do they?*

No, Dan muses, and nor is *he* likely to write one – much less mount a petition. Though at one time, in different circumstances, he wouldn't have hesitated.

> *Finally – and I'm sorry to be bringing only bad news – there is the Chairman of your Parish Council. Mr Earl, as you may know, is an accountant by profession, but he also happens to be, as you probably don't know, a partner in the firm which handles Marshman's accounts…*

Marshman. The speculator. So, that was it, a *fait* only too well *accompli!* Scott's diligent research simply spelt out the details of the stitch-up he'd feared all along, and there was nothing at all to be done about it now. Not, perhaps, by anyone.

Dan sits on with his coffee, wondering about these men and their understanding of truth, their likely on-off relationship with it. Idle speculation, of course, for he doesn't know them, and he will never know the outcome. But truth would be fudged, it seemed, sacrificed, for some grubby little financial accommodation among them: the wider implications of the development – they could claim with a fair degree of certainty – could only benefit the village: thirty-one "executive" families, after all!

But these implications, they went wider still, much wider, reinforcing that equation between genteel rurality and a dull, myopic, seemingly rock-solid conservatism, one that went right across the southern shires, which, time after time, guaranteed the return of Tory governments and their maintenance of age-old inequalities at society's roots.

Had anyone been looking to build thirty-one *prefabs* near the village, houses for the homeless, well, the outcome might have been very different!

Logic, common sense, kindness – they were never enough.

Dan is seething with anger, and finding his coffee stone cold, has to stop himself flinging the earthenware mug at the wall.

And then, somewhere, out in the cold, icy whiteness, an owl cry, a long, mournful, seemingly anguished cry.

Twooooo… And it comes again. Twooooo…

A little later, he returns to the letter and reads it over again. And only now, laying it back down on the table, does its date catch his eye: "13th February". Is today St Valentine's, then?

St Valentine's Day. Alpha and Omega.

Another blizzard is blowing ferociously outside, but as he stands again at the window he smiles. The owl-cry, he remembers, is not one, but two: the second that of an answering mate.

Tw…ooooo…

And out of the drift and swirl of his years a flurry of snowflakes through a broken window, falling on silence; a steel-hard brightness sharpening the stillness into trembling expectation, reflecting on silence; and he hears her hurrying footsteps on the stair and her breathless words as first they touch. And only now does he remember how the snowflakes in her hair and on her lips were melting, even as he kissed her.

It had been Holly's mother dying, of course, that had changed everything.

***

'I have to go back home, Dan. Up to Sunderland.'

'Of course you have. You must.'

'Just a few days, to sort things out. But it's half term next week, so a bit longer, maybe. Anyhow, *you'll* have to take over the production. I know I can count on you. But watch out, it's coming up to critical.'

'Ok. No, don't worry. I'll see to it.'

Holly reaches out and pats him gently, on the shoulder, 'Keep it simmering, Dan, but don't let it go on the boil.' And away he goes.

As the first few actors come into the gym, around nine o'clock, Dan explains the arrangements, as well as Holly's absence, and then these pupils do the same with the later arrivals. One or two, who have to come in from outlying villages, are very late. Buses are struggling.

By this point in the week, Wednesday, the weather has turned bleak. There is already a thick covering of snow, and it is snowing again.

Glancing over to the window wall he notices Liz, plain and bespectacled, forlornly watching the falling snowflakes. He walks over to her and puts his arm lightly around her shoulder. Is she crying?

'What is it, Liz. What's the matter?'

He tries to comfort her, half-watching the snow gusting in through an open window at the far end of the gymnasium.

'Look,' Liz mumbles, thrusting a piece of paper into his hand before covering her face again.

A letter, barely a page in length, from James, her boyfriend. She was too young... he'd met someone else at college... she'd soon forget him. Dan sighs. The usual stuff – but on St Valentine's Day, when she'd have been expecting a card...?

'What can I say, Liz? These things, they always hurt terribly, especially in the moment – and today, of all days. I'm sorry, it's a brutal thing to do. Here...' And he hands her his handkerchief.

The girl nods then shakes her head, quite inconsolable, until Gillian comes in, then Margaret, and Jane, and he motions them over. Full of concern, and curiosity, Gillian begins to ask her things about her relationship with this boy, who'd been in the year ahead until he left for college, and the others join in with their comments. And as he walks away Liz's shared pain is already more contained, soothed. She even manages a smile, he notices.

Someone remarks on how cold it is. Remembering the window, Dan walks over to close it, spotting a wide pool of melting crystals on the floorboards, as he approaches. The window isn't open, he realises, but broken: high up in the corner is a small, perfectly round hole, as though a cricket ball had been driven straight through it! Cricket in the snow? He smiles at the thought, making a mental note to mention it to the caretaker later. And the broken glass? Dan looks about carefully, but not finding any concludes that Mr Morrison must already be aware.

He moves back to where the others are waiting, and briefly outlines what he envisages for both today and the next day. And the rehearsal gets under way.

After each of the pre-selected scenes has been run through and approved, though not allowed to 'go on the boil', he nods, comments, and crosses it off his list. More organised, yet much less experienced than Holly, he needs his lists.

***

In all the years since, whenever Dan's thoughts have run back to that Wednesday, there is something he can never quite make up his mind about. Had he already decided what to do before the rehearsal began? Or had it come to him as the morning wore on?

Standing over the stove, waiting for the mocha's hiss and rush, he ponders the question anew. If there *was* a list of scenes to be rehearsed – and he thought he recalled one – and he'd known how it would pan out, how had he kept going the whole morning? His methodical calm, which he distinctly recalls, the business with Liz, the window, the many scenes they rehearsed…

But if the idea had come to him only during the rehearsal, well, he could just have changed the *order* of the scenes to be played through, couldn't he?

It had to be so. For when they went into that fateful scene, the two of them, he had been brittle with apprehension. And he couldn't *possibly* have got through the morning, knowing it would be so, that this one throw of the dice – and Titania's response – would decide everything, irrevocably.

So…

So did he say, at eleven o'clock, or quarter past, something like: 'Look, it's obvious we're not going to get through all I'd hoped to, so what we'll do now is take two, maybe three, of the shorter sequences...' And did he scan his list and name them individually, then say, 'So, if you're not involved, off you go home and try to be back for two fifteen.'?

***

As each sequence finishes, its actors don coats and scarves and gloves, pull on wellingtons or overshoes and shuffle off home through the deepening snow.

At long last there are only the two of them. Bottom and Titania in a leafy glade. Will o' the Wisps, with their little shifting lights flickering about them.

A mediated world, which demands to be played out to the last.

'Right,' says the director, matter of fact, 'the last part of Act IV, scene one, from *"What, wilt thou hear some music, my sweet love?"*'

And the actress nods gravely and takes her cue.

'Or say, sweet love, what thou desir'st...'

Can she know already? And with time sweeping by like Niagara, dare he seize the moment as it passes?

'I have a venturous fairy that will seek
The squirrel's hoard...'

With all pasts and all futures hurtling in to meet this moment.

'Sleep thou, and I will wind thee in my arms.
Fairies, be gone, and be all ways away.'

Uncertain, hesitating at their instant scattering, immobile for an age, then one, two, three steps forward; and here she is looking down upon him, a bemused Titania.

> '*So doth the woodbine the sweet honeysuckle*
> *Gently entwist...*'

And she is kneeling now,

> '*...the female ivy so*
> *Enrings the barky fingers of the elm*'

is bending over him, closer, closer still, touching now, and almost in a whisper,

> '*O how I love thee! How I dote on thee!*'

In this moment, in this still moment, all risk embraced, a new-invented world carrying over easily from the old which bore it.

Reaching upwards, his hands gently enfolding her face, gently pulling her down towards him, and she coming so willingly to his kiss.

When they emerge from the school gates, it is into bright sunlight; it has stopped snowing altogether. How radiant she looks, as they slip and slide their way together, heading up towards the park gates, going home for lunch.

'It's silly, we've got to stop,' she says, walking up the steep hill from the school. 'There's your wife, your little ones. It'll only get worse.'

Then, halfway across the market square, just as earnestly:

'Why should they stop us? We're doing no one any harm...'

And at the other side of the square:

'If we finished it now, cut it off now, it would be like killing a child, a child that's been born to us...'

He listens, ponders, and willingly assents.

And once through the park gates, the glistening, blinding snow urges them on, carries them above cares into a suggestion of long summer hills rising from a dusty plain, a torrent of tomorrows wafted on wind-wings, leaping and sparkling in eyes which see their country reflecting in other eyes, lilting down wind-path and water-flow, a music that touches her gentleness with shaping fragments of a summer symphony – or merely wind-tricks of a slowly melting spring?

They must hurry, now, though – there is the afternoon rehearsal in little more than an hour. And they part at the fountain: she, soon toiling up towards the church at the top; and he, slipping and sliding still, along the curving paths to the bottom-most gate.

And every now and again, she turns to watch him, as he her, laughing and waving.

Less than an hour later, he is back in the gymnasium, standing by the window, alone, his heart pounding, straining to listen, to hear.

The snow is powdering in again through the broken window.

Then footsteps mounting the stairs, hurrying footsteps.

'I ran, and I ran. I was so afraid that someone else might get here before me!'

And as he reaches out to take her in his arms, he sees the crystals in her hair and on her lashes beginning to melt, he feels her coat damp, as he holds her.

All too soon, other footsteps, and she darts away, exclaiming brightly about the snow, unwinding her dark red scarf as she moves, shaking a fine, glistening spray from her hair.

The doors burst suddenly open, and in comes the bouncing Hippolyta, who stands there as the doors bang shut behind her, her eyes moving from one to the other of them, a sly grin beginning to spread across her face.

'Oh ho! What have we here? Caught you red-handed, Titania!'

Titania giggles. 'Not quite,' she says, 'but nearly!'

Hippolyta's eyes open wide.

And in the brief silence that follows, looks dart back and forth, from one girl to the other, until they begin to laugh, though each, perhaps, at their own different perceptions of the truth of that moment.

XII

Had she already guessed what that whole rehearsal was really about?

Reaching upwards, his hands gently enfolded her face, gently pulled her down towards him, and she came so willingly to his kiss... that kiss in which he would lose himself for half a lifetime; and she – an aery spirit – would first taste the fierce vexation of a dream.

But then maybe all our "first times" – whatever their nature – are always played out in the long shadow of Eden.

'It's silly, we've got to stop... It'll only get worse.' Her words echo round now, in his mind. Titania-Eurydice merging into mist.

And once more, Dan checks his text for Titania's kiss, but in vain.

Yet the kiss had been real enough, had played a crucial part in that unfolding drama inside him, had overturned his whole life. Not the very first kiss in rehearsal, for that had been a scene of shy hesitation for both of them, intensified by the giggling, whisperings, even ribald comments, of the others – disruptions resolved only by Holly's (for once) calm persistence.

He frowns, perplexed even now, for what had that diffidence, the shy reticence, been born of, for either of them? In his case, a slight turn of her head, perhaps, a hand reaching out to touch, a sudden smile, lips parted – any of these things might have had the power to arrest him; and in gazing after its image departing, he would surely have sensed a hint of… of his life re-focusing, of something momentous, even.

He sighs. Truly, can we ever really know when love, that cleaving towards another, takes hold? Or why?

Looking down the dark, further side of the hill where he seldom goes, Dan's eyes narrow: near the bottom the snow is all churned up. He takes several wary steps diagonally down the hillside and then stops halfway and stares at… hundreds of footprints! All still clear and distinct despite the morning's further dusting of snow.

Nearing the bottom, cautiously, for the snow has drifted deep in parts, he realises they all head in the same direction: animal or bird, large or small, and however much they meander or veer from their course, they are all directed from west to east.

Evidence of a mass migration. A diaspora. Silent testimony to the destruction of the wood. But of course.

Deeply disturbed, slowly, and taking care not to disturb them – though quite why he cannot say – Dan follows their trail. Rabbit and hare he identifies at once, but others he can only guess at: partridge or pheasant maybe; his fox almost certainly; and two or three sets of deeper, longer tracks, which have surely been made by deer. They pass round the hill, through the snow-filled hedge, and thence down the embankment to the narrow strip of deciduous woodland between his field and the long-defunct railway cutting.

Following and trying to identify distracts him momentarily, but not sufficiently to displace his consciousness of the finality that these marks express. The insane grammar of possession, enclosure, constriction, and exclusion at work again, as it had been for two hundred years and more, and far too close to be ignored. How long will it take, he wonders, for it to dawn on people with power to make such change that overstepping certain limits must lead to the irrevocable end of all that went before, and the imponderable consequences of this? Will it ever dawn on such people? He shakes his head in true despair. Some things surely *have* to be beyond dispute, otherwise all values, and the world of mankind they underpin, however imperfectly, were destined to crumble away into chaos.

And, while not to him personally, it matters, oh how it matters.

Dan walks back to the house, an anger smouldering deep in his belly, fuelling his contempt for the "developer": people like Marshman, for whom being alive seemed to mean no more than the quick fix, the fast buck; all those who overstepped limits in pursuit of short-term gains, who trod on others and hurt, regardless of the consequences; who demolished and ravaged. The same old, reckless buccaneering… in this newest, uglier phase now gripping the world.

Reason's sleep!

***

Rosalind sneers. 'Don't you ever remember anything I tell you? I already told you about it!'

The two girls are huddled in the park shelter, out of the icy wind.

'That place I used to go to with him. You know, before.'

And Rosemary listens, wondering why her friend is so edgy, agitated.

'There was… is… this long slope down. It was all green like grass, but more like ice, or glass even. And I slipped and slithered on it, down, down towards the trees. Then I…'

She pauses, dramatically.

'Then you… what?' Rosemary pulls her legs out from under her, already feeling the pins and needles beginning.

'Well, there are these dark tress, and just as I get to the start of them, squinting into the darkness, trying to take it all in, this man comes out – from the trees. His face is turned away, but what I fix on is that he's spattered all over with mud. But then he looks at me and he says…'

'He spoke to you, this man?'

'Oh yes.' Rosalind looks smug. 'He says… And he's coming towards me, and I open my arms to him, like in the love films, you know, feeling all… thrilled. He was *really* good looking. And he says:

"You are so beautiful Ros, adorable, as beautiful as a butterfly, and I could make you into a star. You deserve to be a star. You would excel at that, shining so... brightly." And I...'

'Oh, how *exciting* for you, Ros.' And Rosemary looks away as she says it, to hide her smiles, her ironically raised eyebrows. Always the best, Rosalind, the prettiest, the star.

'Yes. And I was feeling all shy, you know.'

'Mm...'

'And I say, "Do you really think I would?" But then he, well, he rushes straight past me, brushing against my sleeve and he vanishes into thin air! I couldn't believe it. And I just stood there, rubbing my eyes and feeling so disappointed, and upset. Then I saw there were splodges of mud all over my white cardigan. It looked a real mess. I tried to wipe them off, but they just spread and spread as I watched them, and I started crying. But I was telling myself all the time, don't be silly, it's just a dream, just a dream.'

'What? In your dream you were telling yourself it was a dream?' Rosemary barely hides her scorn.

'Yes!' Rosalind shrugs. 'But I began to feel... worried in case anyone saw me. And there was someone, a long way off. Whoever it was seemed to be trying hard to get up the hill, to the main road, but he kept slipping back down, like a... a spider trapped in a bath. So I decided to go in under the trees, and get out of sight.'

'Oh, did you?' Deftly, Rosemary turns a yawn into a cough.

'Yes. Because I remember thinking that if I went right to the end of the avenue...'

'The avenue...?'

'*Yes*, Rosie, the *avenue*... in the *trees*. If I went to the end of it, everything would come clear. Wasn't that weird?'

'The whole thing is if you ask me! It doesn't go anywhere, does it? Nothing joins up with anything.' Rosemary barely stifles her next yawn.

'There's more, though – it went on for ages.'

'*Ages*?'

'Don't worry, I've forgotten the rest. Ah, but no, there's this one bit I've just *got* to tell you… It's ok, I won't make you late… I was sitting on the ground, at the far end of the avenue, in front of one of those benches like the ones down by the lake. And I had two stones, one in each hand, and I kept pressing them together on the seat then letting go and they fell apart every time. But I kept on trying. In the end I had to give up, and I put them down on the bench, one at either end. Then…'

'Ros, I have to be… is there much more?' Rosemary ventures.

'Then it all changed.' Rosalind ignores her, speaks over her. 'A bus came, only it was more like a boat. I held out my hand. And then…'

Rosemary starts thinking about bus times, and her mother, and tea and… Vaguely, she hears something about pigs swimming, which makes her think of the pig woman, and then something or other shining, but who cared. It was a dream. A stupid dream with no point.

'… but it was my bloody mother, Rosie.'

'What?'

'Yes! My mother – are you deaf? She'd switched on my light! She said I'd shouted out in my sleep and wakened them up.' Rosalind's lip curls. 'She even manages to ruin my bloody dreams, the miserable cow…'

Rosemary begins to laugh. She covers her mouth with her hand to try and smother her laughter, but she can't, and she really doesn't care any more.

And after a moment, Rosalind joins in, the two of them in stitches. And Rosemary wishes she could stay here in the shelter, and not go home ever again, to her real world.

'Silly, stupid cow', Rosalind snorts. Then she turns serious again. 'But Rosie… do you think dreams mean anything?'

Rosemary shrugs. '*He* always said they did, do you remember? All that stuff about advertisements and wish-fulfilments and things. Really interesting it was. And sometimes he…'

'Oh, fuck *him*!' Rosalind says savagely, and starts walking away, up the hill towards the rose-beds.

Suddenly she spins round. 'Why do you always have to bring *him* into it?' she yells back. 'Anybody would think you had a crush on him. Honestly!' And she turns on her heel and flounces off.

Rosemary stares after Rosalind, startled at her insinuation, but also seeing that silly red face of hers, all twisted in anger, ugly, just like a… a pig! Rosalind was a pig, a pig! So why had she told her the stupid dream if she didn't want to talk about *him*? Because it *was* all about him, sort of, wasn't it? Tossing her head, she saunters up towards the gates, making no effort to catch up with Rosalind.

Once in sight of the bus stop she quickens her steps, and then stops dead. Hadn't her mother mentioned going shopping first, before coming home? Relief washes over her. So she won't be late after all.

So… was it true, any of Ros's dream? Or was she just making it up? That place probably didn't exist – how could it? But if it did, and she found it? Hm. It might tell her something more than Rosalind's disjointed rubbish did, and get her away from her moody friend, and from school and… and pigs, and her stupid parents. And Rosemary starts to laugh again, a rough, sarcastic laugh, rolling her eyes.

And then she bursts into tears.

That night, her parents have their church friends round, and Rosemary sits there, in the cold front room, bored out of her mind.

She listens to the clock ticking, counting the ticks, adjusting her breathing to them for a whole minute, and then for two minutes. And then she slows it to every other tick, then just to the tocks, and then…

'Rosemary…? Rosemary! Tea now, if you please!'

Absurdly grateful to her mother, Rosemary hurries from the room. A dog barks outside. And as she waits for the kettle she thinks about the place in the dream. Ros had said where it was, which bus route, even. But Ros was like that, making things up to glorify herself. A star? Huh. You didn't have dreams like that, or *that* long.

It probably didn't exist. But maybe one of these days she'd go there just to see for herself. Just in case.

XIII

A thrush precariously balanced on a slender bough among the oaks, bobbing in the breeze, chirrups elation into sunlight, with a defiant 'I fear you no more I fear you no more,' banishing the winter for good.

The second snows have departed as suddenly as they came.

Completing the terrace seems easy now, and Dan sets about it with renewed vigour, unrolling its austere beauty from his mind, as if it were a carpet. The paving stones... how bright they are in the morning sunlight, their radiance dazzling the hillside, and at times he must look away to protect his eyes.

And the colours! Of late, he has been finding he cannot look at everything hard enough. And each time he does look there are battalions of green spears, daffodils and narcissus; with grape-hyacinth and anemone, all pushing through in profusion around the house, and the graveyard below him; and every shrub is tipped with a brighter green, like butterflies emerging. Everywhere birds building, leaves thrusting. All this going on as it has always done, and – he owns – until now, he has never really *looked*, just taken it all for granted. All of it, so dependable, so unlike the *human* race.

This earth... too wonderful to be realised. But he will try, persist, all the same.

Minutes later, kneeling on a paving stone to firm in a final broom, his eyes and mind are full of the motionless upsurge. And he marvels at time and sunny days and rainy days and snow, their endless cycle, and how they quietly, imperceptibly, transform the land, the landscape, our perceptions, and our moods.

Yet for all that, and because of it too, perhaps, it is what he has his back to up there on the hillside that really matters; something higher up still, calling him imperiously. But he has no clear notion of what it is, no sense of what it means.

***

Rosalind is nowhere to be found.

Where she goes when she disappears like this, and who with, Rosemary has never dared ask. Does it matter? Does she care, even? Well, yes, she does, a bit. More than a bit, really.

For days, now, she's been trying to make up her mind. Does she have the courage to go and find Rosalind's dream place, if it was a dream… to see for herself if it is anything like how she had described it? Does she?

She rounds the corner, and the bus is standing there at the stop, as if waiting for her to come to a decision. And before she really has she's on it, and it speeds away, bouncing away down the long hill.

The conductor, a lanky young lad, comes upstairs after her, for her fare.

'Where's it you're going, love?'

Rosemary shrugs, flustered, then smiles helplessly at him.

'Um, well, I don't know its name. It's a sort of park, I think.'

'Ok.'

'I know it's on this route only I've never been before. It's about halfway, my friend says… I'm supposed to meet her there, to go to… her auntie's.'

The conductor grins. 'Victoria Park, yeah. That'll be threepence, love. We stop at the main gate – I'll give you a shout.'

Rosemary, on tenterhooks in spite of the conductor's reassurance, peers hard out of the window. What if she misses it, if he forgets? And whenever he comes up to the top deck, she tries to catch his eye. But soon enough she recognises it herself – the great green slope down, after the houses have ended, the green slope, like glass.

As she stands, the conductor's face bobs up the stairwell.

'Here's your park, love!'

And Rosemary nods down at him, like a grown up. But her mouth is dry, her legs feel all wobbly, and she holds the handrail tightly.

It was true, then. Rosalind *had* been here, more than two years ago. With him? Really with him?

The moment Rosemary steps off the bus, she sees the line of dark trees at the bottom of the hill, and, zipping up her thin coat against the cold wind, she half runs, half walks down towards it, as though afraid it may vanish before she can get there. And her eyes open wide in wonder: it really is like stepping into Rosalind's dream, with the grass all slippery, and yes, just like glass.

The morning is bright, a spring morning, almost sunny. Nevertheless, though the leaves are not yet open, the closely planted trees with their trunks thick and black are still enough to shut out much of the light. And standing there, looking up at the canopy of branches, feeling dazed, Rosemary recalls something else Rosalind had said, going on about the dream the next day too, adding things, embellishing...

"It was like walking into another life once I got between those two rows of trees."

Rosemary shivers, suddenly cold. She waits for her eyes to adjust, then wonders whether she too will have this same feeling.

"It always seemed to be evening under those trees?"

Very slowly, Rosemary starts to walk forward. And as her eyes get used to the lesser light she begins to sense something, yes, like Rosalind had said. And she peers out, into the brighter world outside, feeling enclosed, apart, safe. Like being in a tent when it was raining – just once she had been, when her parents had got it into their heads to actually use the ropey old tent someone had given them.

As she nears the end of the avenue, she can see the bench all right, backed up against some ragged beech hedging: a dull green, all carved into with initials and obscenities, more bare wood than paint.

Oh, my God!

But how could they?

Rosemary starts to shake, and her eyes fill with tears as she stares from one end of the bench to the other, at the two stones.

So it wasn't a dream but what *really* happened? But when? Rosalind in that thin, red nylon dress of hers, the one that shimmered and trembled at a touch… here with *him*.

But when was she? Back *then*, when she'd said, or…?

Rosemary screws up her face. It didn't make any sense, and she groans in misery, her head a whirl. And she wants to sit down and shut it all out, bridle her racing fancy. But she cannot bring herself to go near the bench.

The stones are there, plain as day. What did it mean?

She stands there, staring at the bench, a kind of reverence mingling in her head with despair. And then she slumps to the ground, miserable in her desperate aloneness.

But *when* had it been?

Rosalind… a rosebud. Her mouth in flower…

No! Oh, please, noooo!

A jealous anger suddenly rips through Rosemary, and she beats the ground with her fists, screaming and shouting and cursing Rosalind for her betrayal, for *all* her deceptions – dressing it all up as a dream. How dare she!

And then she starts to run – to get away, be anywhere but here.

Behind the seat, where the ground has worn hard, where the roots are exposed, where lots of feet have passed, and through the narrow opening in the straggling beech hedge. Out onto a narrow asphalt path, which she crosses without noticing. Plunging into a copse at the other side. And still running, running, furious with her gullible self and her stupid life, pounding on and on until, pushing through the undergrowth, she comes out into a rough stony lane. And there she stops, panting, gasping, and beginning to feel ridiculous. Suddenly hating her panic, and the absurd unreality of it all. What is she doing in this stupid place?

The grassy slope. The dark trees. The two stones on the bench.
It was no dream.

When her head finally stops spinning, Rosemary sets off walking again, head down, trying to feel calmer and failing utterly. She looks up, and to her horror realises she doesn't know where she is any more. She has lost her bearings, all sense of direction.

Taking a grip on herself, she stands stock still and makes her resolve. She'll walk in the direction she's facing – along this narrow, tree-lined lane – and if after a hundred paces she hasn't reached the main road, or even just heard it, she'll turn back, and follow the lane in the other direction. She'll be sure to find herself this way.

Feeling brighter, her face set in concentration, she starts counting.

Just around a bend, emerging from the tunnel of trees, she reaches a hundred and stops. She looks round her and sees the hedge on either side has opened out to leave a sort of clearing. Over to the left there's an entrance to... she takes a few more steps... a building site. What, in the middle of a wood? Is she perhaps dreaming now? And she stares at it, sullenly.

Directly in front of her the way is blocked by another high hedge, and following it to the right with her eyes she sees a wrought-iron gate, almost hidden away in the hedge, a bit like the one near the pig woman's pen. Urged on by curiosity, she goes up to it and peers through the bars.

An old church, with a hill rising up behind it. The graveyard is full of roses. Rosemary turns away; then, having half-glimpsed something, peers back in to watch a tiny figure far up the hillside, dragging something up the steep slope, but he is moving very slowly, as if in slow motion, and her patience gives out.

Rosemary turns and starts walking quickly, back down the lane.

XIV

There is that day (a Saturday?) when they meet ("by chance") in the great forecourt of the University, each absorbed in the paintings (or was it lithographs, etchings, or photographs, perhaps?); at an exhibition by an artist whose identity, if once known, has long since slipped away, beneath the sea.

Sequence, our security, is of little value to Dan now, so why does he persist with this sifting and conjecturing, fiddling with the pieces, forever trying to find those that are missing or trying to force them to fit snugly together to complete the puzzle? These rugged outcrops of memory, weathering time and rearranging themselves into a different pattern, do they not represent the archipelago wherein the one rocky islet beckons... with its shading tamarisks, its crystal waters, its pure white sands, reminiscent of Theokofti?

And this slowly shaping garden, another *res amissa*?

Neither (naturally) is at first aware of the other.

Well, hello!

What a coincidence!

What a surprise!

Each later leaving (not quite at the same time but almost) and going, as chance would have it, in the same direction. He, trusting, not daring to look back; leading the way along the maze of corridors familiar to him from his not very distant student years there.

A meticulous catharsis, and played out (in all likelihood)

before an unheeding audience, yet appeasing some vague notion of propriety; a ritualised dance before indifferent gods.

What can they say, as they sit in the crowded coffee lounge, able to touch at last, though briefly, warily? Or later, in the Chinese restaurant, holding hands under the table? The words (now long gone) are unimportant in themselves, their significance less complex than their syntax or the landscape over which they range. The ache eased only a little, and for a little while only, never enough.

And was not this day, the day of the Chinese restaurant, also the day of the play? Of that *other* performance, when the legitimatised, permissible, make-believe words are proclaimed before the whole world, and applauded? And their kiss, in the staged realisation of *The Dream*?

This, anyhow, is the way it has come down through the conduits of his memory.

Oh, how I love thee! How I dote on thee!

But if these words, then so too the cruel reawakening later.

Be as thou wast wont to be;
See as thou wast wont to see.

Dian's bud and its faithless prose.

And for him, ever after, *methought I was... And methought I had...*

And now?

Words after speech leach into... what? The intrinsic perfection of an unprinted negative, that still silent image? You in your no-time-no-place tormenting sleep I dream to wake from?

Those mornings when Titania, in her prefect's role, fetches his fourth-year pupils from their classroom and herds them towards the assembly hall, and then, when the last one has disappeared around the corner, hurries back to stand a moment in the doorway, arms stretched across its opening or pivoting on its jamb to smile or shake her head… in an instant shaping his own spirits for the day ahead, until she shall come again.

And it shocks him even now to remember how vain it all was; how once what had been longed for was realised, it still did not span the void around which they circled continually. And so they remained precariously poised, gripped by the tension, that gnawing fear of new, irreparable loss.

*'It would be
like killing a child,'
she had said,
at their first meeting,
'a child
that's been born to us.'
And he couldn't deny it.*

*Then, years later,
he was less sure,
pondering that child
– defective as it was
in mind and body –
he couldn't help thinking
there might,
after all,
be a case
for euthanasia.*

O my pelikan daughter.

A prayer that might have been Rosemary's also. Rosemary, whom no one remembered.

***

Dragging aimlessly through the park along its deserted avenues, across wide lawns, past sodden rose-beds and silent statues, Rosemary pauses for a moment to catch a distant echo or peer intently into a frozen pond, till she merges, once again – like the dripping trees – into the sombre mist.

Truanting again.

Some days the extreme cold drives her back to school, though not always to her classes. She has found a way in, which brings her into the bottom corridor near the girls' cloakroom, where she's taken to hiding out. But one morning, Miss Drake finds her, and she is forced to lie, in her confusion.

'I came all over faint, miss, and I… I needed to sit down.'

The ensuing inquisition had wrung from her an embarrassed confession – it was all she could think of in the moment, and it sounded hollow, even to her.

'My period… it started this morning, miss, and… and the pain's *really* bad… always is, miss, on the first day.'

And ludicrously, the whole charade ends with Rosemary wrapped in a blanket, sipping hot sweet tea and swallowing aspirin, then lying on a low camp bed in the senior mistress's room until lunchtime. Bored, uncomfortable; pointless.

After this episode Rosemary gives herself up to the caretaker's mercy, hiding in the stuffy old boiler room where no one ever comes. But all too soon the acrid fumes from the coke start to choke her and she has to be outside again, coughing and gasping for air, despite the cold and damp.

But even this is preferable to facing the others.

Why do they look at her like that? Why are they always whispering about her? If only she could talk to *him* – the "him" she'd believed in, before – not *this* one, the betrayer, the fake. Already she couldn't look at him without thinking of the things Rosalind had said, about him and her before. But now she'd made it *far* worse, telling her about the stupid park, and the two stones on the bench… Rosemary sighs loudly. Now when she sees him down the corridor, she really can see him with Rosalind, in that park. And she has to hide until he's gone by, or turn back and go another way, just as she does with the others.

Rosalind, in her thin red dress.

Being seen, spoken to. This constant dread. Always straining to see ahead, always glancing over her shoulder. Not that anyone seems to notice. Sometimes, for a day or two, it gets better, and she can slip into school at the last minute and go to her classes, even. But still she avoids the places the others will be. Still she is tense, uneasy, scuttling away before the final bell stops its ringing.

And, beyond these fears of the immediate moment and the next and the one after that, Rosemary also lives in terror of her parents finding out. For find out they will, when her fitful attendance is reported, as sooner or later must happen. Truancy? Her mother and father will throw a fit!

And so, as autumn gives way to winter, Rosemary starts to take precautions.

Usually, the post comes before she leaves home each morning. And so she starts jumping up, helpfully, from the breakfast table, or rushing downstairs from wherever she is, so she can intercept anything that looks like a letter from school. She darts here and there, a bundle of nerves, and it's far far worse when the postman doesn't come before she leaves.

On such mornings Rosemary frets all day, in dread of getting home too late after school. What if the letter's come, and they're there, both of them, waiting for her like fierce, angry dogs? Teeth bared, salivating, working themselves up?

Why has everything changed so quickly? And where is Rosalind when she needs her? Rosalind, who had been so insistent about her... feelings, when she herself was so unsure. Rosemary cannot remember the last time they'd spent an afternoon together. Once or twice, she's caught a glimpse of her in school, and once Rosalind had waved to her, but that was all. Why doesn't she come over? Some friend she was.

And Rosemary is left fretting this loss also.

***

Rosemary has no monopoly of anxiety, however.

Titania may wear her guilt gracefully, half refusing its premises, believing she is doing no wrong. But she lives in fear of discovery, none the less; a novice in deceit, tyrannised by so much love and gentleness around her.

She loves him!

Her heart leaps, her stomach churns when she sees him; and then it's passed and she can't wait until the next time – really, she thinks of little else. But she loves her parents too. Is there nothing, nothing at all she can do, to make this right? Hitherto in her life, love has flourished wholly in the absence of conflict, while this eddying cycle, this different love, terrifies and transfixes her.

At the performance of the school play, aware of all the eyes on her, she had just acted her part, the part she knows so well, and her parents hadn't noticed a thing. 'Proud of you, love,' her dad had whispered afterwards, and she'd almost sobbed with relief. If only they knew what was going on inside her, all the fluttering, the restraint…

A week later she's at the public library, with most of the sixth form, to see a 'rewarding film' – Mr Kelday's words. And a new despair and a new hope make their rapid entrance to torment her, by turns.

Saturday Night and Sunday Morning.

She feels it too – the anticipation and excitement of finally seeing him, after only glimpses all week! But then, all that squalor, and the indignities, laid bare by the film.

And after the film, willing herself not to think, she hurries off to their pre-arranged meeting place.

'Well met by streetlight, fair Titania…'

But his quip is ill-judged: he can see at once she's in quite a state.

'That's how they'll see us,' she sobs, pulling him over to the wall out of the streetlamp's glare, 'even though there's nothing squalid about what we have. But they'll all make it so, won't they? Words can do that.' She lets go of his hands and turns her face away, fighting back tears. 'I can't bear it.'

Understanding only too well and sharing her anguish, Dan takes hold of her shoulders, gently draws her to him and kisses her. The gentlest of embraces, comforting, enveloping. And he wishes...

A moment later he pulls away.

'You're right,' he says, looking into her eyes. 'Transgression of any norms, whatever they are, has its price.'

'So...?'

'So, you live it and pay up... if you think what you are doing is worth the suffering. Otherwise...'

'Otherwise?'

'You stay with the norm. And you accept the other suffering, or tedium or whatever it is, that this norm imposes.'

'Is that what's going to happen to us?' she whispers, close to tears again.

'I don't know, but, well, I think it depends on how we feel, the two of us, on how important *we* feel it is.'

Titania looks away, perhaps not trusting herself to speak.

'The great problem is,' he goes on, 'we're seldom allowed to choose the choices we have to make our choices from.'

'No...' And she sighs softly, shaking her head a fraction.

'But come on,' he says, also mindful of the time, 'let's get you home. We don't want to catch our deaths in this freezing fog.'

Slowly, silently, they walk up the deserted lane towards the top end of the town, but in a short while he stops once again, and pulls her to him. And after a long moment in which they just stand there, holding each other, he tries to put into words what he has been thinking these past few days, spent wondering how he can best... prepare her. A crazy notion, he knows, and far from easy.

'There is another way...' he starts.

'What?' she says, looking at him through tear-filled lashes.

'Refusing to choose at all.'

'I don't...'

'Not an "either-or" world,' he says quickly, 'but a "both-and" one. You see, if you accept the usual premises you have to accept the usual, or likely, consequences, but if you change the rules, well, that alters everything.'

'Does it?' Titania takes his arm, and they walk on. 'I don't see how...'

'Well, your parents...'

'Yes, my parents. And your...'

'Yes. But your parents, they're hardly likely to throw you out, are they?' He smiles, takes her hand in his. 'After the initial storm, things would...'

'Storm?' Titania stares at him. 'I don't think I could...'

'I know, but things would calm down afterwards, and...'

'No. I couldn't. I just *couldn't* hurt them like that.' Titania looks aghast. 'And your wife, your twins, what about them? I couldn't hurt them either. Could you?' She tugs at his arm. 'Well, *could* you?'

He shakes his head, trying to find the words to express his confused thoughts mingling with the new ones now filling his head, his mind, oh somehow he must, somehow...

'But isn't that the point?' he says, eventually. 'Your parents, my wife, or anyone else for that matter, they're hurt because we suddenly stop being who they believe us to be. They've shaped an image of us, but one that reflects only in part who we really are – do you see?'

'Well yes, but...'

'I'm not sure I've thought about it quite like this before, but it seems to me that this means... and perhaps we've fed their misconceptions, but anyway, it means that the person they cherish is not us, it's an idealised us – a phantom that squeezes and pinches us, and takes our breath away, sometimes our very life. And that's why...'

Titania draws away a little, and he stops, unsure any of this is helping. She is no doubt aware that however reasonable he sounds these are only words, that their realities, both his and hers, are something else and much more complex, as of course, they are.

Then she turns to him.

'Maybe you're right,' she says, surprising him. Then she pokes him. 'But it doesn't alter the fact that I couldn't hurt them like that.'

Dan closes his eyes, trying to suppress the desperation inside him; the terrible fear of losing her but a breath away. He feels numb, disoriented, as if he's lost her already, and makes a last, valiant effort.

'Well, I thought you said it was the deception you didn't like!' he says gently, trying to lift the mood, 'above all the deception! And here you are telling me that you won't risk hurting them, preferring to maintain their self-deception.' He squeezes her arm and laughs, trying to lighten his words. 'Whatever else, it's hardly a model of truth, or logic, is it?'

Titania looks him straight in the eye. 'I don't think love has to be a "model of logic," she says, 'do *you*? *Do* you?'

He smiles ruefully and pulls her gently towards him again.

'Sorry... No, it doesn't. It isn't. Quite the opposite, in fact. But that's not what I meant. He sighs. 'In the end, it will come down to a decision about which of our different loves is the stronger, I suppose, as what I was leading to...'

But Titania can keep back her tears no longer, and he holds her tightly against him for a while, without speaking, until the worst sobbing is past. Then, quietly, he tells her.

'Penny knows.'

'What!'

'She knows. Watching the play last Saturday, well, she guessed there was something, and she confronted me the next morning, over breakfast.'

Titania looks aghast. 'But I don't... after what you just...'

'I know. So, I told her how it was – there was no point in denying it – and, well, now she's asking if you'll come, so we can... talk together.'

Titania stares at him, clearly unable to reconcile this new knowledge with the tenor of the conversation that has just preceded it.

Dan holds his breath. Has he ruined it?

Suddenly, she breaks away from him.

'But that's... Why didn't you tell me right away? *Why* have you saved it till now, you *horrible* man?' And her clenched fists pound his chest and shoulders. 'A whole week you've made me wait before telling me! Oh, but this means... So what did she say...? Oh...'

And as he catches hold of her fists she twists nimbly out of his grip, laughing and crying at the same time.

'So, why?'

'No reason at all,' he says, belying the many hours he has agonised over this very point, all the preamble, the reasoning. And he pulls her back into him, laughing with her, exhaling his own relief into her hair. 'Except that it was *you* who started talking right away, about the film, and that led on to...'

'*Me?*'

'Yes, about the film and how it had made you feel about... us.'

'Well it *did*!'

'I know! So it wasn't right to just... and then there was no opportunity, I mean, *until* now.'

'Stop it,' she chides. 'Stop teasing me! Tell me what she said! Her *exact* words. Was she very upset, very angry? Does she hate me? She must hate me – I know I would. What did she say?'

'Well, of course, she *was* upset, *and* angry.' Dan closes his eyes momentarily. It had been an awful day. 'But when it came to evening she had calmed down. And she asked a lot of questions about you.'

'Did she?'

'Yes. She was concerned, you know, about school, and your parents, how they might react if they found out. And how it would affect you – and me, of course – if rumours got around at school. But hatred?' Dan shakes his head and forces a smile. 'She doesn't hate you, no.' And even now, Dan cannot quite take it in himself, this transformation from storm into calm.

Titania is crying again, silently now. He starts to dry her eyes with his handkerchief, but she takes it from him.

'She sounds... lovely,' she says through her tears, handing the handkerchief back. 'And it would be something to come, if only to say... to reassure her she's got nothing to be afraid of. But...'

'I'm sure you'll like her, and she you, if she doesn't feel our relationship as a… threat. And of course – he hurries on – that is up to both of us. So, how do you feel about it?'

He looks intently into her eyes, overjoyed to see her brighten, in the vague realisation, perhaps, of what this new turn in events may mean.

'But this is what we've been hoping for, isn't it?'

'Yes.' Dan smiles. 'It's what we were saying about not choosing. Now we don't have to, do we?'

Suddenly, she starts giggling. 'I suppose this makes me your mistress, doesn't it?'

And he laughs too – at her tinkling laughter, and her naiveté, both of which he finds irresistible. 'Well… technically, no, not quite.'

But instead of responding to her quizzical look, he quickly reminds her that even if things do work out for the better at his end, there is still the question of her parents.

Titania comes to a halt. And she stands there, in the shadows, in silence.

'So,' he goes on, 'Wouldn't it be better, all round, if we were to…?'

But her hand suddenly covers his mouth.

'Don't say it!' she whispers. 'Don't even think it! *I* know them, and I just *know* they couldn't take it.'

But for all that, her gloom has passed, and she takes hold of his arm and guides him now, up the deserted, ill-lit avenue towards her home.

It has begun to drizzle again.

XV

But it didn't work out well. How could it?

At the time, after the play and the film, a future had seemed possible. And he'd lived each day with senses and expectations sparking – loving her, missing her, feeling it all so deeply with every fibre of his being. But it had all quite exhausted him, and increasingly alarmed Penny.

Gripped by love's blind urgings… pure joy, deep pain, and the agonising unreality of it all… could he have embraced it differently, acted in a calmer, more *mature* way? Could anything have been said or done that would really have changed anything, in the end?

Dan stands up and stretches, looking down at the neatly paved terrace a few feet below him, and away beyond to the steeper garden that lies between the upper and the lower steps. His look of satisfaction would have been evident to any observer, had there been any, but what he has crafted is not inflated into a show of pride. His contentment is prompted entirely by the quiet calm of the image alone. Yet its true object originates in the tangle of undefined intuitions and subliminal urges to which, despite an almost instinctive inclination to rationality, he has gradually acquiesced.

Or so it seems. Since – as he recognises in this moment – between these intuitions and the manifold, created icons there is the endless, inescapable, exhausting process of physical translation… bringing with it all its imprecisions, hesitations, and doubts – so many, in fact, that the garden's final outcome still appears to depend largely upon chance.

Recognising all of this is part of his commitment. But so too, it slowly dawns on him, is an obscure sense of expiation, which seems to increase the further upward he battles his way. But for what? For whom?

Whatever the answer to these questions, it hints at a purpose beyond the emerging realities of the garden itself.

Dan turns back to his wheelbarrow to finally tip out the large rock he has hauled up the slope, like Sisyphus, and manoeuvre it carefully upon the gravel of the bed to complete it. And standing back, he recognises how effectively the sand-coloured gravel conveys precisely that sense of aridity he is seeking.

Yet the first rains will soon darken the gravel. And the dry, desert-like garden, with its random shrubs, its hostas, all seemingly struggling to endure, will not stay this way. For staying is nowhere. Soon enough, roots will tap into the subterranean springs that feed the hidden river coursing beneath the hillside, stems will swell, leaves sprout, miraculously burnishing.

Illusion upon illusion.

Oh, when the chance had been there, if only he had… If only they'd…

But what is the point of these regrets now, other than to signal a life that could have been lived, but was not, being stillborn? It could never have worked.

Or could it?

***

Whenever the three of them are together, it seems easy enough; when Titania stays behind to mind the twins while Penny and he go off to a film or a concert, it all seems easy. But it is never enough.

He realises it all too soon, or too late. They too need their moments of togetherness and temporary exclusion, an acceptance of "them", too. Occasionally it is made possible, or, more often, stolen.

But he sees Penny's insecurity and resentment, her very natural fear. And the meetings stop.

And after a while they drift into a new sort of deception, doubly heinous because consciously betraying those earlier concessions and a trust which warrants gratitude. They are young and desperate. But preoccupation with this new strain of guilt, both his and hers, soon blights all contact, contaminates their every tryst.

Yet, separately chained though they are, the more they lean together: blind beggars craving crumbs and crusts.

At home now, of an evening, there are often long, painful silences.

And all this on top of the misery and hassle he's been experiencing at school, with the fifth-formers.

'Your Tuesday letter, Mr Teal.'

Miss Milton, the school secretary, gives Dan a sly grin as she turns on her heel, at the staff-room door.

He sighs. There are seldom letters for staff, and these letters have been coming for weeks now, regularly, so no wonder she's started commenting on them.

Others look up, raise an eyebrow or smile, but Dan ignores them, burying his head in his lesson preparation, or his marking. But he fancies he can hear his colleagues whispering, speculating on the letters' origin or significance, and he can no longer concentrate.

Pieced together from women's magazines, the letters – if you could call them that – used adverts referring to deodorants, toilet soap, or other aspects of bodily cleanliness: silly childish stuff; and so these he had shown around, laughing at them, to allay suspicions. Recently, however, their character had changed. Clumsily printed in capitals on paper torn from exercise books, they'd become cryptic, menacing even, making it very clear that he is being watched.

There is nothing to betray the letters outright, to attribute them directly, unequivocally, to a specific author. Yet to Dan, it is obvious enough, and he is angry and frightened by turns. One moment, he decides on a confrontation, the next he realises there will be risks involved in such an action. But this continuing dilemma feeds his sense of persecution and frustration and gnaws away at his work, as well as his relations with those about him.

No, he is in no doubt at all about who their author is.

Dan snaps his file shut and leaves the staff room, with the envelope still unopened. Getting on with things, hoping from week to week that each letter will be the last. Telling no one.

A bright autumn morning, but he barely raises his head as he walks across the yard to the row of prefabricated huts. Reaching his form room without encountering anyone, he enters gratefully, but with something like shame too that, like a rabbit in its burrow, he has taken to returning here at odd times during the day, whenever it isn't in use as a classroom. Even at home he's been taking every opportunity to slip away to the room which might one day become his studio… which last night had caused an argument, Penny misinterpreting it as relating to Titania, further fanning the flames of mistrust.

Damn these letters, with their violent, speculative obscenities…! Their poison seeps through him, more corrosive than their author could ever have imagined.

Then one Monday morning at break time, he's sitting quietly in a corner of the staff room, when Freddy comes over.

'Dan, our Minister was asking about you, yesterday. Any idea why that should be?'

'What?'

'Yes, after the service – accosted me as we were leaving. His name's Arnold Braithwaite.'

'Name rings no bells,' Dan says, levelly.

'Well, he was asking about you. I thought maybe you'd known each other, in the past.'

'Don't think so. What sort of things?'

'Oh, how you get on with colleagues and with the kids here, and whether you have kids of your own. Just general, everyday stuff.'

'I see. A bit odd, wouldn't you say?'

'Maybe. Or just curiosity.'

Dan nods. 'So why, I wonder? Given that I don't know this

gentleman, and that my own Baptist past eventually led to me signing the pledge – with the Devil that is – to have no Baptist future?'

'You did no such thing!' Freddy chuckles briefly. 'Anyway…'

'Yes, thanks for letting me know.'

Dan smiles, and turns back to his book, forcing himself to remain calm. But a chill has entered him. For hadn't one of the letters hinted that his "extra-curricular activities" were being looked into elsewhere, *with great interest*?

That bloody Saunders.

A couple of days later, Dan summons Rosalind to his form room for the end of afternoon school. This time, he has resolved, he will come straight to the point – unlike that fiasco with Saunders. Does she know anything about the rather nasty letters he was receiving, every Tuesday? Does *she* have any part in them?

'I haven't the foggiest idea what you're talking about,' Rosalind snaps.

Standing just a few feet away, her eyes dart from his intense scrutiny down to the floor, where she traces silent patterns with the toe of her left shoe.

Dan removes his coat and lays it over the back of a chair. The bluntness of his opening question has clearly shocked her, suggesting she is aware. And so, he presses home this presumed advantage.

'Are you sure about that, Rosalind? Well, *are* you?'

Rosalind glares at him, then jerks her head away.

Outside, from the distant playing fields, a muffled cheer goes up.

'And would you or your friends know why a Baptist Minister, whom I have never met, would publicly be showing "great interest" in me and in my private life?'

'I haven't the foggiest *what* you're on about,' she repeats. 'It has *nothing* to do with me, *nothing*… whatever it is.'

'I'm sorry, but I don't believe you, Rosalind.'

'No? Well you can just… Look, *why* don't you just *go away*? We don't *want* you here, we all *hate* you!' The girl's face, now staring at the closed door, is contorted, her words spat from lips which barely open to let them pass.

'The letters, Rosalind,' Dan goes on, ignoring her outburst. 'Who composes them? Who posts them? Well?'

She flushes, then, though whether from guilt or in anger he cannot be sure.

'You're mad!' she snarls, taking a couple of steps backwards. 'I've said I don't know *what* you're talking about… and I don't!'

'Do you know what defamation of character is?'

Rosalind rolls her eyes.

'I asked you a question,' he repeats. 'Do you under…?'

'Of course!' she snaps, 'I'm not stupid, you know!'

'Do you also know that it's an offence punishable by law?'

'And so is… a lot of other things too!' she shouts, flashing a look at him, her anger almost choking her.

'What are you saying, Rosalind?' he challenges. 'Come on, out with it!'

Stubbornly, she stares past him, over at the window.

He walks towards her then, in a sort of arc, trying to get her to engage with him, but she pirouettes away, fixes her eyes on the back wall.

He tries again, but with no more success. Then, just as he is on the point of giving up, she jerks back round again.

'And another thing. What about that girl – the one in the sixth form? Does *she* know about you?'

Dan flinches. What was that supposed to mean? And even though Rosalind has half given the game away with her "And another thing", he feels a cold sweat breaking out. However he answers, he is in danger of revealing something…well, something he may regret, later.

'Girl in the sixth form?' he says, playing her at her own game. '*What* girl in the sixth form? And *what* "other things" did you mean, exactly?'

'You're putting words in my mouth,' she parries, scowling.

He spreads his hands. 'Rosalind, come on. What is it that this girl – whoever you mean – is supposed to know about me?'

'I never said that,' she repeats, looking fixedly out of the window. 'I never said that, and I don't know what you're... Anyhow, you're *not* my teacher and I *don't* have to stand here and be questioned by you.'

She whips round and makes for the door.

But Dan, sliding backwards and sideways, gets there before her.

'Oh no, Rosalind,' he taunts. 'It's not quite as easy as that.' And he stands with his back firmly against the door, blocking her escape. 'You've started something – you, Saunders, and whoever else – I've no idea why. But it's all making *my* life very difficult. So, you'd better start coming up with some satisfactory answers, right now! I'm in no hurry, and you are *not* leaving until I get them!'

After a moment's hesitation Rosalind flounces off to the back of the room. She sits down at a desk, takes a textbook out of her school bag, and makes a great show of beginning to read it, holding it up to her face to block him out. She can neither see him nor be seen by him.

It is outrageous behaviour. And as with Saunders, Dan completely loses patience.

'Some answers!' he barks at her. 'Now!'

He launches himself away from the door, marches down the aisle, snatches the book out of her hands and throws it onto the desk behind him.

'You can't keep me here against my will,' she shrieks, almost in tears, 'You're *not* my teacher!'

Exasperated, Dan jerks a chair from beneath a desk a couple of rows away from her and sits hard down upon it, concentrating on slowing his breathing to a more acceptable rising and falling.

Rosalind folds her arms, turns her back on him, and stares up at the blank wall.

And in these moments he realises he is unlikely ever to reach this girl, so hard, so intractable is she.

But he must at least try.

He looks across at her. 'Is all this really necessary, Rosalind?' he says, quietly, wearily. 'Does all this hatred make you... happier? *Why* is it necessary? What's happened to make you like this? *Why*, when as a class you used to be so...?'

He stops there, waiting for some response, some small concession from her.

But Rosalind remains as she is: obdurate, silent, her back to him.

There is nothing else he can say or do.

And so he stands up. He walks back down the aisle. He picks up his briefcase and his coat. And with one last glance in her direction, he quits the room.

Preposterous, the whole thing. Such a waste of his time and nervous energy. Such a waste.

It was the last conversation they ever had.

Up and down up and down here and there and up and down…

XVI

Why was Rosalind like that? Why had it all changed, and so very quickly?

Sitting in a once-grand, wrought-iron Victorian shelter, musing again on far-away things, Rosemary is not at first aware that another person has crept in seeking refuge from the fury of this sudden storm, until a large white Alsatian nudges her knee and whimpers for her attention.

'Don't be afraid! He won't harm you,' says a breathless voice. 'Jason! Come here! Jason! I'll not tell you again!'

But Jason, unheeding, remains by Rosemary's side. She smiles down at him. Cupping his head in her hands she turns towards his owner, a small, slightly built old lady, still panting, over in the corner, her coat collar pulled up all askew against the driving wind and rain.

The lady smiles back at her.

'It came on so suddenly, didn't it?' And she tries to mop her face with her tiny handkerchief.

Rosemary smiles, shyly.

'He's taken a fancy to you, right enough! Are you sure you don't mind him? He pays no attention to etiquette, I'm afraid – nor to me for that matter.' And she chuckles, but then sighs heavily.

Rosemary, wondering at this seeming change in mood, looks up.

'The truth is, I don't know whether I shall be able to keep him much longer, poor mite. He's getting too much for me. He's only four but he's much stronger than I am and once or twice lately I haven't been able to hold him and off he's gone.' She feels behind her for the seat and sits down. 'One day he was away for over two hours till a neighbour found him and brought him back. I'm terrified he'll get run over or cause an accident.'

'What will you do, do you think?' Rosemary asks, only too pleased to have the monotony of the morning broken by this unexpected conversation. She fondles the dog, aware of the sleekness of his body, the wiriness of his coat against her hand.

'I don't know. I just don't know. To tell you the truth, dear, I'm at my wit's end. My son and his wife, they said they'd have him, but now they're expecting a baby, and I can see they're not too keen. You see, he's away a lot for his job.' She sighs again. 'It would be as difficult for her as it is for me. Besides, they live away…'

Rosemary nods sympathetically, trying to think of something to say next.

'I don't want to think about it, really,' the woman goes on, 'and I keep pushing it to the back of my mind, but I think… Yes, sooner or later, well, I'll have to have him put to sleep.'

'Oh, no!' Rosemary cries, suddenly alert to the hovering realities behind the woman's words.

'You see, my husband died last March – just a year ago. By rights it should have been me, not him. I'm the one who's always been ailing, off and on. And now, well, I just couldn't bear to think of Jason being left. He's such a treasure. Whatever would become of him?'

The woman smiles weakly. But Rosemary can see her eyes have misted with tears. Pretending not to notice, however, she fusses the dog, who has settled by her feet.

'It's always on my mind, these days…' the woman mumbles, eventually.

And she dabs at her face again.

'It's the walks… He's a big dog. He needs to be able to run around and work off some of his energy – don't you, Jason?' She reaches out a hand towards the dog, who lifts his head, briefly. 'You don't reckon much to being on a lead or being cooped up indoors, do you, eh? But – she turns back to Rosemary – I daren't let him off. It's too dangerous.'

'Um... whereabouts do you live?' Rosemary asks, her voice brighter, her thoughts racing on ahead of the woman's words.

'Where? Oh, not too far away. Just along the lane opposite the bottom park gates – which is handy enough for the walks I *can* manage with him... I'm Mrs Appleton, by the way, and...'

'Oh... Yes. I'm Rosemary.'

'That's a nice name, dear. Anyway, I thought I could get back before the rain came on, but it was so sudden, wasn't it? Were you caught out in it, too?'

'I can... I can take him for walks, if you like?' Rosemary blurts out.

'Oh, but I didn't mean to... I was just...'

'I could even take him right up to the moor, so he can be off the lead!' Rosemary laughs, happily, and rushes on, before she loses her nerve. 'You'd like that, being off the lead, wouldn't you Jason? Though... I'm not sure about Sundays... And I could go to the shops for you, Mrs Appleton... if you wanted anything. It's quite a traipse into town isn't it? But, whatever you... need.' She pauses, anxiously.

'Oh... Oh, could you really?'

And the pact is soon sealed, though not without some genuine embarrassment on Mrs Appleton's part.

***

Perhaps it was the silver coolness of the myriad stars, flocks of them grazing the grey, distant hills, or maybe their utter tranquillity, each in its own isolation, but by the time Dan is standing among the newly laid rocks at the upper limit of the garden, the anger he'd felt only a short while before, only yards from this spot, has quite abated.

Once again, he had ventured out beyond his gates; once again, he had slipped out into the "development", the ghostly hamlet displacing the wood.

Not without misgivings about his curiosity, which has no rightful place in the life he is trying to carve out now, Dan wanders along the starlit roadways.

Remembering the noise of the machinery grinding away day in day out, the rhythmic roll of the cement mixers, all the tearing and uprooting, he stares at the opulent houses with their Georgian fronts and pseudo-colonial porticoes, all of them minor variations on a basic theme. And he stops every now and then, to peer in at a window or enter a door-less building – for a little while yet, throughways to wind or breeze.

Here and there, trees have been randomly spared, either singly, or in pairs or clumps of four. But the old watercress beds are unrecognisable. Sanitised and landscaped into a central pond, enclosed by a low wall. What exploring child could ever have adventures in a place like this, now?

And a surge of anger whips through him, soon displaced by a lingering sadness. How many times had he been here with the twins, together or singly, to watch newts or frogs or the occasional migrating elver gliding through the crystal waters? How many times? 'Look daddy, look...'

In winter they'd race through the wood to be the first to break holes in the ice for the birds. In spring, there was the new frogspawn, then myriads of sprouting tadpoles, and later, in the warmer months, mayfly and dragonfly, rippling rainbow wings reflected on water; while thick, emerald forests swayed gently in the undertow of feeder springs which bubbled in at different points along the beds. The sun-dappled silence.

'Look daddy, look...'

Dan wipes away the intrusive moisture in his eyes. For his children this had always been a wild and magical spot, full of contingency. And later, with their teenage years behind them, they'd still loved to come here on their, in truth, ever more infrequent visits home – venturing across the lane as if absent-mindedly, even secretively, as if ashamed to admit the place's lingering hold upon them.

Until not so long ago, bits of old machinery and curious implements had lain rusting here – from the nineteen-fifties, when wages, transport costs and changing tastes had put paid to the local watercress industry. Well, not a jot remained of it, now.

And then he sees it.

Away up the slope, behind the pond, a giant excavator lurking in shadows, a tyrannosaurus awaiting its moment. He walks slowly up to it, and round it, noting the bricks beneath its wheels. He launches himself up into the cab and feels for the gear lever, which he finds in the reverse position, with the handbrake engaged. Then he closes his eyes. All quite safe, then. Quite, quite safe. But he sits on awhile, pondering, calculating.

Is it the irreparable loss of "his" wood he objects to, one of his own, inviolable spaces? He shakes his head; few people today would understand his isolation here, or his motives, but then – he chuckles – he doesn't entirely understand them himself!

He purses his lips, tries again. This isolation of his is self-imposed, like that of a monk or hermit, though not tied to a particular rule, or vital purpose, or none he can put a name to. Isn't it that he's simply given up on the world of people? Certainly, he misses them less and less. Not to mention all the follies and hypocrisies of the world, which... Yes, they too are part of this hiding away, of his unwillingness to share, or give any thought to needs beyond his own.

So, has he found the right path? The right way? How can he be sure, whilst he is still groping his way through hard, painful, physical toil?

Dan sits on, surveying the shadowy site, imagining this and that, and trying to remember some story about a landowner who had had the trees around his gate cut down because beggars were in the habit of sheltering there from the sun or rain, or of begging a crust. But then, who needed such stories, when certain Tory councils had been doing their damnedest to make it impossible for a homeless person to sleep on a park bench, or drowning the fleeing victims of others' wars in the Channel?

Like these speculators, trampling over people, violating virgin sites like this one, destroying so much to "develop" them, their "development" aimed solely at wealth, while elsewhere people begged and fed from food banks or soup kitchens. "Countless" people, their numbers conveniently obfuscated in "official circles". Embarrassingly "countless", not that those in a position to change things ever seemed "embarrassed".

So much for "humanity".

Releasing the handbrake and jumping down. Kicking the chocks away, it would be so easy, wouldn't it?

Dan looks around the cab, and then stares over at the mock sentry boxes standing at either side of the entrance to the Park. He snorts in disgust and climbs back down.

Yet to the casual eye, would there be very much difference, in intention, between these, and his towering, virtually impenetrable hedges?

Now, sitting calmly among these rocks, where a drifting smoke from the previous day's garden fires seems to cling about him, Dan still has no ready answer to the conundrums that had plagued him in the night.

In the early days here, his locked gates and high hedges had provided a refuge, while he began to gather up the splinters of his former life to try and turn them into something new and meaningful. But now the world from which he has chosen to absent himself, however temporarily, is outpacing him, outmanoeuvring him. And soon, when the ghostly hamlet has gathered in its inhabitants, even a midnight walk to the post box at the end of the lane would run the risk of unwanted encounters. The very presence of the hamlet, of its as yet undefined life and habits, just beyond his hedge, will turn his refuge into something resembling a prison cell or a citadel besieged; it will limit his choices, and also take away its necessary, its *vital* context of space, distance, isolation. Letters, postcards, the occasional ringing of the telephone… they were as nothing when set beside this approaching tsunami.

And there he'd been – Dan shakes his head in almost amused disbelief – sitting in the cab of a mechanical digger in the small hours, trying to justify releasing the handbrake and letting it roll down into the pond, crash into a house side, or demolish a portico!

Futile, of course, for such wild gestures could in no way stem this tide, the insistent world clamouring at his very gates.

XVII

Rosalind did come back, of course: she had no one else to turn to.

It is already quite late in the afternoon and Rosemary is returning to Mrs Appleton's with Jason, just passing the shelter in which the dog had first introduced himself so insistently and triumphantly. And suddenly there she is: Rosalind, leaning awkwardly against the back of the wooden seats.

'What are *you* doing here?' Rosemary asks, trying not to seem too surprised, much less, interested.

It has startled her, seeing her here, in *this* place, and for a moment she has the idea of just carrying on; of waving, casually, but going straight on.

But she can't do it. 'Well?' she prompts.

Rosalind gives her a cold, stony, superior look. 'Waiting for you, of course!'

'What? But how did you know I'd be here?'

'My note.' Rosalind says scornfully, as she stands. 'The note I left you in your locker. I pushed it under the door.'

'Did you?' Rosemary bends down to fondle Jason's head, determined not to react. 'I wasn't in school,' she says loftily, without looking up. 'So, I didn't get any note.'

'Playing truant again, were we?' Rosalind sneers. 'Whose is the mutt, by the way? It's not yours, is it?'

'He's *not* a mutt,' Rosemary flashes. 'He's a dog. And he belongs to a friend of mine, called Mrs. Appleton. She's asked me to walk him and that's what I'm doing.'

'Oh... I didn't know you even liked dogs,' says Rosalind, her tone suddenly less aggressive.

'Neither did I,' Rosemary confesses. 'Not till I met Jason. But Jason's special... aren't you?' she says, turning back to the dog. She pats his strong shoulders, feels him strain to move on. And suddenly, she feels strong too. She's got Jason and Mrs Appleton, and she doesn't have to be bullied by Rosalind, not ever again.

There is a moment or two's silence, as Rosalind stands there, one foot stubbing at her other shoe.

Rosemary looks away, off into the park, sensing Rosalind's tension. And she feels torn, caught between an instinctive sense of loyalty, and her own self-preservation.

'Well,' she says, patting the dog. 'I'll have to be...'

'No, wait!'

'What is it?'

'It's something important.'

'Important?' Rosemary shrugs, cynically.

'Yes. Look, I've got to talk to you. It can't wait.'

'Can't wait?' Rosemary spins back round. 'What? After ignoring me for months, you just turn up here telling me it *can't wait*, and you've got to talk to me? Well, I can't. I've got to go.'

'I know, but...'

'No. I can't, and that's that!'

Rosemary pulls on the dog's lead, but a moment later makes the mistake of looking back. Her eyes stray to Rosalind's crestfallen face. 'But I could... I would be back in twenty minutes.'

Rosalind can barely suppress a smile.

***

Dusk again. More days, weeks even, have passed, with their labours and their musings, which have led Dan to the decision that he must look to his hedges which he will no longer be cutting back on the outside. And he comes on, now, as most days, out of the thinning, wispy smoke and up the short, gentler, final slope to the outcrop at the top.

Standing there silhouetted against the darkening sky, he finds himself wondering what will become of the garden after his day. And the house from which it had all begun, what of that? Will the twins want it, with their far-away lives? Unlikely, and certainly not for its own sake. Or Penny, maybe? He would dearly like her to see it, if nothing more.

Yet it is an idle, detached wondering.

'It won't matter to us, will it, Ben?' he catches himself whispering. 'Not then it won't.' It was just one of the many stations they had stopped at in the distractions of life, quite forgetting they could only ever be just passing through... on their one-way ticket. 'It won't matter to us, however much we have loved it, for all we thought it meant.'

Unless the poet was wrong; and place was more than place, and time much more than a passing of unrecorded hours.

Dan sits down, leans back against the largest rock, and lets his eyes wander slowly over the world in shadows. For a little while, they fix on the dull red glow of the distant city, which for him, now, might as well be at the ends of the earth: a furnace-glow of crimson light under which many thousands cluster; seeming the smouldering embers of a burnt-out world.

But then, as they have on so many nights in these latter years, the great patterns of stars capture and enrapture him, drifting in and out of lingering clouds; hints of light, of worlds to be in. And as he marvels he laughs, quietly, at this habit so difficult to grow out of – still pinning thoughts of infinity onto the physical, the corruptible, however remote. How many lives and deaths, he wonders, would it take to fill the vast spaces between just two of those worlds?

He stands up and stretches, takes a step to go back down, and then, without any warning, over to the east the moon bursts through its cloudbank, flooding the hillside and the woodlands, flushing out the deeper shadows... all in a trice. And he looks down at the small, sedum-covered island of earth, a few feet away, it too washed in the glimmering sea of moonlight, and he shakes his head, at the... yes, the wonder of it.

This sudden translation of darkness to light has released something in him, an immediate surge of elation far beyond any meaning he knows or can put a name to.

'I'm getting impatient, Ben,' he whispers, 'and I mustn't. I mustn't, or else my project will fail. A little while longer, and, just a little more patience. Then we shall see.'

***

'Hold me,' begs Rosalind. 'Please hold me; like… like you used to.'

And Rosemary, who has taken even less than those 'twenty minutes' to get Jason home and come back to the shelter, cannot resist this vulnerability, even though she knows well enough it means embracing her own betrayal; it's hardly the first time.

She takes Rosalind in her arms, and as the tears begin to flow strokes her hair and tries to calm her.

Rosalind cannot seem to stop crying. Tremor after tremor. Sob after sob. Then without warning, she breaks free, and raises her head. She doesn't look at Rosemary.

'I'm pregnant,' she announces.

'What!' Rosemary's eyes open wide in horror, her breathing suddenly ragged. 'Oh…'

Rosalind twists round, her tear-stained face dark and sullen. Then she flops back down into Rosemary's arms, snuggling in. 'I'm pregnant, I'm sure I am,' she mumbles, and her body is convulsed by further violent sobs.

Rosemary strokes and squeezes, but her mind is now coursing madly round; and then it empties, so that she is hardly aware of the person she is holding against her. All she can think is that the betrayal is complete, and that it is greater, *far* greater even than she could have imagined. Distastefully, fastidiously, almost, she removes her arms from Rosalind's back, and pushes away from her, so that a gap of a foot or more separates them, on the bench.

Then she glowers at her Judas-friend. 'False Rosalind. False. False,' she taunts.

Rosalind moans and covers her face with her hands. But Rosemary forces them down, forces her to turn round and look directly into her eyes.

'False. False. False,' she chants.

'Yes. Yes, it's true. I am. I am,' Rosalind sobs. 'But I didn't want to be. I never wanted this, honest, I didn't.' She hangs her head, as if to avoid looking into Rosemary's terrible eyes.

'Then *why* were you if you didn't want to be? You didn't *have* to be.' With no warning at all, hardly aware of what she is doing, Rosemary swings her arm back and with the flat of her hand aims a stunning blow to the side of Rosalind's bent head.

'Ow! That hurt!' Rosalind reels with the force of it, keels over to her right and bangs the other side of her head against the wall and the seat they are sitting on. Furious, she yells at the pain and the yell turns at once to a renewed, disconsolate sobbing, her face pressed hard against the wooden seat back.

Rosemary gasps, appalled at what she has done, at what she'd thought she never could do. Her eyes brim with tears and she looks away into the grey dusk. Nothing can be undone now, be unsaid or unfelt. She must wait on Rosalind, and try to make amends in some way, if she can. She glances over at the cowering, alien thing Rosalind has suddenly become, and she doesn't know how to approach her. Her own body contorted, rigid, she stretches out and touches her.

But Rosalind, perhaps fearing another blow, shrinks away.

Rosemary feels sick. She stares at the ground between her feet, suddenly distracted by the slow progress of a spider across the paved floor. It disappears finally beneath the bench at the far end of the shelter, and she sits on thinking, thinking… and then wondering how long they've been there. Abruptly, she springs to her feet. And the spider, which had reappeared, darts back under the bench.

Darkness is now falling fast.

'Who was it, Rosalind?' Rosemary asks calmly, eventually, resisting the temptation to touch her. 'Who was it with? Tell me!'

Rosalind straightens up and shakes her head. 'I can't tell you. I can't. I mustn't.' Her eyes are still averted from Rosemary's.

'Please Ros. Was it... Was it Saunders?'

'*Saunders!*' Rosalind looks up, stung by the suggestion. '*Saunders!* You think it was *Saunders*?' she repeats, her face registering her scorn. He's only a kid, you idiot! Saunders is only a kid!'

This vehement protestation alarms and confuses Rosemary, and her thoughts whirl away again, probing possibility. And then there it is once again, inescapably, starkly. The only possibility that she can imagine.

And if she's right?

Rosemary winces. She can't be. She can hardly credit it, much less voice it.

But she can't get rid of the thought either, of the only possibility that makes sense, despite Rosalind's hatred for... But maybe she doesn't hate him, maybe she's just...

'Anyway, I've stopped seeing him, Rosie. We've stopped... you know...'

But Rosemary isn't listening. Oh! How terrible if she is right. And she cannot convince herself that she is not right. Wildly fascinated by the horror seized upon by her intuition she imagines this, sees that, and inside she burns to know the details of it all: where it had been and when and how many times and what it was like to have *him* on top of you and thrusting away inside of you...

'He doesn't even know about... you know, about what's happened...'

She wants to watch it happening, yes. To Rosalind, but more, oh much more, to her. She wants to stand outside herself and above, and see the two of them become one. She wants it to happen to her and she wants it badly, because by being used, humiliated even, she would feel she counted for something at last. Counted for him too, maybe. Yes, oh please, for him. But for Rosalind too, yes. And if only...

Rosemary walks slowly home. How foolish she has been all this time. She realises it now. Thinking there was some other way to count for someone, for something. Sly Rosalind had been right all along, and she, Rosemary, has been left behind, thinking there was this other, better, purer way. Refusing to accept the awful truth of it all, cutting herself off.

She sighs miserably. Rosalind forging ahead of her in her knowing, in her experience. In everything. Without her.

And she was right about *him*. *He* was a fraud. Making all of them feel everything was… was all bigger, grander, more miraculous, when clearly by his very actions he didn't even believe it himself. Rosalind was right. And probably about a lot of other things too.

He was a fraud, a fraud after all. Him, Ros, her parents, all of them.

False. False. False.

XVIII

There are times when Titania confesses to herself that she isn't at all sure what she really feels, or even knows what she wants.

Being with David, or daddy, when they are doing things in the workshop, or the garden, or helping mummy about the house, or out with Prince chasing away up the moor, those times he seems to be a million miles away from her life, and often, guiltily, she realises she has not thought of him all day. In her bedroom, reading, or planning her essay. Sometimes she looks up from the table and lets her eyes move slowly round, dwelling on each object in turn, and she feels the completeness of it all, the cosiness, its warm light, its gently glowing fire. So where does he fit into all of this with his complicated mind and his complicated life?

She knows she shouldn't be thinking such things, for she does love him, of course she does, but she can't help wondering, at times.

With a sigh she turns back to her schoolwork and tries to shut herself in it once more.

Later, in the weeks leading up to Easter, so persistent, so insistent have these renegade thoughts become that she determines to have done with it, once and for all. She knows he will be hurt but she will try to express it in such a way that does not even hint at finality, not sure she even wants that herself. Not to see him again… no she couldn't bear that. So she will… yes, try to shift everything onto a different plane. After all, doesn't he always say that love and friendship are essentially the same thing, the difference being no more than a question of degree of feeling and need?

Can she bring herself to tell him? But when and where, and… And how will she put it?

The words are finally composed, and uttered. And Titania hates seeing his sad, stunned expression, that ironic look, and his… and this she hates most of all… his silence.

But it's done. And as she walks away, she has this powerful, suddenly expanding physical, almost giddy sense of release.

At the sea, when they go, she's busy like everyone else on the first day, cleaning up the caravan and then unpacking, and he never once enters her thoughts.

On the next day, a cold wind whips in from the sea in ferocious gusts, shaking the caravan quite frighteningly at times. The sky sinks beneath its ever-increasing load of grey-black cloud and by mid-morning it is raining steadily.

And in these conditions the constant, close proximity of the others makes it quite impossible to read or do anything she would like to do, needs to do, and anyway, David keeps pestering her to play cards or scrabble or I-spy. On the third day Titania can stand it no longer, and the wildness outside seems far preferable to the noise and the irritations, the coffee she doesn't want, and the steamed-up windows. Nodding gravely, though impatiently, at her mother's steady accumulation of things she must be careful not to do, she fastens the lead to Prince's collar and marches him off through the dunes to the head of the beach.

All the way along the shoreline the breakers keep crashing in, sending spray and sand flying in all directions, and though she must be fully fifty yards away from the water she can feel its spray cold against her face and hands. All the same, she pulls off her hood, releases her hair, and thrusts the Alice band into her duffle-coat pocket. She breathes in, deeply, and pauses to watch the churning waves for a minute or so before heading off into the wind. A couple of miles away, though the sea-spray mist makes it difficult to see anything with certainty, it seems that the waves are breaking high and white against the towering cliffs.

She sets Prince free and away he dashes in all directions. All ways away, she thinks, watching him go.

How she misses the rehearsals, their... magic, despite the... even though they were... And immediately brushing aside her search for words to encapsulate whatever it was she missed, she breaks into a run after Prince who, sensing her approach, tauntingly lurches away even faster and further than before.

They come to the first rocks and the pools are opaque. She notices too how, even though it is only the very beginning of the season, new caravans are already spilling over onto the dunes. Paper and plastic bags seem to be blowing everywhere. What was the sense in it? Maybe there really was no stopping all this breakdown of things she used to think were forever. And maybe the day would come when she'd have no option but to move away from them simply because they were moving away from her. Maybe, after all, what Dan had said about...

Faintly, she catches the sound of Prince's barking, and looking around she sees the dog up beyond the dunes near some of the new caravans, backing away, barking, being followed by a man who is waving his arms and silently, angrily shouting. Hurriedly, she goes to the dog's rescue, clipping on his lead from behind, and apologising to the horrid man whose words are thankfully dispersed by the gusting wind.

And only now, walking slowly back, does she allow herself to think, to let the waves of sadness wash over her, and to wonder if, after all...

***

Penny finishes tying the twins' scarves and adjusting their bobble hats then fastens them carefully into the pushchair. 'Who are we going to see?' she asks, and their faces light up at her question.

'See daddy!' they chorus.

'That's right,' she says. 'We're going to the park to see daddy.'

'Wave to the boatman,' she tells them, for she'd noticed him waving at them. And she acknowledges his wave, stopping to point down to the lake. The twins, however, barely raise a hand, so she shrugs to the man in a theatrical sort of way, before turning off along the middle path, which leads up through the rose beds, past the ornamental pool to the aviary beyond.

As the path steepens she slows her pace, for the wheels are small and badly need oiling. Of course, he never notices things like that, and certainly not now. And a flash of anger furrows her brow.

'Soon we'll see the flowers and the water in the pool,' she entices.

Matthew chuckles. 'See water. See water,' he repeats excitedly, his refrain taken up immediately by Simon. But the water does not appear there, and their shouts turn into whines of frustration.

Penny stops then, and points down the hill.

'Look, there's lots of water there,' she says, flatly, and they brighten again as they see the lake below them, with the thin sunlight glinting off it.

'Water!'

The wind is chill, and Penny wishes she'd brought a warmer scarf. She jerks the pushchair on, ignoring the new howls of protest, wanting to reach the pool before there are real tears.

'We're almost there now,' she assures them.

'See water. See water,' Matthew insists. And she leans over him until her face is almost touching his cheek.

'Nearly there,' she whispers. 'Just up here a bit further.'

Restricted by the pushchair's harness, the little boy tries to twist round to face her, laughing with excited anticipation.

The pool has been drained.

'What luck!' she says, half aloud, 'I'm sure there was water in it a few days ago.' And the three of them look down disconsolately at the broken glass glinting at the bottom of the drained pool.

'The men have taken the water away,' she tells them. 'But never mind, we'll go and see the birds instead. They can't have taken them away as well.'

'Why have the men taken the water away?' asks Simon.

Penny shakes her head. Then she points at the drinking fountain. 'Look. I'll bet there's no water in that, either.'

But the little boys have no interest in such abstractions.

'See birds! See birds!'

Penny smiles and hurries across to the branching path beyond the fountain.

Once at the aviary, she unfastens their reins, and the twins totter out. They clamber laboriously up the three high stone steps, then rush back and forth the whole length of the cage, shouting in an endless monotone which sets the birds squawking and twittering in their turn, fluttering about from perch to perch in sheer panic, high up, close to the roof.

Breathless, Matthew stops near his mother and contemplates the chaos they have achieved.

'Why don't the birds fly away?' he asks, his voice tinged with disappointment.

'They can't fly away; they're in a big cage, see,' she explains, with her habitual patience.

'Why are they?'

'Because the men put them there.'

'Why did the men put them there? Why did the men take the water away? Why? Why did they?'

Unsure what to say, Penny doesn't answer immediately. Then she shrugs: 'So the birds will be safe, I suppose.'

'Do the birds like it in the cage?' the boy persists, all innocence.

'I'm not sure,' she answers, feeling a curious sense of conflict rising within her. 'No. Perhaps they don't like it very much.'

'Why did the men put them there? Why did the men take the water away? Why did they?'

She glances away; and thank goodness, there he is, coming towards them over the grass.

'Oh, at last!' she says, 'you're here!'

Her husband looks at his watch. 'At last?' he teases, feigning an expression of pained bewilderment, 'but I'm ten minutes early!'

'Daddy! See daddy, see daddy!'

Penny watches as the twins bound towards him, as he stoops down towards Simon and sweeps him off his feet, swinging him high in the air, round and round. Then it is Matthew's turn to fly.

Elated, the little boys stamp and shout, vying for his attention.

'You're like the birds,' he says, flying! Whee!'

And at this new intrusion on their uneventful world, the birds fly about too – twittering, squawking, and flapping in all directions. All ways away.

XIX

Head down, her brow furrowed in concentration, Rosemary pounds on down the path to meet Rosalind, at the shelter.

No, there simply was no other solution. And of course, Rosalind *had* to come to *her* with this... this treachery, with the evidence of what she'd been getting up to, as if it were *her* problem too: she was *always* doing it, coming to her with things she didn't really understand but had to try and help with.

And now, just when she was managing to wean herself away.

Tears of anger and frustration wet Rosemary's lashes. Whenever *she* was sad or hurt, where was Rosalind then? *She* just got ignored, didn't she, treated like a leper. For sure, Rosalind was no friend to *her*.

Anyhow, there wasn't anything else. There was no one else she could think of. So that was that!

Rosalind is full of scorn.

'If you think for one minute I'm going there,' she storms, jerking down to retie her shoelace. 'In fact, I don't believe she even exists! She's just another of your bits of fantasy, isn't she?'

'Mine? And what about all yours?' But the pig woman, this strange, rather frightening woman, is real enough and also, Rosemary feels sure, very wise. 'Anyway, I'm not forcing you,' she says, sitting down again. 'It's your choice, Rosalind. You're the one with the problem.' And she spreads her hands, like her mum does in the church group, when she thinks something's just obvious.

Rosalind screws up her face.

And Rosemary smiles to herself, pleased to have come up with the 'your choice' bit. But still, all too familiar with Rosalind's wiles, she must be wary.

She sits on, staring out at the tarmac path, and waits.

Soon enough, Rosalind darts a glance at her. 'All right then,' she says, with a shrug. 'So show me, come on!' She leaps up. 'I'll bet you can't. Like last time!' she taunts. And she stands there, openly defying Rosemary to confess her deception, her voice hard and cold.

But Rosemary is tired of the convoluted games she's always being made to play. She folds her arms, resolute.

'Look, Rosalind, if you want to see her, we'll go. Otherwise, we'll just have to think of something else, all right? It's up to you. You're the one that's got herself… pregnant.'

A brutal, blunt reminder.

Rosalind's eyes fill with tears. Suddenly, it seems, she has the greatest difficulty in getting her words together. 'I can't… I can't think of anything else, Rosie,' she mumbles plaintively, sinking back down. 'Can you?'

Rosemary shakes her head. 'No. I've tried and tried but I can't.' She lets the silence hang a moment or two. Then she stands up.

'Come on, then,' she says quietly, 'It isn't far.'

***

Was that voices, downstairs?

Dan listens for a moment or two, but there's nothing more. With a sigh he turns back to his marking. Or rather, to his blank staring at the page, his mind-drift, able to concentrate on nothing.

How many weeks has it been, now?

***

If Rosemary had entered the undergrowth at the far end of the lake like the first time, maybe she would have had no difficulty in finding the place again. But coming at it from this side she is at first quite disoriented.

Rosalind, seeing her friend's old self-conscious confusion returning, begins to taunt her again. 'You're just trying to bluff your way out of it, aren't you! So all of this, it *was* something you made up. So, what are you playing at? What's it all for?' She sighs dramatically. 'I suppose you'll just say she isn't there, or something like that, won't you?'

Rosemary ignores her. She plunges on into the trees, not looking to see whether Rosalind is following, and without too much hesitation she reaches the wall not far from the high, rusted gate. Reassured now, she waits for Rosalind to catch up.

'Just fancy... putting such a big gate here,' Rosalind says, her tone changing, full of curiosity, 'where nobody ever comes.'

'Maybe it wasn't always like this,' Rosemary says. 'I mean, this park wasn't always a park, you know.' She takes another step. 'And the houses over there, outside the gate, they weren't always there. A century ago, this was the grounds to a big house. The museum up the hill – that's all that's left of it, now.'

'What? How do you know that? *I* didn't know that,' says Rosalind, uncertainly.

Rosemary doesn't bother to answer. She takes another couple of steps along the wall, but again Rosalind stops her.

'Look, it's got an inscription over it.' Slowly, she spells it out. 'aznarepse...' What does *that* mean? Doesn't sound English. Or French, for that matter.'

'You need a looking glass to read it properly,' Rosemary says, tiring of Rosalind's arrogant ignorance.

'A looking glass... in the park! You're screwy!'

'It'll read properly from the other side, it's probably Latin.' Rosemary glances impatiently at the still uncomprehending Rosalind. 'Oh, come on, never mind that.' And she strides off several yards. 'It's about *here*,' she says, confidently. 'Give me a bunk up onto the wall top and I'll have a look, see if she's there.'

But Rosalind makes no move, so she grasps hold of the iron

railings and is soon kneeling, then standing on the wall, without any help at all.

And there she is: over in the corner, just as she had been the first time. Rosemary gazes round, breathing out slowly, as if she were suddenly in some hallowed place. All that is different, she sees, is that she now has a third pig. All three of them are standing close round her, jostling for position, sensing that their… swill, yes, that's the word, is coming.

The woman wheels round and looks up.

'I thought I hear you come,' she says, smiling broadly. 'I *say* you come back – and I am right, look.'

'Yes, and I've… I've brought a friend,' Rosemary stammers, not knowing what else to say. 'I hope it's all right.'

'Ok. It all right. Let me look. At friend.'

Rosemary hesitates a moment before answering. 'She's… She's got a problem, a big problem, and I… we wondered if you might know, well, what to do about it.'

The woman doesn't react. And Rosemary starts to wonder if perhaps she hasn't understood. She'll just have to try again, try and explain… Oh, but it was *so* embarrassing. Annoyed, she can already feel herself colouring.

'I not much time, now, girl. Feed pig then go. Where is friend? Let me see friend.'

Rosemary bends down to help Rosalind up.

Rosalind takes her hand and manages to scramble up the wall, scuffing her shoes, laddering her stockings and cursing all the while under her breath.

Her face is pale, and she is trembling, and Rosemary squeezes her hand before releasing it.

The woman scrutinises Rosalind closely. 'So! You are friend! More pretty than she. But you have *problem*?'

Rosalind looks to Rosemary for some guidance or reassurance, but Rosemary offers no more, merely nodding at the woman, who is now standing directly below them, with her squealing, snapping pigs around her.

Rosalind looks down at the woman, blushing madly. She opens her mouth, struggles, and turns pleadingly to Rosemary yet again.

'It ok,' the woman says. 'I understand, I think! You, girl – she gestures at Rosemary – maybe better *you* go 'way. Just two minute.'

Rosemary nods, gratefully. Quickly she lowers herself back down the wall and moves away, out of earshot. But then she positions herself to keep Rosalind in view.

Much to her surprise, Rosalind clambers down almost at once and rejoins her.

Rosemary draws her away. 'That was quick. What did she say? What did you tell her?'

'Actually, she'd already guessed,' Rosalind whispers, 'so I didn't have to say anything. But we have to come back on Thursday, she says, but not here. To her house. She told me how to get there and we have to go as early as we can, you know, early in the morning. Oh, and we have to bring a big bottle of gin.'

'What? Gin?' Rosemary laughs. 'What does she want that for, are you kidding?'

'No.' Rosalind frowns. 'She was *very* serious when she said it. Look, you weren't there, so...' Then she sighs and suddenly looks miserable. 'But Rosie, how can *we* do that? We can't, can we? We don't have any money, nothing like enough.'

'And we're not eighteen. They wouldn't sell *us* gin, or anything like that, even if we did have enough money.'

'No.'

'So, we'll just have to go without.' Rosemary shrugs. 'And explain.'

Rosalind shakes her head. 'Personally, I think she's a bit... she's off her rocker. But she said there was no point going without it. So, we have to get it, somehow.' She frowns again. 'It's a kind of payment, maybe, for... whatever she needs to do, do you think?'

Rosemary shrugs. 'S'pose so.'

And the two girls sit there, back at the shelter in the park, swinging their legs, racking their brains to try and think of something.

'We'll never manage it,' Rosalind sighs. 'We've no idea what it costs, but I know it's dear.'

'We could check, at Sargeson's.'

'We could, only...'

'I know!' Rosemary cuts in. 'We'll get the money... somehow, don't worry. Then we'll take it to her, so she can buy her *own* gin, ok? That way we don't have to buy it and she can get the sort she likes.'

Rosalind's expression doesn't alter, but she stops swinging her legs.

Rosemary waits.

'Thanks, Rosie,' Rosalind mutters, eventually. 'Come on then, let's go and find out.' And she takes Rosemary's hand as they set off in the direction of the off-licence.

***

Dan opens his eyes. The pile of exercise books on the left of the table has decreased by one. The pile on the right still stands at two. With a sigh, he turns again to the book open in front of him, awaiting his judgement. He takes up his pen.

But then footsteps on the stairs, not Penny's, so, who...?

A light knock, then as the door slowly opens, he realises his deepest longing has been answered. Even before he sees her, he is on his feet.

She comes in, timidly almost, closing the door carefully behind her, then she turns. And quickly, without a word, she is in his arms, her head on his shoulder.

'At last! At last!' she gasps. 'I had to come back, I just had to. I've been able to think of nothing else... I thought I could get along without you, for a few days. But I can't. I can't. What have you done to me, you horrible man?'

How many times this scene is acted out, in one way or another, during those few short months of fleeting togetherness; like rehearsals, but rehearsals for what?

XX

Bindweed, or Convolvulus to give it its proper name, ground elder, thistles, nettles and couch-grass: all are a perpetual plague. With their roots burrowed deep they break easily and frequently, emblems perhaps of Adam's original sin. They tax his patience and tempt half-measures, with any victory only momentary, a prelude to more struggle. Yet there are several areas of the garden which are real only in his creator's eye. Is there no way to keep these finished sections free of corruption?

For want of better, Dan has lately intensified his efforts to propagate plants that will provide abundant, low-growing ground cover – sedums and saxifrages, creeping Jenny and ajugas – and he has been planting these sentinels wherever invasion seems most likely: near the hedges, in particular, where the bindweed especially is a constant menace.

Plunging his fork, turning the soil. Trying to root them out, to recreate a sense of order in the garden, to more nearly reflect that in his mind.

This last week, interrupting his more engaging work on the third terrace, he has had to turn his attention to the first level again, down in the bottom-most corner on the lychgate side. It had become badly infested, and he has had to use the spade and the heavy fork continually, whilst battling to remain vigilant against his own failings, of endurance and of will, in this endless struggle.

And now, taking stock, it strikes him anew that there must come a moment in which the garden will be as complete as ever anything can be in a world where nothing is ever complete. And, in that moment, it must also be as near perfect as ever anything can be in this world in which ripeness is *all*, beyond this, the long hill would commence its gradual process of reversion: rampant, chaotic nature's helpless captive, once more.

And then…?

Straightening up gingerly, stretching, shaking the pain out of his back and thighs, he sits against the handle of the fork, close in to the overhanging hedge, trying to decide whether to go on a bit longer or finish the day with a lighter, pleasanter job, when suddenly, the crack and whirr of a low-flying helicopter.

After the initial shock he watches it disappear directly overhead, then dismisses it. But a minute or less later it is back, and hovering, as near as he can tell, just above the wedge of trees over to his right, between the new development and his sloping garden's thick hedge.

He adjusts his position to observe it casually as it swings round, surprised to see it then edge back over the garden, dropping much lower as it does so. And he retreats under the hedge, his breath quickening.

The craft moves slowly out over the garden, and he sees its black and white markings: a police helicopter. And he sees the pilot point down towards the house, his arm jabbing insistently, as two or three others crane their necks from the passenger seats to get a better view.

Thoroughly bewildered, he cowers down, pulse racing furiously.

The helicopter hangs there, its propeller whirring for what seems an eternity. Then it swoops off once again, whirrs away in the direction of the city. And very awkwardly and shame-facedly, Dan steps out from under the hedge.

So, what was that all about?

Collecting his tools together, he scrapes the clayey soil off the fork and spade as best he can, and lays them across the barrow to begin his descent.

Odd, the police so obviously interested in his house. Were they looking for something specific? Should he expect further intrusion, a house call, even? Or maybe they'd simply noticed the garden as they were passing, and been curious.

Thus speculating, Dan walks back down the hill towards the kitchen door, leaving the tools in his barrow.

A chance passing? Idle curiosity? Perhaps. Yet there was something about the pilot's insistence, his insistent looking.

Dan goes upstairs, selects a small volume off his shelves, and runs a bath, immersing himself in the comforting warmth, and in the long poem he knows so well until, uncharacteristically reading the verses aloud to himself, the sense of unease gradually dissipates.

A few days later, while he is fixing a couple of laths that have become detached from the side trellis of the arch, just above the three steps, he suddenly has the uncanny feeling he is being watched.

An involuntary tingling up and down his spine, yet he resists the impulse to turn round. And when he eventually does, his movements are studiedly casual, giving every appearance of total absorption in his task. Thoroughly and systematically, however, his eyes rake the hedge down the eastern side of the field. Then, seeing nothing unusual there, they move round past the house, through the narrow gap between the house and the end of the greenhouse, to the postern, where they come to rest.

Someone is standing there, looking in.

Too far away to make out any detail, Dan heads down towards the house, still trying not to give any indication of his awareness of the intruder's presence. Besides, he has no desire to become involved in any way, and certainly not to be drawn into conversation. But then the figure pulls back into the shadows, pressing up against the gate post, obviously not wishing to be seen, yet unwilling, perhaps, to put an end to his scrutiny.

What is he doing here? It wasn't as if people passed by his house, it being the last and some way up the lane, near its end.

Dan strides on down but next time he glances up the figure has vanished. Reaching the gate, he steps quickly outside into the lane, then sprints to the bend.

But there is no one.

Over to his right, now, lies the development. Warily, he takes a few steps through its entrance, scanning the site for any sign of movement. But all is still. There is nothing, no one, not a single workman. Is it a weekend, then? Even the few trees here are motionless, the whole image seeming flat, artificial, a half-finished backcloth.

So where has the man got to? Or has he imagined the whole thing, just a trick of the light, maybe?

Unless...

Discounting the thought even as it enters his mind, that there is a connection with the helicopter, Dan walks this way and that, then exhales loudly.

'You're getting paranoid, Teal,' he declares, shaking his head, laughing at himself. And for a moment, his better humour returns. He saunters back to the entrance, across the lane and on up to his gate, wondering about the effects of solitude, and whether this is the sort of thing you can expect, being too long on your own.

Well, he'd better expect more of it, he supposes, grinning.

But when he reaches the gate he stops short, catching a whiff of cigarette smoke. Then he sees the still-smouldering butt under the hedge. So he hasn't imagined it! He glances further left. And lying there, neatly, is a white lace handkerchief.

A lace handkerchief? He picks it up, stares at it, at this seeming incongruity, and, newly on edge, casts it down, and walks smartly back inside.

XXI

Rosemary is waiting at the street end. She hears the town hall clock striking and realises she's been here for almost half an hour and there's still no sign of Rosalind. She sighs her impatience. So, what now?

She had glanced at the house as she passed it, on the other side of the street. Its windows were covered with net curtains, which looked clean enough, and the green paintwork seemed fresh. She sighs again, decides she'll wait another five minutes and then go and knock on the door and explain that her friend hasn't shown up yet. And then, she'll… well, come back here, she supposes, to the corner, and wait a bit longer. What else can she do?

Five more minutes go slowly by.

So where was Rosalind, as she couldn't have slept in, not with her mother waking her, making sure she was up for school, so…?

Rosemary feels a flash of anger whip through her, as it suddenly occurs to her that Rosalind might already be inside. She'd got there early for once, and not waited. She was always doing it, not keeping to an arrangement.

Had she really gone in without her?

Rosemary's irritation smoulders into real anger. She looks up the main road for one last time, turns, then, heaving an enormous sigh, tramps back along the street towards the house. She crosses over, and knocks.

The door is opened at once.

Startled, she steps quickly back.

'Friend not come?' the woman inquires, but without any trace of surprise. 'I see you wait half hour. She not come. Maybe she ok now?'

Rosemary frowns at this new possibility, but then finds herself beginning to apologise, to explain how Rosalind is. But the woman interrupts her.

'It is no matter. *You* come.' And almost pulling her inside, she leads Rosemary down a long, narrow, poorly lit corridor, to a room at the far end of the house.

'Maybe she come soon. Maybe not come…You sit. Here. This chair.'

The woman also sits, in a rocking chair by a table on which there is a large bottle. Rosemary stares at it, reminded about the explanation they'd decided to give about the gin. Is this gin, maybe? It has a white, obviously home-made label with something scribbled on it, in pencil. She feels in her coat pocket to make sure the money is still there, but decides not to mention it just yet, or the difficulties. Maybe now she'll be able to return it to the box in her mother's dressing-table drawer, and hope it's not even been missed, yet.

She smiles and looks up at the woman, expecting her to say something, but she just sits there rocking gently back and forth. Once or twice their eyes meet, and Rosemary looks away, embarrassed, hoping the woman will now say something. But when she looks back, the woman just smiles and nods her head slowly back and forth, back and forth, and still nothing happens.

Rosemary clears her throat, and the woman becomes attentive. But no words will come to her, she can think of nothing to say; and she flushes, looking away, out of the window into the stark back yard and its row of empty troughs and flowerpots.

Suddenly, the woman stands, nods brusquely, then leaves the room by a door behind Rosemary's chair, returning a moment or two later with two tumblers. She sets them down, half fills them from the bottle on the table, then hands one of the glasses to Rosemary.

Rosemary's eyes open wide, and she starts to explain that she isn't allowed alcoholic drinks.

'I've never even…'

'You try. Goooood! You like.' The woman laughs and gulps down some of the clear liquid from her own glass. 'From Ukraine. *Good.*' And she drinks down the rest in one final gulp, reaching immediately for the bottle and replenishing her glass.

Rosemary smiles wanly, fiddles with her glass, and then tries a sip of the clear, white spirit. It burns her throat and makes her cough, but then tastes sweet, and she has another sip, trying not to let too much slip down all at once to avoid the burning sensation. She feels pleased she hadn't refused outright: the woman might have remembered the bacon sandwiches, and been offended this time.

The woman drinks steadily, sipping and sighing her contentment, and Rosemary begins to feel uncomfortable again, unsure why they are sitting here in complete silence. She looks at the old-fashioned clock, tick-tocking loudly on the mantelpiece: five past ten. When it gets to quarter past, she thinks, if nothing's happened, I'll say I have to be going.

Reassured by her decision, she leans back into the chair – at which the woman leans forward and tops up her glass, which is now brim-full. Rosemary's brow furrows and she looks for somewhere to put the glass down, but there is nowhere near enough. And now, when she announces she's leaving, she'll have the embarrassment of having to apologise for not finishing it, for wasting it – almost a whole tumbler-full of the drink.

The pauses between her sips become shorter, the sips become gulps, and the burning sensation brings tears to her eyes.

The woman keeps on nodding and smiling. 'You see, you like. Good. Very good. From Ukraine.'

Back and forth her chair goes, with her nodding and smiling. Nearer and farther. A smile coming and going. In and out of shadows and misty light, and the clock hammering at the silence.

Nodding and smiling…

Coming and going. Going and coming…

Then the woman speaks, but a long way off, such a long way off. Another voice joins her voice, but far away.

And someone helps Rosemary lift her glass, lifting her, up and up and up, among clouds.

Her arm moves slowly, into regions which are cold and colder. Arm full stretch. Fingers full stretch. Her senses gather, but slowly, and she draws in her distant arm till it lies cold against her side.

Rosemary opens her eyes, but they do not focus at once. And when they do, she is still not sure that they have, and she rubs them, and she is surprised that her arm is cold, and that it is cold because it is bare. Her head jerks up, and she sees she is lying in a large bed. Then she feels at her body with her hands, and it is completely naked.

Naked? Her stomach lurches at the shock of it.

She turns her head, and sees the woman sitting there, still smiling and nodding. But they are in another, different room, a bedroom.

'You sleep long. Long. Long time.'

Rosemary sits up, clutching at the covers, dragging them up to her throat.

'Why am I in this bed? Why have I no clothes on? Where are my clothes?'

The woman chuckles: 'Clothes? I wash. Little accident. Too much you like Ukraine gin!' And she wags her finger, laughing.

'What time is it?' Rosemary asks urgently. If she is late home her mother will be furious, and she'll never hear the last of it, and…

'No late. Four and half nearly. No late.' The woman shakes her head reassuringly.

'My clothes… please, may I have my clothes back?'

'I go see.' And the woman leaves the room.

'All dry. All dry,' she says as she comes back, a couple of minutes later, and puts them down at the foot of the bed before sitting down once more.

All too conscious of her nakedness beneath the bedclothes, however, Rosemary feels unable to reach for and get into her clothes, without revealing… all of her nakedness. So, she stays put, hoping the woman will take the hint and leave the room.

'It's so cosy and warm here,' she says, trying, self-consciously, to sound grateful, and not reveal the confusion and rising panic almost suffocating her, 'and… and I wish I could stay here all night, only,

I have to be going… I'll have to get dressed. Could you…?' And she motions vaguely with the back of her hand, trying to hide her desperation.

The woman nods her understanding, and smiles. But she makes no move to leave her chair even, much less quit the room.

Rosemary closes her eyes, uncertain what next, but then opens them with the sudden realisation that the woman must already have seen her naked, if she'd undressed her, and made her… this way. And she blushes deeply at the thought of it.

She tries another ploy. 'Did I faint or something? What happened?'

Again, the woman chuckles. 'Oh yes. You faint. Too much you like Ukraine gin!'

Rosemary frowns, half remembering that also, in that moment, there had been another voice. A man's voice.

'Was there a man here, too?' she asks, timidly. 'I think I heard a man… just before I…'

The woman stares at her, seemingly bemused. 'Man?' she says. 'No man. You girls… all same. Only think of man, man, man.' She laughs, bitterly. 'No man,' she insists, 'no man here.'

'And my friend, Rosalind – did she not come?'

'Not come,' says the woman, quietly, gently. Then she smiles broadly. 'Not come. Just you. And me. You and me.'

Then she rises from her chair.

And Rosemary closes her eyes tightly as the woman draws back the bed clothes, and with slow, purposeful movements, begins to dress her, as if she were a little child, or a doll.

XXII

Had he always intended the garden should be this way, right from the start?

As far as Dan can recall, his mind had conceived the idea of it, but had been less than precise about how it should take shape, or what its shapes might be.

And what of his solitary life?

Years ago, whenever he'd confessed his strong attraction to the monastic life, friends had dismissed his words with amused incomprehension, or some ribald reference to Boccaccio: at table, or in the course of some languid conversation over wine. Yet friends know only that part of us they are witness to – or which they create for themselves and defend as best they can against these occasional, inconvenient spectres from another, perhaps more truthful world.

And effectively, yes, he was living such a life now. But what do we really know about intention, what finally determines the direction we actually take?

Dan finishes his coffee, feels at the pot, and gets up to make a fresh one, but before doing so slips on his boots and steps outside to bring in the box of groceries which will be waiting for him in the shed.

Maybe he had only intended a temporary withdrawal, a few months at most, to enable him to give the garden his undivided attention in its early stages. And if the temporary has now slipped into the permanent, with such permanence as time ever has, it is too late to go back even if he were inclined to.

Is it too late? And if so, does he regret it?

On mornings when he is up before daybreak, Dan stands by the kitchen window, his eyes squinting into the darkness outside, straining among shadows up the past and future field. Sometimes he returns to the question of the police helicopter's visit; to the intruder, and where he went if he didn't vanish into thin air; to the cigarette butt, and the mysterious handkerchief: things whose incongruity nourishes something in him which, if not quite fear, comes very close to it. But mostly all his eyes see is his own image, mirrored against the darkness in the glass by the light that is all behind him. And this is the threshold.

The large cardboard box is lying just inside the shed door. He picks it up and heads back towards the house. Does he regret it?

He stands a moment at the door, and then smiles, pushing it open with his knee. Certainly no more than any other such endings, or slippages, in his life.

With his groceries all put away, Dan goes up to his study and fetches down the box of old sketch books he has been intending to look through for a while now, engaging with the possibility of painting and *its* ideal worlds, even if after half a lifetime away. Could he paint again?

His mind meanders back to the question of "intention" and "realities". Even now, the choice is still his – insofar as there is choice – in the absolute… or the abstract, perhaps? And he smiles, not thinking about painting now. So yes, he could, as it were, breeze back in from "America" or "Australia", or wherever it is he's been, and resume his old life where he had supposedly broken off.

Of course he can. But for whom, and how, and to what purpose?

He sits there a while, then turns to the box in front of him, refocusing on its contents, and whether he could paint again. If he does try, there'll be much to relearn, but also to discover, as his perspective will surely have altered: earth colours would abound now – burnt umber, sepia, rose madder… the new Adam; light would be darkness, the apparent real, and images might simply be… images.

He pulls out a couple of the Greek sketch books, and leafs through their fragile pages. How would these translate into paint, here? now? He pulls out another, then another; and passing slowly through them, all these hills and rocks and skies, the seas, he wonders at the colour notes he had made then, all pointing to light and brightness.

Brightness, light… No, he very much doubts he could paint in these vivid colours, now. But Isixia, what a place. All that marvelling and speculation and hopes for the future. And for a moment his attention wanders back, over the soft white sands and warm waters, the steep slopes. But wasn't there…?

Suddenly, Dan is rummaging deeper. Ah yes. Gently extracting another book, he flicks through the first pages. The little white church, perched defiantly on the ledge high above the village. The busy street at dusk. The fish market on the quay, when the boats were back in the early evening. And those solemn rocks crowding away up the hillside towards its old Venetian fortress, in the clouds. An idyll, Isixia.

He looks up, calculating the span of time during which these representations have stayed locked in, unseen by any eye, then runs his fingers over the rough texture of the pages, looks through them both forward and back, but also beyond. For beyond the edge of each faded page, like two-way mirrors, are the minute, unnoticed, unpaintable things that had grafted onto their lives, his and Penny's – inextricably, and (doubtless they'd thought it at the time) forever.

He turns another page, but then a frown creases his forehead.

Pressed between the leaves is a page from a letter. And similarly, he quickly ascertains, between all subsequent pages to the end of the sketchbook. The notepaper is of different sizes and colours, but the handwriting is always the same. Different lives from different times, interfusing. And meaning what, now, exactly?

Dan shakes his head. And his chair scrapes back as he goes over and stands looking out of the window, at the high containing wall.

Meaning nothing. After many years in their darkness, their silence.

He turns back, and smiles ruefully. They were like ammonites turned up from their million-year-old beds of Kimmeridge clay, glistening but only momentarily, like mother-of-pearl.

> *In my little dream world in which I live about 50% of the time I have now excluded all possibility of ever marrying you, as even in my make-believe world I realise the difficulties & upsets that it would make. But don't think for a moment, though, that you are not included in my dreams; you are always there, the two of you, & I am married to another man (not that I've any particular longing to get married, but things are much tidier if it is that way & it overcomes a lot of difficulties). The 4 of us actually do something worthwhile with our lives (& I'm more convinced of the necessity of this than ever, after working a week in the snack bar here). We're always in a foreign country and working in the poorest of conditions (oh dear, I'm terribly romantic & frightfully impractical!). You must forgive this escape of mine from reality, but I have to do it sometimes, or events would become intolerable.*

And there it ends, for the next page evidently belongs to another time and a different letter. Today's memories, yesterday's dreams; shells vacated and beached far beyond the reach of any tide.

> *Before I went away, I thought there was a possibility that all this would change, but now I am almost positive that that will never happen. You are my first thought on a morning just as you always were, my last thought at night & are with me all day long. Oh! What a cruel, cruel letter! How could you say that it would probably mean little to me? Every time that I read it, it is as though a knife was being pushed through my heart.*
>
> *I can understand a little, but not forgive, as yet, why you believe all these awful hard things about me. Oh, how superficial and unfeeling you must think me. The last letter which I sent you should never have...*

Nothing but words, words in a vacuum, yet still pricking curiosity.

What could he possibly have written back then, the way he felt, that was 'hard' or 'cruel'?

Dan snaps the pad shut in something like despair. That all of this had once been life and death to him... and to her too, if her words, however loaded with schoolgirl cliché and melodrama, had conveyed something of her truth, her earnestness.

What fools these mortals be!

He stands abruptly, angry that his long-nurtured tranquillity can still cleave to, and dissolve in these empty echoes from the past. 'Outside, Teal! You've dallied too long already,' he admonishes, and snatching his rain-proof jacket from the hook behind the back door, he steps out into a blustery wind.

Once outside he pauses as if scenting the air, as Ben always did; then suddenly deciding, he heads right, diagonally across the paved area, to the trough. And he stands there, looking down into its crystal-clear waters.

Moments later, there is a sudden silvery flash, of something startled, too quick for him to see. And he hears again the cries of gleeful excitement from the swing in the oak beyond the apse, and those distant shouts from up the field, from over the ridge, from within the wood. Like the letters, like the sketches, all fading, their former being, nowhere.

Then he whips round, mounts the steps, and strides up through the garden, proclaiming out loud to the wind:

'This is no place for us! This is no world for us to be in! Do you hear me? This is all wrong!'

For the rest of the day, he gouges earth, tips stones, hammers posts, drags, beats, and pushes, with barely a moment's pause.

Towards dusk, however, when he finally straightens up and looks back over the patch the storm has raged through, it is with something like satisfaction. And he knows again that nothing, or no one, is ever wholly, exclusively, what we take them to be, so that at last, walking back down to the shed, a sort of peace settles in his mind.

***

Why had Rosalind not come?

Bewildered, though seemingly none the worse for her odd adventure, Rosemary has to wait almost another week for an explanation. Nor is it that Rosalind comes and tells her. One morning, instead of avoiding her, as she normally does, Rosemary just stands in her way along the school corridor.

'So, what happened to you?' Her dark, accusing eyes flash in anger.

'I forgot,' Rosalind mumbles, her face sullen.

'You *forgot*!' Rosemary is incredulous. 'But how could you forget a thing like *that*? I thought that it...'

'Because it didn't matter anymore, did it?'

'What?'

'My thingy started. It was a... false alarm.'

Rosemary's heart misses a beat. 'What?' she gasps? 'What...?'

Though why she should be shocked at Rosalind's fecklessness after all this time is beyond her comprehension. Her eyes fill with tears, and she stands, unable for the moment to speak or to move. She scrutinises Rosalind, searching her face for... something, at least. But Rosalind's eyes are averted, staring into space, quite unforthcoming. Rosemary bites her lip, and then, when she has regained a little composure, gently touches Rosalind's hand.

'But... couldn't you have let me know? Instead of...'

'I told you,' Rosalind snaps, barely audible, 'I forgot! I forgot! That's all.' Her fierce blue eyes pierce Rosemary to the core, and Rosemary looks down and then across at Rosalind, still hoping for an apology, for anything at all.

But Rosalind says nothing. She stands there, rubbing at an invisible stain on her skirt.

Without another word, Rosemary turns and marches off down the corridor, and out of the swing doors at the far end. Does she hear Rosalind's voice calling behind her, or does she imagine it? She neither stops nor turns. She has Rosalind's measure now. There is nothing to turn for, nothing at all.

XXIII

Vision diminishing, myopia of the moles whose mounds dot the rise. Intermittent bird cries settling into silence (the wood, they say, was once home to nightingales). White flash of a haunting owl so near its flapping wing-beat fans his face. All inclination stilling. Knot garden and foot maze now pushed away to his mind's horizon.

Dusk again, and Dan's deep feeling of lassitude pervades the gloom. In such moments as these, where does the next moment come from? And the next?

He turns to stand at the very edge of the made garden, surveying the emptiness sloping gently away up into the thickening darkness, to the now almost invisible ridge behind. For a moment his eyes strain into the dark to make out what seems to be silhouetted there, upright, coming-and-going darkly to his sight; and in the next, he is shocked rigid, his heartbeat racing.

'Ben?' he whispers.

For this is how Ben would sit, pert, eager, in anticipation.

He takes a couple of steps up the slope, and instantly, the figure dissolves; it breaks out of its stillness and dissolves into the darkness.

'Ben, come back!' he cries, his mind in turmoil, yet with a sense of measure already scrambling over the wreckage of illusion.

'You're losing your bloody marbles, Teal, that's what!' he mutters. 'Come on, don't be ridiculous.'

All the same, the after-tremors remain. And he stands there, his palms still damp, trying to control his breathing, but still staring up into the blankness. At last, he turns, and slowly, reluctantly, moves away towards the steps, then on down to the house.

Only as he crosses the threshold into the lighted kitchen does it occur to him that it was the fox.

***

… I spent most of my time wishing that I could meet you. Perhaps just see you, conjuring up the most unlikely situations and it was not until the last day when I was passing the school on the bus that I realised that I just couldn't have faced it. I felt the beginning of that horrible, frustrated feeling which I used to get every time that I had to leave you. The feeling which prevented me from concentrating on anything or doing anything and which took ages to get rid of. Always trying to make possible the impossible. Although everything is all right here, I don't think I'm yet ready to cope satisfactorily with the situation of seeing you. You said friendship and love are the same. The love I felt for you when I was with you, was not; the love that I feel here is verging on it, and soon I hope will always be entirely it – even when you are there. I do so want to be completely open to you, to feel that I can tell you anything and everything and that you really care. This was what I was getting at when I asked you to promise that you would always be there – at that time, the idea that such a thing might be possible was absolutely overwhelming, and it had every right to be, for it was not possible, only for an entirely different reason to the one that I thought of then. It was not that I didn't want to give myself or that I didn't have anyone to give myself to – I was afraid to; afraid of the consequences – I soon became quite aware of that. I always had to be holding myself back, for I was never sure just what you might do if I showed too much, and when I did – do you remember, the night before Emma's wedding, at the University, when I showed more than ever before just how much I wanted you? Did you think that

was the only time that I felt like that? And look what the result was! I shall never risk that again, never.

Please, I don't want to see you before Christmas ('don't want to' are utterly the wrong words, but I can't think of any others) as not only would it completely overbalance me or make me as tight as an oyster – but it would also have to involve lots of lies and deceit, and once again I would start building barriers against all and sundry because of them. It will not always be like this, and surely that is worth waiting for. Please don't try to persuade me to do differently...

Titania puts her pen and pad down on the bedside locker. Time had flown by. Yet the effort of writing... oh it was exhausting. She switches out the light. She would read it over in the morning, then finish it.

***

Rosemary tries the front door, a thing she's never done before, but it is clearly locked. She knocks again, then goes round to the side of the house and tries the high gate, which leads through the garden to the back door, but that too is locked. And not a sound from within.

So where are they? Was Mrs Appleton away, visiting her...? But wouldn't she have said?

Rosemary frowns. And then remembers. The baby, her son's baby, which was due any day now.

'I may have to go, dear, you know, lend a hand... These things always happen suddenly, taking everyone by surprise.'

'Even though they've been expecting them?'

Mrs Appleton chuckles. 'Oh yes. But I shouldn't be away very long.'

Rosemary closes her eyes, hearing her words, feeling disappointed and lonelier than ever. Today especially she had felt a need for

Jason – to ruffle his coat, bury her head into it, to lose herself in his warmth... Then to walk with him in the park, walk briskly, and not worry about being seen... to feel proud even, proud of having a fine-looking dog to walk, and doing a kindness for someone.

In through the lower park gate she goes, along the path towards the lake, head down, brooding. A bird cries, and, as if newly directed, she veers off to the left, across the grass and up to the gardens round the bowling green, where she doesn't often go. Once there, she sits down on a low wall, her back against a huge ornamental urn, scrolled and flowered, such as finish off the corners of each of the surrounding walls, her feet against a stone acorn finial. And again she closes her eyes, this time turning her face up towards the sun.

She would *so* much have liked Jason to be with her. It's like an ache, lodged deep in her stomach.

Too much on her own, her parents said. They often said it, encouraging her to make more friends, as if it was something you could just, well, decide and it would happen. But last night...

Rosemary's head falls forward. And when she looks up again her face is wet with tears.

'That girl of ours. She's hopeless!' her father had said – deliberately within her hearing, as she carried their tea things away to the kitchen.

Stung to the core, Rosemary had simply dumped the plates by the washing-up bowl and fled upstairs. She'd not stamped her feet, not cried even. But the words had kept coming back, all evening, and she'd stayed in her room, not even responding to her mother's feeble 'night-night' call. Ok, so she hadn't said much at teatime – Rosalind's callous indifference had been too much on her mind – so maybe that's what had made him say it.

But whether it was or it wasn't, it was clearly too much of an effort for her father to talk to her, to raise his head from his paper, or the Bible. Anyway, she wasn't good enough for them – that was obvious. Never had been, never would be. Not for her father, not for her mother, who just knitted on, like a machine.

And sitting on the wall, on this cloudless summer morning,

Rosemary starts kicking her feet against the acorn finial, angrily, rhythmically. Left, right, left right, with her eyes tightly shut.

A dog barks somewhere, and she stops, her thoughts immediately turning to Jason again. Dear old Jason, who never let you be on your own. You were always with Jason if Jason was with you, that was for sure!

Rosemary smiles at the image of him in her mind, sleek and solid and warm, and she opens her eyes.

On the far side of the green an old man is lowering himself onto one of the benches, almost exactly mid-way between an old lady and another gentleman who is leaning forward, with his chin resting on his hands clasped around the handle of his walking stick. Dotted around are several other old people; one lady, like another Mrs Appleton, has a little dog sleeping at her feet; and another man, younger-looking than the first one, puffs at his pipe, its smoke drifting upwards, making a bluish haze around his head.

On the other two sides of the green there's an outer circle of chairs facing into it... so they can move them, maybe, or maybe as they'd run out of benches... And these have people on them too. All in the same place, but none of them together. She angles her head, squinting at them in the light. What are they all doing here, all silent and still like the roses in their beds? All separate and staring at the empty bowling green, like statues. Perfectly still like statues. Twelve... no, thirteen of them, with the little dog. No one speaking. No sounds. Not a whisper. Where are they all, then, these separate people, these... these... gargoyles? Then immediately, it strikes her that if any of them were having her thoughts, then she would be a gargoyle too! Or a rose, maybe... Rosie, as Rosalind sometimes called her.

And she sighs and closes her eyes again, tilting her head back to feel the warmth of the sun on her face, wondering how things are going with Mrs Appleton, and the new baby. And Jason, of course.

***

Between Easter and Pentecost. A time of tension.

Between words and other words. A time of expectation, of passions crossed.

Rising and falling, into and out of hope and despair. Each moment a decade, her fleeting smile fading, then curling away at the edges of his memory.

Whole days when she does not come, days which have no memory because she doesn't come, isn't a part of anything. His mind sowing tares. The same page holding its place for aeons of time, blank, wordless (despite the gusting winds within him), held in place by a hand he barely takes account of.

'I think they're going to be away this weekend,' she'd said, 'at the caravan, by the sea. I shan't go with them, though. Too much work – an essay on *Lear*...'

His spirits had soared. But now... after yet another whole day lost in agonised suspense... in desperation, a few words hastily spoken, a lame, unbelievable excuse – 'a walk, to clear my head,' was it? – away he'd gone, to seize an hour with her, leaving behind a woman's puzzlement and fears he dare not contemplate.

On one occasion, even very late at night, so great had been his sleepless desperation.

How much cruelty could silent love absorb?

And once there...?

'I just knew you would come.'

She in her night clothes. Coffee. The biscuit tin. The living-kitchen with its peculiar, homely smell, its battered sofa. Once (or is it more than once?) she shows him her room with its table, its soft lamp, its wide, upright armchair.

'This is where I read, and where I think about you,' she says. And he kisses her, surely not unaware of her firm nakedness through the thin night-dress and the nylon robe, pressing towards him, beneath his fingers.

He remembers her high bed, and that her room was at the back, overlooking the garden.

Languid talk of films, of books, of thoughts stemming from

others' fancy but never quite sweeping them up as it ought to. Never quite. It would have been so simple. Falling silent. Sitting close. One movement. Two. Once, it almost happens like this, but he fights and fights against this "base calumny" and in the end lurches off in the direction of the bathroom, sick. *Per ardua ad astra*. Futile heroics on the mocking field of chastity. Rooted Apollo.

In the end, faithful to whom? To what?

Words fail him.

And hurrying back that next morning – a desperate Sunday – on yet another, hardly plausible pretext, taking the twins with him, whooping in their push chair. She has barely had time to dress.

'I was half expecting you,' she confesses.

He takes a seat, angles the pushchair, hands the boys their picture books, as she stands close, her fingers running through his hair already tousled by the wet summer wind. And, clasping her around her thighs, he is tormented by that particular scent still faintly clinging to her from the evening... as if she had, perhaps, learned to take her own pleasures, obscurely confusing them with love, in the night.

Such a notion would never have entered his head; not then, with the vision he had of her, then.

Glancing beyond her, he is trapped by Matthew's wondering gaze, by Simon's peevish whimpers, two small heads twisting round. And, full of love, his heart bursting with it... for them, for Penny, and for Titania on whom his gaze rests briefly... he scurries away, with nothing gained, to pine all over again.

***

For Titania also, any step in any direction would be the wrong step in the wrong direction. Stifled by these newly awakened demands pressing in upon her, and this outward urging from deep within her, she gasps for air, to grope blindly away, to implore...

She takes up her book, imagines herself in the role, beseeching, longing, and pleading…

> *for love and courtesy,*
> *Lie further off, in human modesty;*
> *Such separation as may well be said*
> *Becomes a virtuous bachelor and a maid,*
> *So far be distant; and good night, sweet*
> > *friend:*
> *Thy love ne'er alter till thy sweet life end!*

She tries to read on and can't. She tries to sleep and can't. 'Which way can I turn? Where is there an end of it, this anxiety, when all my hopes are other people's fears, and prohibitions…? Which way can I turn?'

***

Hammering blindly at the door with clenched fists, another girl might have asked herself the same question: Rosemary, feeling in her heart of hearts she is too late.

Oh, poor, poor Mrs Appleton. Whatever can have become of her?

She stands back, thinking hard, then on impulse, pushes the crumpled envelope through the letter box and watches it drop into the so familiar, now distant, deeply silent hallway, whispering her prayer. Please, oh please someone find it, and send me word.

Days later, after anxious mornings at home watching out for the postman, the unwitting messenger of her deepening despair, she is again looking through that letter box. And… her envelope is lying exactly where it had fallen into the silence.

The next day, she is back again, and so intent is she on the letterbox that she doesn't at first see the 'For Sale' notice planted by the door, a bizarre weed among the climbing roses. Looking up at it, at last, she is stunned by its implications of finality, and her face drains of all colour.

Mrs Appleton's house… for sale?

'Oh….'

And passers-by who might have noticed a girl on her knees, or heard her cry out, now turn their heads, startled to hear sobbing; and they stare on as she runs off, a handkerchief stuffed in her mouth, the back of her hand raking over her eyes. Stumbling on, away, lost.

Not many minutes later, drained, exhausted, and sobbing uncontrollably, Rosemary is banging at another door, one which opens readily, to admit her.

Clasped in encircling arms, feeling the woman's hand up and down her spine and in her hair, Rosemary, even in the extremity of her distress, realises this is not quite how it ought to be. Maybe it is the faint animal smell the woman exudes, mixed with lavender, which repels her, or the monotonous clucking into her hair that has no currency in her own emotions' vocabulary. And yet, this woman is also her angel of consolation – the only angel she is ever likely to know – whom she can turn to, now, in her distress.

'Oh Jason, Jason, Jason,' she moans into the woman's shoulder. And soon, unresisting, she is led gently away, along the corridor into that room at the back of the house. There is nothing that can happen to her, outwardly, that can match the hurt in her mind and in her being, and she longs for oblivion, so as not to have to keep on suffering the loss she has not yet begun to understand.

Gently, she is lowered into a chair.

Then, for a moment or two, she is alone, until a glass is proffered, and an arm once more about her shoulder, comforting, kindly. Recognising the smell, and then the burning sensation, Rosemary feels the spirit's warmth spreading slowly through her body.

She gulps down more, and then more.

The woman has started stroking her hair again, and Rosemary falls in easily, now, with the slow rhythm of her hand. Back and forth it goes, back and forth, subtly drawing her away, along another pathway, where the hurt is less acute, though the aftershocks of her sobbing still surge in waves through her whole body. A sudden memory of Rosalind once, like this, in her muddy shoes, ghosts across the fragmenting landscape of her mind.

Rosalind, another kind of loss.

But Jason. Standing on his hind legs, his paws on her shoulders, licking her nose... 'Oh Jason,' she cries. And her tears fall again and submerge her.

When the worst of the fit is past, her glass is replenished and she is led away, led into a lightsome world which is blurred and soft at its extremities.

Hands now gently moving over her arms, her legs, her face, her breasts, the warmth of a naked body pressing upon her own nakedness, smooth and warm, covering her nakedness, absorbing her grief, already more muted. Flickers starting up, now here, now there, always on the point of... floating off. Tingling music, in a dream, until she fades.

Rosemary's return is inevitably to tears. She lies silently remembering and grieving, her eyes tightly closed, shutting her in with the loved, lost image of Jason – so unjustly, so pointlessly, the victim of Mrs Appleton's failure, and her own, to make provision for his future.

Has he been "put to sleep", as Mrs Appleton had said might need to happen? And has Mrs Appleton really... departed this world? She shakes her head, miserably. Why else would her house be for sale, and so quickly?

Maybe she will never know. And this thought adds yet more weight to the burden of Rosemary's sorrow and plunges her into more tears. She tries to contain them, biting hard over her bottom lip, trying to hold it all in, but she can't, for her tears, it seems, are all she has left of him.

Her hair is gently stroked, her hand held, and a voice is singing to her, words she does not recognise, but so sweetly and sadly they penetrate her grief and mingle with it, strangely diluting it. Rosemary finds herself captivated by the lilt, by the sounds, which gradually displace the sad pictures in her mind.

At last, she opens her eyes and turns her head. Through the prism of tears hanging on her lashes, the woman is quite transfigured; she seems softer now, leaning over her to wipe her tears away. Her hair, which Rosemary had always seen tightly bound in a plain, severe knot, close to her head, is loose about her shoulders and, though flecked with grey, makes her look much younger. Her face is less round, her eyes sharper, her breasts full.

Strange that she's only ever thought of her as "the pig woman" – which she at first seemed so totally to be! And a frown wrinkles Rosemary's forehead, and then the flicker of a smile, for how can that image of her poking the pigs with a stick, in the pen, have anything at all to do with this kindly creature, soothing her hurt, applying a balm to which she feels herself more and more easily responding?

'Thank you for being so kind,' she says, raising her head a little. The woman chuckles softly, pats her wrist, and whispers something incomprehensible, though its tone is soothing, so very soothing.

Rosemary sighs, then shifts sideways a little, her head turning towards the window. Through the net curtains, her eyes follow the slow progress of an old man and woman going by along the other side of the street. Each carries a heavy shopping bag, shuffling along in slow motion, in a world which is so very remote. The light is failing fast, and she realises it must now be late in the afternoon. Yet she sinks back, feeling no inclination to exchange this haven of warmth and security for that darkening world outside.

There is a faint crackling sound, like the static she hears sometimes as she brushes her hair, and she turns back to look in the woman's direction. In the fading light she sees her standing over the bed, clutching against her body the nylon night-dress she has just removed. Rosemary hesitates, but only briefly, and then she slides over to the other side, her movement an invitation, not a rebuff. And sensing this, the woman slips into the bed beside her, dropping the night-dress as she does so.

***

You can catch a train or a bus. Take a ship, or fly. You can walk away. But it isn't only a suitcase and a shadow that go with you.

Titania can see it so clearly in her mind's eye. She has dreaded it and longed for it too. 'It's awful' she had practised, 'It's like knowing you were going to die.' She has been remembering these words of hers, all the way here, and they're true, but does this make them any less sincere? Acting a part, feeling it…

And he holds her now in silence, unable to speak, knowing, she trusts, that it is for the last time. And she feels so much pity for him.

Knowing. She hopes he does, and she fears it too, knowing…

The July evening draws in slowly. Over his shoulder she watches the sky turn pink then mauve then grey and still they stand there, leaning together in the kitchen, in the darkness. She stifles a yawn – it must be the sudden, evening chill catching the air. But then she can bear it for not a moment longer, and ever so gently she slips out of his enfolding arms. She must be going; it is the end but not the end. A while away; time heals – of course, she will write, though not at once. And so this last, still lingering kiss, then she walks away, knowing that he will watch her all the way to the end of the road, until she is swallowed by the darkness.

She walks slowly at first, then quickens her pace as she nears the bend, but she does not look back. A burden has slipped from her; she has done what she thought she could never do. And once round the corner a rapidly rising sense of exhilaration takes hold of her, and like a grasshopper, she launches away into free air. She begins to run and keeps running until she is quite out of breath.

Mummy will just be making the hot chocolate.

A wisp of smoke curling away down an empty street, drifting into stars, one rose-tinted evening, in summer. And watching still I stand, the stub ends of your words clutched tightly in my hand, scorching my fingers.

The silence in your eyes, the blindness in your kiss, suggest one certainty at least – that you will never know, nor miss, the light which dies in me (a shadow stays), now we have turned and left, to lose our different ways.

Titania is herself now always away. After the summer sea, then Holland, then the sea again. Then the first few weeks of college, with everything so new and to discover. New friends, a new old town. And daddy popping in every now and again when passing through. Everything so exciting and fresh and… and, yes, just so different.

But soon there are also his letters. Long letters full of hurt and hurting, and they leave her sad, angry, remorseful, and guilty, by turns.

And as the new and exciting turns slowly into routine, she is surprised to find her thoughts returning more and more to the things she believed she had left behind for good and all. And she finds, after all, that she cares, and she needs to see him. Needs him, oh yes. His gentleness, their discoveries, all the little things. She sighs deeply now, and often. The need is still there, when she had fully expected, hoped fervently, even, that time would dissolve it.

And now, with this new, shocking awareness, she swings back, like a pendulum, into that old, familiar frame of mind, and longing, so that by Christmas she cannot wait to get back home, to see him, to know – and she will know at a glance – that for him everything is as it had been since the very beginning, that it always would be.

And yet… And yet… still, she makes no real effort to see or to meet him, always putting it off till the next day. Writing for hours, letters she never posts. Going once or twice to the places she knows he might be, her eyes flicking all ways at once, ever expectant, riding the rising tide of anticipation. Why, oh why, does she go on writing these letters, page after page of words that are leg-irons to her true feelings?

Titania has been at home a week, just over, before it happens. And when it does, when she does finally meet him, it is by chance, crossing the market square late in the afternoon. By chance. No words. No lingering.

Back in October, at half term when she was home, there had been the same unmistakable desire to see him, to be with him, and she'd walked to "their" places as now, though she'd never waited long. Once or twice, she had gone past the school in the bus. And then, even when it was too late, and daddy was driving her back up to college… always looking for him.

Was it enough to know that he was there, somewhere, in that particular place… a kind of surety, maybe?

Anyway, now it wasn't enough, it simply wasn't. And here they are.

A quick, furtive, sweeping glance, then he is taking her by the arm, bundling her roughly through the park gates, off the path into the darkness, pushing her against a wall, covering her face, her throat, her eyes with kisses. Breaking off to take in her face, her features, then kissing her again, gentle, fervent. And oh, this is it, this. The realisation. Dizzying precipice, pivoting on the very edge of ecstasy. At last, oh, at long last…

Back in the town, though, when the words start, the questioning, it is like stepping back, not trusting their new wings.

And when the lamps around the square come on, she can see his eyes, their pain, their anger, as plain as if in daylight.

XXIV

Another time. Another, far-off place. So far off it might have been a dream.

A gust of wind flicks the tent flap, once, and again, then again. It sounds like someone coming in, like the boy bringing the tea in the morning. Dan – *Tuan* Teal, as they call him here – looks up from his book because it was that sort of sound. But there is no one. He sits listening, his concentration gone. Occasionally, the deep silence is brushed at its edges by the high-pitched voices of the recruits, drifting up from the water's edge, where they are still digging for hermits. He thrusts the book aside and crawls forward to fasten the flap back.

Reading in such an idyllic setting… it always seems a better idea than it turns out to be. And yet, there's Ray, some little distance away, still sitting in the sun's full glare, still reading – maybe his third detective or western in as many days! Six or seven he's brought for their five-day trip. 'Just enough – he'd said – to see me through…'
    A few pages at most, that's all Dan ever seems to manage.
    But Ray will no doubt read them all, sitting out in the sun, his lower limbs swathed in that chequered sarong, the white bath towel turbaned round his head. Reading on and on, while his back and shoulders gradually take on the colour of the earth.
    Dan ducks back into the tent. Looking out, he can see only the blue of the sea and sky across the wide sandy beach, stretching away northwards into haze, then nothing. Here the silence is physical, like

a gong in his head. Sand. Sea. Sky. Sun. And this mighty, booming silence.

He reaches for his book again, turns a page or two, but his thoughts snake and glide away.

Sri Pantai. Earthly paradise. To the east and north is the conical island, Pulau Tioman, floating in the haze, shifting and sliding as though shaken by tremors. But running away northwards, much further than any eye could see, are silent, empty, silvery, palm-fringed beaches all the way up to Kuantan – and beyond, for all he knows, up to Trengganu, and still beyond. But over this curving horizon, and the next, and the next, as total a rejection of this notion of paradise as humankind could ever devise is taking place, right now.

Vietnam. And, of course, it is not so many years since this very spot, Johor, had been engaged in its own sadistic, human savagery.

Sand, sea, sky, sun, and silence; infinitely neutral, patiently waiting, like an empty stage set. Maybe it is only our North European, forest-bred myths, which shy away from the thought of atrocities in sunlight.

What could ever compensate for man?

Giving up, finally, on *The Durian Tree*, Dan crawls outside and starts walking purposefully, as though bent on crossing the horizon – all too aware, though, that not even the merest manifestation of the soul's squalid alchemy is necessary for this or any other place to be infested by demons, the unseen flock of them we shepherd before us. Or perhaps not. For once spawned, is it not they who are in charge and we who are goaded, driven, or dragged along over our trampled hopes, wills, and reason?

This sudden despondency… oh, he knows well enough what lies behind it and leadens his steps: yesterday's discoveries, still raw, still nagging away at him; these, and everything else he had fervently hoped to leave behind him, in his own far country.

The day – their second out in the *ulu* – had begun well enough. The first batch of trainees had gone off early in the two three-tonners which, after an hour or so, had returned for the rest of them.

Ray had finally sat all the recruits down in a wide semi-circle in a clearing, and talked to them in his quiet, confident way about the "fears" of the jungle and the rationale behind jungle warfare.

Essentials – like water, camouflage, parang, stepping lightly, eyes and ears always alert...

After ten minutes or so of polite listening, Dan rises quietly and walks off along the path, vaguely hoping for glimpses of whatever wildlife is in the area – gibbons, tigers, snakes, and *dik-dik* deer, perhaps, as well as elephants. He'd not seen any on the two previous occasions he'd been up here, though you heard gibbons often enough.

A noise makes him turn, and to his annoyance, Clive is swinging jauntily down the path towards him, waving as he comes. Nice enough fellow, but one of the decidedly less able students who had come his way on the Malay language course.

'I say, old chap, where are you off to?'

'Nowhere in particular.' Dan shrugs. 'Just having a look around.'

'Jolly good. Are the others close by?'

'The far side of that stand of rubber,' he says, turning and pointing, hoping this big boy-scout of a man will trespass no further on his solitude.

'Good. Well... Look, I'll synchronise with Ray and Pete, then tag along with you, if you don't mind.' And he beams his great boyish grin. 'Back in a jiffy!'

'Fine...' says Dan, his flat tone unnoticed as Clive trots off, circling round the trees.

Cursing his luck, Dan remembers what Ray had said about him, on their first trip out here.

'Clive? Oh, he's always like this when we come out in the bush. Never settles to much, always flitting backwards and forwards between the groups.' There had been no resentment in Ray's voice, no disloyalty to his superior officer. He'd merely stated a fact.

'Does he know much about this sort of thing – the jungle warfare, I mean?'

'Not much. Of course, he knows it in theory, I imagine, but certainly, he's never had to put it into practice. In this respect, he's just the equal of these kids. Still, it's not his fault there's no war on. Leastways, not this side of the Straits. Whereas...'

'Ah, there you are!'

Clive strides up, laughing. 'Listen, I passed through what looked like some interesting country earlier, on my way here, and I was thinking, well, we might take a look at it, and then press right on through the *ulu* until we meet the river, which we can then follow down to the road.'

Dan looks away, as if considering the thought.

'Well...? What do you say?' Clive grins, and slaps Dan on the shoulder. 'Can't be more than a couple of miles, five at the most, could be fun! Besides, the others won't be leaving for another four or five hours, so there'll be *plenty* of time to get to the bridge over the old *sungai*... And they can pick us up there, on their way back down to the coast. Look, I've already told Ray, so they'll keep an eye open for us.' He rubs his hands together gleefully, his eyes alight. 'So, are you game?' he asks.

Not that it's a question, really.

They walk along side by side when the path is wide enough, but when it's not, Dan drops behind. After not many minutes, they come across a postman on his rounds, which seems... incongruous, though why it should escapes him, for even people living in a Malay *kampong* surely received mail from time to time.

The postman raises his hand and smiles and would have gone by had not Dan stopped him, thinking that he, perhaps more than anyone else they are likely to meet, would know about things happening hereabouts. And after the customary polite exchanges, in Malay, he asks about animals and learns that a couple of days before, there'd been a small herd of elephants – *beberapa ekor gajah dekat sungai* – down near the river.

'Elephants? Did you see them?'

The postman hadn't, but he'd heard them. And he'd seen their footprints early on this morning, noted the dung where they'd crossed over the path.

Dan frowns. But why hadn't Clive said? He'd come this same way less than half an hour ago – he couldn't have missed the signs. He looks across to see what Clive is making of the conversation. But the man's not even listening, just glancing at his watch, impatient to be off.

As they part, the postman turns and shouts back at Dan, '*Tuan sangat pandai bercakap Melayu!*' Your Malay's very good, sir.

Without turning, Dan raises his hand to acknowledge the compliment. He'd worked hard on his own training, and it always pleases him to hear it acknowledged.

'*Tuan sangat pandai bercakap Melayu.*'

The bar girl had said it the previous evening, talking with them, though it was doubtless part of her "sales" patter: the one from Kelantan, with her exquisite, flawless features. She couldn't have been more than seventeen at most, and her beauty, perhaps her only asset here, had been for hire at twenty dollars a time.

Down in Singapore, or in Kuala Lumpur, she might have made something of herself with a minimum of training. But not here. Here, she was probably already at the end of the line.

'*Tuan sangat pandai bercakap Melayu...*'

She had spoken shyly, almost, but then they all did, the bar girls. That or not speaking but blushing furiously. It was a part of their attraction. And he'd wanted her all right.

Ray had kept pushing him.

'Go on, Dan, I'll pay, my treat. Go on. I'll make it all right back at camp... Don't worry, I'll send the jeep in for you first thing tomorrow morning, ok?'

But Ray had misinterpreted his hesitation, and an hour later, after thinking it through without reaching any conclusion, he'd left with the rest of them. And as they went out, it had been the other one, her more experienced, much less attractive friend, or minder, who had thrust a grubby card into his hand. 'If you want me, I Mariam; you ring this number,' she'd whispered.

He didn't, and he hadn't.

Returning to camp in the darkness of the jolting truck, he'd tried to figure out why he'd passed up the chance of the lovely Miss Kelantan. Where was the virtue in it? Apart from the obvious, of course, his own tussle with the moral question. But even now she was very likely being crushed half to death beneath some fat Chinese *towkay*, making just enough to see her through tomorrow. So, what, in the end, had he saved her from?

He'd gone round and round it, but then the badinage back in camp had turned his mind to other things. And by the time the briefing and the material preparations for this morning's manoeuvres were over, he'd moved on.

So why now, stumping along behind his guide, does he find himself thinking about the girl again, trying to make sense of the ironical – in a way – courtesy he'd shown her? And seeing her face in his mind, he realises…

'Just a mo…' says Clive, stopping in his tracks.

Dan hangs back, not wanting to engage with him, or with whatever it is that has put him off his stride; not now, just when…

Clive sets off again, and he sighs his relief.

A parallel, yes, there is one, if not something he can quite… pin down. It wasn't the girl's face, or any likeness. Nor was it the same reticence that had always made him hold back with Titania.

No likeness, no, Titania being so tall and willowy, and… oh, so very far away.

Dan follows on, still trying to fathom it out. Was it innocence, or the appearance of it? Miss Kelantan, with her child-like prattle… And maybe she was still innocent, if not sexually – not that he necessarily subscribed to the notion that loss of sexual "innocence" was the end of all innocence. But next week, next year? How long would it take for her to be blunted and blinded in a struggle to survive even that small town's uncomplicated brand of human degradation?

So not that either, really.

The path broadens out again and Clive drops back to walk alongside him, placing a hand on his shoulder.

'There's a track coming up, off to the left I seem to remember, just a bit further ahead,' he says. 'I think we'll take that.'

Dan nods almost dismissively, content to leave the details of their excursion to his companion.

It was a year now, with no word from her. A whole year.

At first, he'd written every day – for weeks – until it had dawned on him that she was not going to write, not ever. That realisation had felt like a death to him.

'It's terrible,' she had said, maybe at their first parting, 'it's like knowing you were going to die.'

Weeks and weeks of turmoil, of gaping emptiness. The long, sticky nights, sitting out on the veranda, well after Penny and the twins had gone to bed, sipping tumblers of whisky-water, slipping gently into mist… when Penny believed him to be reading or preparing classes; sometimes, with her eyes full of sleep, she'd stumbled out to find him in the dark and bring him to bed. The days had been less difficult, for they were full of teaching and then the children, going to the pool or shopping; but unless they were invited out to friends', or going to the cinema, he'd dreaded the evenings, when he had not been able to settle to anything, over-canopied as they were by her fathomless silence.

Why didn't she write?

Eventually, having no choice but to accept, he'd drifted into something resembling normal life. But then, after several more weeks, he'd started writing to her again: ordinary accounts of how their days were spent here, and always written in seeming expectation of a reply… though she must be incredibly busy, all the work she had to get through, teaching practice… It was difficult fitting everything in, he understood.

He'd not written regularly, just now and then, but each time…

He sighs. Deep down, he'd known no word would come. And

during those many months, his only comfort had been in the knowledge that, even if she destroyed the letters without opening them, she was made aware that not many days before, for an hour or more, she'd been at the centre of his life.

If only he knew the reason for her silence.

If she'd taken the decision to make a *final* break then he would find a way to cope – he'd have to; but then, why could she not write – two lines, no more – to tell him so?

She could be dead, for all he knew.

Is she dead? Some days, he lives in terror that it is so. And yet, his letters have never been returned… In them he has mostly tried to reason, but sometimes he'd threatened or accused or pleaded. Once, he'd even written to her parents. But her darkness remains total.

Does she intend to punish him for his love, for the deep love he has for her? Or is she – are *they* – oblivious to the effect all this emptiness and fear can have? He closes his eyes. And if not oblivious, why have they chosen this most powerful of tortures, and how can she… this gentle girl, running to him, crystals in her hair… be party to it?

Is she? Does she still… feel anything?

Il mio amore è un sapore d'altrove, una superstizione pudica nell'osceno. My love has the flavour of another place, a chasteness in the midst of so much dross.

Tous les claires et toutes les ombres…

But now, what?

Clive has stopped again in a small clearing. He looks this way and that, clearly perplexed. 'This doesn't seem right,' he shouts back.

What doesn't? Jerked back into the moment, Dan tries to refocus.

'From what I remember,' Clive is saying, as though to himself, 'we should already have come to the river, then turned right to follow it down to the road.' He stands peering into the dense wall of undergrowth. 'And even if we *had* come in along the wrong path, we should still have got to the bally river by now. So, where the devil is it? I can't see how… Odd, old chap, decidedly odd!'

'Well, let's have a look at the map,' Dan suggests, coolly. 'Take a bearing.'

'Oh, we'll come to it in a minute or two.' And Clive moves off, without turning.

'Never mind. Maybe I just underestimated the distance.'

A few yards down the track he stops again.

The path has petered out.

As they push through thick bush and thorn, the forest floor becomes wetter, and Dan grimaces, remembering the horror stories he'd heard about leeches.

They enter into a brake of bamboo, the real *belukar*, and the mud squelches beneath their boots, making the going more difficult. Clive stops and twists round, shouting back over his shoulder, 'Lend me your *parang*, old chap. It's really quite thick just up ahead.'

Dan unsheathes the heavy knife, then steps back, watching Clive's frantic hacking. Ten minutes, and the man's barely moved forward at all. Then he stops swinging the long blade and stands back himself, panting hard. He is red in the face, his arms torn by briars and his shirt wringing with sweat. But he is laughing.

'Wouldn't like to take over for a bit, would you, old chap?'

'It's not worth it,' Dan counters. 'Look, you've cut through only four, maybe five feet in ten minutes. At this rate we'd both be exhausted before an hour was up. No, I suggest we go back, and find another way through.'

Clive nods, still gasping to get his breath back. 'You're probably right. Jolly good fun though!'

Dan looks away, trying not to show his annoyance. He leads the way back to the little clearing where they had stopped initially.

'Right, so let's have a look at the map. See if we can make sense of it. Clive...?'

'It's a bit stiff...' Clive fiddles with the fastening of the pouch at his side for what seems an age. 'New stuff just come in,' he confides, cheerily.

Then Dan hears something snap.

'Ah, there we are.' Clive has forced an entry. But soon he turns to

Dan. 'You'll find this hard to believe, old chap, but – he chortles – I… haven't got it!'

'What?'

'Nope! Everything but, though!'

'You mean, you've…?'

'Best of a bad job, I'm afraid! Here, have some chocolate instead.' And he breaks off a generous piece of the sticky bar, proffering it in its silver paper.

'No thanks.' Dan flings his arms and palms wide. That "instead" has stuck in his gullet, almost choking him.

'You're sure?'

'Maybe later,' he says, it suddenly occurring to him that later the chocolate could become dire necessity.

It was the barest of amends, and Clive rummages on.

Dan nods at the pouch. 'You have a compass do you, among your… provisions? And shouldn't we go more or less south to reach the road?' he adds, placatory.

'Nope!' Clive confirms, brightly. 'No compass either. Forgot to pick the bally thing up. Left it on the bed, I expect. Never mind, we'll manage somehow.'

'How "somehow"?'

'Well, you see, there's an old trick with a watch.'

'I see, so…?'

'You don't know it? Ah, well, something I learned in the scouts, Dan, years ago. You just point the twelve at the sun and then you divide the angle between that and the actual time and that tells you where the south is… or is it the north? Anyhow, something like that,' he finishes heartily.

Dan's anger is now tinged by panic. 'Right, so, Pathfinder. North or south, which is it?'

Clive looks blank.

'The watch!' Dan nods furiously. 'Point it… at the sun!' And he gestures at the wan sky. 'Should it read south or north?'

'Ah, yes. I see what you mean,' Clive mutters. 'Well, I'm sure it's one or the other. Blessed if I can remember.'

'Well, I'm sure you're right,' Dan spits. 'So, do you have any more… ideas?'

'Not at this moment in time. Sorry.' Then Clive clears his throat. 'I'm for going on.'

'On? Fine! And which way *is* "on"?'

Fuming, Dan turns and splashes his way in the direction of what he hopes will be the track they'd been following before it ended so abruptly.

No map. No compass. What an idiot! Supposed to be responsible for training a bunch of recruits in the finer points of how to survive in… 'It's the jungles of Johor we're in, Clive! Not Never-Neverland!'

He twists round, and seeing the misery of failure written on Clive's face is immediately gripped by remorse. Anger won't solve their problem. Calm, clarity, and concentration – that's what is needed – and another way.

And maybe, just maybe, this is what Titania's silence is about. Maybe she too is battling her way back through her own *belukar*, to find another way.

To go forward. Is that what her silence should really be telling him? To go on and not look back, for if he does, like Eurydice, she will be lost to him forever?

It could well be so. But is it?

Getting back even to their last chartable point proves far from easy. Dan recognises nothing since he had noted nothing. There had seemed no reason for it, Clive appearing so sure.

Justification or excuse?

Dan closes his eyes, furious with himself for having carelessly drifted into this absurd situation, the more so since his companion's fecklessness was hardly a secret. But he had been too much entangled in his own. Never-Neverland. He had barely been present himself.

He opens his eyes again and hears Clive humming quietly, tunelessly, a few steps behind him.

'*I will sing that they shall hear I am not afraid*,' flits across Dan's mind, and he smiles grimly. The irony of it… remembering how it goes on: '*if I had wit enough to get out of this wood…*'

And if they don't get out, like that American millionaire a few years back? What was his name? Never found. Not a trace.

If they don't get out, he is to blame too, as his mind has been away with her, in this maze: with Titania, beguiling, beckoning always, chasing after, to catch the wind in a net. Here and there and up and down.

Amor condusse noi. Love that led us on…

Cause. Effect. Cause.

***

Kneeling and firming in another laurel with his hands, Dan pauses a moment. Then he straightens, and looks around him, letting the present moment filter back in.

The day is almost over, and the first stars are showing faintly against a rose-tinting azure. A lifting breeze bustles through the newly planted shrubbery. Kneeling, still, in the swelling darkness, there is a lingering sense of the menace of the close-meshed net of natural profusion wrapped about him, as with increasing awareness of the fanciful connection his intuition has spun (*Grasshoppers are Gyants there*), his eye moves, in panic almost, among the towering bushes, seeking the merest gap through which to catch a glimpse of… To catch a glimpse of what? Something dependable? Something concrete?

The ground is suddenly dank and cold, and he clambers stiffly to his feet.

And now it is all different again, perforce, with his perspective as tallest tree now among the lesser. The light is more, the air is more, and gaze can once more outstrip memory. But he does not turn away. Time – his time, forced on him gradually over many years, by human contact, with *its* own endless incursions and jostling priorities – had required change after change of him, in direction and mood, always demanding more than time and patience could give. But all that, at least, has now thankfully receded, beyond the lychgate.

Time is his now. For a while yet, anyway.

And in this new dimension, this continuous present, inner and outer, past and present embrace easily. This darkening swathe of evergreen, this laurel, that daphne, those junipers, each and severally, he now perceives more clearly than ever before, since all are being reborn, recast in his mind: the same shapes rooted in the same earth as before, but waymarks now of a new order unfolding, unhurriedly, from within him. *Apparenze d'apparenze.*

Inner silences made visible.

***

The jungle had "released" him. But only into another kind of jungle.

XXV

'Hello, I'm home, mam!'

Closing the door quietly, Rosemary senses at once that something is amiss. The silence that falls on her cheery greeting proclaims it.

Steeling herself for whatever comes, she slowly hangs her coat, her beret and her schoolbag in the hall, then pauses at the dining-room door, which is barely ajar. But she has no alternative.

She pushes at the door and slips into the room.

'I'm sorry I'm late...' she begins cheerily once more, hopeful still she may be able to retrieve the situation – whatever the situation is. But then she sees the open letter, like a gash, on the table, midway between her stony-faced parents, each of whom seems clenched in airless space, masticating slowly, so slowly they seem almost to be grinding the morsels of food they fork into their mouths at ever longer, more desperate intervals.

So, it's come then, from school, the letter.

She stands waiting some way behind her father's chair as if frozen. No words will reach her lips. Her pulse is racing.

After some moments, her father turns and stares at her. He stares for what seems forever.

'Are you our daughter or are you not?' he asks finally, in that stentorian voice he always assumes whenever, a smallish man, he counterfeits growth in stature, and authority.

'Am I...? I'm sorry, I don't know what you mean, dad.' Rosemary's face twitches, as she tries to keep herself from laughing out loud.

But dad's moment is already over, shouldered aside as her mother blusters in, impatient, irrational, truculent.

'This Mrs Appleton, who is she? How do *you* know someone in Sheffield that we don't? In Sheffield!' And she picks up the letter, brandishing it like a sword, in triumph, above her head.

The tension in Rosemary's face vanishes, and her eyes open wide with wonder, and joy. Mrs Appleton! Mrs Appleton, she's alive! And so, therefore, surely, is Jason. Laughing and ignoring all this ridiculous rigmarole, laughing, though with tears welling up in her eyes, she steps in closer and makes as if to take the letter from her mother's hand.

But the hand is snatched back, and Rosemary loses her balance over the table, knocking over a jug of milk in her attempt to save herself.

Her mother leaps to her feet.

'You clumsy, stupid, deceitful girl!' she shouts, smacking a hand hard across Rosemary's cheek, even as her daughter opens her mouth to say she is sorry. 'Now, answer my question at once,' she demands. 'Who is this woman? And this Jason she speaks about, who is he? We have a right to know!' she shrieks, in her hysterical, stubborn fury.

Overwhelmed by this absurd ignorance and its unjust consequences for her, all Rosemary can do is slump down onto a chair, and let the tears come. It is all too much.

But her mother is remorseless. 'There. I thought as much. What did I tell you, Percy?' And she turns to her husband, who nods slowly, sadly, sagely, chewing on.

How Rosemary despises them and their narrow-minded obsessions! Why can't her mother just send her to her room, as she usually does, and put an end to this meaningless charade? Then later she can come down and explain and…

'Oh yes. We've really caught you out this time, haven't we, young lady? Seeing this… Jason… and the woman, whoever she is – how long did you think you could…?'

'Mam, Jason's a…'

'Don't you dare interrupt – do you hear me? How long did you think you could get away with it, eh? Now, we demand to know who he is and what you get up to and where you go, and… and another thing. In future, you're to come straight home from school, you hear me? And there'll be no going out, oh no, not unless we can be absolutely sure where you are going. Church and Sunday school – that's all – unless you're going somewhere with us. Do you understand? Your father and me, we've had quite enough of your sly, underhand ways. Do I make myself clear? So, come on, who is this Jason?'

'Mam, Jason's…' But Rosemary's throat constricts, her conflicting, pent-up emotions all vying with each other for instant release. And her father, his eyes gleaming with self-righteousness, leaps into the silence.

'Ah, so now we're getting to the truth, Ethel, and not before time.'

'Well, what are you waiting for you stupid girl?' her mother barks. 'Tell us!'

'Yes mam….' And still sobbing, Rosemary starts to explain how Mrs Appleton is an old lady she met in the park, and… 'And I help her, Mam, she's very kind, and… and she asked me…'

Rosemary's eyes then fall on the crumpled letter lying on the table, beyond her reach. And now, more than anything else in the whole world, she wants to be able to read it, to know that both of them are all right. 'Mam, I just need to know she's… Please, mam, could I just…?' And her begging eyes fix on the letter. 'It's so important that I…'

'Oh, no! First the explanation, young lady, then we'll see about the letter. So answer my question, right away. Who *is* this Jason?'

Rosemary steps forward. 'Jason's a dog, mam,' she announces into their suddenly stunned, bristling silence. 'He's a beautiful Alsatian dog!'

Happiness, anger, frustration, and impatience all rage within her. Surely *now* it will be all right and she can read the letter, *surely* she can. Maybe they can even laugh about it, later… But just now she must wait, she knows that, and there is nothing for it, not if she is to have any hope of seeing the letter. Why don't they say something? Crestfallen, she stares at her mother, then sharply away, trying to free her voice, to bridle her erratic breathing, still curdled by sobs.

But this supreme effort at control throws her off guard. She starts to explain that she has been taking this old lady's dog out each day for weeks now, and she stresses her dedication to her charitable task. They'd even been up on the moorland.

'Yes, mam. Most days. Even whole mornings, or afternoons sometimes...That is...'

Realising her slip at once, she tries to backtrack, but, too late. And her mother pounces.

'Did you hear that, Percy? Did you hear? She's been missing school, as well as everything else!'

Rosemary opens her mouth but her mother's wild, staring eyes are back on her in a flash.

'You've been playing truant, haven't you? Haven't you? And we thought we could trust you! What fools we've been! Does your deceitfulness know no limits? And how often have you played truant, eh? Answer me!' Then her voice changes key as a new realisation breaks in upon her. 'So *where* have you been when you should have been at school? What *else* have you been up to, and who with?'

Rosemary slumps in her chair, helpless before this onslaught of cold, cruel anger. Is there really no way out of the snare she has blundered into? She hangs her head, shaking it from side to side, unable to speak, to find words which are big enough or whole enough to say the things that have grown inside her in these past months, perhaps years.

Yet her mother, floundering in her own self-pity, interprets her daughter's silence for stubbornness, for dumb insolence. She leaps to her feet, and even as she is uttering these new accusations, relishing the drama of it, snatches up the letter and starts to tear it into tiny shreds.

'Mam...!' Rosemary screams, 'what are you doing...?'

'There!' her mother gloats. 'That'll teach you! That's a lesson you're never likely to forget!' And in a final flourish of triumph she crosses the room and flings the shredded letter at the fireplace, where, as if counter to the thrower's desire for effect, it cascades, like myriad snowflakes, into and around the hearth.

Wide-eyed, Rosemary grips the edge of the table, aghast at this act of wanton cruelty. Dumbfounded, she leans forward to scrutinise her mother's blotched, red face, searching for some clue to this incredible violation. And slowly she nods, miserably to herself. Yes… Loud and hurtful on the outside, and all meanness on the inside – oh, she knows all about this sort of thing; it's Rosalind all over again. And any reaching out, false, any show of softness just calculated to…

'What are you staring at, you little fool…?' her mother cries. And she plants her feet and sets her arms akimbo, gearing herself up for yet another onslaught.

Her father leans forward, placing his forearms firmly on the table.

'Now calm yourself, Ethel, d'you hear?' he cajoles, perhaps sensing that some sort of limit has been reached, even crossed. 'She's not worth making yourself ill over.'

This cautionary note notwithstanding, he cannot let the matter drop.

'See how you've upset your mother, young lady! I hope you feel proud of yourself. How you must hate us to treat us like this. We've tried to give you a decent, Christian upbringing; we've tried to give you everything you ever wanted. And this is how you repay us…'

But Rosemary can take no more. She stands up, full of cold anger, and rounds on her father.

'"Christian"? "Christian"? What's "Christian" about it?' she shouts. 'Where is all the love there's supposed to be, the understanding and the forgiveness? Your sort of Christianity's a sham, a show-off – strutting up and down our street on a Sunday with your bible in your hand, so the neighbours can see! That's what it is, and something to chain *me* up with. What *she* just did to *me* was *far* more hurtful than she even hoped for, and I'll *never* forget or forgive it as long as I live. *Never!*' Red in the face, breathing hard, she turns away from them and stares, stonily, at the patterned wallpaper. But then she becomes aware that her father has risen and is moving towards her.

'Who do you think you're talking to, eh? Who d'you think you are to talk to us like that?'

And if, a moment or two before, the man had been trying to

pour oil on troubled waters, now he too is beside himself with rage. He rises over his daughter, like a storm, and hits her hard across her mouth with the flat of his hand.

Rosemary staggers backwards with the force of the blow, against the wall. Yet, even though the blow stings, seeming to intensify as it spreads all over her face, she is beyond tears. Livid with cold, indignant anger, she growls through clenched teeth: 'If you *ever* do that to me, again, you'll be sorry. You'll regret it for the rest of your days.' And she thrusts herself forward to stand and face up to him.

Taken aback, the colour drains from his face, but then blustering, flustered, he croaks: 'Go to your room at once! At once, d'you hear me? And stay there! There'll be no tea for you, tonight!'

Rosemary glares at his flabby, white face, at the saliva at the corners of his mouth and flecked on his chin and then at her mother, hunched up on her chair, snivelling into her handkerchief, contemptible victim of her own stupidity, wallowing in self-pity. How she loathes them.

She turns on her heel and quits the room.

The owl's cry comes loud. And listen. There it is again, loud as before.

XXVI

Weeds, weeds weeds – scourge upon scourge of the damn things at every completed level, and the higher up he goes...

The garden's upward reaching is also Dan's own, but however much he seeks to embody within it the notion of perfection in as intransient a form as possible, he is ever more aware of the stealthy, creeping, all-consuming corruption that is everywhere hell-bent on havoc.

His energies and patience are stretched to the utmost.

And his original notion of a good earth? It seems naively romantic, now.

Washing lettuce at the sink after a day of moiling and toiling up the wet garden, Dan sighs heavily. The "good earth" – like the "body beautiful" – had latent within it all the poisons needed for its own dissolution back into chaos. It was full of noxious gases, suppuration, melanomas, all endlessly demanding their own actualisation, always at the expense of everything else. The seemingly passive earth was in fact no different from whatever crawled upon it, endlessly devouring to endure, to be devoured; the massacre was everywhere and total.

And this, it comes to him in a flash, was the overriding tragedy of life – this competitive insatiability, *the* driving principle of all physical being. And the convolvulus – misshapen chaos of well-seeming forms – was its epitome!

Pretty to behold, with its exquisite white trumpet heralding its manic zest for life, it outrooted, out-grew, outdistanced all its rivals, pulled them down and throttled them, if the gardener were not attentive. An endless struggle. The lion and the wildebeest played over in endless, imperceptible slow-motion.

Dan shakes his head, then smiles bitterly. Here it is again, the ironic realisation that his purpose demands recourse to the brutal manner of a stronger, bolder, uncompromising enemy – the convolvulus invading his garden, his peace. And he, alone, cannot prevail: the best devices of his mind are as nothing when set against its wiles.

Is it only aspiration that matters, then, this entire world, blossoming within him which might just carry him away beyond the interminable struggle with blind physicality, which always ends in a heap of excrement, then dust?

Dan rises from the table and carries his plate over to the pedal bin. Raising the lid, he tips his half-eaten salad into it. What a waste, he thinks, making a mental note to buy less of it in future, before he turns away, back to his book and his wine.

Of late, he has been trying, yet again, to read Cervantes' masterpiece, realising, as he slowly progresses, that he and the perhaps not-so-mad Manchegan were travelling parallel roads. What is his garden if not a barely manageable act of defiance? And is it not also representative of a radical change of state, from chaotic and destructive to the prescribed and orderly – as is Quixote's faith in an antique chivalry, itself just such a combative, ordering principle?

Yes, he thinks, the garden is fragile. It is but a fleeting glimpse of a state which, though attainable, cannot long survive in the prevailing circumstances of this world. Chaos is the ever-returning constant. Still, here is his quixotic… what? hope – *not* faith – that it may yet prove to be a kind of antechamber… or anti-chamber?

Like the lychgate: setting down the bier between two worlds, waiting for the storm to pass, for the mediating priest to come.

Close on midnight, after an evening in his study, Dan finds himself still battling with these speculations, since there is something he cannot get into focus, but which feels relevant. Something he'd come across once, perhaps in a play, where, in order to bring a desired state into being, physical things normally associated with that state are accumulated, as in a shrine, until the absent ideal, no longer able to resist the attractive power of its habitual context, has no choice but to reappear.

He stands, suddenly, and *Don Quixote* slips to the floor, momentarily unnoticed. Isn't the garden just such an accumulation? But to attract what, precisely? Oh, why, why is he always on the edge of something, something momentous even, but which eludes his grasp? Is he too distracted, or are there simply too many disparate elements to piece it all together?

Or is he imagining it, sensing it because he desires it?

Dan bends to retrieve the book and place it respectfully on the table. It is sleep he needs more than anything else, just now. His eyelids are heavy, his mind weary.

But still he stands there. The garden... the garden... His purpose drives him forward, that is obvious, but its nature is vague, incomplete, and tonight he feels disoriented and vulnerable. What is this...?

Oh, to Hell with it!

He snaps off his desk lamp, and, once his eyes have adjusted to the sudden dark, gropes his way through into the bedroom. To sleep.

***

Hints and guesses, sweet honeysuckle threading in and out, bindweed, woodbine. Letters also, gently intertwining.

In my little dream world... Yes, suddenly, this seeming... flurry... of letters, letters which stop time in its tracks but whose relevance diminishes as time resumes and leaves their worlds behind in utter isolation... and yet still able to affect; and sometimes devastatingly so, years after.

***

Rosemary wakes with a start, though in truth she had drifted only momentarily across the borders of sleep. Peering into the darkness of the bedroom, she listens intently for any sign of movement, either upstairs or down. She feels almost faint, worn out by her tears of grief and relief, and by her frustrated desire to retrieve the tattered fragments of her happier future, lying in and around the dining-room hearth. Faint, yes, and nauseous, as the emptiness of hunger relentlessly tightens its grip on her stomach and her mind.

Her thoughts circle round and round, impatient at this silly waste of time, wholly intent on her quarry; like a huntress stalking those little white birds, glimpsed, then lost, then half-perceived again in the thickening gloom.

And still she waits.

The town-hall clock strikes the quarter… or was it the half? Then, after an age, disappointingly, comes the half, so again the agony of waiting. Quarter to, now, is that? And on she goes, casting her mind's eye this way and that, coming always up against the wall of darkness, the emaciation of a world she had once believed in as so plentiful.

Leaning back into her pillows, she once again straddles the border country between sleep and waking. Then her mother appears from nowhere, eyeless, and gaunt, her father a wraith hovering over the tattered fragments, a great long pen extending like a finger from his hand, jabbing at her, towards her eyes, and she is unable to back away, and…

Her panicked cry wakes her.

She sits up, counts the distant chimes. Three, or four… or has she missed some, catching only the last few of many? Three o'clock now, surely. It couldn't *still* be before midnight… could it?

Her fists rise, then beat down on the eiderdown, in her frustration that nevertheless must be contained. Then suddenly she decides. She will creep out as if she were on her way to the bathroom. Then when she reaches the top of the stairs, if all is still silent…

Beyond this point, she knows there is only defiance and her own truth. And off she tiptoes, and quietly descends, counting each step.

Kneeling in front of the fireplace she gropes around blindly, and then more urgently, but her fingers light on nothing, not one single shred of paper. She shuffles forward and tries again in the hearth, but in vain. Where is it all? Her heart starts to pound as she realises that she must risk the light if she is to be sure, one way or the other. Moving carefully, she crawls towards the corner until she reaches the standard lamp, and feels her way up its length to the switch beneath the shade.

The sudden flood of light blinds her. After rubbing her eyes in a frenzy of impatience, blinking, she looks round, towards the fireplace.

Empty.

She sighs, glances up at the clock on the mantelpiece which shows a little after four, and back at the hearth. Empty, yes, but nothing seems to have been burned there.

Scrambling to her feet Rosemary crosses the room to the sideboard, holding her breath. She peers into bowls, behind ornaments, under tiny lace mats, but there's nothing, and despair surges up inside her. She turns back towards the tell-tale light, her heart newly pounding, then makes her eyes travel in a wide, slow arc around the room.

And there it is! A little heap of torn paper stacked neatly at one corner of the polished table! Maybe her dad had gathered it all up.

Quick as lightning, her frantic hands scoop it up and slip it into her dressing gown pocket. Switching out the light, she stands for a moment, trying to bridle her heaving emotions and re-accustom her eyes to the dark, before beginning the perilous ascent back to her room.

Fighting her impatience, she counts the steps, wondering which of them has recanted. Oh, how she scorns their crabbed, mean, little world! Eight, nine... No, more likely the torn-up letter had been placed there by her mam, to use as further torment in the morning. Twelve, thirteen... Well, too late, *she* has it now!

Back in the safety of her room, Rosemary drapes her black underskirt over the bedside lamp, and, using a tall atlas as a tray, sets to work to piece the letter together, fighting weariness. She has to do it now, for if they discover it's missing, she'll be forced to give it up.

Oh but, Mrs Appleton...!

Rosemary is almost crying with relief. Her face lights up and she chuckles to herself, realising that once she has the letter's message – and the address, she mustn't forget the address – she can... Oh, she'll show them. She'll creep back down and replace the pile on the table, just as she found it! Yes, and she'll grab three or four biscuits from the tin in the larder while she's at it. Oh, she'll show them all right! Then her face turns serious. When *she's* a mother, she'll make sure she isn't mean, and shows her children love and kindness, always. If she ever has any.

Rosemary turns to her task with a will, and it isn't long before she has the address and the opening lines before her on her makeshift table. Just as well she'd done all those jig-saw puzzles when she was little – she'd been famous for doing them; on wet Sunday afternoons when, well, what else was there to do? Quickly, taking no chances, she copies down the address and telephone number, and slides the slip of paper between the pages of a story book which she repositions on the bottom shelf of her little bookcase. There! Then she jumps back into bed and turns her attention to the remainder, anxious to know everything at once.

Oh, but... what had happened to Mrs Appleton's handwriting? She'd admired it so many times – on letters she posted for her, or on those little shopping lists, written on the backs of last year's Christmas cards: firm and round and ever so neat. But you could hardly read it now, in places. The letters were like squiggles, with some words not even finished, making it more like guesswork than reading.

'Poor Mrs Appleton,' she murmurs. 'Whatever can have happened to you?'

Rosemary's sadness is spontaneous, and real enough, yet she is all too conscious that the old lady's primary importance is as *her* only link with Jason... although, if they'd killed Jason... oh she can hardly bear to think it... but if they had, Mrs Appleton would be even more important: there was no one else who could talk about him with her, help keep him alive in her mind. No one at all.

But five minutes later, there are tears of joy in her eyes. 'Oh

Jason… you're safe,' she whispers, 'you're all right! Thank God you're all right.'

And she leans back in relief against her pillows, before reading on.

But Mrs Appleton isn't safe. She's had 'a bad turn', leaving her feeling 'very queer' and 'not quite my old self'. Oh no… 'I don't know when Jason and I will be home again, dear, but as soon as I do, I will let you know, and in the meantime, we must keep in touch by letter.'

By letter…? Rosemary's face clouds over. And… how *can* she come home if her house is up for sale?

It didn't make any sense. And the more she thinks about it the more she feels something else is wrong.

The son and his wife, had they taken the decision to keep her with them because Mrs Appleton is far more ill than she thinks she is…? Could they do that? Keep her there and not tell her, or about her house? Rosemary's heart lurches suddenly. But… if Mrs Appleton stays on in their small house that would be even smaller when the baby came… what about Jason?

Jason, with his coat so smooth, his cold nose nestling into her.

Rosemary starts to cry again, softly. But then, in a flash, she knows what she has to do. She has to go to this son's house *herself* to know the truth of it. And she *definitely* has to to find a way of having Jason. She *has* to. Because if… if Mrs Appleton died, they'd just get rid of him.

So she needs a plan.

***

Consoling though it is, the letter is only a reprieve. And maybe that is all one can ever hope for in a world that has gone so wrong.

XXVII

Dan's time is always precious up on the hillside. And whatever he does each day, however quickly, he is always conscious of it seeping away, for it is all the things he is not doing that he feels he has to do, now, at once, endlessly.

Like a cat chasing its tail.

Nevertheless, he drops the secateurs, the dibber and the twine into his pocket and straightens up, stiff as a scarecrow, contemplating his achievement both above and below him. Consolatory, yes, but not sufficiently so to wipe away his consciousness of earlier failings.

'Rosalind' he murmurs quietly, then more loudly, again. 'What was it that turned to hatred in you?'

Sometimes there are faces, or images of doing or saying, which memory frames for him, yet – like cinema stills, with no future or past – so often fails to name, so that they die a second time, withering out of their half-life through lack of nourishment at the root.

Of all those second-formers – as they'd been when he first knew them – it had been Rosalind who had first stood out. At the staffroom door, a little insistent, pleading: she just couldn't get the hang of colons and semi-colons, couldn't see their point, like with apostrophes, so could he just…? And so he'd spent half an hour with her in their form room after school, explaining, giving examples. Later, it had been parsing, then clause analysis, and while focusing on these problems of English, inevitably, little by little, the girl's intelligence, her winsome spark had come through, but also, hints about her home life. Her father, a gambling man, always out of work and often drunk; her mother never at home, out every evening dancing; and the rows, the never-ending rows.

"Disadvantaged", yet bright and eager to learn, she'd garnered his sympathy with ease, a "worthy cause", and so he had persevered, given his time. Then one evening he'd met her parents at a parent-teachers' meeting. Holding hands, smiling together, talking earnestly, genuinely concerned about their daughter's education, and nothing like the monsters Ros had described. Perplexed by the stark contradiction, he'd asked around in the staffroom. And it transpired that far from being unemployed, her father was a weaving over-looker at Lister and Moss's, while her mother, formerly a staff nurse at the Royal Infirmary, was a full-time housewife, on the local WI committee, and worked as a volunteer in the Oxfam shop.

So, what was Rosalind up to? Why the self-dramatising untruths? From then on, he'd been more wary, and not quite so "available" when the girl came calling. Not that it had diminished his liking for her, her ready smile, her cheek, but had his gradual "cooling off" been at the root of her eventual hostility? Was that it?

Thus, it is not only the hoeing and weeding that slow Dan's progress towards the summit, but these frequent upsurges of memory, memories that time has pruned, coppiced, transplanted and patiently teased out, until they blossom before him like roses, newly living in their colour, their shapes, *and* their thorns.

Will he ever reach the topmost height, he wonders, pausing as he mounts the steps, looking up the field and realising how much yet remains to be done? And if he does, will this crowning be the kind of triumph his toiling has so tentatively surmised?

Once, in her enthusiasm, Rosalind had said it was his different way of talking to them that mattered: 'as if we *count* for something, we're not just silly, ignorant children.' And maybe it was so. Now, of course, he talks to no one, and hasn't in a long time – unless you count the odd word in passing to the Taylors, or the Earnshaws, in their beds of roses, and to these tumbling images from a distant past, their *pastness* perhaps disturbing him most of all.

At the school back then, he most probably *hadn't* fully understood what he was about. A new teacher after all, plying continually between the "traditional way" imposed by his own school years, then by Albert Kelday's well-meaning guidance – and what he had so newly learned at university, and was still learning, an instinct for something deeper. But was it his "lack of experience", as some older colleagues had decided, or these different, more urgent criteria of relevance and engagement that had propelled him? He had felt it so powerfully – this need for openness, for questioning, and making connections between things, and learning to differentiate. Later of course, such "rebellious" ways had become fashionable, the new norm – when the world really had seemed to belong to the young. But this world had changed again all too quickly, had hardened into a new "order" of rhetoric, of control, of commercialised passiveness and conformity: with their blue jeans turned inside out, as it were!

Dan picks up the hoe and moves on to the next bed to tackle the young thistles before their roots thickened and tangled.

Considering it now, though, how honest had he been, then? Even with himself? Hard to say, now, of course, half a lifetime later… But at first, whilst ever the pupils had remained at a distance, hardly known, his questioning approach had been easy. Yet once they began to emerge as individuals, with their differences, even in their attitudes towards his approach, then other expectations had started to take shape in them. And he'd been flattered by this sudden "elevation"; it had seemed to confirm the validity of his method, his "success" in engaging their curiosity and interest.

All those discussions after school, arranged or extempore, with the brightest of them, those who had engaged, like Saunders, Rosemary, and Rosalind; the various diversions from his planned lessons; his readings from Steinbeck, Hemingway, Packard, and other "adult" books; and the occasional visits he'd organised, to the theatre or cinema; once, he'd even had some of them home.

And then what? Perhaps too self-congratulatory, he had allowed his ideal to lapse into something else: having this "following" among pupils had meant that he'd then become *their* prisoner. His approach, or strategy, if you could call it that, had borne its own nemesis.

Dan shakes his head, wistfully. Thus entangled, he'd had little time for anything else. And so the other pupils, the less attractive or less sure of themselves, had felt excluded, and resentful. And of course they had – easy to see, now. But at the time he had probably seen this as their choice, rather than his failure to bring them on board. And that was worse, far worse.

Automatically, unconsciously almost, Dan gathers his tools together, then walks smartly over to the main path to begin his descent. But every few yards he stops and stares into space.

Why *hadn't* he recognised these defects at the time? Why do they plague him still? Why should *any* of this matter to him now, after half a lifetime?

Feeling suddenly gloomier than he has in a while, Dan quickens his pace, anxious to slough off these plaguing shadows.

Yet still they persist.

It had all gone wrong, of course, then. But later, when their Mr Teal was long gone and far away, what had they taken with them of him, he wonders? Had his teaching counted at all? When Saunders and others were at university or college, or in some job, trying to make sense of a world seemingly turned upside down, had any of them made the connection between the air they breathed now as young adults and what he had shown them then, through his questioning of their previously unquestioned "values"?

And all that hostility, had it subsided as soon as he'd left, or eventually? Had the ghosts been laid to rest?

Dan leans across to rake up some stray thistles. He will never know, of course. He can only hope, as would any teacher, that the abiding memory of him might have been of appreciation. But who could say? 'Rosalind' he murmurs, almost smiling, 'whose snowy lamb put out claws…'

Abruptly, he checks his pockets for secateurs, then veers away off the path, towards a rose bush. Pulling on his gloves to protect himself from the thorns, he snips away at its suckers, all the thrusting, unproductive green stalks.

***

'I can't talk now,' Titania whispers, quietly putting down the receiver. And she jumps round and prepares a smile for mummy and daddy just then coming through into the sitting room after supper.

And the next night, and the next, on tenterhooks, listening out for the phone, and after all's been cleared away, she hurries through again. Of course he'll phone… but… watching the door… please, now, it has to be now…

And he will. If it is something urgent, he will. Of course he will.

But it's not until the Saturday afternoon, three whole days later, that Titania will hear those low, resonant tones that send tremors up and down her spine.

But, but what is he saying? What? *Where*…? She can't seem to take it in. *All* of them going?

She knows from his letters that he's been looking for a new job. But it had never crossed her mind it might be so very far away. For good and all, and…

Next *Tuesday*?

'I've got to go now,' she says, fighting back the sudden tears… and keeping the receiver pressed to her ear.

'I have to see you. When can I see you?' he whispers.

Gently, ever so gently, Titania lays the phone on its cradle. Then she runs upstairs, throws herself down on her bed, and sobs into her pillow.

'Supper's ready – it's on the table!'

Vaguely, distantly, Titania hears her mother's call. She sits up, but can't even begin to compose herself before her mother is there, in the room.

'Whatever's the matter, my darling?' And she sits down beside her daughter, stroking her hair, slowly, rhythmically.

Titania starts crying again. 'Oh mum, I can't bear it…'

And for a while, they just sit there, mother and daughter, the mother perhaps understanding long before her daughter finds the words.

Slowly, hesitantly, Titania explains how it had continued even after she went to college.

'Just sometimes, mummy, by letter mainly.' How could it not?

'And now?'

'And now he's going away... not just leaving, mummy, they're going overseas, and I can't.... You *can't* just stop loving someone to order, you just can't.'

And her mother silently comforts her, sparing her daughter the sharpness, the admonitions of the previous summer when it had all first come out.

'I did try, mummy. Honestly, I did, but... it kept coming back.'

'Shush, now, that's not important, not now. Come on, love, let's go downstairs.'

Titania eats a little, grateful that no more is said, but then returns to her room, desolate in the darkness.

Why is he abandoning her? Why now, and so suddenly, so cruelly? Just when...

It was like knowing you were going to die.

On Sunday, she takes Prince out for a long walk on the moor, in rain which gradually turns to sleet, then snow. She *has* to be alone, to think, to try and understand her newly empty, lonely, horrible world.

His last letter at college, less than two weeks ago, it hadn't even hinted... not at *anything* like this. What did it mean?

On Monday, in town, she looks out for him, goes where he might go, even sits reading fitfully for a while in the library. But she knows it's unlikely; they'll be busy getting ready, packing up. And her tears well and spill over at the starkness of this thought. But she just *can't* let him go like that, without a word, some explanation, with so much left unsaid, without at least saying goodbye.

Tuesday comes. And Titania's whole being is reduced to this one, overwhelming need.

Nervously she fiddles with the gate-catch, walks up the path.

The back door is ajar. And even before she knocks, the finality of it all bursts in upon her. Through the kitchen she sees into the living room, the tea-chests, the boxes, cases, the bare walls, so much emptiness.

She gasps and stares at it all, not having taken it in till this moment, not really, that *this* is how it is, and they aren't coming back here. Not ever.

She steps back, afraid now. Shouldn't she just…? Or…? And she turns, hesitates, frozen in indecision.

'Hello… Titania.' The calm, friendly voice.

And she is trapped.

'I… I came to say goodbye and… and good luck!' she falters, trying to compose her features, while surreptitiously looking for him, listening for him.

But he isn't here, her heart just knows he isn't, even before Penny confirms that he has slipped into town with the twins.

'…Cancelling the bread order, the papers, taking books back to the library. All these last-minute things, you know.'

She nods, her stomach churning. 'Is it… this afternoon that…?' And the absurdity of the question strikes her, even as she speaks it.

'Yes, we're just about ready. We're leaving after lunch, about two. But – Penny shrugs – you'll probably see him. He'll be on his way back, by now.' And she moves the door, just a fraction.

Titania half smiles, half turns, and steps back. 'I'll go now,' she murmurs, hating him for having put her… them… in this impossible position. 'You must have… things still to do.' She fights back her tears. 'I just thought…'

This time, Penny doesn't help her at all, and they stand facing each other, passing over, already, into an unending silence.

Titania looks down. She must say… something. 'I'm sorry that… for all the pain and worry I must have…'

'It doesn't matter.' Penny pulls her cardigan round her. 'Not now. It wasn't anyone's fault, I always understood that.'

The sky is clear, the grass laced with frost, reflecting a cold, white sunlight.

Then, already backing away, awkwardly, the thought – a lifeline.

'Please,' she says, softly, earnestly, 'will you write, let me know how things are going? And… may I write too, every now and again?'

Penny smiles, seems to consider her request, but then pushes the door a fraction more. 'Let's… see how it goes,' she says.

'If I don't see him… them… please, say goodbye for me.'

Closing the gate behind her, Titania knows she must hurry. He will be looking for her, she knows that, and she wants him more in this moment of piercing clarity, more than anything else in the whole world.

But she *cannot* meet him. She could not survive meeting him. No, not now. She must take another road – one he will not come by.

It begins to sleet again. Titania huddles down into her duffle coat, thrusts her hands deep into its pockets. The moment, and the world, have slipped between her fingers and are falling endlessly away.

***

'When can I see you?' he'd asked. But she hadn't answered. And for her, perhaps, whatever she'd felt, then, had come to matter a little less each day, as she slowly, gradually forgot.

Yet for him, these last, whispered words had echoed on, day in, day out. Even in times of distraction they'd been there, the shadow world they framed suddenly reappearing, to corrode all hope, ambition, belief.

'When can I see you? When will I see you again?'

On and on. Two years in the East had felt like an abysm of time, then. But he'd had to do it, do something to cut the net, to free them all.

And after two years, who was to say what their worlds would have become?

Dan picks up a hoe lying against a rock, but it slips from his grasp and falls with a dull thud on damp earth.

'When a plethora of words brings love tumbling to its knees, we prod about in dust piles, seeking conviction still that in the beginning is the word, the word is made flesh… and all that supposedly follows…'

Something he'd written at the time, or some time.

Alpha and omega. A gossamer-like thread leading up from the labyrinth.

He had eventually lived beyond it, of course, that time of darkness and its miserable revelations. That state of exile, which had come to seem like a destiny, with its empty longing slipping always between aspiration and fulfilment. Like a tree clustering shadow fruit, goading the child into throwing sticks and stones to bring them down, the child ever impatient for their season, which never came.

Nevertheless, here he is now, bending his mind, body and will to this stubborn hillside, tending this garden as if his dedication may yet heal the scars and disfigurements lodged in his being, this long legacy, scooped of all goodness. Living on beyond it all he had prospered and diminished, adjusting always to less and to more, in permanent exile.

Retrieving the hoe, Dan finishes off the long bed, cleaned now like a confession. The tares are out. The fires have died down, the smoke – blinding, choking – has drifted and finally cleared, and now only their fine ash remains. And now it is time, again, to go up and start into the new.

But is this peace?

Just beyond the hedge everything is massed and threatens as it always has: all clamouring for attention, if for just one brief flick of time's lashes; all clawing and struggling to survive a little longer; all seemingly eager to display resilience, whatever the circumstance.

He feels a light breeze blowing on his forehead, bearing with it the faint scent of roses. Is it roses? Wings move within his hearing. Colour flashes briefly then dissolves back into the green shade. And he smiles, increasingly certain now, as in other interludes like this, of something imminent, though what it may be he still cannot say.

XXVIII

Her mother can't abide animals, so there's no point in asking, is there?

Scorn passes momentarily across Rosemary's face. And what's more, if she suspected it was important to her, she'd not rest till she'd found some way of using it against her – it's how she is, her mother.

Appalled by the stark truth of this last thought, she climbs to the top deck of the bus and sits at the front.

No, her parents are not an option. Pointless even considering them.

The bus speeds down the hill, past the school, and Rosemary moves with it, smiling smugly to herself. For two consecutive Sundays, now, morning and evening, she's done it! She has stared down the collection box shaken persistently under her nose, simply stared past it until its bearer got the message and moved on along the row. And she'll do it again next time too.

As they pass the drab factories, the run-down estate at the bottom of the hill, she smiles again, thinking how bread and potatoes, tea and sugar, indeed anything she has been sent to buy at the corner shop, have all suddenly become a little dearer. Ah, the cost of living!

A tax. Yes, that's it. A tax they have to pay, the Jason Tax – she giggles at the thought – and they haven't even noticed!

And thus, to her steadily mounting hoard of small change, Rosemary has added the sweet satisfaction of outwitting her spider-eyed mother who has been so flushed with the seeming success of her iron regime – with her daughter's now eager obedience to run errands, wash dishes, sweep steps – that she always finds a way of turning every conversation to that topic, with no matter whom, regardless of whether Rosemary is present or not.

'Spare the rod, I always say, and you spoil the child.'

Rosemary snorts. How she despises her parents' pettiness! A million miles from the world Danny had shown them. But that too, sunk now without trace.

But soon, soon, it will be all right. And the runaway bus, bouncing along the road, lends wings to this morning's elation. Soon now she'll be with Mrs Appleton and Jason! Just for a while, but with time enough to decide things.

Rosemary's trip has been planned down to the finest detail – she's been over it time after time, covering every eventuality.

And with her mother paying for it all!

Still smiling, Rosemary folds her hands in her lap, and sits back to enjoy the ride.

'It's Rosemary, isn't it?' An extremely pregnant young woman, Mrs Appleton's daughter-in-law, waves her inside. 'I'm Juliette, by the way,' she says, smiling broadly.

Rosemary nods, but she can hardly contain her excitement. She can hear Jason whimpering and scratching at another door, perhaps sensing her own presence, and she stares anxiously past Juliette, who puts a restraining hand on her shoulder.

'I must tell you,' Juliette whispers, 'you'll find mum much changed from when you saw her last. She's paralysed all down one side, and it's very noticeable in her movements and speech. And her face, it's quite… distorted.'

Mrs Appleton… paralysed? But what…?

'The doctor says she's not likely to improve much, if at all. And another stroke, well, she wouldn't survive it. I thought I should warn you before you see her.'

Rosemary nods, forcing herself to comprehend, to counter this sudden shock. 'Thank you for warning me,' she says, trying to sound calm and grown up. 'I shan't stay too long so as not to tire her.'

Then the door is opened, and Jason is through it in a flash, and on her, almost knocking her to the floor in his excitement.

'Oh, Jason, Jason… lovely Jason!'

The dog licks her face and Rosemary cannot hold back her tears, remembering all that time, that endless time in which she'd believed she would never see him, never hold him again.

Then she sees Mrs Appleton, and her tears perhaps also serve to cover this new shock. For whatever the daughter-in-law has just tried to convey in words is much worse, in reality, and she gasps, involuntarily.

Her friend's face is all twisted, her whole body twisted round, like that old tree in the park which they said had been struck by lightning.

'It's all right,' Juliette soothes, and Rosemary nods, embarrassed, then wonders if these words are meant more for Mrs Appleton than for her. She pulls Jason towards her, patting him, fondling his head and his ears. But then, conscious of paying too much attention to the dog, she tries to disentangle herself.

Would she be expected to… kiss Mrs Appleton? She feels her insides shrinking at the thought, and she hates herself for feeling like this.

With a supreme effort of will she goes and sits on the chair beside Mrs Appleton, and tries to picture her friend as she had been, to remember her many kindnesses, and all the little routines and formalities which had pleased her and kept a slight distance between them, ensuring both dignity and respect on both sides.

She closes her eyes, and then opens them again, but it makes no difference. It is still terrible seeing her like this, as if… as if an earthquake had gouged out her body in its single strike.

'So… so… kind you… come… Rose… Rose…'

'Oh but I wanted to.' And Rosemary tells her about coming on the bus, about never having been to Sheffield before, and about this, and that, babbling on in her continuing discomfort.

Then she comes to a halt. 'So… have you been out at all?' she asks, immediately hating herself for sounding like her mother.

Mrs Appleton starts to speak, but the physical effort of trying to find and form words frustrates her, and her awareness that her words, when finally out, are incomprehensible, causes her even more distress.

Drawing her chair in closer, Rosemary can see now that her friend is crying, the tears welling up and bursting in slow motion, though strangely, only in her right eye. Yet even as she tries to stop herself from staring, she sees a thin, slow stream of saliva starting to trickle from the left corner of Mrs Appleton's mouth, down her chin.

Rosemary looks anxiously, helplessly, at Juliette, who shrugs slowly, and shakes her head, standing behind her mother-in-law's chair. Then as Rosemary watches, Mrs Appleton's right hand slowly rises, and she dabs clumsily with her handkerchief at her eye, then at her mouth, and as she does so, she shakes her head, and looks away, in her distress. And Rosemary can't help thinking how strange it is that all three of them are pretending that everything's normal and behaving as if the old Mrs Appleton and this new one are the same person! As if people's tomorrows are the same as all their yesterdays – when, clearly, they aren't – or this new person doesn't really count, and that's not right.

But maybe, she thinks a moment later, it's just what you do, and if her grandma hadn't died when she was tiny, she might have known.

Did Juliette know these things already, before all this?

She looks round again at her, but Juliette is speaking quietly to Mrs Appleton, murmuring something that Rosemary can't quite catch; then she quits the room, closing the door quietly behind her.

Rosemary bites her lip, feeling even more awkward. She leans back in her chair, and then forward, looking at Mrs Appleton and thinking how brave the poor lady is being, really brave. How would it feel knowing you are dying and that a part of you has died already? She glances at her again, and shudders inwardly. But then maybe she doesn't know, or doesn't have thoughts any more. But she *is* dying, withering away. And all this, all their normal-sounding words and actions, she decides, are there to keep her from knowing it for a little while longer… from realising that so many bits of her are drooping or dribbling away.

Rosemary searches for her handkerchief, and blows her nose, conscious of the tears still on her lashes, all the while smiling and nodding at Mrs Appleton and hoping the old lady can see that she *understands*, that she *knows*, and that she *also knows* how *she* must be feeling.

But as Mrs Appleton nods and tries to smile her own understanding back at her, Rosemary suddenly feels a sort of emptiness inside. All the time she's been planning and scheming to be able to come here, Mrs Appleton has been like a shadow, just this vague figure in the background. Whereas Jason, dear Jason, he has bounded towards her time after time. And this meant, well, that…

Rosemary goes hot and then cold, like she does when she's about to be sick or faint. She swallows hard a few times, then glances over at Jason now lying on the hearth rug, and he raises his head and wags his tail at her. But she looks away, shamefaced: she's not being honest; she's a fraud, isn't she? Oh, but… Feeling terribly guilty, she looks around her, unsure what to do next. If only she could be more like Juliette, who clearly knows how to be, and what to do and say to deal with a sick old lady. Whereas she, she's just hopeless… like her dad said.

Out of her depth, Rosemary hangs her head, then looks about her through her lowered eyes, trying desperately to think of things to say, and she turns to Mrs Appleton and tries out a few of them, feigning enthusiasm for the colour of the curtains, the wallpaper pattern, even her lessons at school… But she hates herself – for being a fraud and not thinking all this through properly before coming; for only thinking about herself, and Jason. And when Juliette comes back into the room, she straightens up and says she'll have to be going, soon.

Juliette nods her understanding.

And after another failed attempt at conversation, Rosemary stands up, but almost immediately sits back down again, a gasp escaping her.

Mrs Appleton's right hand has shot up and is waving about in the air!

Wide-eyed, Rosemary sits there watching and waiting, so tense she almost forgets to breathe. It's as if the old lady wants to say something, so she sits on, expectant, but the silence only lengthens so she transfers her gaze to Juliette, who is fussing around behind Mrs Appleton's chair, pulling up her rug round her knees and straightening her head on the cushion. And as Rosemary watches her she wishes *she* could do something important too, for Mrs Appleton.

But then, with a flick of her ponytail, and a wan smile at Rosemary, Juliette moves towards the door. 'Let me make you a cup of tea before you go.'

And when the door is closed, slowly, Mrs Appleton's tired arm flops down, and trembling all the while, she begins to speak.

'Wha... abou... Jas...?'

'Jason?' Rosemary repeats, rather stupidly, frowning and cocking her head to one side.

Saliva dribbles from Mrs Appleton's chin, and she becomes agitated, her arm circulating again, furiously.

'Jaso...' she croaks again. 'When... I am... gone... Very soo...' And she slumps back in her chair, clearly exhausted.

Shocked by Mrs Appleton's unshrinking honesty, Rosemary's mind is racing to find words that will reassure, while not denying the truth of what she has so bluntly expressed. Has the doctor told her, then...? Beginning to tremble, she looks helplessly across at her, only to find those fierce, blue eyes already fixed hard on her own, eyes that will permit no falseness. She hesitates, shivering with emotion, holding Mrs Appleton's gaze.

And then it is suddenly as clear as day what she must say.

She leans forward and grips Mrs Appleton's wrist. 'When... that time comes,' she says, solemnly, 'Jason will come to me, I promise.' Then she sits back to observe the effect of her words.

And for the first time this afternoon, a smile struggles out from Mrs Appleton's weary eyes until it covers her twisted features. She reaches out her good hand, and Rosemary takes hold of it, and the other one again, and squeezes both gently.

The hands are cold and clammy, but they squeeze back affectionately, in a trust sealed, something important and shared. And Rosemary finds herself thinking that maybe this is what love is, these things together. And she smiles too. She stands then, releasing the hands, and bending forward she kisses Mrs Appleton on her papery, white cheek. And with a whimper Jason starts up from the hearth rug and nuzzles his way between them, and their smiles become open laughter. First, she, and then Mrs Appleton, lay a hand upon him, and ruffle his coarse coat.

'You will… co… again?' Mrs Appleton murmurs.

'Of course, I will. Just as soon as I've managed to…' Rosemary stops, embarrassed by what she was on the point of saying.

But Mrs Appleton has understood.

'Yes… yes…' the old lady says, 'you'll nee… your… your…' And her good hand tries its best to make thumb and fingers meet.

Rosemary smiles and starts to protest that she can manage. But Mrs Appleton seems no longer to be listening.

'Ma ba…' she raps out inarticulately. 'Ma ba….' And she gesticulates impatiently, wildly, with her good hand.

Rosemary looks about her, frowning, then recognises the handbag on a chair by the window. She opens it and holds it out towards Mrs Appleton. The old lady makes another impatient gesture, and, nodding, Rosemary begins rummaging inside it until her hand lights on the familiar purse. She takes it out and Mrs Appleton motions to her to open it quickly, as if there were not a moment to lose. And then she herself, her hand shaking visibly, takes out two pound notes and thrusts them into Rosemary's hand.

'But I don't need…' Rosemary starts to say, politely. But Mrs Appleton, looking as stern as she can manage in her pitiful condition, waves her protests away. So Rosemary folds the notes carefully and places them in one of the press-studded compartments of her own purse, which she immediately returns to the zip-pocket on the inside of her windcheater. She then replaces Mrs Appleton's handbag on the chair.

Mrs Appleton sighs and smiles, looking contented, peaceful even, now, nodding her head slowly, approving all.

The eventual leave-taking is swift and sudden, with Juliette intervening mainly so that Rosemary can slip away before Jason realises what is happening. And while Rosemary hates doing this to him, and to Mrs Appleton too, she knows it's for the best, especially now that it's certain she will be coming again. And she walks swiftly to the bus stop, to ensure she is home before her mother.

Only when she is on the bus does she realise she hadn't told Juliette about their arrangement for Jason – that he'd be coming to *her* when, when *the time* came. And she'd not drunk the tea she'd made for her, either. But – and she chuckles, feeling at the purse in her pocket – she can tell Juliette next time. Or maybe Mrs Appleton is telling her right now. So they'll probably have worked something out between them, before her next visit.

And smiling to herself, she settles back in her seat.

XXIX

The herb garden had not turned out well. Or rather, if aesthetically it may have pleased anyone who saw it, in structural terms it was altogether too precarious, clinging to the steeply sloping side of the bluff between the shrubbery and the rose arbour above it, squeezed where it should have stretched over a wider terrace.

Dan looks down at it, gloomily. It seems anything but the calm, decisive statement he had hoped for. He has miscalculated, leaving himself too little space for the last three levels, and thus a foot maze, which would also have required another quite considerable expanse of terracing, must remain a vague image in his mind. So much for perfection!

It is a disappointment, and his face puckers into a frown, recognising too that something has changed in him of late. In the early days, the bluff would have been levelled first to create a substantial terrace. If he had worked it all out properly in the beginning, he would have constructed all seven terraces before planting anything, wouldn't he?

It may be just the effects of an accumulating weariness, but Dan feels particularly impatient today at his limitations, both physical and imaginative.

Circling the top side of the bluff, his thoughts meander on, nevertheless, into the what-might-have-been. Working and planting from the top down, he might have avoided much traipsing up and down the whole length of the garden in that endless war with ever-latent chaos, particularly in the lower reaches.

Well, too late now! Such wisdom, always too late.

Another flawed Creation?

Scanning the newly planted herbs, first from this angle, then from that, he clambers up to the little space left, into which he has crammed the arbour and its roses, and his mind races for a moment, wondering, even now, if there may be some way of correcting it. But there isn't, not unless he uproots both the herbs and the arbour, and pushes the latter further back towards the pinnacle... which he could do, unmaking the herb garden, filling in the bluff until it was all *properly* level, giving it its own retaining wall, maybe. He ponders the idea awhile, until the thought of barrowing many tons of soil and rocks all the way up sinks in. It would be a Herculean task! And he no longer has the energy or the strength or the patience. And perhaps not even the time.

He shrugs, resigned. No, this is how it is, now. The vision has been trimmed, of necessity, and he must now live with it, for a little while longer.

The air grows chill. Yet there is something else his mind won't leave alone: this sensation of being watched, which has never really left him, not since the first time.

But who is doing the watching and why?

For a while, to try and dominate his growing discomfiture, he'd sought to reduce the unseen watcher to a shadow, as insubstantial and transient as all the other agglomerations of molecules in the garden – like a flower, a tree, a stone, the present and the past, each with its own shadow extending towards him and from which his own emerging universe has been taking shape. Then he'd tried to tell himself he was imagining it, that it was a sort of paranoia, the result of too much time spent alone. But the handkerchief, the cigarette butt, and more recently, what looked like footprints in the rain-soaked soil among the graves, they told a different story. The watcher is no flower or tree or stone, but an alien will with a different purpose, where only his purpose should be, alone.

The coiled spring, the latent strike. The snake in the garden.

Dusk falls. And yet, jaded and irritable though he is, he does not return immediately to the house but leans against a high flat rock near the crest of the hill, watching the stars switch on across the deepening dark blue vault of the sky. Then after a few moments, from behind a patch of low, thick, billowing cloud, the moon bursts through, flooding the whole garden, its silver light instantly liberating beds and pathways from their swaying shadows.

On how many nights has he climbed to this point to peer into this same deep mirror which, strangely, through its ever-changing, changeless criss-crossing of lights, seems to hint – like the garden itself – at a different ordering of sense, which lies beyond, and far outstrips mere substance? And each time that a shaft of moonlight singles out the small, rounded hummock and its sedum cover at his feet, as it does now, he feels a childlike thrill. And he marvels, disbelievingly, how he of all people has come to this point, surrendering half a lifetime's faith in reason to these flimsy scraps of... what, in this patch of star-and-moon-lit earth, through the lychgate?

Tonight, a long cloud slides slowly across the face of the moon, to eclipse it again, leaving only the stars. And suddenly, from this momentary preoccupation with light in the firmament, Dan is pitched back inside the vast space of the Great Pyramid where, plunged without warning into blackness, he had seen stars through an air vent, at three in the afternoon.

Stars in the daytime... had it really been so?

Closing his eyes now, he can almost feel those ice waves, shivering up and down his spine, in that fearful, impenetrable darkness. And even when someone had given their little group a plausible-seeming explanation, those tremors had remained, their icy fire far more real than any words.

But that experience had only been a beginning, hadn't it? For other, equally curious events were to follow.

***

The great cavernous space, whose extent seems endless on the inside, despite its precise external, geometrical configuration, is made bearable, though only just so, by the pinpoint of light moving slowly up towards them on the long steep slope. And huddling together behind the torch of 'McTavish', as their not-wholly-to-be-trusted guide had laughingly proclaimed himself, they hazard step after step, down, down, occasionally thrusting out a hand to touch a shoulder or a back for reassurance. And then, after what seems like agonised aeons of time, the lights finally cross, and the upward-coming column files silently past them in the confined space, some pausing briefly to let their opposite number pass, like ants touching in the emphatic dark. Then they are gone, worlds receding, a silent funeral. And under the immense weight of this crushing blackness, Dan's whole being is contracted into hope and fear, centring absolutely on McTavish's little point of light moving downwards, ahead of them.

But it comes to him in this darkness that he had been no stranger to these two extremes during his time in Malaysia, nor to looking always for some flicker of light ahead.

And when the members of his group are at last gathered in the great burial chamber, adjusting their eyes to the dim light offered by the naked bulb on the back wall, without warning *all* light is extinguished; and the echoing, floating, mocking voice of McTavish invites them to feel the weight of the darkness – and to wonder at the stars through the air vent. Sighs and gasps and little startled cries signal the reawakened terror. And Dan knows, in this moment, that all he has ever learned is as nothing when confronted by this fear, this primeval fear, which reconnects him instantly with the universal chaos of before and after his own brief transit.

Then, with a sadistic snicker, the guide snaps a switch. The atmosphere recharges instantly, and time and history resume.

McTavish's monologue, not always intelligible, drones on, but many of the group cluster tightly around their guide, in his long white burnouse, still visibly shaken. They hang on his every word, nodding vigorous approval at this new High Priest of Amon… or is he really Seth in disguise?

Moving noiselessly, detached, wide-eyed, about the great chamber, Dan senses the endless tramp of the frescoed figures round the walls.

He looks up at the painted ceiling, and down at the catafalque itself, absorbed instead in these silent witnesses of the agonies, hopes, and fears of a time long returned to dust. And, so possessed is he, that he does not notice his companions drifting towards the low doorway and the long, dark, upward slope. But then, suddenly realising he is alone, that flicker of panic again, and he hurries towards the low, shadowy opening by which they had entered. And already the point of light seems far away, and even further off another is inching its way down the higher slope towards the burial chamber.

He turns for a final glance before plunging off into the darkness. And then his heart skips a beat.

There is a shadowy figure near the catafalque – a woman, outlined in the wan light – and he gapes in bewilderment. Then he recognises her, though is no wiser as to why she's here: it's the woman he'd seen at lunch earlier, in the Hilton; Rufus, the ship's engineer, had pointed her out… her plunging neckline, and popping, overripe breasts as she reached towards a bowl of fruit further up the table. And he had sniggered along with the rest of the men.

But what is she doing? He takes a step or two towards her, uncertain. And even as he hesitates, she drops her dress to the floor and, entirely naked, clambers up onto the high slab. She is aware of his presence, he realises, though quite unconcerned, as if he were not there at all.

Slowly, sighing audibly, she lies back on the cold marble slab.

What…? With a sharp intake of breath he wrenches his eyes away, and peers back up the long tunnel. The points of light are still some distance apart. They should leave, follow on at once.

He glances back at the bizarre figure on the catafalque. After lunch, he'd caught sight of her again, when she'd passed through the open French windows onto the hotel's wide veranda: the intense sunlight had cut through the thin fabric of her dress, stripping and silhouetting her; and the engineer had unleashed more of his ribald, cutting wit.

'What was that verse of Ogden Nash's?' he'd mused, theatrically. And then, as if hauling in a distant memory:

Lovely form, decked in splendour,
How I love that form, my sweeting,
What grace, what poise, as you advance,
But have you seen yourself retreating?

And yes, the sight of her ample haunches had detonated an explosion of cruel laughter, while the engineer pulled hard on his cheroot, smugly savouring his own triumphal wit.

Stepping towards her now Dan assumes, as he had then, that her flamboyance is as transparent as her Indian muslin. He stoops and picks up the dress, and the knickers lying beneath it, and stands beside her. Her eyes are closed. And in the dim light he sees her no-longer young skin, parched and wrinkled with too much sun.

He speaks gently, leaning over her. 'There are people coming. You must hurry.'

But murmuring softly, she holds out her hand towards him, its fingers splayed. He makes to take hold of it, but deftly she slips out of his grip and her fingers tighten about his wrist. She pulls his hand down onto her breast, which is cold and flaccid, and she sighs deeply.

He whispers into her ear. 'Put your dress on, they'll soon be here!'

She sighs again, her eyes still tightly closed. Then abruptly she sits up, and he thrusts the dress into her outstretched hand. She pulls it over her head, swings her legs over the side of the catafalque, and as she slips to the ground yanks the dress down, but rejects the proffered underwear, which he quickly stuffs into his trouser pocket.

'There we are,' she murmurs, as the next guide stoops through the low doorway to usher in his blinking group, 'conveniently hidden from the world again.'

Dan takes her hand and pulls her towards the entrance, where they will wait until this new party, of Japanese tourists, has finished filing in, each one bowing to them, ceremoniously, as if they were departing deities.

And from these shadows, in limbo, half-way home from the Far

East, suddenly, and for just a moment, he is back with Titania on that warm midsummer's night; after Holly's farewell party and their long, joyous reconciliation in the park.

Almost three years, and yet… as if only yesterday.

'Promise me. Please, promise me, you'll always *be* there…'

And now, in the adjacent churchyard, she lies back upon a high, stone slab and pulls him down towards her. The stars, perhaps, or the unaccustomed cider she has drunk, desire churning away inside her…

All or none of these things. But her breath quickens, and she seeks his hand in the dark and places it over her young, firm breast. Holding each other, so close.

'Promise me…'

It had been a promise oh so readily made, and one which he had meant, had wanted so very much, to keep, always.

Dan releases the woman's hand. The new band of pilgrims has finally passed through into the chamber, and as the new 'McTavish' launches into his own litany, they duck out into the darkness.

With the woman now clutching tight hold of his upper arm, almost hanging on his body, they begin the climb back up the pitch-dark slope. Whatever had she been thinking, back there on the catafalque? And what was she thinking now, surely not unaware of the fire she had stirred up in him?

Titania clings tightly to him, as he to her, as slowly, so very needful of each other, they leave the churchyard; wondrous, heady moments, which he would gladly have lived forever.

Their arms round each other, heads pressed together, stopping here, kissing there, even outside her grandparents' house.

On and on and right up to her garden gate, where he stands and watches as she silently lets herself in with her key, before turning away, enraptured.

The midnight streets had been deserted, and that too had contributed to their recklessness. But he had held back, sacrificed desire and opportunity then, as now, in this dark place, to vague notions of honour, honesty, and in Titania's case, to the hope of a rosier tomorrow, when all would be well... all would be well.

And here in the stygian darkness, Dan sighs and smiles at these ironies, for the ache is always there.

But his fear of stumbling, of perhaps bringing this woman crashing down upon him, injuring one or both, even, compels him to concentrate on the moment, on placing one foot carefully before the other, and guiding her. There are no steps, only the centuries-old sand and dust upon which one could all too easily slip, if in too much of a hurry.

Yet progress up and out of the Pyramid, cautious though it is, seems much quicker than the earlier, crowding descent, and Dan can hear the woman's breath catch and quicken as the slope becomes steeper. But she does not speak, for which he is grateful.

Far above them, another torch is suddenly visible, and soon he hears the slow, uncertain shuffle coming towards them, as yet another group is shepherded through the blackness, to marvel, and to fear, in the burial chamber. They pass without a word. Moments later, he feels a slight movement of the air, a warm, quickening breeze playing on the cold, clammy skin of his face. And here, at last, is the entrance. Covering his eyes, squinting into the sun's harsh glare, he emerges with the woman, under a serene, azure sky.

When Dan can properly open his eyes again, he looks around to see whether any of their party are still about. But the woman gives a little cry, shouts a name, and waves both arms at a distant someone nearing the Sphinx. And away she goes without a word or a backward glance.

Without a word or a glance.

Bemused, still, at this whole bizarre interlude, he watches her go, to thrust her body between two sauntering male figures, link up with their arms, and laugh up into the face of one of them, then turn to the other, as they pass the Sphynx. And that is it.

Titania too had hurried away that very last time, when the school year had ended, hurried off without a backward glance.

It had seemed like the end of the world. Like knowing you were going to die.

After the Cairo interlude, during the remainder of the voyage Dan had hardly seen the woman. If she passed him along the ship's corridors or in the lounge or the grand dining room, she simply smiled sheepishly, or lowered her eyes.

But then on the morning they tied up at Tilbury he is saying goodbye to one or two people in the bar. And as they turn away to go to their cabins, the woman catches his arm; he hadn't seen her sitting alone there, on a high stool. She is wearing a crimson suit, already wrapped to face the English winter.

'I owe *you* a drink,' she says.

'Oh, no... really, I don't think so,' he says, feeling this second intrusion into his life an inconvenience even more pointless than the first. Releasing his arm politely, he tries to push between her and another group which is standing close.

But again, she catches hold of him.

'Look, I just wanted to say, "thank you". I've been wanting to, ever since that day you brought me – and she giggles like a schoolgirl – back from the dead. But I've been too...' She looks away, blushing, even now. 'After all...'

'It was nothing,' Dan says quickly. 'For me, anyway. I just sensed that, well, a Muslim country, and pretty hostile at that...' He shrugs. 'Anyway, we managed, just in the nick of time.'

She inclines her head a fraction, then glancing round, makes as if to take his hand, but doesn't. Her make-up, he notices, is meticulously applied, sculptured.

He shakes his head. Belated sincerity, or ploy, or what? He looks at his watch, realising he can delay no longer.

'Forgive me,' he says, 'but they're waiting for me – my family. I must go.'

She smiles, wistfully, perhaps. Then she half-stands to kiss him on his cheek. 'I understand,' she says. 'But I guess… Anyway, *you'll* never know, and *I'll* never forget your… kindness.'

He nods, and on impulse, brushes his lips against her forehead, then away, leaving her sitting at the bar.

And that is where she remains for Dan, even now, all these years later.

Not so Titania. For that vision of her at her front door that night, on the threshold, her lingering, wistful, tender, saying-everything look, is with him still.

XXX

I'm so sorry to have to tell you...

Rosemary reads the letter, over and over, struggling with its finalities, the suddenness, this flat and empty translation into words on a page.

> *It was the same day I brought the baby home from the nursing home. She'd been so excited about the baby, and she even managed to hold him for a moment or two. Peter had made a nice lunch for us (mercifully, he hadn't gone to work that day) and afterwards she said she'd have a nap because she hadn't slept too well during the night. I helped her through into her bedroom and saw that she was comfortable, then went back to feed the baby.*
>
> *After about half an hour, Jason started whimpering and scratching at her door. Peter went and pulled him back, afraid he might disturb her, and most unusually the dog snapped at him.*
>
> *We knocked gently and went in.*

Over and over, she reads it, hoping that somehow...

But it is always the same.

> *She was lying exactly as I'd left her and looked just as though she was asleep. Jason went and brushed his head against her hand – we couldn't stop him; and it was then we realised she had gone, for her arm slipped suddenly over the*

edge of the bed, heavily and quite lifeless. Her end had been swift and sudden, but very likely quite peaceful, the doctor told us. She had probably passed away in her sleep, almost at once, he said.

We tried a couple of times to ring you to let you know about the funeral, but I'm afraid we got no reply either time. I'm very sorry. We know how upset you will be because she did manage to tell us how good you'd been to her and how she'd come to rely on you, especially for Jason.

Mentioning him reminds me that she also said to me (and on another two or three occasions to Peter) that if anything should happen to her, you might like to have Jason, since we'd find it difficult to keep him, what with the baby and all. I wonder if you could possibly give us a ring to let us know. Peter will be coming over to see to the house and could easily bring Jason with him.

If you can't have him then I don't quite know what we shall do.

There are also one or two little pieces of jewellery I think Mrs Appleton would have liked you to have, to remember her by.

All at once, it was as if Mrs Appleton had been a dream.

Stunned though she is, Rosemary realises she has to work something out fast, if Juliet's husband is bringing Jason soon.

She draws her chair nearer the little desk in her room, and starts thinking about who might help. Her parents, huh! They hadn't even *told* her about the phone call. No kind neighbours, no friends... But there was Marya. She was a kind person, and she loved animals, didn't she, not just her pigs? Marya would help, she feels sure of it. She'll go and talk to her, explain... No, she'll call her first. So she needs some coins. And then...

Rosemary's eyes suddenly open wide in horror and she starts to tremble. Tears fill her eyes and spill down her cheeks. And she hangs her head in embarrassment and shame as she remembers the last time she was there, ages ago now, when she thought she'd already lost Jason, and there'd been the gin, and… all that. Her shoulders shake, and she sits on, crying, in utter misery. How *can* she go back, after all that, and ask for help?

Then just as suddenly, her head jerks back up. What choice does she have? Wiping her tears away brusquely, with the back of her hand, she resolves to put the things that had happened there out of her mind. She just has to. Marya is her best bet – maybe the only one, if she is to save Jason.

Sniffing, dabbing her handkerchief over her eyes and nose, she opens her desk drawer and takes out the hand-written copy she'd made of the text Mrs Appleton had had in a frame. And as she reads it Mrs Appleton is smiling at her still, as she had on that day when, impetuously, she'd copied it, to keep forever.

'It's lovely, don't you think? And so very true', her friend is saying, 'something to hold on to, dear, words to treasure.'

> *We are beset in our daily lives by fret and worry and frustrations. We find ourselves too readily pinned down to thoughts of what seems obstructive in our immediate environment. But it is possible, and wise men have proved that it is possible, to live in so large a world that the vexations of daily life come to feel trivial and that the purposes which stir our deeper emotions take on something of the immensity of our cosmic contemplations. Some can achieve this in a greater degree, some only in a lesser, but all who care to do so can achieve this in some degree, and, in so far as they succeed in this, they will win a kind of peace which will leave activity unimpeded but not turbulent. This state of mind is what I mean by wisdom, and it is undoubtedly more precious than rubies.*

More precious than rubies.

And thinking about the words and seeing kind Mrs Appleton by the fireplace in her cosy sitting-room, where the framed text had hung among the horse brasses, remembering Mrs Appleton and Jason, and Marya, and all her problems. Rosemary throws herself onto her bed, sobbing into her pillow, her whole body shuddering as the tears keep on coming with the realisation of the stark finalities that have suddenly wrapped themselves about her.

***

The double trellis curves round beneath the crest in a broad arc, with a wide, central opening on its lower side. To reach the rocky pinnacle, one now passes through this opening and along the corridor, either to left or right, and out through a narrower exit at the end. A few steps and you are there, at the crest.

The structure stands in an exposed position, and he has already linked the front and rear posts over the top with sturdy struts to strengthen it. But then this morning, as an afterthought, he'd fixed some narrower lengths of planking, diagonally between the struts, effectively turning the construction into something resembling a cloister, and with all its associations the notion pleases him; its piecemeal realisation, however, leaves him rather less than satisfied: contemplating his "folly", now, from the rocks, he knows a real creator would have seen it all, whole, from the beginning – as with the herb garden – and done a much neater job.

Dan sighs regretfully. And, with the sun sinking down the sky, its bright rays falling where all the splendour of the all-important red climbing roses will soon be, flaming proud towards the crest and transfiguring his defective arbour, he finds himself wondering if his many failings will also, perhaps, turn to ash in that wall of flame.

Rose time, yes.

And he stands on, his thoughts stilled for a moment. For rose time is not only splendour, scent and hue, it is also the memory of long-faded blooms, their petals fallen… of Titania, of Penny, and others, too.

'What did you think you were doing when you suddenly went so far away, when you'd promised you would always be there for me? Whatever did you think you were doing?'

'What did you think you were doing every day, leaving me sitting there absurdly knitting, always in shadow, out of the sun's hard glare, with Ah Kim forever bringing in yet more tea or juice, the children fractious with the heat, counting the hours, then the minutes to the grocer's daily visit, highlight of the morning, for *two whole* years? Whatever did you think you were doing?'

Closing his eyes he exhales slowly, trying to ward off these other, more heinous tares, these more significant failings in his life.
    Wounding to heal, he had failed them both, garnered no peace or merit, having nothing of the healer's art.

Under the trees, once, in a dead season, Penny had planted aconites, daffodils and snowdrops for the spring, and he had barely noticed them – not then, *a temps de ma dolor*. Some little way ahead he may yet have time to marvel at their silent splendour; to sit or walk among them, feel a healing breeze hushing among the leaves, and recall her slender hands coaxing flowers; to contemplate a quiet joy.

Later, that same evening, Dan is still trying to unravel, and to piece together. Not that it is complete quite yet, but this garden of his, what is it?
    In its making it has taken into itself many things, ghosts from different phases and places and pasts.
    It is Penny, perhaps a completion of what they started all those years ago.
    It is Titania, with him here as she was in the tangled wilds of Johor, the Great Pyramid, the quiet churchyard.
    People and pasts and phases still adrift.
    All ways away.

Once in the house, Dan goes into the lounge and across to the drinks' cabinet. He turns the key, pulls back its doors and surveys the array of long-neglected bottles. Deciding quickly, he reaches for the Isla, ever his favourite, takes a glass from the compartment below and pours himself a measure of the straw-coloured liquid. Then he sits down.

'Oh, this *is* good!' he murmurs. And for a while he leans back, savouring it, murmuring a silent homage to Titania, his long-ago-friends and colleagues, his lost family; remembering those initial weeks here, his blind determination as he assembled tools, plants, provisions; then toiling each day, season after season, year after year.

Then so many thoughts start to tumble out and cascade uncontrollably, but he can perceive no coherence in any of them. He stands, trying to shake them off, then paces round, tidying stray books and cushions, trying to clear his head, force his mind to reframe and rephrase. And a moment later, in his mind's eye he is once again in the garden.

He is sauntering up through it, this place now so familiar to him, with its seven interlocking terraces, its many islands, its significant plants set in appropriate places and proportions in an attempt at symmetry. These many decisions he has willed, imposed on the land, seemingly, have led to a sense of wholeness, a feeling new and unaccustomed to him.

And now he rests, quiet in the notion that it is this state, fragile and transitory though it is, that comes nearest to the impulse that has been driving him. Like being on a journey, a new path, setting out not to fulfil a purpose but to discover it.

And most surely, he has not done so yet.

***

Marya's anger sprang from hurt, and Rosemary, stung, dares not even raise her eyes to meet it. A torrent of anger, raging sounds, making little if any sense. Words flaking. Sentences falling apart. No, all she can do is wait until the storm has blown itself out.

Silent, submissive, and contrite. It is the only way. For she cannot risk jeopardising her plan for Jason. She simply cannot.

Besides, what other truthful response she can make?

So she waits. She cries. Then ever so humbly, she acknowledges her fault. Yes, yes *of course* she should have come; it was thoughtless, unforgivable of her not to. She's sorry, but... but it's been difficult, still is. Her mother, she...

But Marya seems hardly to be listening.

Rosemary tries again. She takes a deep breath and explains about her mother's new, stricter regime, about Mrs Appleton's stroke, and about Jason. Head drooping, mouth askew, she even tries to mimic how poor Mrs Appleton had been. But Marya doesn't respond, and while her head and shoulders jerk this way and that, Rosemary fears she hears neither her words nor her contrition.

She waits a while longer, then on the spur of the moment, her heart thumping away in her chest, chances all on one, desperate throw.

'I think maybe I'd better go,' she says. 'I'm sorry, truly I am. I can see how it must seem to you, as if all I want is to... make use of you. It isn't like that really, but to you, clearly it is. And I have no right. I was wrong to come.' And she stands up, smartly, as if to turn her words into action.

With a shout, Marya leaps up and almost throws herself at the door as if possessed by demons; hands raised, as if to stop someone on the other side from coming in. Then she spins about and comes at Rosemary, seizing her roughly by the shoulders, forcing her back and down onto the settee, all the while jabbering away shrilly in her Ukrainian.

Rosemary struggles, half-heartedly at first, then as hard as she can. But she is no match for Marya's greater strength. And with the woman half kneeling, half lying on top of her, she suddenly ceases all resistance and lies quite still. Both are panting hard, each eyeing the other warily, to see what happens next.

At length it is Marya who speaks, spitting words like bullets.

'You *not* go!' she shrieks. 'Not go! Not let you!'

She shuffles forward onto Rosemary's chest, her knees pinning her down so that Rosemary's neck is bent painfully against the back of the settee and all she can see is the ruck of Marya's rough skirts, just inches away. And it is in this awkward position, twisting slightly to relieve the pain in her neck, that Rosemary sees the numbers on Marya's wrist. Why hadn't she noticed them before? Trying to ignore her pain, she thinks back. Didn't Marya usually wear, yes, a big, man's wristwatch?

'Marya,' she says, breathlessly, unable to repress her curiosity, and as if the present incongruity of their respective positions were normality itself, 'Marya, why did you have those numbers put on your wrist?'

Once again, she is wholly unprepared for the woman's violent reaction.

'You not ask!' Marya screams at her. 'You not ask about number! Never you ask! Never! Never! Never you ask!' And repeating herself, time after time, she slaps Rosemary's defenceless face, first one side then the other, until, unable to bear it any longer, she too screams in pain and humiliation, and writhes and bucks in her anger until she succeeds in dislodging her tormentor.

Marya slips to the floor. Rosemary stares down at her, still gasping for breath, still wary. The prostrated Marya makes no move, breathing heavily among her sobs, quite spent. Eventually, she kneels up and blindly clasps her arms around Rosemary's thighs, meekly pleading forgiveness, softly at first, almost in a whisper, but the whispers rise to a mournful wailing, which seems as if it will never end.

Rosemary holds Marya, whose body pitches and heaves with her sobbing, and she remembers Rosalind in a similar state. Yet this outburst, she senses, this sobbing of Marya's, is different. Rosalind was shallow, hollow, and she got over things in a flash. But not this woman.

Rosemary struggles to put it into words, but this pain, she feels, comes from long ago, not just a reaction to today and whatever offence she's caused, but to something in the past; something bigger, a whole lifetime's sorrow, maybe, whatever it may be. Had she been hurt badly? Instinctively, she begins to stroke Marya's hair.

And when at long last the sobbing subsides, Marya sleeps where she is. And Rosemary, trembling still, sits there quite alone, keeping a dark, silent vigil.

But surely, now, dear, dear Jason is safe.

XXXI

The little boys gasp and whoop as each new present is handed out, only to be replaced by another and another in breath-taking succession, many from back home, from fairy-tale England.

'Mummy, look! Daddy! Ah Kim...!'

But Ah Kim is away with her family, to celebrate Christmas Day.

When their noisy excitement has abated somewhat, and they are intent on a more detailed examination of their presents, Penny, in her dressing gown and sleepy still, begins to assemble things for breakfast.

Dan steps cautiously round bits of Lego, an assortment of vehicles, colouring books and story books, collecting up the ripped, widely strewn wrapping paper to restore a modicum of tidiness and order. But he is distracted from his task: by Matthew, intent on building the big ship which will take them all the way back to England; by Simon, trying to retrieve one of his Dinky cars from beneath the huge, ornate Chinese sideboard; and by a vague sense of the incongruity of it all.

Eventually, he goes out through the kitchen into the sun-washed garden with a boxful of paper and shambles over to the farthest corner, beside the banana tree.

'Don't start burning that now!' Penny calls after him. 'Breakfast's just about ready.'

He quickly empties the box into the cold incinerator and packs its colourful contents tightly down into the square wire basket. All this brightness, these fantastic garlands, for so little time and even less consequence. But the boys' faces, so joyous... Smiling vaguely, he stoops to take the box back inside ready for the next load, after breakfast, and sees a sheet of newspaper still wedged at the bottom. Always one… Reaching in to dislodge it, his eye catches a small headline in block capitals.

'TRAGIC ACCIDENT IN LOCAL LAKE'

Banal alliteration, he thinks, barely scanning the piece, his mind already halfway towards breakfast; their old local rag after all.

But then his blood runs cold.

'Dan! Are you coming?'

He looks up, trying to quell the panic rising within him, to see Penny peering out, then taking a step or two towards him across the lawn.

'Come on! We're waiting to start.'

'Yes, yes, I'm coming,' he calls back. He drops the paper into the incinerator and turns as if to follow her back inside the house. But as soon as she has disappeared, he darts back and snatches up the brief report which he reads rapidly, his heart now thumping hard in his chest.

> *Yesterday, three boys playing in woodland by the boating lake in Handscombe Park caught sight of a large object which had become entangled in the low branches of a willow tree and the thickly growing rushes near it. At first, they thought it was a log, but on closer inspection it tragically proved to be the body of a local girl, who was later identified (by her father) as Rosemary Wardle, aged seventeen.*
>
> *She was fully clothed, and first reports suggest that she had been in the water for several hours. There were no signs of a struggle, but the police are puzzled by the fact that she had a long daisy chain around her neck and foul play has not yet been ruled out.*
>
> *A sixty-three-year-old employee of the local parks' department is said to be helping police with their inquiries.*

In a daze, Dan folds the sheet of paper, puts it in his pocket, then plods back across the lawn.

Not Titania, no, thank God; but Rosemary... Oh that poor girl. What on earth had happened to lead her to such a desperate act, if it was as it seemed? But when had it happened?

Adrift in the chill unreality of this chance knowledge come to him out of nowhere, Dan realises he has no choice. He must find a way back at once, shake himself out of this sudden turmoil, his bewilderment, his distress, back to the children's pleasure; to Penny, and Christmas morning.

***

Dan wakes in panic, perplexed, eyes wet from a complex, emotional dream; yet moments later only a few images remain: Ben, Hare Hill, and fragments of an elusive hymn tune.

It's not that Dan doesn't often dream of Ben, but this time it had been the dog's eyes: eyes that commanded, with their ink-black pools, never shifting, drawing him in towards them, seeming to grow and grow till they consumed him entirely, till he had felt such powerful assurance that he had cried out in despair at their fading.

And that tune, still eluding him.

After breakfast, these ragged images persist, seeming disinclined to desert him as he sweeps crumbs, washes plates, wipes surfaces. And when he gathers up his tools from the shed and heads away up the field, still they accompany him, drifting in and out of his mind, with half snatches of that tantalising, far-off tune.

He labours and rests. And staring about him, he reminds himself that like dreams, everything he has made here will vanish and be buried away, whether by wilderness, or incivility: that other kind of – human – wilderness.

After an early lunch he takes a fork and having cleared two or three roses of thistles walks slowly down to the lychgate. This he finds, with some relief, is now entirely overgrown, completely absorbed into the high, wild hedge. And yet despite its density, as a barrier it is by no means impregnable. Some days, he cannot quite escape the pneumatic drill buzzing, a dog barking frenetically in the distance, or a motor bike revving – even soft-drink cans or cigarette ends thrown over, a crisp packet thrust through.

These things, the merest inferences of a dull, brutalising, alien world which is never far away. Like the convolvulus, the aphids. All gradually slipping, or suddenly leaping, into his consciousness.

Tam grata rerum novitas, he muses, ironically, before stabbing the earth once more with the heavy fork still in his hands.

An hour or so later, however, having gathered up his tools, he abandons his work up the garden, feeling a new sort of despondency.

Thou most kind and gentle death – that was the hymn tune, at last. And he recognises, once again, that there is not one vision we conjure in our minds that we have not already encountered somewhere before. That moment when gently, ever so gently, they had laid Ben on the vet's table, the moment before the needle. Those dark, soulful eyes, which had never left them for one instant until they closed, nor ever would. Eyes that penetrated deeply, were unmoving, consoling, unperturbed by the immensity of the moment. Trusting. And in the end, their own human sorrow had had to give way to *his* trusting serenity.

Thou most kind and gentle death.

Modicum, et vos videbitis me. Just a little while longer, then you will see me.

In a little while, yes. Surely.

And soon a comforting feeling takes hold of him, tapping away in his mind, and staying with him for the rest of the afternoon. A suspicion, a superstition, maybe?

Towards evening, Dan sits down at his desk to write a letter. He does not address it to anyone, but tries to explain, in so far as he is able, why his life, since "retirement", has been centred on the creation of the garden. Certainly it is bound up with Ben, he acknowledges, with his dreams of the dog, though drawing in other images too which, in their coming together, seem to suggest a quite different dimension from his habitual, day by day routine.

Subsequently, in this process of trying to transform chaos into order, the first image has insisted on the one direction to the exclusion of all others, he realises, though he does not write this.

He explains too, as best he can, about the form of the garden, its several twists and turns, the paving, the flowers and shrubs, the daily battles with aphids and weeds.

When the letter is complete, he bites into a large, crisp apple, and turns his attention to sorting through his papers, though with no sense of urgency or clear purpose. Skimming through some, destroying others.

> *Thank you for your letter – he begins to read – though why I say thank you I don't know. I must admit that it was a shock to receive it, although I thought you would get in contact with me when you returned to England.*
>
> *What can I say, except that I don't want to see you again, no matter whether you promise there will be no complications or not? What happened, happened a long time ago, and yet just a letter from you out of the blue has the power to upset me. To meet again would be madness, and this I do not intend to indulge in.*

But of course, even then dreams had led him on, only to be dashed in their turn.

> *You say that for you basically nothing has changed. Surely this is a good enough reason for you to avoid me. Don't you think we caused Penny enough trouble all that time ago without starting anything afresh?*
>
> *Perhaps things haven't changed for you – and believe me I am very sorry if they haven't – but they have for me. I had a wonderful three years at college with loads of ups and downs, falling in and out of love as regular as clockwork. I also sorted out myself a lot, and believe me, it took a lot of doing. It took almost three years and a very patient friend who sat up night*

after night until three and four o'clock in the morning for months on end to listen to me talking when I couldn't sleep. Then, just over a year ago I met somebody that I am going to marry. We knew that we would get married after only knowing each other about 8 weeks, and this Xmas our engagement will be official. I can feel you turning cynical and hard at this point – please don't – he is very different to you. He is very open and straight forward and can't understand how anything can get complicated and mixed-up. He is just the person I need. Apart from looking at him in this detached way, I love him very very much, and he is crazy about me.

He knows all about our little saga, and I'm afraid – though naturally I suppose – he has taken an intense dislike to you. This is, of course, the main reason why I cannot meet you. He is very possessive (… pause while you think nasty things!) and I am glad, glad of it. I want to be owned, loved, cared for and to feel secure and this he will certainly give me.

I cannot see you. I don't want to see you. I can't see you for his sake, for Penny's sake, for the twins', for mine, for yours. Please don't try and take anything that I've said and twist it and try and convince me that I ought to see you, that I love you etc. etc. – I know perfectly well in my own mind what I must do, and what I want to do. I love him very much and I would do anything in the world not to hurt it or him.

Obviously, you don't want Penny to know that you have written to me as you haven't given your home address. I don't want my parents to know that you have written – there was enough fuss and bother last time – please do not phone me as I will not change my mind and it will only cause more upset.

If you want to reply to all this, write to me at school… Just write and tell me that you, Penny, and the twins are well – nothing else please. Make it a nice one, as I want it to be our last. Please do this for me, and let our memories be pleasant ones, not over-shadowed by anything we may do or say now…

Dan reads her words again for the first time in a quarter of a century, maybe more. With memory forever leaking, who can say for sure what we have done or when? He reads her words, and he understands them, of course. But how had he understood them *then*? Evidently, after their return from the Far East, he had written to her, and this was her reply – after more than two years of incomprehensible silence.

Leafing through the same file, he finds another letter in her hand, written only six days after the first.

Forgive the writing paper – but I'm at school and this is the best paper that I can find.

Thank you very much for your letter which I received this morning from our very unpleasant caretaker. I know I asked for one, but oh, why did it have to be such a nice letter? You make me feel absolutely rotten about the one I sent you. Did I really snarl? It wasn't a very pleasant thing to have said about one – but if it was true, I'm glad that you said it. Please believe me when I say that there is not the slightest bitterness in me towards you. There never was and I am sure there never will be. That letter of mine was written in a state of panic. For some reason you seemed to threaten my future life and I had to defend it with every weapon I had. Your letter today made me see everything in perspective. Forgive me for being so silly.

I'm glad that you think it is better we do not meet. No doubt we shall run into each other sometime. Well, if we do, we do and please don't walk past me as if you didn't recognise me – I suppose it is me who should be promising this.

Must finish – I've had an exhausting day sitting in the middle of a piece of corrugated paper the length and breadth of a classroom wall directing operations while 25 kids aged between 5 and 7 years sloshed paint all over everything in the attempt to make it look like Aladdin's cave. I have 2 blue knees and a yellow and red splattered face, and my feet are the colour of the rainbow.

Congrats. on your job, by the way. It sounds very grand.

Thank you once again for your letter. Please, I'm sorry that I must ask you not to write again. I tell him just about everything and it will only cause upset and misunderstanding if you write.

Love and God Bless…

So, he had written again. But from the echoes picked up in this, her reply, he is glad he will never have to read his own words – those that had elicited it. Yet wasn't her mood a little too rounded, perhaps, her words a bit too pat? Were they?

Whatever had he been thinking, *then*?

He hadn't insisted. But if he had, had had enough courage or desire, or will to press her, with what word, he wonders, might he have unlocked all that accumulated hurt?

Dan lays the letters aside. Seeking solace, he stands and crosses to the window to stare up at the crescent moon, but still his thoughts stampede. After enduring those two years of hurtful silence, why, not knowing, not being sure, had he simply accepted her words and walked away – into yet more longing; trying endlessly to heal, to not lose himself in his sense of loss?

Had she then found happiness, satisfaction in life? He hoped beyond hope that she had. But if not?

His eyes mist over, as slowly, gradually, he sees the scene building, unfolding before him. Years later. In a theatre, of course. For where else could it have been?

No, that last letter of hers had not quite rung down the final curtain, had it, even for her?

***

It is not until they are seated, at the end of the third row from the front on the left of the central aisle, that they realise they have no programme.

'How could we have missed them?' Dan explodes, annoyed with himself.

Penny stands and puts a hand on his shoulder. 'I'll go and find one.'

The small auditorium is filling up. Penny is not back yet, and the play is about to begin. Anxiously, he stares at the door.

Then a stooping figure, a quiet voice asking if 'these seats' are taken.

'Only this one,' he says, absent-mindedly, still looking out for Penny coming through the last-minute, milling crowd.

There are several seats unoccupied further along the row, to his left, but he is aware of the woman settling into the one right next to Penny's, then standing again to remove her coat.

Then, just as the house lights are fading, Penny scurries in, breathless and cross.

Dan stands to let her pass. His eyes stray beyond her. And in a flash, he knows. The long scarf, the duffle coat so long out of fashion.

His heart skips several beats as he sinks down into his own seat, then thuds and pounds away, mercilessly. He goes hot, cold, hot.

More than twenty years since he has seen her.

In the soft orange glow cast by the stage lights he observes her minutely, discreetly: the profile is the same, the hesitant smile that flickers once, twice, before bursting into laughter, the same; the toss of her head, the cut of her hair, the spread of her fingers. All, all are the same, there is no mistaking them. But there is no ring on those fingers.

At the start of the interval, Penny stands.

'Come on, let's get some coffee.'

Trance-like, he tears his eyes away. Moving like an automaton he crosses the auditorium, and at the door, finally glances round. But her eyes have not followed him.

As they are coming back, Titania turns away to rummage through her bag on the seat to her left. Once they are seated, she studies her programme, assiduously. And not until the lights have dimmed and *The Dream* resumes, does she raise her eyes again – to the stage: her eyes fix on it, and not once throughout the whole performance does she turn her head towards them.

Such absorption – intensity and indifference alike – is a performance in itself. For unlike Penny, she knows well enough where chance has led her.

Yet he sits and waits and hopes that she will make some gesture, some more positive kind of acknowledgement.

After the play, as they are nearing the exit she hurries past them, down the steps, towards the car park, and into the night.

Some minutes later, he fancies he sees her in a dark-coloured saloon, pulling away in the opposite direction to their own.

And that had been that. Each vanishing into a different darkness; though hers, of course, might have been no darkness at all.

And nor should his have been.

And *if we do, we do…* and… *Please don't walk past me as if you don't recognise me.* The words ricochet back and forth in his mind. *Please don't walk past me…*

***

Twenty years. Hardly surprising he had seen nothing of what transpired on stage, in that evening's version of *The Dream*.

But the clarity of those stills unfolding out of that distant memory, they mesmerise him, still.

Dan sits back from his desk, finding he has been gripping his chair arms tightly, his whole body tense.

In those stultifying periods in which for days on end he had not been able to free himself from the memory of her, he had often wondered just what he would do if ever they came face to face. Of all the scenarios he had imagined, it had never occurred to him he would… could… do nothing.

He had never really become free of her, never. She could emerge from almost anywhere, at any time. And always, the vague belief, or hope, the foolishly romantic notion that somehow, somewhere in the future, the better part of their fragile, long-distant past together could in some way be recovered, remade.

But it couldn't, could it? Not now, for his tomorrows were well-nigh spent. And besides, his darkness back then had had many layers, meaningful ones too: he had lived on through a loving marriage, been as good a father to the twins as he could be. And managed a career.

Nevertheless, central, dominant, though all of this was, he had always been aware of an otherness in exile. And it had never occurred to him, not until long after that tormented evening in the theatre, what a tremendous load that "exile" had borne in the whole structure of his life. Faced with the stark reality of Titania's rejection (her rejection, or his own inaction – whichever it had been that had affected the other), he had collapsed into a despair that had lasted many months.

And when he could at last raise his head again, not surprisingly Penny had already left.

How came these things to pass?
Oh, how mine eyes do loathe his visage now!

The clarity of those stills unfolding, yes, they mesmerise him, still.

XXXII

As soon as Dan enters the darkened house, he knows something is amiss.

Mid-morning, heavy rain had prevented much progress up the garden and soon driven him back inside, where he had chafed and fretted, and then taken more trouble over lunch than usual, even setting the table first. Some little time later, however, the sun had emerged, the garden beckoned, and he'd set to work again with a vengeance – up at the top, between the trellised, not-quite-satisfactory "cloister" and the rocks – most of the time giving little thought to anything else. Occasionally, though, he had glanced back down the garden, which in its created order was once more at that point at which everything was about to burst, straining into blossom or leaf, or was already, shyly, in flower.

When exhaustion brought his session to a close, curiosity had taken him right over the crest and a little way down the other, northern side, where he'd not even looked, much less been, not in a very long time. And he had stood there, startled by how much the undergrowth had spread, already well advanced up the hill from the bottom hedge with some slender ash saplings even three and four feet high. A foretaste, maybe, of the whole garden's eventual fate.

Walking back up to the rocks, he had gathered up his tools, then glanced down at that advancing wilderness one last time, his foreboding quickly subsiding into indifference.

Dan stands poised, just inside the back door. But hearing nothing, his hand moves to the switch and the long, narrow kitchen is flooded with light. He sees the door opposite him, the hall door, standing wide open, and at this his eyes widen, knowing for certain he had closed it before going out. He hesitates for a moment then steps boldly through it into the main body of the church. At the foot of the staircase to the upper floor, holding his breath, he snaps on the light.

Even before his eyes adjust, a sharp movement of air tells him that his front door, the south entrance to the church, must also be wide open. Quickly, he crosses the nave and steps outside, walking, now marching almost, towards the postern gate. And as he nears it in the gathering dusk, he sees that it too is standing open.

By now, Dan's pulse is racing. He is slightly breathless, tense, and puzzled. Intruders, again? But why? What were they looking for? Strangely, however, he has no sense of fear.

As he pushes the gate shut it comes to him that it may have been his entrance at the back that occasioned their sudden flight – through the front door. He had probably missed them by mere seconds, if that's how it was. But if not?

Back inside, he shuts the front door behind him and leans heavily against it, pondering other possibilities. Could there be someone still upstairs? He glances across the nave at the staircase. Maybe the door and gate had been left open to facilitate a speedy getaway, which he has now forestalled… maybe?

He cannot be sure, of course, but nor will he risk any sort of encounter. Whoever they are, and whatever they are seeking or have taken, does not really matter. Not now.

He turns and reopens the front door, leaving it wide open. Then he walks back across the nave, switching off the lights as he goes, and through into the kitchen, banging the hall door behind him. The kitchen light he leaves burning, and after pausing to zip up his coat, he steps outside again.

Slowly, purposefully, he climbs the steps up into the garden, aware that the light from the kitchen will make his actions plain to anyone watching from an upstairs window. Taking his time, he meanders up the garden, past alpine rockeries, ornate flowerbeds, the rose arbour… right to the crest, where he sits on the rocks, knees drawn up to his chin, looking back down, contemplatively, at the house.

All remains still and silent.

And still he waits.

After some little while, he stretches, yawns, and starts to walk back down towards the house.

'Not long, now, I think,' he says out loud, running his hands over the satin-like sedum covering the grave, before making his way round the rose-budding trellis screen.

Once inside the house again, he sees that everything is as he had left it.

Calmly, unhurriedly, he goes upstairs.

With all the lights on, he takes in the signs of a hasty, perhaps inexpert search. Drawers have been pulled out, and overturned. Piles of papers and other objects litter each room. Has anything been taken?

Impossible to know, and he hardly cares, but makes a half-hearted effort to tidy his study – ignoring some things, and pushing others back into the nearest drawer or cupboard and shutting it. It is a bother, nothing more, and when he has done, he flops down in the armchair. He needs to focus now, to make sure everything is ready and in place in his mind.

But a moment later, he levers himself up and goes over to the window. Resting his palms on the cool sill, he stares out into darkness. The helicopter, the figure watching, the cigarette butt… and now this latest disturbance… are they all connected?

And if they are, which the manner of them seems to suggest? No, he must clear his mind of them. They are of no consequence now.

Dan paces the room, his thoughts veering in all directions, but the thing that keeps coming back to him, that defiantly evades all attempts to dismiss it, is that the MoD is still pursuing him – the paranoid MoD, yes! Even now, after however many years it has been since his retirement.

He thinks back to the prickly business with Dale-Denton and the Chemistry department, his speaking out. The MoD was the sinister arm of a government that had legislated itself into dictatorship even before his own "exile", a government that was also paranoid, not least about "national security"; viciously class- and race-driven, xenophobic in its motivation and promised actions.

He thinks about the anti-nuclear or anti-Thatcher marches in the eighties, but now he is being paranoid, isn't he? There'd been thousands of marchers, and the MoD would hardly waste time and public money on all of them. They'd pursued Wilson, all right, but people like him, and after so long?

Round and round it he goes, though with no sense of urgency, not reaching anything like conviction.

Anyway, if it *was* the MoD, they were in for yet another disappointment, no mistake!

Shaking his head, he strides purposefully back to his desk, whose surface is covered with files evidently lifted directly from the still-open filing cabinet, and cascaded from one end to the other: from left to right bank statements going back years and years; from right to left, utility bills, also stretching back to the year dot. For goodness sake! But why would they be interested in these, why now?

Irritated, he takes up one of the folders and begins to cram the files back into it, and as he does so his eyes light on an old Basildon Bond envelope lying, incongruously, between the two lines of splayed files. Titania's hand. He picks it up, wondering vaguely why it's here and not with her other letters, then with a start, sees it doesn't seem even to have been opened.

An unopened letter, and from Titania? But how...? Penny, maybe?

A thousand questions crowd Dan's mind as, hand trembling, he takes the envelope back to his armchair. The hard glare of the lamp shows a postmark dated some months before his departure for the Far East. So why hadn't he...?

Has he *really* never seen it until this moment?

A sudden gust of wind hits the window; torrential rain lashes against it. And Dan leaps up to close the curtains, half conscious of not minding this interruption, this slight delay in confronting the letter's words.

Then, his breathing still ragged, he tears it open and extracts its two closely written pages. He scans rapidly, but nothing seems remotely familiar. Concentrating hard he reads it again and reaches the same conclusion. A failure of memory or truly his first sight of it?

> *The reason that I have not written was that I wanted you to have a chance to forget me. If I see or write to you now, I am always going to feel that, though unintentionally, I am influencing your decision about the future. I am sure that if contact is broken off between us there is more likelihood of you deciding to stay with Penny, & as you know that is what I want above all else.*

Uncompromisingly stark, her opening words would certainly have thrown him into deep consternation at that fragile time, blunted his reception of whatever followed, had he read them *then*.

> *Can't you see that while the possibility of you leaving Penny hangs in the air, I will always feel that I ought to behave in an aloof manner towards you & perhaps even say that we ought to stop seeing each other altogether, for I would go to any lengths to stop you from taking that step.*
>
> *Oh, Dan, no matter how much either of us may want it differently, I believe that the only capacity in which we will ever know each other is as friends – please don't ruin this as well. All right, perhaps at this moment this is just wishful thinking, but time is a good cure, I'm told, and please, don't be cynical about what I say, for you will only hurt yourself even more, and consequently me as well.*

'Time is a good cure...' How ironical, and sad. And to read it only now.

> *Do you remember telling me whenever I felt depressed to think about the Saturday night in the park when everything was so beautiful & we felt raised above the petty day to day routines & squabbles? Please, don't you forget it either... Perhaps it is easier for me than for you at the moment, as I am far away from any concrete reminders & this helps enormously...*
>
> *Yesterday, Christine and I went for a long walk on the cliff tops...*

Dan closes his eyes. Of course he remembers that night; it was after Holly's farewell party. In the parish churchyard. And their long, tremulously slow walk, right up to her front door! Bound together, carefree both of them, at midnight, one in the morning. He had never forgotten that night, nor would he ever.

Nevertheless, its vital message – *Please, don't you forget it either* – he *had* lost sight of, hadn't he?

Outside, the rain has ceased, and the wind dropped. The air however is chill, and deciding a hot, rather than a stiff drink is what he needs, Dan goes down to the kitchen.

Back upstairs, he undresses quickly and sits back down in his dressing gown, warming his hands on the large, earthenware mug of drinking chocolate.

Yes, he sees it clearly now. Whatever we are engaged in, moment by moment, we are also willy-nilly constructing our very selves. And so being, so doing... cramming all his desperate longing and pleading into his own letters... this person he seemed to have become had eclipsed the one she had known and loved at the outset. Small wonder she had maintained her silence over those two, long years – a silence she explains to him here, in this letter, a silence she had not intended to be endless but a slow, patient way forward. It is all here: in this letter which explains and warns; in this letter which, with its genuine sharing, its intimacy, and its, yes, maturity of outlook, is anything but a shrugging off; in this letter which he doesn't ever seem to have read, or if read, had understood differently.

Either compromise or confrontation. She had understood that, even then, and had pleaded for the former, while he had offered her the latter, it having taken him more than half a lifetime to attain to her wisdom.

Long into the night, Dan's thoughts career this way, then that, wistful, wondering, and full of regret. If only he'd been more patient, more trusting, their love might have survived into a different future as she had envisioned it: a loving friendship, offered as something precious, and above all attainable.

Yet even as these thoughts take hold, unfold their delicate, gossamer-like wings and take flight, he knows well enough that he has strayed over, fallen into a world of speculation: a world where everything is possible, however complex, however fragile.

But… truly, what fools these mortals be! Forever setting and resetting their compass on the strength of dreams, shadows, feelings of the moment, and losing sight of the whole. There can be no redemption for once possible lives – not now, or ever; they have diverged too much, and for far too long; and moved into very different realities.

After breakfast next morning, Dan gathers up the files still littering his desk, slots them back into the cabinet, and slams it shut.

Then he sleeps.

Deeply at first. And then, half-sleeping, half-dreaming… of Penny, of his sons, of his "Beatrice"; of all futures and all pasts. And a curious notion starts taking shape, flickering in and out of consciousness, a conviction growing wings, that the intrusions, all of them – the helicopter, the unseen watcher or watchers, and now this break in – have indeed had a purpose. Nothing to do with the MoD at all. No, another agency has been at work here, one whose playful interventions, whose artful designs, have brought this letter to him, have placed her ignored words, now, into his hands.

Superstition, perhaps? Like the conviction that has taken hold of him of late, that has been gaining traction and substance over the years he has spent here... that the garden – the making of it – has been something required not *by* him but *of* him.

It is this last thought which, on waking briefly, sends him back to the letter he had written a few nights before, the letter addressed to no one, and everyone, and taking it from the drawer in which he had left it he begins to read it over, sinking down into his chair.

> *It is astonishing that, even now, after living for so long, from choice, without the company of others, I should think of writing to someone about what I sense is about to take place. Not my impending disappearance, since that event effectively took place some years ago and caused not the slightest stir, but something about its cause and possible meaning. I write, because I am well aware that we human beings fear any silence that follows a question mark: dust settling upon a void; and maybe that is sufficient explanation in itself.*
>
> *But who am I communicating with? With Penelope, with Titania, with Matthew and Simon, whom words, conniving with a cerebral alchemy, have transfigured into beings they might never recognise as themselves? Or with you who are reading my words now, someone I never knew and who did not know me?*
>
> *A vaguely directed message, then, like one sealed in a bottle by a child and tossed into the sea.*

> *To all intents and purposes, the garden is finished. In a short while I shall step out into it. And if what I have come to surmise proves true, I shall leave it, leave everything, once and for all.*
>
> *Am I anxious at all? If I am, it is that my surmise has been wrong, my intuition has misled me, and I shall have no choice but to return here to drag out the rest of my days without purpose. I say intuition, not quite belief – for belief must be directed at a goal circumscribed by consciousness, which this is not.*

But is it truly intuition? Perhaps no more than speculation. For there have been precedents, of course, though these, quite unlike my own, were enshrined in the belief systems which gave motive and measure to all actions of their times. Their sources are literary, mythical, and so, as fictions, are always suspect. I am thinking of Odysseus, of Aeneas, of Orpheus, and of Paul, and others who came after, of their other-worldly journeys, which history, and especially that of our own times, has variously interpreted as mere metaphors for individuation. These "journeys" were verbal events, professedly reflecting earlier, lived experience; but with the weakening and collapse of the socio-religious systems which sustained them, only the words lingered, shells beached, husks devoid of their former sense and transforming power.

And we know, of course, that words alone cannot save us, since, like the shrine or saint's tomb, the word is simply a reliquary, which awaits – requires – its catalytic agent. It is aspiration untranslated, a whisper echoing round the galleries of the soul... whatever we mean by that quaint, perhaps outmoded notion. And at a certain point, I, who have spent a lifetime submerged in words, became conscious of a need, impatient for something quite beyond them and the comfortable redoubt they represented.

Just suppose though, as I have done, that the miracle can be called forth, not by words but by actions, and not the spectacular kind either. Just suppose that the context and the substance of our unrealised, visionary self may be reconstructed in spite of – indeed whatever – the times, though necessarily abstracted from those times. And if we can suppose this, what then?

In a little while I may have an answer to my own vaguely Pascalian, vaguely Kierkegaardian surmise. But let us be clear about this one thing: my penance – if such it is – my expiation, has been enacted in the name of no god, nor out of fear, nor out of sure and certain hope of any reward. A growing disappointment propelled me along this path – a disenchantment, if you like – with all the pettiness, sinuosity and viciousness around me, a sadness at the general failure of our wonderful humanity; and within this, my own guilt, and different human failings. And when I found myself cast adrift from my professional life and absorption in my work, my need became urgent: a calling; a calling back too, perhaps.

Being for oneself, alone, gradually tempers you. Priorities and circumstances are radically redefined, for one owns one's days at last, for better or for worse. How different this life is from my former world!

For many years, I went in to the office full of optimism, of enthusiasm for the day ahead and all the tasks I planned to accomplish – only to be met at my office door by my secretary or a student, requiring my time and undivided attention. The phone would ring even before my coat was off. Or the post would come, or a fax. Or an email message from France, Italy, or my colleague along the corridor. Any one of them, or several, would take control of me and of my day, and re-mould me in their image. Whole lives, I came to realise, are squandered in such contingency.

In good measure, if not quite entirely, I have here freed myself from all of that and become… well, by the likes of the world of social intercourse, probably quite strange, I suppose! Eccentric, because solipsistic, dutiful to my own purposes. The keeping up of appearances, which dominates us when we live among people, has played no part in my life here. Even words assume a different status and purpose, are thankfully less intrusive yet more vital, being brief and to the point. Most days, according to the day or the season, I have laboured, like the convicted; some days I have experienced the glow of the climber who senses the summit is close. I have kept going, striving always to take myself above and beyond… in a sort of secular monachism, perhaps. Some might say I have taken the easy way out, renouncing responsibilities as well as comforts, and perhaps this is so: who can say for sure? Whatever the outcome, turning back now would feel like a return to prison.

And really, it is time to leave; though curiously, knowing what I know now, I would dearly love to be at the outset again, to live it all over again, but differently, perhaps very differently.

When you have reached the top of the mountain, where else is there to go but the stars?

Dan Teal

XXXIII

It is the full moon filling his window, its blast of light cascading over his bed, which wakes him, and he lies there enthralled for a long while, his mind racing. Then, sleep having now abandoned him, he gets up and goes to the window where he stands watching the harlequinade of light and shadows up the crystal garden, glistening like molten glass, swirling, its forms endlessly translating on a capricious breeze.

Then, darting into the bathroom, he quickly rinses his hands and face under the cold tap, and runs downstairs.

At the bottom, a rush of cold air hits his body, and he realises the front door has been open all night. And he smiles to himself, thinking how such an omission would once have been so grave a matter. He opens the door into the kitchen, consciously leaving it ajar also, and goes through, again catching the sudden breath of air drawn in from across the nave. Ignoring the light switch, he turns the back-door key and crosses the threshold. And he stands there, astounded at the garden's moon-swept immensity, with everything appearing to overstep its own limits so that he feels almost compelled to begin naming things all over again.

Stepping away from the house he is sensible of the dewy grass cool on his feet, the gurgling spring, and the splash of water spilling from the trough into the marsh, of the whispering yews, the rustling oaks. He walks slowly towards the front corner of the house and pauses there awhile, contemplating the quiet graveyard, moving his thumb and forefinger gently up and down a rosebud, almost savouring its latent glory. And the lychgate, set back, ivy-covered now, and bound up in shadows.

He turns and walks over to the stone trough where for a while he watches the water departing, spilling in two distinct rivulets away down into the still, dark wood below. He stoops, cups his hands, and raises them to his lips, feeling the refreshing force of the sweet water filling his mouth; then stooping again he splashes more water all over his face, and feels it running icily down his naked chest.

He is ready.

Sensing neither warmth nor cold as the desultory breeze goes by him, he is conscious of the nodding response, the approving rustle of young leaves, and of imminent flowers, with the breeze gliding easily, a sprite among them

He wanders along pathways, sometimes to their very end, sometimes no way at all, to peer, to inspect, as fancy directs him

With unhurried steps, he makes his way upwards, from terrace to terrace, pleased at his handiwork, even now bending to pull a weed, or set a pot upright, toppled by an earlier wind, sometimes pausing beneath an archway before passing on, up to a new and different level, and all that he inherit

All with weary task fordone

A new rose peering white in the silver moonlight poised to burst into momentary perfection

A caterpillar haloed in moonlight on a gently bobbing leaf awaiting its time

Trellised branching corridors soon to be aflame with roses

And with the spinning stars like wheels revolving, the moon and velvet sky already tinting towards the new dawn before the morning watch…

His eyes strain towards a motionless silhouette mirrored darkly in the lea of the rocks

He pauses still struggling with reason and shadows and he whispers 'Come on then…'
    And he kneels as the shadow bounds towards him in a blur
    'So, what now, Ben?'
    Yet even as he speaks, he is aware of other shadowy silhouettes moving above him along the skyline… Penny, could that be? Young Simon? Matthew? Titania? At the tipping point of sight…
    And he rubs his eyes with the back of his hand

Delirium of stars flung out across an endless twangling sky a miraculous garden of light clearer now nearer now than ever before

The season of reversion beginning beginning

Contrarieties forging new conjunctions

Conjunctions dissolving into vast new configurations

No more words

***

Rosalind wakes with a start.
    Standing at the other side of the bed the young nurse is leaning out of the shadows into the little light cast by the bedside lamp, bending over John.
    'Oh, I'm sorry, Mrs Saunders, if I woke you. Your husband seems peaceful enough, just now.'

'That's all right.' Shifting her weight, she too leans forward towards the bed, feeling stiff from sitting too long in the same position, keeping her vigil.

'Would you like some tea?'

'Oh, yes. Please.' Rosalind stretches her arms.

'I'm going to make some. I generally do about this time when I'm on nights.'

'What time is it?'

'Coming up to a quarter to five. It's been a fine, dry night. A full moon too. I looked out a little while ago, it seemed like day already, a silver day... Anyhow, I'll go and get us that tea. Milk and sugar?'

Rosalind straightens up. 'Just milk, but just a splash.'

And the girl smiles, glancing back at her sleeping patient and nodding slowly, giving the impression that everything is as it should be.

But nothing is, is it? Nothing.

Rosalind closes her eyes, shakes her head and sighs. Poor John. Fifty-two – no age to be leaving this life. And suddenly she wants to ask... is on the point of asking...

But when she opens her eyes, the nurse has slipped away.

Rosalind stares blankly at the door. She knows the answer to her question, anyway. It will be the steadily increasing doses of morphine now, and not, in the end... the very end... the cancer, for its work is well-nigh irrelevant now.

Repositioning the cushion she leans slowly back into her chair.

This numbing inwardness into which Rosalind knows she is spiralling has a long pre-history in their thirty-odd years of marriage. So many events have seemed to her like a judgement on them: her early miscarriages, their baby's cot death... and the fizzling out of her promising career, and John's too, while they were still only in their thirties.

And now this. This final... retribution. Her brow puckers, as she thinks how it had all started much further back than that, even, with poor Rosemary's death.

It had been an awful shock. Just awful. And *all her fault*. How *could* she have been so… callous? Rosalind shudders, the tremor rippling through her like a current.

They were only seventeen. She still at school, Rosemary having left by then, their paths already diverging.

All *her* fault, yes, because of earlier, what she'd made them all believe, taunting Rosemary mercilessly. *Why* do I hate him? What, are you stupid or something? It's obvious why. It's what he did to me, remember…?

And she shakes her head, despairingly. Poking, prodding, on and on. Not that John was blameless, with all his messing about with that oaf Willetts – both of them making snide remarks and mocking Rosemary at every opportunity – *and* Mr Teal of course. But it was *far* more *her* fault – all of it was.

Crying, night after night, after Rosie's death, unable to sleep and worrying her parents half to death.

And then marriage, and still that nagging sense of guilt keeping her awake, wearing her down, and finally goading her into a half-confession to John – on their fifth wedding anniversary.

Poor, patient John. He'd listened to her for hours, questioning first this statement then that fear, trying to reassure her, or at least reason her out of her "superstition", her "penchant for self-flagellation", as he'd called it. He'd genuinely tried to help her, rescue her from herself, telling her Rosemary's death *wasn't* her fault, that the girl had *always* seemed unhappy, or that there had been other things going on in her life, which was true – what with her sanctimonious parents, and that dog and its owner's death. Why oh why hadn't she got it over with, told John the whole story there and then?

But she hadn't, had she. She'd kept up her half-truths, let their poison seep insidiously into every corner of their lives. And one day John's probing had resumed. And this time he'd unpicked her deflections and diversions, one after another, all the layers of deceit. And the two of them, finally engulfed by it all, had beached in a bleak, barren land.

The truth was out. Her false witness. The original sin.

And from that moment on, this full realisation of trust betrayed, an icy wind had swept through their marriage. They'd barely spoken after that, communicating solely through cold formalities – for years.

She had been the fraud.

And all trust was gone.

'It was that first morning back at school, John, after Mr Teal had left – for good, as we thought, then. Do you remember?'

'So, we're back with Teal, are we?' John looks hurt.

'Well, yes.' She pauses a moment, acknowledging his feeling.

'So, do you remember? We were all sort of... vying with each other in condemning Teal for leaving, for abandoning us.'

'Yes. So...?'

'But we were also, at the same time, trying to claim... all of us, not just me... that we'd each had our own special relationship with him.'

John shrugs.

'Well, caught in the... spin, shall we say, of that mood, that moment, I... *made up* that story about our affair.'

'What?'

'The *secret* affair between Teal and me. I made it up.'

'Made it up...? You made it up? But you told us...'

'And I did it – Rosalind raises her voice over John's – so I could seem more important than anyone else, in his regard, and my loss. And it shocked you *all*, didn't it? It shocked *everyone* into silence.' By this time she is almost shouting. 'Do you remember? I was crying as I said it. Maybe already half believing it myself.'

She falls silent, not daring to look at her husband. And suddenly she is seeing them on that long-ago day, sitting together in their form room – John, Willetts, Rosemary, and the others – seeing them where they always sat, being there with them as if it were yesterday. All of them gaping, gasping, all agog at her revelation, her triumph.

Her triumph, *then*.

'For God's sake, Ros. You *told* us he'd *seduced* you!' John is beside himself with anger, his face ashen. 'What were you thinking?'

'I'm sorry.' Her body sagging, pathetic.

'And… all those rumours going around, you feeding them with your… your lies. *Why in heaven's name* didn't you put a stop to it, nip it in the bud? Instead, making us *all* believe… Oh, how *could* you? And you didn't tell *anyone*, not even later on,' he says, bleakly.

Hanging her head, openly admitting her shame. At last.

'Not even me. You just let it fester.' He turns away. 'Why, Ros, why?' His voice, a thin, rapier-like whisper. 'Not even me.'

Openly admitting it. But far, far too late.

Rosalind breathes out slowly. Swept along by her story's momentum, its trailing consequences, she'd been unstoppable. And soon, prompted by their new, prurient form teacher, Mr… Wilcock, or something, Teal's replacement, she was telling *him* too, going back over it, elaborating and embroidering… with Wilcock incensed, of course, outraged, and wholly sympathetic. So she'd stuck by her story, she'd had to, until she really did almost believe it herself. Trapped in her own lie. Oh, how *could* she have been so stupid, so stubborn?

Teal had left the school again, not long after. And who knows what *his* life had been, after that. Rosemary had left too – even before Teal; poor Rosemary, who'd always tried to temper her, and her vicious outbreaks against Teal, or anyone else.

Why, Ros, why?

So as not to lose face, that's why. To *protect* her stupid lie.

John wasn't innocent – far from it. But he'd believed her, perhaps as he was already smitten. And thus, trying to prove himself to her, he'd carried out her wishes, orchestrated all her meaningless reprisals.

'*You* conned us all! You *changed* us!'

He'd raised his hand, and it was all he could do not to slap her, to bring it down hard on her unhappy face. How *could* their relationship have survived after that? How could anyone's?

'So, what *else* have you been keeping from me? Come on! Let's have it all, now!'

'False Rosalind. False. False….' Rosie had once chanted.

False witness, yes. She had long known it for what it was.

Rosalind slumps back in her chair, and yawns, utterly spent. Cowards or cowed, they'd led separate lives under the same roof after that. No more anything. Sucked dry of all life.

A sound outside, beyond the heavy curtains, has her suddenly bolt upright, listening intently. And there it is again, just as before, that one eerie note. An owl, is it, in the hospice garden, anticipating the dawn?

She stands, crosses over to the window, and peers round the curtain, to stare into the garden awash with silver moonlight.

And she starts as the door opens, and the young nurse backs in, bearing her tea-tray. 'So sorry, Mrs Saunders, I got waylaid.' Very carefully, she sets it down on an empty chair.

Rosalind takes hold of the proffered mug. And the charade judders on, down towards its inevitable conclusion.

***

Titania bends her head once again over the book open on her shawl-covered lap.

Her persistent insomnia, it had at least yielded something positive over the years – this time of quiet, pleasurable reading. *This* had been her real education. And she smiles in grateful acknowledgement at the near negation of the "ill wind". Truth was, her days had always been too full: of children, paperwork, meetings; then Keith and the girls at home, with their enthusiasms and anxieties, to say nothing of the washing and ironing and cooking. And then marking, preparing the next day's lessons, while the others cleared away, washed up... sometimes. And then always... with weary task fordone... exhaustion, brief, heavy sleep, and her time of creative wakefulness: all this for the past thirty years.

She glances down at the book, but distractedly. Keith, still sleeping like a log each night, barely stirring as she slips from their bed an hour or more before dawn. The girls gone now, of course.

College – that's where the sleeplessness had first taken hold, when... Jenny, was it? Yes, Jenny had sat up with her night after night, when she was fretting over... Titania shakes her head. Why is her mind so unfocused? She can't even remember his... Not that she's really trying. Another world, and such a long time ago.

She lifts the book up a little nearer to her face, keen to read on. College had trained her well for her job – the social bits, too, in a way. But there was no doubt about it: this had been her real education, here, by the sea.

Note my words well, and when you give them breath,
repeat them as I said them, to the living,
whose life is no more than a race toward death...

True enough, yes, all in the batting of an eye. Keith's dad, grandma and grandpa, long gone, Daddy and mummy too now. And yet it all seems like yesterday. Life choices working out, or not. She smiles. He'd dreamed of being a painter, hadn't he, went on to teach in a university, when really, he'd wanted...

Leaning backwards, she lifts the corner of the curtain to try and get a sense of the coming day, but she is caught off guard by an intense silvery brightness that makes her blink and close her eyes.

Out over the sea that shifts and shimmers like molten glass, the full moon is still riding high. She stands, impelled by the shock of it, and wrapping the shawl about her shoulders she sets the book down on the little table beside her ancient chair and opens the curtains, just sufficiently for her to stand between them, and gaze in awe at the silver sea.

And still his name won't come back, that of her first love.

With Keith, it had been very different – love at first sight. And even though that ecstatic state hadn't... well, it couldn't, and that was the truth of it. But they'd rubbed along pretty well together despite their several drifts and peccadillos. It had been a good partnership, a good life on the whole. None of that romantic nonsense about going off and saving the world together! And she shakes her head catching at wisps of distant memories.

She closes the curtains, takes up her book once more, and settles into the comfort of the wing-back chair, determined to concentrate or she'll only have to read it all over again. She glances across at the small carriage clock on her desk. Ten to five. Now, where was she? Ah, yes.

> *But I assure you that I shall select*
> *the simplest words that need be from now on*
> *to make things clear to your dull intellect…*

Well, thank you for that! she thinks, smiling at the irony of it. She raises her eyes, trying to give the words something like their due merit, then reads swiftly on towards the end.

> *lead him… to the brim*
> *of that sweet stream, and with its holy waters*
> *revive the powers that faint and die in him*

Lead who to the brim? Recognising now that she will have to read the whole canto again in a more compliant mood, Titania skims a little, until her mind battens on words that merit her renewed concentration.

> *I come back from those holiest of waters new,*
> *remade, reborn, like a sun-awakened tree*
> *that spreads new foliage to the Spring dew*
> *… in sweetest freshness…*

But she soon looks up again, frowning, unsure who the 'I' is, or where it is all happening or leading… Not easy reading at all, not for a mind inclined to stray, as is hers, especially this morning, goodness knows why! Still, whoever would have believed it, all those years back, that she would find her way to this? In the Italian, of course, it would be much more satisfying to read – in its first world of words. Far richer, she doesn't doubt.

Strange, though, this business of names. Names that have been with you all your life, even. Yet you wake up one morning and they have slipped away, gone forever, maybe.

And not just the name in *his* case, but a whole life that in other circumstances could have been but was never lived. Ah, well.

***

'No, mum. Although we've had this place, oh, more than two years now.'

'Two years?'

'Already, yes. But we never have enough time, not for what we have in mind for it. Or for the garden – the "grand design," you know?'

'So how often *do* you get down?'

'About once a month, if I'm lucky – just for the weekend, though. Di and the kids come more often – it's only an hour or so by train from Melbourne. But she can't do much, beyond pulling out a few weeds, deadheading the roses, that sort of thing. The kids take some watching!'

'All sounds familiar. Your dad and I, we always had great ambitions for our place in the country. You remember, and that hill beside the house?'

'I do. We loved the woods.'

'But they never came to anything.' Penny sighs heavily. 'The Department, and the interminable writing… that all had to come first, always. But still…You've got it nice here. All neat and under control. You'll do it someday, I'm sure.'

'So, do you ever hear from him, from dad?'

'Not any more. No, it's been quite a while now, despite sending him…' She shrugs. 'So, how is he? What's he up to these days?'

Matthew looks suddenly uncomfortable. 'Sorry. I just presumed that you…'

'So, you're not in touch, either?'

A sudden breeze rushes in from the sea. And the serenity that had enveloped them since their arrival here an hour earlier seems to have dissipated – in an instant.

Penny takes off her sunglasses. 'So how long is it, actually, I mean since you last...?'

'It's been quite a while. Frankly, years. Since taking over the Department here... Well, I'm up to my eyes. It never stops. Like dad, I suppose.' He looks embarrassed for a moment, then shrugs. 'Maybe Simon keeps up with him. He's coming over in September, if he can get away from the ranch for long enough. And he's bringing the whole family this time.'

'That'll be nice. They seem to have settled permanently, now, wouldn't you say? I do hope that...' But Penny stops, aware her youngest grandchild, his face tear-smudged, is hovering for their attention.

'Daddy. Daddy. Judy's got my rocker, and she won't come off. I *said* she could, but now she won't come off... and... and...' And he is clearly on the point of tears, again. Matthew rises from his chair, pushing it back from the table.

'That girl! She never lets up from teasing him! Won't be long... So, James, where is she, then?'

And away they go, hand in hand, up towards the house.

Oh, Dan... Always somewhere else, never where he should be. Now too, apparently. And even when he *was* at home... all those times when... whatever her name was had gone away somewhere he was moody. Forever shutting himself away pretending to work, maybe even trying to work, but brooding, getting nowhere. Always licking his wounds. Either that or going off to the school to "get things ready for next term". Or maybe they'd quarrelled (she'd hoped), maybe it was all over.

Though it never would be for him, she'd realised, after the theatre episode. The last straw.

She stares out at the vast, silver-grey Southern Ocean and watches the crimson clouds rapidly silvering at their edges. She can just hear the distant shrill of the children's voices, away over in the shrubbery at the far side of the house, but hardly disturbing the immense silence that has settled about her.

She closes her eyes. It ought not to matter after all this time. What he does. Where he is. It is none of her business, now. And it doesn't, not in an everyday sort of way, with so many things to occupy her. And yet somehow...

Feeling a sudden chill, she thinks to head back indoors. She gets out of the deck chair and turns towards the house, but then stops, bending down to attend to a couple of plant pots that have fallen off the plinth on which the pergola stands.

Matthew comes back round the corner of the house, humming softly. And then he sees her in arrested motion, statuesque, either bending down towards something he can't see or straightening up from something. Quite motionless, she seems... suspended.

'Mum. Are you all right?' And he quickens his pace.

Another moment and Penny raises her head. She sees her son running towards her, and she smiles, then waves.

'It's nothing,' she shouts. 'It was as if... you know that saying... as if someone had just...'

And now, almost upon her, he realises she had simply been setting a toppled planter back in its place.

'Oh, mum, you shouldn't have bothered about that. They're always falling. It's the gusts of Antarctic wind we get down here – they can be really fierce. Come on, let's be going inside. It can get quite chilly at this time of year when the sun dips. Di's just put the kettle on, you'll be pleased to know.'

'That's actually where I was headed, Matthew, inside. Just got distracted, that's all.'

Chilly, yes. It is. For the bright day of a few minutes ago is rapidly turning to ashes.

XXXIV

Knock. Knock. Knock.

Milly Tomelty has had another exhausting morning – an exhausting week, in fact. She's lost count of the number of visits from the police, local radio, local newspapers, friends and other curious villagers, then the regional tv, the national newspapers… all of them eager to know what she'd seen, what she'd heard.

But now this. She could happily have done without *this*!

Knock. Knock. Knock.

Wearily, she eases herself up from the sofa where she'd lain down not ten minutes before. Mrs Talbot had been away for several days, visiting her sister-in-law over in Cambridge, but this knocking announces her return, sure enough. And then a sly smile creeps over her face, as she toys with the idea of ignoring it, of pretending to be fast asleep.

But too late, alas! For here she is, bobbing up and down, weaving to right and to left, waving and yoo-hooing through the window, over the nets.

Mrs Tomelty sighs deeply, her smile turning sour. She waves peremptorily, slips on her shoes, then shuffles across the room to open the door.

And Mary Talbot, breathless and eager, bursts in the moment the chain is off.

'Have you heard the news, Milly? Have you heard the latest?' She glances swiftly round the room, clearly in a state of some agitation, her left eye twitching furiously.

And in that split second, Mrs Tomelty fears that her neighbour, despite her absence, already knows more than she does herself – she who has been here all week, on the spot!

Typical! Just typical! And annoyingly, her bottom lip starts to tremble, and she turns away, fussing over a potted plant.

Mrs Talbot's excitement bubbles over: 'I heard it on the local news last night, Milly,' she confides, 'just after I got back. Did you hear it, about old Professor what's-his-name? He's disappeared! Did *you* know that... *did* you?'

Once more, the faintest of smiles flits across Mrs Tomelty's face: for once, then, she hasn't been upstaged by know-all Mary!

She spins round. 'Well, yes, Mary, of course I've heard! And, well, you... being away... Such a pity you missed it, all the excitement here! In fact, *I've* become a bit of a celebrity. They even showed quite a bit of the long interview I'd given them on *Look East* – on Tuesday evening, and...' But Mrs Tomelty looks suddenly crestfallen. 'Oh, but Mary, you mean... you didn't see it? I thought you *always* watched *Look East*?'

'No television.'

'No television?'

'Sister-in-law. She doesn't believe in them.'

'Oh dear, Mary, what a pity! But never mind. Do sit down!' And, savouring her good fortune, Mrs Tomelty charges on with her story.

'Well, what with the police and the television... Mary, I've never made so many cups of tea in my life! And the radio and the newspapers, and all. I've not had a minute to myself these past few days, and Inspector Chambers and me, we've become quite pally – always knows where he can get a nice cup of tea, does Inspector Chambers. Oh yes, things have been fairly buzzing around here, I can tell you!'

'So, what's happened to him?'

'Inspector Chambers – he's...'

'No, Milly! To old Professor what's-his-name!'

'*Inspector Chambers*,' Mrs Tomelty repeats, refusing to be deflected, 'is the detective in charge of the investigation. And *he* says Dan Teal was his name, Daniel Teal. Did *you* know that? *I* didn't, not till he said. Anyhow, *no one* knows what's happened, Mary. Just that he's vanished… puff… into thin air!'

'What? But…'

'And he were married… that is, divorced. Did *you* know he were divorced, Mary? His ex-wife, she lives in Ireland they say, and his two sons, one of them's in Canada, and the other in… Austria, I think, or Australia. Somewhere like that.'

'But Milly…'

'But *they* haven't heard from him in ages,' Mrs Tomelty continues firmly, 'none of them has, even though they'd been sending him cards and letters and things, and even tried to phone. But not a peep. Everybody else believed *he* were abroad, somewhere. All in all, it's a bit of a rum do.'

'Oh it is, it is! And before he… vanished, where was he? Do they know?'

Mrs Tomelty shrugs, then gestures expansively. 'They're saying he's been living there all along – at that house of his down the lane. But we never seen him, did we? Not in years, I'd say. And no one else has neither, leastways not them the police have talked to.'

'All seems a bit… odd, doesn't it?'

'*Very* odd. But it seems he emptied his letter box regular like, Mary, and paid his grocery bills… Mr Longwill says he used to leave groceries for him in some shed he has, by his front gate. That's how they come to discover something was wrong.'

'What do you mean?'

'It were Mr Longwill what phoned for the police.'

'Oh. I see.' Mrs Talbot's brow furrows. 'But… *why* did he?'

'Last lot from the previous month was still there, when he went back. Never been taken in.'

'Well, I never!' Mrs Talbot sinks back in her chair, trembling with the emotion of it, her left eye twitching fifty to the dozen and her fingers all twisted up in her tiny, lace handkerchief. 'So he phoned the police,' she repeats, nodding, and untwisting her fingers.

'Yes, that's right.'

'So what did they find?'

'Nothing much. Leastwise, nothing that adds up to anything. There were a letter, but nobody at the police station can make head nor tail of it.'

'But your Inspector, what does *he* say?'

And Mrs Tomelty, who had been on the point of offering her neighbour a nice cup of tea, sits down again.

'Inspector Chambers told *me*... in *strictest* confidence, mind... that both his doors was wide open – and had been for a week or more, judging by the leaves and things what had blown inside, back and front. But everything else looked normal, he said, apart from papers everywhere. And his bed, it was just as he'd have got out of it, with the covers thrown back, and... Oh, and this is the strange thing. His clothes were still on a chair by the bed. And his dressing gown and all.'

She pauses dramatically, inviting the comment or question she is sure must follow.

'Well, Milly.' Mrs Talbot's eyebrow rises a fraction. 'I always said he was up to no sort of good, didn't I... whatever he was up to down there?'

'You did, Mary, yes.' And Mrs Tomelty folds her hands neatly in her lap, delighting in seeing Mrs Talbot flopping helplessly, well-and-truly hooked. How satisfying it was, playing her in, slackening a little, then reeling hard, by turns.

'But that's as maybe,' she goes on, suppressing a sudden desire to tell all in one breath, 'but have you *any* idea what he *was* up to? *Have* you, Mary? I have to admit I hadn't, nor had anyone else, it seems.'

And again, she pauses, sadistically, to force the next question.

'What was it then?' Mrs Talbot complies, all agog. 'Drugs, was it? Sex? I always said...'

'Oh, dearie-me, noooo!'

'So, what then, Milly? What?' Mrs Talbot's impatience is almost choking her. 'What *was* he up to?'

'It were gardening he were up to.'

Mrs Talbot fiddles with her hearing aid, as perplexed as she is meant to be. 'What? Gardening, did you say?'

'Gardening, yes. That's what!'

'Well, if that was all...' And Mrs Talbot sits back in her chair, deflated, every now and then sneaking a covert glance at Mrs Tomelty.

Then she leans forward. 'So it was a cover, then. Growing cannabis or something, was he?'

Mrs Tomelty smiles, magnanimously. 'Well, the police are suspicious, of course. And they've done a lot of digging, themselves. But they've not found anything. Except...' And already her mind's eye is seeing her neighbour wriggling this way and that. 'Anyway, it seems he'd turned that useless old field behind the house into a beautiful garden, a Paradise on Earth!'

'Well I never!'

'I'd not been along there, myself, not in years – don't expect you have neither. But I went a couple of days ago just to have a bit of a nosy round. It were a bit difficult, you couldn't really see much through the gate, which the police have locked in any case, and what with it being so far away and all, and the old church, and trees and things blocking your view... I think there used to be one of them gates you find in some old churches, round by the side. But anyway, that's gone. I suppose he had it blocked up, maybe when they built the new estate, or it just got growed over. Still, if the old church yard is anything to go by, he done a good job, all right. You remember it were all overgrown with weeds – thistles and nettles, brambles and thorns and such like, all them years back? Well, peering in, I could see it's a real picture now; all roses it is.'

'All roses... What is?' Mrs Talbot is lost, having missed much of Mrs Tomelty's description, since there is something her mind has *not* missed. 'Never mind that. Except *what*, Milly?'

Mrs Tomelty looks blank.

'Come on, Milly! You said the police hadn't found anything, *except...*'

'What? Oh, yes, that's right, I did!' Mrs Tomelty covers her smirk with her hand. 'Well, up at the top of the long field there are some rocks, do you remember? And just below them, the police found what they said was a sort of... crater. As if there'd been an explosion, or an eruption or something. There were ash and cinders all round it. And round about the soil were turned to… glass, they said.'

'Glass!'

'Yes. Can you believe it? But… and this is the funny thing… they say their forensic people haven't been able to identify what these things are. And there's no traces of gunpowder or anything like that. So, all things considered, it's a bit of a mystery. Oh, yes… at first, they thought he'd been experimenting, being a professor, like, and blowed himself up. But it seems he hadn't.'

'Hadn't blown himself up?'

'No – been experimenting! Because, you see, he were a *history* professor.'

'Oh, well, I could have told them *that*,' says Mrs Talbot, primly, striving to retrieve some vestiges of her fast-dwindling authority. 'And I'll tell you what I think, Milly. Milly…?'

But just in this moment, Mrs Tomelty is scurrying over to the window, to peer up and down the lane.

'Wasn't that a police car going past? I'd best be getting the kettle on.'

***

The gate swings open and shadows flit quickly in, flowing out around the old church and towards the bottommost corners of the garden, shadows in shadows, gliding noiselessly. Pausing only momentarily at the open door then in and through and out at the other side they go, dark and silent, and on again up through the garden, swift, all-pervading, like a river in spate. Up and up, from terrace to terrace, the garden seething but with only darkness visible; passage of a malevolent wind without shiver of stalk or flicker of leaf in the cold, thin moonlight. They flow up and around the rocks, around the small crater at their foot, and over the brow of the hill and down, down, swirling round and back, eddying round and back, breasting the hilltop, brushing the hedges, all ways away, swift over the dead leaves, turning transient beauty into shadowy chaos; settling dusk; leaving a gate swinging on rusted hinges.

This book is printed on paper from sustainable sources managed under the Forest Stewardship Council (FSC) scheme.

It has been printed in the UK to reduce transportation miles and their impact upon the environment.

For every new title that Troubador publishes, we plant a tree to offset CO_2, partnering with the More Trees scheme.

For more about how Troubador offsets its environmental impact, see www.troubador.co.uk/sustainability-and-community